SOMEONE IN TIME: TALES OF TIME-CROSSED ROMANCE

Also edited by Jonathan Strahan

With Lou Anders

SOMEONE IN TIME: TALES OF TIME-CROSSED ROMANCE

Edited by

Jonathan Strahan

First published 2022 by Solaris
an imprint of Rebellion Publishing Ltd,
Riverside House, Osney Mead, Oxford, OX2 0ES, UK
www.solarisbooks.com

ISBN: 978 1 78108 509 9

A CIP catalogue record for this book is available from the British Library.
Designed & typeset by Rebellion Publishing

Printed in Denmark

For Marianne, the only person I would travel through time for…

ACKNOWLEDGMENTS

THESE PAST TWO years have been strange, difficult, and unexpected. I'm grateful beyond words to my incredible editor, Michael Rowley, who got *Made to Order* out into the world during what proved to be the hardest of years and who has been fabulous to work with on every book we've done together. My sincere thanks also to David Thomas Moore and everyone at Rebellion who had anything to do with *Someone in Time*. The team has been fabulous over the years, and it's a joy to work with them. My agent Howard Morhaim continues to be the best person I could be working with in this business, and I want to thank him and everyone at HMLA for their work on this and on all of my projects. And then there's everyone else, the people who gave time, suggested stories, and helped in so many ways with this particular book. Thanks as always to my dear friend and podcast co-host Gary K. Wolfe; Ellen Klages; Ian Mond; James Bradley; and to all of the authors and their agents who let their work appear here.

FINALLY, AS ALWAYS, a special thank you to my wife Marianne and two daughters, who were the best people in the world to be locked-in with, even if it wasn't for too long.

CONTENTS

off through time and space. There have been more—perhaps too many more—till you get to the point now where we have superheroes travelling through time by running really *fast* and spaceships warping or folding or something to do stuff and travel in time. Very sciencey. Very timey-wimey.

So, there are a lot of ways to travel through time, and a lot of famous time travel stories. Some of them are hard science fiction, some of them are fantasy, some of them are horror, and some of them are, well, romances. *Someone in Time* has its origins in two stories, neither of which appear here for reasons of length, but both of which I'd recommend to you. About four years ago I edited *Passing Strange*, a long story by Ellen Klages about two women living in San Francisco, one a famous pulp artist of the time and one not. They were both very much in love, but being queer in the 1940s was a fraught and difficult thing, and being together was even more difficult, if not almost impossible, and certainly dangerous. The story moved through time, from present day San Francisco and back to the '40s, giving us an overview of how their relationship developed and evolved, how the world responded to it in different times, and whom it affected. It was, and is, quite marvelous. And then a year or so later another, not completely different story came across my desk. Ian McDonald's *Time Was* is the story of two men during World War II who fall in love but, following a military experiment gone awry, are left falling through time. They leave messages for one another in books, meet up years apart in strange ways, and are ever lost.

Both of these stories left a nagging feeling in me. There were more stories to be told, more romances to be allowed to unfold. And the more I thought about it, the more great stories and movies came to mind that sat in exactly this space. The film adaptation of Richard Matheson's classic *Bid Time Return*, *Somewhere in Time*, had something of the right feel, and inspired this book's title. So too Nicholas Meyer's *Time After Time*, the perennial classic *Groundhog Day*, and books like Robert Nathan's *Jennie*, Ken Grimwood's *Replay*, and Diana Gabaldon's *Outlander*. So, I did what I tend to do in these circumstances. I reached out to writers around the world and asked them for their time travel romances, their stories of love lost and found as time slips away. And I was not disappointed.

Someone in Time features sixteen stories, fourteen original to this book and two that are long-standing favorites of mine. Ellen Klages's 'Time Gypsy' was published in a landmark book of queer science fiction, *Bending the Landscape*, back in 1999 and was nominated for the Hugo and Nebula Awards and long-listed for the Tiptree, so I knew it belonged here. Elizabeth Hand's 'Kronia' is something else again, a short tale that takes a romance and shatters it through time around the events of 9/11. These two wonderful tales are joined by stories of scientists falling forward and backward in time, using both elaborate machines and something not a lot unlike the dreaming of those classic tales of the 19th century to visit alternate versions of the past, to touch people who would otherwise be out of reach, and to join them together. Some of the stories are funny, some are sad and poignant, some are tales of fresh love and some of love forever lost, but they all are rather wonderful.

No editor should single out favorites, and I won't do that here, but I was honestly delighted as the stories came through, one by one, over a series of months through our pandemic year of 2020, and was able to fall back in time to ancient England to see a heart broken, and then could fly far forward in time to see love blossom anew. Romance itself is something that's open to interpretation. There are straightforward matters of the heart and there are literary and scientific romances of many kinds. What you will mostly find here, sometimes unexpectedly and delightfully, is a mix—matters of the heart blending with matters of the world, as they do. For the most part, though, I think you will find, as I did, stories that delight. I hope you enjoy them as much as I have.

Jonathan Strahan
Perth, Western Australia
May 2021

ROADSIDE ATTRACTION
Alix E. Harrow

Alix E. Harrow (alixeharrow.wixsite.com/author) is an ex-historian currently living in Virginia with her husband and their semi-feral children. She won a Hugo for her short fiction and her debut novel, *The Ten Thousand Doors of January*, was nominated for the Hugo, Nebula, Locus, World Fantasy, and Goodreads Choice Awards. Her second novel, *The Once and Future Witches*, was named as one of the Best Books of the Year by NPR Books. Her novella, *A Spindle Splintered*, was released by Tordotcom in 2021 and a sequel is due later this year.

THE DAY AFTER Candace Stillwater broke his heart, Floyd Butler decided—with the reckless haste of a twenty-one-year-old who knows they must act quickly, before good sense intervenes—to go time traveling.

It wasn't a difficult proposition: you simply took Exit 52 off I-70, halfway between Junction City and WaKeeney, and followed the signs for The World's One and Only Time Machine. You bought a ticket from the amiable drunk at the front booth and waited while he unlocked the gate, and then you walked through a grove of cottonwoods until you came to the time machine, which isn't really a machine at all. It's a rough pillar of sandstone weathered into a shape not unlike an hourglass, carved all over with names and initials and faded hearts.

There was a lot of fuss when it was first discovered—minor wars, international espionage, secret government agencies with a bewildering array of acronyms—but when the stone failed to provide either profit or power, the land was quietly sold to a private entity. The Ticket Through Time Theme Park opened in the early '70s, boasting a Chronological Museum, an overpriced supply shop full of pocket dictionaries and period clothing, and an extensive system of waivers. It lasted four or five years, when it became clear that the number of people willing to pay exorbitant prices in order to fling themselves like deranged darts through space and time, with no guarantee of return, survival, or even a good time, was sadly limited.

So the private entity sold the acreage to another, smaller entity, which eventually sold it to a Mr. Anthony Barton, who found that there were just enough cultists, conspiracy theorists, true believers, historical re-enactors, and desperate escapists to cover the salary of one full-time employee and send Mr. Barton to the Bahamas every January.

If Mr. Barton had been there the day Floyd Butler paid for his ticket, he would have put him without hesitation in the 'desperate escapist' category, and he would have been half-right: Floyd was running away from plenty of things (his next shift at the QuikTrip 24-Hour gas station; the deadly flat of the Kansas horizon; Candace Stillwater's blue, blue eyes when she broke up with him; and the dizzy sense that he'd lost the plot of his own life) but he was also running *toward* something. He just wasn't sure what it was.

He thought of it as an apple hanging just out of reach, perfectly ripe, gold-limned in the light of some new dawn. If he'd ever spoken of it to anyone, which he had not, he might have called it his destiny.

Floyd had to tap the glass of the front booth to wake the ticket seller, who squinted at Floyd's bright blue backpack—stuffed with all the necessities a person might need on a journey through time or, more accurately, all the non-perishable food that was available in his mother's kitchen before dawn this morning, when the idea had occurred to him—tore an orange ticket from a large roll, and said "Good luck" in a tone suggesting he would need it.

Floyd was undeterred. He walked through the gate with a swelling, billowing sensation in his chest, as if he were finally reaching out for that red, ripe apple. He would have touched the stone without breaking stride, without a second's hesitation, if it hadn't been for the man standing in the way.

He was a little older than Floyd, somewhere in that nebulous range between *early-twenties* and *old*, which were Floyd's only categories. Floyd thought he might have been handsome, in a tensile, whippet kind of way, if he shaved those embarrassing sideburns and wore 21st-century clothing. His outfit looked as if it had been stolen from the cover of one of Floyd's mother's romance novels: high-waisted pants, a collared shirt, and a stiff red vest that Floyd suspected was called a waistcoat or a cravat, or possibly a cummerbund.

Floyd knew some time travelers chose to dress in period clothing, but this man's costume had a geographical and chronological specificity that struck Floyd as thoroughly silly.

If he'd heard Floyd's approach, he made no sign of it. He stood before the stone, staring at it with a strange, lost expression, as if he didn't know why he'd come or what he ought to do next.

Floyd waited a polite minute before saying "Morning" in the same soothing tone he used to greet stray cats.

The man startled so violently he tripped over his own feet and very nearly fell against the stone. Floyd caught one flailing wrist—so slim and sharp it was like catching a tossed butter knife—and stood him gently back upright.

The man blinked several times, panting and rubbing his wrist. "Thank you." He had a nasally BBC accent that made Floyd suspect he'd traveled much further than three counties to be here.

"No problem." Floyd nodded at the stone. "I'll give

you some privacy, if you're going first."

"Going…?" The man looked at the stone, then back at Floyd, squinting as if Floyd were standing in much brighter sunlight than he actually was. "No, I wasn't—that is, I'm just the, uh, groundskeeper." He nodded vaguely at the trees, which seemed to be keeping themselves perfectly well. "You go ahead."

But he looked so pale and alarmed, his pupils dark beneath the long fringe of his eyelashes, that Floyd found himself lingering. He extended the travel mug he'd stolen from his mother an hour earlier. "Coffee?"

The man took the mug with long fingers, sipped cautiously, gagged, and said "How kind" in a slightly hoarse voice. He must have been the sort of person with a Starbucks order and a French press; Floyd generally just microwaved yesterday's leftovers and stirred in so much powdered creamer it left a pleasant chemical film on his tongue.

"You keep it," he said magnanimously. "I'd better be heading out." Floyd tightened the straps on his backpack, hoping he looked like a dashing explorer rather than a Boy Scout.

"Where are you going?"

For some reason—because the man's eyelashes were really quite long and he was looking at Floyd with such a pleasingly wistful expression, or because Floyd was filled with the ebullience of someone who has a feeling he will not be in Kansas for much longer—Floyd told him the truth.

He shrugged, smiling, and said, "To find my destiny."

He touched the stone and disappeared.

* * *

THREE DAYS LATER, he was back.

Floyd staggered away from the stone, sunburnt and hungry, a little dizzied by his split-second journey across thirteen hundred years and several thousand miles, but otherwise perfectly fine.

There he was again, standing under the dappled shade of the Kansas cottonwoods as if he'd never left, and there, too, was the nervous groundskeeper, although he'd exchanged his Regency outfit for a shapeless pair of coveralls. He was raking ineffectually at the dead leaves between the trees, looking as if he'd read about manual labor in books but had not tried it himself until now.

The groundskeeper looked up so quickly he must have been listening for footsteps. His eyes didn't do anything so dramatic as *light up* at the sight of Floyd, but their corners crimped.

He nodded at the dramatic folds of Floyd's caftan. "Where did you get that?"

"Tajikistan. But you should have asked *when*."

The corners of his eyes crimped a little further. "Very well. *When* did you get that?"

"The early seven hundreds, I think."

The man's gaze moved up to Floyd's jaw. The crimps disappeared. "And where did you get that?"

Floyd rubbed his palm across the scabbed line between

his throat and cheek. "There were a couple of men attacking a caravan. I got in the way."

The story sounded very good told like this, all pride and scars, but at the time it had merely been dusty and confusing and full of men shouting in languages he didn't know. Neither the merchants nor the bandits had seemed particularly pleased with his involvement, and afterward the caravan had taken him in more out of pity than gratitude. It was not at all the hero's journey he'd been expecting.

Floyd shrugged it all away. "Anyway, I'll let you get back to work. I'm starving." Caravan rations were not generous, and something in the water had violently disagreed with his digestive system, to the general amusement of the merchants.

The groundskeeper fumbled at his breast pocket and withdrew a silvery packet of off-brand Pop-Tarts. "You can have these, if you like. The ticket seller gave me an entire box, but I don't…"

Floyd ripped open the packet and ate the first tart in three bites that would have made his mother swat him with a dish towel. "Thanks. Mister…?" Floyd wouldn't normally call anyone mister unless they were wearing a uniform and asking him if he knew how fast he'd been going, but something about the groundskeeper indicated a certain sense of decorum.

"Wells. Edmund Wells."

"Floyd Butler." He extended his hand. Edmund shook it once and let go.

"Well." Floyd dusted multicolored sprinkles off his shirt. "See you next time, Edmund."

Edmund cut him a look, sharp and quick. "So you didn't find it then. Your destiny." Floyd squirmed a little at the word, but there was no mockery in the groundskeeper's voice.

He shook his head. "No. But it's just a matter of... time. I've got to run a couple errands"—like making sure his vaccinations were up to date and stopping at Walmart for a box of granola bars, an atlas, sunscreen, and three bottles of Imodium—"but I'll be back."

Floyd clapped Edmund on the shoulder, waved to the ticket seller, who did not appear to be conscious, and left Edmund raking the leaves with his eyes crimped once more.

OVER THE FOLLOWING two months Floyd went through the stone six times. His shortest trip was two hours in northern Siberia, which he spent swearing and dying; his longest was thirteen days in Zanzibar, which he spent climbing clove trees and bathing in the wild cerulean sea. It was true that he hadn't met many famed men of history or witnessed any significant battles—one of the government's great frustrations with time travel was the dull but inescapable fact that most of human history was occupied by ordinary people doing the ordinary work of survival, and their statistical chances of killing Jefferson Davis or winning the space race were very low indeed—but he had hunted wolves with the Khan's nephew and made out with a pirate, and that wasn't nothing. It just wasn't quite enough.

If he wasn't destined to be the handsome high school point guard who married the homecoming queen, he imagined he was meant to be some other kind of hero: a knight, a rebel, a soldier, a saint. The sort of man who stood at the end of the movie with his arm around a pretty girl and his eyes on the horizon.

He imagined, when he finally fell into the right time and place, the story he was destined to have, he would feel a tiny, silent *pop*, like a puzzle piece snapping into place, or teeth breaking the skin of an apple.

But until then, at least there was Edmund. The groundskeeper was odd and reserved, but Floyd liked his long lashes and silly sideburns, the Pop-Tarts he kept in his breast pocket, and the crimp at the corner of his eyes each time Floyd returned.

"Did you find your destiny?" he would ask, without irony.

"No," Floyd would answer, without embarrassment, and the two of them would sit under the cottonwoods while Floyd described the grand mosques of Songhai or the mammoths of the Pliocene. He tried not to hog the conversation, but Edmund answered every question with such tense brevity ("When did you start this job?" "Recently." "Where are you from?" "Ayrshire." "Whatever happened to that outfit you were wearing when I—" "Burned it.") that Floyd gave up.

If Edmund wasn't near the stone when he came through,

Floyd wandered until he found him pulling thistles or failing to pull-start a weed-eater, and they worked and talked together until the Pop-Tarts ran out and the sun set.

One day, when Floyd was in the middle of a story about falling out of a Tlingit canoe and being rescued by an extremely irritable fisherwoman, it began to rain.

Floyd stood and said he should probably head home, but he didn't move, because he didn't want to head home, because he'd spent most of his journey composing this story in his head, picturing the precise moments that would make Edmund laugh or shake his head or bite his lower lip.

Edmund smiled up at him, rain splintering against his eyelashes, and said, "Come with me." He led Floyd a quarter mile past the chain-link fence to an RV so old and sun-bleached it wouldn't have looked out of place in an elephant graveyard.

Floyd had imagined Edmund living someplace with matching curtains and glass coasters, but the RV had old sheets tacked over the windows and stained linoleum on the counters. The front seats were overflowing with Natty Light cans and waxy burger wrappers, and the carpet squished underfoot.

The bench seat was the only habitable space, with a stack of blankets folded neatly at the bottom and a row of very fine books with leather bindings stacked along the top. Floyd knew instantly that this was where Edmund slept, and found this information made his palms itch.

"The ticket seller said I could stay here as long as I kept the place up," Edmund said, and Floyd said, "That's nice." Neither of them seemed to know where their eyes should go; they'd never had a conversation without the plausible deniability of happenstance.

Eventually, Edmund cleared a seat for Floyd and poured tea into two chipped mugs, and Floyd asked about the leather-bound books, which proved to be the one thing that could provoke Edmund into volubility. Floyd didn't know who Blake or Shelley were, but he liked the way Edmund's hands moved as he talked.

The rain let up just before sunset. Floyd might have gone home then, but Edmund said, without meeting his eyes, "You know, that seat folds into an extra bed."

Floyd didn't often leave the grounds after that.

He helped Edmund haul the beer cans and rotten laundry out of the RV, wedging open windows and disinfecting surfaces until the only smells were cut grass and bleach. He plugged in the coffee maker, put out the subsequent electrical fire, and decided he could survive on tea after all. He made a run to town and stocked the cabinets with instant noodles and Pop-Tarts. They kept no schedule but lived like Lost Boys or Boxcar Children, a pair of homeless boys playing house.

Floyd found himself lingering longer and longer between journeys, until one morning he woke in the soft hour just before dawn, when the RV was silent except for the unhealthy moaning of the mini-fridge and the soft rush of Edmund's breathing, and found he didn't want to leave.

He was out the door and running for the stone before Edmund's head could lift from the pillow.

FLOYD RETURNED SEVERAL hours later with wind-chapped cheeks and a sealskin cape. He was tempted to go back to the RV and make a cup of tea that would stretch into a lazy breakfast with Edmund on the front steps, their knees sometimes brushing together, but instead he spun on his heel and touched the stone again.

Over and over Floyd flung himself into the mad river of time, staying just long enough between journeys for a hurried meal or a few hours of sleep, no longer sure whether he was running toward or away from something, clinging desperately to the vision of that red, red apple.

He knew it was beginning to wear on him. He accumulated scabs and scars, gathered bruises like blue flowers. He got frostbite in the Kiso Mountains and caught a nasty cough in Spain, which lingered, settling like sand in the bottom of his lungs. He spent a hungry week in the Reagan administration and had to carve a new hole in his belt when he came back.

Edmund didn't ask questions or complain, but he didn't laugh during Floyd's stories anymore, and he watched Floyd tightening his belt with something bitter and dark brewing beneath his lashes, like a distant storm.

To the extent that Floyd had considered the mortal perils of time travel, he'd worried about saber-toothed tigers or dysentery, but in the end it was a little old white woman on the Western frontier that got him. She found him sleeping in her corncrib and sent a bullet through the meat of his neck, just beneath his left ear.

She might have put another one in his brain but the fabric of space and time dissolved around them, leaving Floyd kneeling in the dirt beside the stone, blood slicking hot and fast down his throat. He clamped a hand against the wound and broke into a shaky run toward the RV. He would wonder, later, why he didn't head for his car or call 9-1-1, but at the time all he could see was the soft amber glow of the RV's windows.

Edmund was still up, sitting in the passenger seat with his legs crossed on the dashboard and an open book in his lap.

He didn't look up from his book when Floyd stumbled through the door. "Did you find your destiny?"

Floyd would have answered, but his tongue felt very heavy in his mouth and the lights were flickering strangely, as if the fabric of time was considering dissolving again.

Edmund sighed. "Is the faucet leaking again? I thought—" He turned around. His gaze landed first on the floor, where Floyd's blood was dripping against the linoleum, startlingly red, and then on Floyd's left hand, still clamped against his neck.

"No," he said, very firmly.

Floyd tried to say he would clean it up later, that he was

sorry, so sorry, but he passed out instead.

HE WOKE UP, which struck him as lucky, in Edmund's bed, which struck him as miraculous, given the distance from the door to the bed and the circumference of Edmund's biceps. The mattress was littered with ripped-open packets of alcohol wipes and sterile bandaging, and when he touched his throat he found a wad of gauze and tape instead of a bullet hole.

Edmund was sitting beside the bed with his elbows on his knees, long fingers buried in his hair. There was a streak of rust on the inside of his wrist.

"Since when do you have a first aid kit?" Floyd's voice sounded like it was coming out of a punctured garden hose.

Edmund looked up quickly, his hair standing in wild peaks, his face slack.

Floyd met his eyes and swallowed, painfully, at the naked relief he saw there. He tried a rueful, casual smile; Edmund did not smile back. The relief ebbed from his eyes, leaving nothing but weariness in its place. It was a bleak, suffering sort of weariness, of the kind that comes from waiting up late for someone who may or may not come back, who will surely leave again.

Neither of them spoke, until Edmund said, abruptly, "What do you think it is, exactly? This destiny of yours." For the first time Floyd heard a tiny, acerbic slant on the word *destiny*, the faintest suggestion of quotes.

Floyd started a defensive shrug but abandoned it, wincing. "I don't know. A damsel in distress. A revolution. Something better than the ordinary. Something…" He made a fireworks gesture with one hand. "Grand."

Edmund's face didn't move, but a shadow passed behind his eyes. "I see. So what if you find this *destiny*"—oh, it was definitely italicized now—"but you get dragged back here? To the merely ordinary?"

"I don't think that's how it works." Archaeologists had found enough evidence—cell phones in Nubian tombs, ancient skeletons with braces and fillings, paintings of Baby Yoda daubed on cave walls—to confirm that some time travelers simply stayed put. It might have been random, just a roll of the cosmic dice, but Floyd preferred to believe they found something worth staying for. "I think the stone takes you where you're supposed to be. Where you make sense."

Edmund's mouth wrenched into a small, ghastly smile, but the corners of his eyes remained perfectly smooth. "Ah." He caught Floyd's eyes again and held them, his voice lowering almost to a whisper. "Doesn't the stone keep taking you back here?"

Floyd swallowed again. It hurt, again.

In Edmund's eyes he saw everything he'd been running from: hurt and hunger, desire too long deferred, the truth itself. And the truth was he hadn't run away because Candace Stillwater broke his heart; he'd run because she *hadn't*. Because she was funny and sexy and everyone wanted her, and when she broke up with him he'd thought, *huh,* as if he'd read a weather report for a city he didn't live in.

And now here was Edmund looking at him with a question in his eyes, a whole future written on his face, and futures were so much harder than destinies. They were full of doubts and uncertainties, long nights and uncomfortable conversations with your mother. It took guts, to face your future.

And Floyd—who was brave enough to fight bandits and drink gas station coffee—found he was not brave enough for this.

He sat up, head spinning, and wallowed out of Edmund's bed, fumbling for the worn blue straps of his backpack.

Edmund didn't try to stop him. He only watched, looking just as lost as he had the day they met, while Floyd shoved painkillers and bottled water in his bag. He spoke only once, just as Floyd was stepping back into the night.

"I won't be here," he said softly. "When you come back."

FLOYD WAS GONE for a long time. He thought, for a while, that he might not come back at all. The '20s were just as sinful and opulent as Fitzgerald had promised, glimmering with dreams and destinies, or at least distractions.

But one night, after the sort of party that never ends but merely relocates, shedding stragglers, Floyd found himself slumped on a stranger's couch, listening for the geriatric groan of a mini-fridge or, perhaps, the soft rush of someone else's breathing.

It was too late for the future he'd seen in Edmund's face, he knew. He said he wouldn't wait, and why would he? How could he love a man who would choose chance over choice, a man who would spend his life sprinting through the past rather than taking a single step toward his own future?

Floyd sighed, and at the end of the sigh he whispered, "Enough."

Time dissolved once more. It left him standing under the cottonwood trees at Exit 52 once more, simultaneously hungover and still slightly drunk, entirely alone.

He closed his eyes, partly to stop the trees from spinning, but mostly to stop himself from looking for a bright red waistcoat.

A twig snapped under a wary footstep. A voice said, "Did you find your destiny?"

Floyd opened his eyes and there he was: a slight figure standing in the gray glow that comes before dawn, watching Floyd with his hands in his pockets and one last chance in his eyes.

Floyd found himself abruptly sober. "No. I don't know. Maybe." His pulse thumped in his ears, *don't-blow-it, don't-blow-it*. "Maybe there's no such thing as destiny. Maybe every place I went could have been my destiny, only I didn't choose it, so it wasn't. I just wanted to be"— anything other than a queer Kansas kid who needed some serious introspection and probably therapy—"someone who fit. Someone with their story all laid out. But the only place that stone sends you is somewhere else, and the only place I wanted to be, every time, was…" Floyd made himself meet Edmund's eyes, forced the truth between his teeth, "Was here."

Edmund's face didn't move. Floyd wet his lips and added, lamely, "I'm sorry. I was wrong."

"Oh," Edmund breathed, "I don't know about that." It was hard to tell in the half-light, but Floyd thought the corners of his eyes might be crimping. "You asked me once where I was from."

"Yes."

Edmund ran his teeth over his lower lip, tilted his head. "You should have asked me when."

There was a small silence here, just long enough for several pennies to drop. Floyd felt the keen, disorienting embarrassment of a person who has lived his entire life under the assumption that they are the main character in their story.

His voice, when he found it again, was a cracked whisper. "When are you from, Edmund?"

"I was born in 1781," he answered, calmly, and Floyd thought *sideburns!* with the internal groan of a detective who had missed an obvious clue. "The only son of the Marquess of Lindsey."

"The what of Lindsey?"

"It's a title, like duke or earl. That particular title was declared extinct in 1809 after its heir went to see the standing stone on the moor and disappeared."

"I thought the stone—stones, I guess—only went

backward."

Edmund lifted his shoulders in a gesture Floyd recognized as his own. "The one in Ayrshire only went forward. Or so the witch-woman told me, when I went asking."

"Why...?" Floyd began, although he thought he knew.

"I wasn't looking for my destiny, that's for certain. I was looking for a place I could breathe, could just *be*, as I am. A home, I suppose."

Floyd thought of the ticket seller's RV, with its squishy carpets and beer cans, and could not stop himself from asking, "Then why'd you stay here?"

Another shrug. "I was just thinking it was all a terrible mistake and I ought to go crawling back to my father, when I met this tall young gentleman who gave me the most awful drink I've ever had in my life." The sky was blueing fast, and Floyd could see the crimp of his eyes clearly now. "So I waited. The ticket seller was kind to me—gave me a job, and suitable clothes, a place to stay... He's waiting, too, you know. His lady love might never come back through the stone, but you did. Again, and again, and it began to feel..." Edmund looked away, the calm seams of his face finally splitting, his voice catching. "I'd thought a home would be a place, until then."

Floyd took a step toward him, toward the long sweep of his lashes and the slight tremor in his shoulders. "Why didn't you tell me?" he asked, softly now, and Edmund huffed a small, wretched laugh.

"The way you talked about your destiny, Floyd—

you wanted something shining and glorious, something special. And I'm just…" Edmund gestured at his cuffed jeans, his secondhand shoes, and Floyd wanted to catch his wrist in midair. "Ordinary."

Floyd had never had his heart broken, not really, but he wondered if it felt like this: a hunger so sharp it hurt, a want so vast it splintered ribs.

He took another step, and they were so close now that Edmund had to tilt his head to look up at him, his eyes wide and dark.

"Ask me again," Floyd said, softer still. "If I found my destiny."

Edmund's face did not light up so much as ignite, blazing up at him. "Did you find your destiny?" There were no italics this time.

"Yes," Floyd answered, and kissed him, hard and joyfully, knowing he must taste of stale absinthe, not caring.

Edmund tasted much better: fresh and sharp and alive, like the first cool day of autumn, when the heat finally breaks, or like an apple twisted fresh from the tree.

THE PAST LIFE RECONSTRUCTION SERVICE
Zen Cho

Zen Cho (zencho.org) is the author of the *Sorcerer to the Crown* novels, the novella *The Order of the Pure Moon Reflected in Wate*r and a short story collection, *Spirits Abroad*. Her newest novel is *Black Water Sister*, a contemporary fantasy set in Malaysia. Zen is a Hugo, Crawford, and British Fantasy Award winner, and a finalist for the Lambda, Locus, and Astounding Awards. She was born and raised in Malaysia, resides in the UK, and lives in a notional space between the two.

"DO YOU HAVE any questions?" said the technician. "You'll have read the materials."

She peered into Rui's face.

The technician had short hair and square, blunt-fingered hands that gave off a reassuring impression of competence. Rui thought she was probably gay. He would have been sure of it if she were his age, but who knew with Generation

Z? Rui—approaching fifty and coming reluctantly to the conclusion that, if he was not old, he was no longer young—certainly didn't.

"Yeah," he lied.

He'd received the bushel of paperwork about the Past Life Reconstruction Service and all the eventualities they weren't liable for. But who ever read the fine print?

The technician looked skeptical. "You sure you don't have anything to ask? This is your last chance to back out."

Rui raised his head, though the contraption she'd put him in made this challenging. "You're making this sound like it's dangerous. The website said I won't even leave my body."

The technician shrugged. "Your body stays where it is. But your spirit, who knows where that goes?"

"You do, don't you?" said Rui. "That's what I'm paying you for."

"Of course, Mr. Wang," said the technician. "All I'm saying is, just because it happens in your head, doesn't mean it's not real."

It sounded like something Yiu Leung would have said. But Rui flinched away from the thought. He wasn't here to think about Yiu Leung.

Paying a mysterious company an inordinate sum to help him uncover his past lives was the kind of weird rich people shit he'd never envisaged himself going in for. His wealth was so recently acquired that it still hung strangely on him. Even after he'd got to the point that he could afford anything he wanted, his indulgences had remained the same—work, maintaining an enfant terrible pose well past the age of enfant-cy... and Yiu Leung.

Had Yiu Leung been an indulgence? Most of Rui's friends seemed to think so. A boyfriend eighteen years his junior, with the kind of physique Yiu Leung boasted... they'd never taken him seriously, even as the years passed and proved the relationship more than a passing fancy. That had been part of the problem.

Rui wrenched his mind away from Yiu Leung. That wasn't the problem he was here to fix.

He had the impression he was unusual among the clientele of the Past Life Reconstruction Service, in that he'd come seeking not cheap thrills or affirmation or even self-understanding. Rui's subconscious had been a mystery to him all his life and he wasn't about to start digging around in it now.

No. What he sought was inspiration.

There had once been a time when he had never lacked for ideas or the confidence to execute them. In that first hardscrabble decade or two—churning out ads for corporate clients to pay the bills, fitting in creative work as and when he could—it was only opportunity that was wanting.

It had taken years, but slowly he'd started getting traction: recognition at film festivals, invitations to judge competitions. The name he'd made for himself wasn't one the man on the street would recognize, but kids at film school might quote it to impress their peers.

Then Rui had had his big breakout with his fourth

feature film. And it was *big*—big-money big. He became the kind of director your mom might have heard of. That was when the trouble started.

The film he'd made after that sucked, but nobody seemed to notice. Audiences streamed to the cinema in their millions; awards showered down on him. Rui told himself that evidently there had been more to the movie than he'd thought.

But with his sixth film, people did notice. It was a flop, losing an eye-watering amount of money. Rui discovered that the only thing more embarrassing than making a lauded piece of shit was making a piece of shit that everyone recognized as such.

By the time he'd started shooting his seventh feature film, he'd known he was on borrowed time.

Maybe he'd been a little difficult to live with while that was going on. But Yiu Leung hadn't said anything about the late nights, the dinners Rui had blown off, the messages left unread.

If you'd asked Rui at the time, he would have said Yiu Leung was giving him face, that he knew how much pressure Rui was under. In fact, what Yiu Leung was giving Rui was enough rope to hang himself with. Rui only saw *that* once Yiu Leung left.

He blew it with the movie, too. The original plan was to go straight into shooting another project, a thriller that had already been greenlit. Rui had assembled a cast and crew, cleared his diary. And then the email had come pulling the plug.

They'd given some bullshit reason about him being difficult to work with, as if a director having an artistic temperament was anything unusual. The truth was, his luck had run out. He was no longer so successful that people were willing to put up with his shit. Yiu Leung had only been a couple of steps ahead of everyone else.

It was that thought, rather than the email itself, that had made Rui hurl his phone at the wall. Panting in the silence of his apartment, he'd known something had to change.

"What's the worst that could happen?" he said now. "Could I die?"

There was the slightest hesitation before the technician answered.

"The machine puts you in a trance state so you can relive a past life," she said. "You're essentially dreaming, though clients say it feels like you're really there. After thirty minutes, the machine wakes you up. No matter what happens in those thirty minutes, it's unlikely you'll suffer any physical injury to your actual body. But some people have traumatic experiences. One client had a mastectomy without anesthesia in her past life. She found that very difficult."

"*That* was the exact thirty minutes you chose?"

"It's not a precise science, Mr. Wang," said the technician. "You tell us which time period you want and the machine sends you there. But we don't know who you were or what you were doing then. It's a leap into the unknown."

Rui settled back in his chair. It was plush and leather-covered, presumably acquired in the hope its luxury would offset the ominous flashing lights of the machine. Rui still felt like an extra in the old *Frankenstein* films, a subject of the mad scientist's experiments.

"That's what I'm here for," he said, more to remind himself than anything else.

The technician checked the notes pinned up by Rui's head. "This says you want to be sent to the late Qing dynasty, around the 1800s?"

"Yes." That had felt far enough away in time to be exotic, but not too far to be alien. "Will I remember who I am now?"

The technician nodded. "You'll be inhabiting your past self's body and have their memories, but you'll have your own as well. Think of it as being an actor, playing the person you were in that past life."

She paused to adjust a control, then went on:

"I'm going to ask you to close your eyes and empty your mind. Have you tried meditation before? It's like that. You can recall your past lives yourself if you're good enough, but most of us aren't Buddhas. The machine gives you a shortcut."

Rui shut his eyes, but he'd never been any good at emptying his mind. It kept on going, throwing up the usual irritating jumble of half-formed thoughts, ideas, feelings. "Can I diverge from the script? Could I tell people I'm from the future?"

"You can do whatever you want, Mr. Wang," said the technician. "It's all in your head. Your dream won't affect anyone or anything else. The most it can do is change the world inside you. But that's why you've come to us, right?"

The last thing Rui remembered seeing was her conspiratorial grin.

RUI CLOSED HIS eyes in a temperature-controlled room in Hong Kong in winter. He opened his eyes to the glare of tropical sunshine. The air was humid, like the warm breath of a god. Sweat stuck his clothes to his skin.

He was in a shack, with wooden walls, zinc roofing and a floor of bare earth. His friend was sitting with his back against the wall.

Rui flung something down, wrapped in dirty fabric. It made an ominous metallic rattle when it hit the floor.

His friend leaned over and pulled the fabric away, revealing an old-fashioned musket.

Rui was angry, his heart pounding. He heard himself say, "Ah Seng gave this to me. For you."

His friend sighed. "Ah Seng is too pure-hearted. He expects sympathy from everyone."

"You mean he is a fool," said Rui. "But he's not as much of a fool as you."

He felt his mouth move, but the voice that spoke wasn't his own and the words came out without the intervention of his brain. Which was good, because his brain was busy processing the realization that the man in front of him was Yiu Leung.

Rui couldn't have said how he knew this. Yiu Leung was

a five-foot-ten martial artist with the torso of someone who had a protein powder addiction. His friend, sat on a torn, grubby old mat, was five foot and gaunt. Poverty and hardship had engraved lines in his face that made him look far older than his thirty years.

But the spirit gazing out of those eyes was Yiu Leung's own—mocking, quixotic, indomitable. It was a spirit Rui loved. And it was going to get his friend killed.

"What's the gun for?" said Rui.

The man who was and wasn't Yiu Leung gazed at the musket. "Would you believe me if I said it's for hunting monitor lizards? Ah Seng says they taste like chicken."

"I have nine more hidden behind my quarters," said Rui. "What are they for?"

"Ah Seng is really too trusting," said Yiu Leung, but he was relieved. He hadn't really wanted to lie to Rui. "You don't need to worry. They're for Che Long."

"Che Long? The head of the Red Flags?" Rui dragged his hand across his face.

The atmosphere in Penang had been explosive in the past few days. Tensions between the Muslims had been simmering ever since that Red Flag man had killed a merchant under the protection of the White Flag—and if the Flag groups fought, the Chinese kongsi allied to them were sworn to help. Now the Awal Muharram celebrations were approaching, with their riotous processions, everyone knew something big was about to happen.

Rui had known a battle was coming. He just hadn't expected Yiu Leung to be at the heart of it.

But he should have guessed. From the first time he'd spoken to the man—Yiu Leung leaning over from his rickshaw to offer Rui a drink, a twinkle in his eye that promised too much—Rui had known he was trouble.

"Are you *crazy*?" said Rui.

"They're our brothers," said Yiu Leung. "You're a member of the kongsi, too."

"Because I had no choice!" said Rui. "I joined to keep out of trouble with those gangsters. Not to get close to them!"

"They asked me to be a go-between with Che Long and his men, because I speak Malay," said Yiu Leung. "I said yes. What else could I do?" But he wouldn't meet Rui's eyes.

"I've never known you to do anything you didn't want to do." Rui folded his arms. "You couldn't find a way out of it?"

Yiu Leung shrugged. "Maybe I didn't want to." He rose to his feet. "You don't need to worry about the guns. I'll deal with them."

"I'm not worried about the guns," said Rui. "Did you leave your village and come all the way here to fight and make trouble? You should think of your family."

Rui—or rather, the version of Rui who had lived this life—was visited by a vision of his own family. His father and mother, worn from the demands of scraping a living from their poor land, and the wife he'd left behind with them in China. She had borne him a son whom he'd never seen. It was his wife's face Rui saw when he thought of the child—a square, pale face, blank with terror, on their wedding night.

She hadn't seemed to notice that Rui was equally terrified. He'd agreed to the marriage so that his parents would have someone to help them when he was gone, but he couldn't escape the lurking fear that somehow she would know what he was—the way Yiu Leung had known, just from looking at him. But then, Rui and Yiu Leung were cut from the same cloth.

Yiu Leung said, with absurd jealousy, "Think of what? I haven't got a wife to pine for, not like you."

"Don't be an idiot," said Rui. "You have a father and mother. What would happen to them if you got in trouble? You think your precious brothers will help you if you get killed or thrown in prison or sent back to China? They won't care."

"It seems like it, doesn't it?" said Yiu Leung. "Eng Au has been dead two months and nobody remembers him."

Rui paused. "That's what this is about?"

"Eng Au left three children and that Ghee Hin man who killed him walks under heaven without fear," said Yiu Leung. "Is that justice?"

"You didn't even *like* Eng Au when he was alive," said Rui.

Nobody had. Eng Au had been a drunk, a gambler and an opium eater. These vices were common enough that they could have been forgiven, if he had not also been bad company. His killing in a drunken squabble had made no difference to anyone on the island. Rui doubted whether it would even have given Eng Au's family in China much concern to lose so troublesome a son.

Of course, as always, Yiu Leung had to be the exception.

"That's why," he said. "If you were killed, wouldn't you want your sworn brothers to seek justice?"

"If it was me who died, I'd want you to forget about me and concern yourself with your own business," said Rui.

Yiu Leung made to move past him, but Rui grabbed his wrist.

"But when has what I want ever mattered to you?" said Rui bitterly.

He could feel the flutter of Yiu Leung's pulse under his fingertips. Yiu Leung held his gaze until Rui looked away.

"You're right," said Yiu Leung. "If it was you, I wouldn't do what you wanted. I would never forget you and I would never get over it."

Maybe it was he who pulled Rui's head down for the kiss, or maybe it was Rui who bent to meet him. It didn't matter. However they got there, they always ended up in the same place.

"Don't do this," said Rui, when he could speak again. "Tell them the White Flags are watching you. Tell them they need to get someone else."

He knew even as he said the words that they were useless. Rui had never been able to change Yiu Leung's mind when he'd decided something was the right thing to do. That was as true of his own Yiu Leung as it was of this one.

Yiu Leung made no answer. He only looked at Rui, his

expression pitying. He would spare Rui if he could, Rui knew, but he would not spare himself, and so Rui would lose Yiu Leung, whom he loved above all else. He would lose him and there was nothing he could do about it …

RUI WOKE CLEANLY, all at once.

The technician said, "I should tell you that we don't do refunds."

"I—what?"

The technician was unbuckling Rui from the chair, untangling the various wires that connected him to the machine.

Rui sat up, rolling his shoulders. His body felt like that of a stranger's. The length of his own legs took him aback.

"Sometimes people don't like what they see in their past lives," said the technician. "But it's in our disclaimers, we can't control what you experience."

Rui still felt the pressure of Yiu Leung's mouth on his, the heat and despair that had surged through him.

Except that hadn't been Yiu Leung. It had been another man, in another life. Nothing to do with Rui.

"Do people ever…?" Rui's throat was dry. The technician gave him a glass of water. Rui drank, grateful for its warmth. The air conditioning seemed colder after the tropical heat of his past life. "Is it normal to recognize people back then? I met someone who… I thought I knew them."

The technician's eyes widened. "You saw your soulmate?

That's good luck, on your first time. Not everybody gets a meaningful encounter like that."

Rui coughed on his mouthful of water. "No, not my soulmate. Just an acquaintance."

"It probably wasn't anyone you knew," said the technician. "You have to have a very strong fate with another person for you to recognize them in another life. Even our bonds with family members are too weak to carry through. What we've found is clients are only likely to recognize somebody in a past life if it's their soulmate. You know the story about Jyut Lou, how he ties people to their fated partner with a red string?"

Rui snorted. "That's just a story."

"Yes. But from what we see, the part about fate, that's true. Who was the person you recognized?"

"Nobody important," said Rui. He swung his legs over the side of the chair. "I was probably imagining it."

The last time he'd seen Yiu Leung was when Yiu Leung dumped him. He'd done it with what was, for Yiu Leung, a remarkable lack of drama. Rui had come home on an ordinary evening, tired and cranky from the day's work. As usual, Yiu Leung had talked and Rui had grunted, letting the words drift over him.

If you'd asked him then, Rui would have said he put up with how much Yiu Leung talked for his good qualities, like his torso. It wouldn't have been a lie, or at least not an intentional one. At the time, he hadn't known how much he liked hearing Yiu Leung's voice.

There was a lot he hadn't understood about him and

Yiu Leung. Just how much was made clear when Yiu Leung said, abruptly, "Alice's lodger has moved out. She was asking if I knew anyone who might want to rent the room." He paused. "I told her I'd take it."

"What? Why the fuck did you tell her that?" Even then, Rui hadn't realized the danger he was in. Yiu Leung was always overcommitting, doing over-the-top favors for friends. "You're going to end up paying for a room you can't use."

"I'm going to use it," said Yiu Leung. He was standing by the kitchen counter, refusing to look at Rui.

"I want to break up," he said. His voice was curiously flat. "I can't do this anymore. Trying to love someone who won't let himself love me back."

"What are you talking about?" said Rui.

He'd never said 'I love you' to Yiu Leung, but that had never seemed to matter before. It was accepted between them that there were certain things Rui wouldn't say or do. Yiu Leung didn't mind.

Or at least, that was what Rui had thought. In the months since Yiu Leung dumped him, Rui came to realize he'd thought a lot of dumb fucking shit.

"Are you saying I'm wrong?" Yiu Leung raised his eyes to Rui.

The obvious and simple and straightforward thing to do would have been to say, "Of course you're wrong. Of course I love you."

But Rui had been taken off guard and he felt, stupidly, that giving Yiu Leung what he wanted would somehow be a surrender, a loss of face, conceding defeat in a fight Yiu Leung had unfairly sprung on him. So instead he said:

"Where is all this coming from? Has Alice been bitching about me again? She needs to get a life."

"Alice thinks I should have broken up with you years ago," said Yiu Leung, but then his face crumpled.

For the first time, Rui realized this was for real. It wasn't some fucked-up joke and Yiu Leung wasn't about to change his mind.

"You couldn't even say it," said Yiu Leung. "You couldn't even—"

He cut himself off and walked out, leaving Rui on the sofa, staring after him like the prize idiot he was.

Five years together and it was over just like that. Yiu Leung left that night and went to a friend's place. It was Alice who came to get his stuff.

"He couldn't even come himself?" Rui said when he saw her.

"Yiu Leung's very upset," said Alice. "He thinks it's better if you guys have some space."

"He's never going to fuck you, you know," said Rui, because he was angry and hurt and Yiu Leung wasn't there to explain himself.

Alice said, "Aren't you sick of acting like a sixteen-year-old when you're fifty?" and pushed past him into the apartment.

Fortunately, it only took her a couple of visits to pack up Yiu Leung's things. He didn't have much in the way of possessions. Yet when she left for the last time, carting off every trace of Yiu Leung, the apartment felt like a different place. It was only once Yiu Leung removed himself from Rui's life that Rui realized how much space he'd taken up.

That had been three months ago. It was time for Rui to move on. He could bemoan the past all he liked, wish he'd done things differently, but that wouldn't change anything. Yiu Leung had decided he didn't want Rui anymore and Rui had to live with that.

Now he needed to focus on his work. Sure, he'd suffered a humiliating failure, but failure was an old friend. He still had all the skills he'd developed over the years, the vision for which he'd been praised. All he needed was an idea—one that would put a fire in his gut, that would unfold into a story so incontrovertibly good that nobody would be able to deny its power. Even fucking Alice would get madder and madder as all her friends went to watch it in the cinema.

That image gave Rui particular pleasure.

His mission of seeking creative renewal and incidentally forgetting his ex wasn't exactly being helped by the Past Life Reconstruction Service sending him to a life in which he happened to be in love with a version of said ex. But maybe that ragged malcontent hadn't been Yiu Leung, despite the sense of recognition Rui had felt. He must have been imagining things, Rui told himself.

It was either that, or Yiu Leung really was his soulmate and Rui had fucked things up irreparably by being a self-absorbed dickhead who was incapable of expressing his feelings to the people he cared about most. Rui couldn't tell which alternative was worse.

He entertained the idea of not going back to the Past Life Reconstruction Service. But he'd prepaid a significant sum for five sessions and he wasn't quite rich enough not to mind writing it off. He'd just avoid the 1800s next time.

AVOIDING THE 1800s did not work.

In his next session, Rui asked to be sent to the Song dynasty. Maybe he could do a period piece. People went wild for historical dramas. But his would be different—a fresh, subversive take on a classic genre.

He was somewhat startled to wake up as a woman in this past life. The room he was in was handsomely furnished and his clothes, though disordered, were made of a fine cotton, so evidently she was wealthy. Rui would have got up to explore the house, maybe even tried to catch a glimpse of the outside world—if not for the baby.

He had never held so young a baby before and he had certainly never breastfed one. To find himself doing both was a lot to process.

The Rui of this life was extremely tired. She had not slept for more than three hours at a stretch in months. And the baby, who demanded so much of her, was a disappointment.

Rui's husband had taken her as a wife so that she could bear him a son. There had been great excitement, universal approval, when she had become pregnant. To have gone through the agony of childbirth only to end up with a girl was crushing.

Next time there must be a son—and Rui dreaded the idea of *next time*. She did not dislike her husband—he was gentlemanly, kind—but he would not have been her first choice as a partner in the act which produced children. Appalling as giving birth had been, at least it had granted her a reprieve from *that*.

The baby whimpered and she soothed it, loving it despite herself. There were consolations in being a married woman, despite everything. After all, if she had not wed her husband, she would never have met…

A woman entered the room. The young mother turned toward her like a flower lifting its face toward the sun.

Rui thought, *Fuck*. The woman was Yiu Leung.

He felt no surprise, only resignation. Part of him had been braced for this.

This life's Yiu Leung was older than Rui's current incarnation, closer in age to their husband. It was she who had ruled that their husband must find a second wife and chosen Rui for the role. Perhaps she had not worried about the possible impact on her status because she was so beautiful—far more beautiful than Rui. Rui's youth was her chief recommendation. But she had no grievances. Her charms, such as they were, had sufficed to bring her into this house.

"Is the baby fed?" said her husband's first wife, who was and wasn't Yiu Leung. "I will call a servant to look after her. I've made soup. You must drink it and rest."

The servant came and took the baby away. When Rui moved to adjust her clothing and cover herself, Yiu Leung put her hand out, stopping Rui's. She smiled.

Oh, thought Rui. This time he *was* surprised, but the woman whose life he was visiting was not. She was charmed, giddy, in love, and as her husband's first wife lay her down on the couch, she laughed aloud with delight.

"DID YOU SEE anyone you know this time?" said the technician.

"No," said Rui shortly.

IT WAS THE same story at the next session, when the machine sent Rui to the Ming dynasty, except that he was male again. Yiu Leung was a woman.

If Rui had ever thought this might have made things easier, he was incorrect. It seemed nothing between him and Yiu Leung was fated to be straightforward.

Rui didn't know what his face was doing when he woke to his own life, but evidently it was sufficiently intimidating that the technician didn't even ask how it had gone.

This was getting ridiculous. Maybe it was all the time he was spending in pre-industrial eras that was the problem. At the session after that, he told the technician to send him to the 1950s. Before he was born, but not that long before.

The technician raised her eyebrows. "That recent?"

"I want to see what the world was like when my parents were young," said Rui. "It'll probably teach me more than going to the Song dynasty."

"I guess," said the technician, but she sounded dubious. "You never know, with past lives."

She was right. In the 1950s, Rui was a cow.

Rui was never able to remember the details of this past life experience. Cows didn't think; they existed. There were snatches of memory—the sensation of grass tickling his feet, the warmth of the sun on his head, a soft breeze along his flanks. He was vaguely aware of other cows around him.

Even then—*even then*—there was a fly. It kept buzzing around him as he chewed his cud, irritating him. He flicked his ears, but the fly persisted.

Rui's human mind was a speck floating in the cow's consciousness. It was as though, Rui thought blurrily, as though the fly had a vendetta against him. Some kind of personal connection that drew it back to Rui again and again...

Upon emerging from being a cow, he cancelled a promising meeting with a producer and went home to sulk.

Four weeks after he'd started going to the Past Life Reconstruction Service and he was as bereft of inspiration as ever. What a waste of money.

What had he learnt from the past lives they had shown him? No more than that Yiu Leung had apparently been put on this Earth to pursue him across the centuries, purely to torment him. Yiu Leung had never been more recognizable than in the form of that goddamn fly.

It was funny. No matter where he went in time, he couldn't escape Yiu Leung—except in his own life, the one he was actually living.

Rui brooded over a beer on his sofa, surrounded by all the beautiful things his wealth had purchased him. His apartment was shrouded in silence—the silence of stagnation, of emptiness. He could do whatever he wanted, go anywhere, get anything, and none of it appealed because he had lost the thing that had made it all meaningful.

His creativity, Rui told himself. The spark that had driven him for so many years and fueled his success.

But his ability to lie to himself had been eroded by the past few weeks. Staring unseeing at the TV screen, Rui couldn't avoid the truth any longer.

He missed Yiu Leung. Life sucked without him.

He couldn't stop thinking about the way Yiu Leung's face had crumpled the day he'd broken up with Rui. "You couldn't even say it," he'd said.

If only Rui had said 'I love you' then. It wouldn't have magically fixed all their issues. But it might have persuaded Yiu Leung to stay the night and the night after that, to agree to work things out with Rui.

If Yiu Leung were here right now, Rui would say it. It would be true.

* * *

THE TECHNICIAN WAS in an upbeat mood, chatty despite Rui's silence. "Where are we going this time?" She checked his notes and whistled. "Prehistory? That's daring. Not many clients will go that far back."

"Can you send me back to my first past life?" said Rui. "The first one you sent me to, I mean, in the 1800s."

The technician looked at him, her good cheer fading.

"I could," she said slowly. "I'd advise against it, though. It can be... risky. Sometimes people get overinvested in a past life."

Rui studied her. "Is it company policy not to send clients back to the same life more than once?"

"It's company policy to send clients wherever they want to go," said the technician. "You've paid. It's up to you what you want to see." She shrugged. "I'm just telling you my opinion. I've seen clients get stuck, that's all."

"It's my last session," said Rui. "I'm not going to come back. All I want is to know what happened to... what happened after what I saw last time."

"It's a bad idea to seek closure from the past, you know," said the technician gently. "There's nothing you can do to affect what happened then. You can only change the life you're living right now."

"You're very wise for your age," said Rui.

The technician inclined her head. "But you still want to go back to that life."

"I need to know," said Rui, after a pause.

The technician let out a breath.

"It's your life," she said. She leaned forward, tapping at

the control panel on the machine. "I hope you find what you're looking for."

"DID YOU FIND what you were looking for?"

Yiu Leung was lying in bed, looking like shit. He grinned.

Rui had been trying to pretend he wasn't inspecting him, searching for signs of improvement in that bloodless face. He looked away.

"You look terrible," he said. "How are you feeling?"

"If I look so bad, it must mean I feel bad, right?" said Yiu Leung.

Which meant he must feel even worse than he looked. Yiu Leung hated admitting weakness.

Perhaps nearly dying had made him less worried about that. If Ah Seng hadn't found him a hideout at his aunt's brothel, Yiu Leung would have been arrested by the British and he'd probably be dead of his wounds by now. Ah Seng's aunt had a face of stone, but she had a soft spot for her nephew and for his sake she had nursed Yiu Leung with steely competence.

Not that he was back to full health. But they had no choice. They had to move on.

"The British are looking for you," said Rui. "They're saying you're one of the ringleaders of the riots."

"They've got a point," said Yiu Leung fair-mindedly.

"You need to leave Penang."

Yiu Leung smiled thinly. From where he lay, injured

and—like most of Penang's Chinese migrant workers—hopelessly in debt, Rui could well see how flight would seem impossible.

Rui sat next to the bed. "My cousin's brother-in-law is a trader. His boat leaves for Medan tomorrow. He's said he'll take us."

He couldn't make out Yiu Leung's reaction at first. For a moment Rui was afraid he would refuse to go.

But then Yiu Leung said, slowly, "You're coming with me?"

"It's not like you can go by yourself, in your state," said Rui. "You need someone to look after you."

Rui had never seen Yiu Leung look shamefaced before.

"I didn't mean to drag you into this," he said. "You warned me not to get involved. Won't this be troublesome for you?"

Rui shrugged. "I've paid off my bond. I don't owe anyone anything."

That was not strictly true. Rui had finally managed to settle his debt to the agent who had arranged his passage from China to Malaya, but between that and sending money home to his family, he hadn't had the funds to pay the cousin's brother-in-law for a place on his boat. They had agreed Rui could start paying him off once he found work in Medan.

"I don't want to burden you," Yiu Leung persisted, until Rui got annoyed.

"Enough," he said. "What's there for me in Penang anyway? There will be the same work in Medan and the same fools. If you want to join another kongsi and make trouble there, you can."

"No," said Yiu Leung. "I've learnt wisdom now." He leant back in his bed, not even trying to hide his happiness. "How lucky I am to have such a patient friend."

The look on his face embarrassed Rui.

"You'd better rest," he said brusquely. "I'll pack your things."

RUI WOKE WITH tears on his cheeks.

The technician seemed used to this. She made no comment, but gave him some tissues and brought him a cup of tea.

The tea scalded his tongue, but he didn't say anything. He blew on it, watching the steam rise from the surface, and said, "I kept seeing the same person. In every life."

The technician nodded. "Who was it?"

"An ex," said Rui. "They dumped me a while ago."

"Ah." The technician paused. "My boss would want me to tell you that you can get a discount if you sign up for more sessions now."

Rui looked at her. "You think I should come back?"

"I think you should consider therapy," said the technician.

"Maybe I will." Rui finished his tea, then said, "Do you like your job?"

He left with her business card, having given her a generous tip. Rui always kept an eye out for bright, competent people. It was hard to find good staff.

He was in the lobby when something happened that was surprising, yet entirely in keeping with all his experiences of visiting that particular building. He saw Yiu Leung.

Except this time it was actually Yiu Leung, wearing workout clothes. He'd spotted Rui, too. The panic on his face was almost funny. In the past few weeks Rui had had a lot more practice running into Yiu Leung than Yiu Leung had of encountering him.

He wasn't sure if they would speak. Yiu Leung looked like he wanted to run away, but as they were about to pass each other he gave a hesitant nod. It was enough for Rui to say:

"Going to find out about your past lives?"

"What?" said Yiu Leung. "Uh, no. I'm here to do a personal training session with the CEO." He held up a bulky gym bag.

"Of course." Rui wondered if the CEO was attractive. Yiu Leung had always been drawn to older men. "You look great."

Yiu Leung looked wary. "Thanks." He didn't return the compliment. "How are you?"

"Fine," said Rui. He thought he might even be telling the truth. "You OK? Still living with Alice?"

"Yeah." Yiu Leung's eyes slid away. "I should go. I don't want to be late."

Rui was at the exit when he thought, *What am I doing?*

If he wanted Yiu Leung back, it wasn't going to happen unless he went and got him.

What was the worst that could happen? Yiu Leung could

say no, but that would leave Rui in the same position he was in now. It would be humiliating—but everything Rui had ever achieved, everything in his life that he could be proud of, had happened because he was willing to fail.

He turned around. Yiu Leung was almost at the glass door that sealed off the Past Life Reconstruction Service's offices from the lobby.

"Yiu Leung," he yelled.

The woman at the reception desk raised her head. Yiu Leung turned.

He looked a little anxious, visibly dreading being dragged back into Rui's bullshit. But it was too late to stop now.

"I'm sorry," said Rui.

For once he had surprised Yiu Leung. "For what?"

"Everything," said Rui. "You deserved better." He glanced at the receptionist, who wasn't even trying to pretend she wasn't listening. "Look, can I take you out for a coffee after this?"

Yiu Leung's face worked. "Rui…"

"It would be good to talk," said Rui. "You can do the talking if you want. Tell me what you think of me. I don't think I listened enough to you."

"You can say that again," said Yiu Leung waspishly. He paused. "Alice is going to be mad at me."

That meant *yes*. Borne up on a wave of exhilaration, Rui said, "She can tell me what *she* thinks of me, too. I promise to keep my mouth shut. But I want to talk to you first."

"I'm busy today," said Yiu Leung, but before the wave could come crashing down, he added, "I could do tomorrow."

He looked back at the office door, behind which, presumably, a CEO in need of burpees awaited him.

"I've got to go," said Yiu Leung. "You've got my number."

"I'll text you," said Rui. He watched Yiu Leung as he went through the glass door, his gaze following him until he turned a corner and could no longer be seen.

wormwood on the tongue, making the hairs on Tay—on *Bridget's* arms stand on end. She bit her tongue as the tingle spread across her entire body, reminding herself over and over again that her name was Bridget now; this was a one-way trip, and 'Taylor' was not a girl's name in 1575. Or, well, maybe it was—research into the parish records of the time had shown that it wasn't completely outside the realm of possibility—but it was uncommon enough that it would stand out, and everything she'd done in the last five years had been geared toward preventing her from standing out.

Everything. From Invisalign braces designed to undo years of careful orthodontia by un-straightening her teeth just enough to make them look natural, without going far enough to cause future dental problems, to the removal of her fallopian tubes to permanently prevent the possibility of pregnancy without requiring hormone replacement, to the surgical shortening of the long bones in her legs—a process that had required months of bed rest, followed by physical therapy and learning how to walk all over again—to changing her name. That had been the part she'd been most willing to fight against, to delay as long as possible, even as she understood that it was necessary.

Changing her body was trivial. It hurt and it forced her to reassess how she moved in and related to the world— watching the way people's expressions changed when she went from a tall woman with perfect teeth and tasteful glasses to a woman of average height with stained, faintly crooked teeth and perfect vision had made her wish for the world before she'd let them fix her eyes; at least then she could have removed the lenses that corrected her vision and been ignorant for a little while longer—but her body was just the house where she lived. She could redecorate it any time she wanted to, and as long as she was the one doing the redecorating, she was perfectly fine with that. Her name, though...

Her name was the part of her that she had chosen. And yes, she'd named herself after Taylor Swift, an American singer-songwriter from the early decades of the 21st century, but for her, part of rejecting the regressive and patriarchal community where she'd spent the first seventeen years of her life had been about naming herself after a woman she truly admired, shaping herself into the person she had always known she had the potential to eventually become. Sure, she was now *literally* going to spend the rest of her life in a backward, patriarchal society, and sure, she was doing it of her own free will, but that was the important part, wasn't it? Her own free will. She was choosing this.

And Elizabethan England couldn't be called 'regressive' when it was the modern era, the cutting edge of European thought and culture. Which was admittedly an Anglophilic way of looking at things, but after five years of rigorous educational and theological preparation, accompanied by cultural drills and painful surgeries, she had become Anglophilic in self-defense if nothing else. She'd already been fond of the era when she'd volunteered for the deep past embedment program, seeing it as a fascinating moment in the history of both Europe and, thanks to the British tendency toward empire, the world. Now she was functionally obsessed.

She was also, she realized, as the walls crackled blue-white with lightning and shook around her, not nearly as prepared as she was supposed to be. This was supposed to be the greatest moment of her life, the day she gave up the woman she'd been for the sake of the woman humanity needed her to be. "Those who do not remember history are doomed to repeat it" wasn't just a pretty phrase: it was the full motto of the Deep Time Project, which intended to unsnarl the mysteries of history by throwing it the bones of the future.

Fully immunized, to prevent them from carrying back any diseases that could change the course of empire. Sterilized, to avoid the grandfather paradox from warping the very fabric of reality. Prepared to blend in and disappear into the populations they were being sent to study, and unaware of one another's identities, to avoid situations where two time travelers might meet and prefer one another's company to the people they were supposed to disappear into. Bridget knew one other person in the program, a very sweet Armenian-American man who was bound for the 17th century. Their eras had been far enough removed from one another that they hadn't seen the harm, and even that had been enough to trigger a review by the advisory board that had nearly stranded them both in their home time period.

Not an acceptable outcome, given how much debt they would already have accrued if they hadn't finished the trips they'd been indentured to. Joining Deep Time was midway between joining a particularly competitive graduate program and enlisting in the military; the project paid for your education, including all necessary tutors and trainers, and funded any medical procedures deemed essential for implantation in your chosen era. That wouldn't have been enough to convince most people to give up their lives and resign themselves to never seeing friends or family again, if not for the fact that the project also paid a more than healthy stipend to whomever their subjects designated, providing them with comfort, means, and medical insurance for the rest of their lives.

Taylor—Bridget, no, *Bridget*, even in the past tense, she had to be Bridget now—still might not have considered Deep Time as an option, if not for her baby sister. Emily had been born in the same borderline cult that she had, raised from birth to believe that her only options as a woman were to marry well, practice flawless obedience to the man who was her husband, and bear him strong children to be raised within the faith. Emily, who had been the only difficult part of leaving home, because saving herself had meant abandoning her sister to a world that was already threatening to swallow her alive.

Emily, who had been found by the side of the road, beaten almost to death by the man their father had given her to on her sixteenth birthday, for the crime of miscarrying twice in a row. She had been cast out by the only community she'd ever known, with no way of going back, and when the police had called Bridget, as her only family with a listed phone number, she'd found a trembling, traumatized young woman in the place of the bold teen she remembered, cowed by years of discipline, willing to do anything a man instructed her to do without a moment's hesitation, convinced that Bridget, whose departure had been fully voluntary, had been cast out by their father for her sinful thoughts and refusal to obey.

Getting Emily someplace safe had been the most important thing Bridget could consider, and once Emily was safe, paying for the lawyers and doctors and therapists she needed to not only legally separate her from her husband and their family, but to mentally rebuild all the places she'd been broken down. Bridget had been working at an independent bookstore in downtown Chicago when all this happened, making ends meet and thriving in her own quiet way. There had been no possible way she could pay for all the services Emily needed on her salary, and so when Deep Time had come recruiting, she'd signed up with regret but no reluctance.

Emily was her family. All the family she had in the world, and more family than she'd ever expected to have again. And no, Emily had never been able to live with her, unable to handle the noise and violence of the modern world, and still halfway convinced that Bridget was the Devil's own emissary, but that had just made it easier to sign up for the program. The way it was structured, once you signed up, there was no backing out without full repayment for all care and services.

Emily needed her to do this. It meant she'd live and

die centuries before Emily was even born, but that was a small price to pay to know that she had saved her sister.

The walls flashed again, then... flickered, almost, the ozone brightness seizing in a pattern she had never seen in training. Bridget screwed her eyes closed as tightly as she could, clenching what felt like every muscle in her body. She just had to hold on. She just had to keep calm until the lights blew out and she was safely in her new home, where the pre-industrial air would be fresher and cleaner, and the food would taste impossibly different, even after the years of palette retraining she'd been forced to undergo. And the voices would sound different, and the people would be different, and...

Everything would be different. Bridget closed her eyes, breathing deeply of the ozone-scented air. This was her future. This was her past. This was her decision, and even if she'd somehow miraculously had the funds to change her mind before getting into the transit box, it was too late now. Once the process was engaged, there was no stopping it. There was no deciding that no, really, the modern world was good enough for you, thanks. She was on a one-way express to Elizabethan England, and she was going to live there until she died, burying detailed records of her life at the predetermined location. The Deep Time archeologists would already be breaking ground, ready to harvest the fruits of her research, now that she was no longer there to present a paradox. There was no going back. There never had been. There was—

There was a strange buzzing sound coming from the

walls around her. Bridget opened her eyes and saw that the flashing had slowed to a crawl, barely qualifying as a pulse. Before she had time to fully wonder what that meant, there was one final flash and the booth disintegrated around her, exactly as it was intended to, leaving her standing in the middle of a green, grassy field.

In mud up to her ankles. Mustn't forget that crowning touch on her arrival. The booths were set to deposit their occupants near other people, but well out of any possible line of sight. Bridget didn't understand the technology and didn't pretend to. She was, thanks to Deep Time's training, a more than competent historian and oral storyteller, grilled and grilled again until her visual recall was practically perfect, but she wasn't a physicist, or a chronological scientist. How they picked the point where she'd be dropped was as far beyond her as her home in the 22nd century.

2108. A year she had never once, not even for a second, expected to feel nostalgia for. It was a hard, terrible world, still filled with inequality despite centuries of human advancement saying that they should have been better than that by now. The rising sea levels had destroyed most island ecosystems and coastal societies, resulting in steadily increasing numbers of both climate refugees and people like her parents, who had believed the word of a con man who claimed to be a prophet and allowed him to seduce them into his supposedly 'perfect' society, where a return to a simpler time could somehow be accomplished despite living in the same world as everyone else.

But it had been her hard, terrible world. It had contained her friends, her sister, her bearded dragon, and her favorite bands. Bridget felt a brief painful pang of loss as she thought of her books and entertainment disks, sitting on shelves in her room to be boxed up and presented to Emily, should her sister ever come back into synch with the world enough to want the things that had been left behind. She would never hear the new Poison Candy album. She would never eat at the Indian street cart on the corner that had the really good samosas. She would never eat another samosa. Potatoes wouldn't be widely available in Europe until long after she was dead and dust, and even if they had been, she wouldn't have had access to the rest of the spices and culinary concepts necessary to build a proper samosa, and even *if* she'd had access to the ingredients, all she would have been doing was getting herself credited as the inventor of the samosa. That went against both Deep Time principles, which said she could embed herself, and that it was understood that her presence would change the past, but instructed her to avoid changing the past intentionally if she had any choice in the matter, and against her own principles, which said that level of cultural appropriation would be so far from a good idea that it couldn't see appropriate with a telescope.

Suddenly, the fact that she had signed up for a life without samosas seemed like the greatest tragedy of them all. She took a deep, hitching breath, filling her lungs with the past, and paused, looking quizzically up at the pale, cloud-speckled sky. The air was fresher than it would have been back home, absolutely, but it wasn't the crystalline sweetness she'd been told to expect.

"Some of our returning researchers have reported feeling euphoric, almost drunk, after breathing the air in the past," was what her recruiter had said, when they still cared about selling her on the benefits of a program that would first completely remake her body, then her personality, and finally her life. "It's so clean that you won't be able to imagine breathing anything else—and you won't have to. You'll die long before pollution returns to the atmosphere."

The air wasn't like that. In fact, the air had the distinct, if mild, tang of petrochemicals, of gasoline and the combustion engine. Bridget frowned and started walking, gathering her heavy skirts in her hands to keep them from dragging in the mud. Lying about the sweetness of the air, she could understand, but the impossible pollution was harder to accept.

Cresting the shallow hill in front of the point of her arrival, she scanned the fields around her until she spotted a low cluster of wooden buildings and carnival tents. Some sort of harvest festival, given the time of year, or a summertime feast. Either way, she'd find people there, and they'd be able to tell her what was going on. She had trained for this. She knew who she was going to meet, in theory if not in practice, and she knew that they were going to be suspicious of her at first. People in this time period were always suspicious of strangers, especially ones like her, who bore no outward signs of malnourishment or disease. Bridget had been willing to let them make her shorter for the sake of blending in. She had drawn the line at smallpox scars, preferring a personal history that had her tending cattle on her family's farm before they were impoverished by famine and she was forced out on her own.

The insertion booths could target a century easily, and a decade with more difficulty, but an exact day and year was beyond anything the technology had yet been able to achieve. Maybe someday, but those advancements would come too late to help the members of her cadre. Unaware of what year it was, sure that it was summer only from the position of the sun and the buttery quality of the light as it slanted through the clouds, Bridget walked on, through the past, toward her future.

The smell of roasting turkey assaulted her nose when she was about twenty yards from the outer ring of tents. Bridget paused to inhale deeply. *Real* turkey, not synthetic or soy. She hadn't smelled anything so wonderful in years. Maybe she'd be able to survive the loss of her samosas after all. She started walking again, faster, as her stomach rolled and complained. Food was forbidden before the transit process, as the risk of candidates arriving in the past covered in their own vomit was just too high.

A second smell was close on the heels of the first, and enough to give her pause. Apparently, Elizabethan England had possessed a technique for frying turnips or beets or some other root vegetable that caused them to smell almost exactly like French fries. *That* was going to go into her record, for sure. The smell of frying potatoes was virtually impossible in this time period, and if she'd been in view of any other people when she encountered it for the first time, she could easily have given herself away.

Little things like that were the entire point of the program. Learning the pieces of history that had been left unrecorded, either because they were unremarkable or because the people who'd lived them in the first place had had nothing to put them into context and make it obvious how incredible they were. Bridget would find out how to cook whatever they were cooking to make it pass for potatoes, and she would write it down, and one of the Deep Time researchers would unearth it in the present and understand the past a little bit better.

In the future, technically. Linear time was hard to think about once it was broken down into a series of places she could never go again. Five minutes from now, that was the future. Emily and Deep Time and samosas, they were all in another world, one that she could never be a part of again.

She pushed her way between the tents, stepping onto ground packed hard and flat by the passage of hundreds of feet, and stopped, bewildered by the sight in front of her.

It wasn't the bright colors of the clothing worn by the people, which she had been warned to expect, dyes being much more plentiful and popular during this time period than the history books made them out to be.

It was, however, the denim jeans, and the silhouettes created by clearly modern undergarments, which had shifted in style and quality since the invention of the brassiere, but had never returned to the base form of the corset, or the loose-breasted styles that had come before either. It didn't help that there were also corsets on display, although few were worn in the style she had been prepared for; too many were undergarments being worn above the clothing, or incorrectly fitted, or entirely anachronistic.

A child walked by with a cone of what looked remarkably like tater tots. Bridget stared. The image on the child's T-shirt was anachronistic but familiar. Mickey Mouse had no place in Elizabethan England, not unless Deep Time had achieved their dreams of tourism while she was still in transit. Bridget took a shaking step forward, only to freeze again as a loud voice boomed out, "The Queen! Make way for Queen Elizabeth!"

Everything about this was wrong. There was no possible way Queen Elizabeth of England would be attending a small harvest festival, however bizarre. It wouldn't be safe, it wouldn't be sensible, and it wouldn't be happening. None of this was happening.

"Oh, I understand, the booth glitched," she said, before collapsing in a dead faint in the mud.

TAYLOR—NO, BRIDGET—no, *Taylor* woke up on a camping cot in a tent whose walls smelled of reassuringly artificial materials, the light from overhead distinctly electric and run on a plastic wire. She groaned, putting a hand over her face, and once again missed her glasses. Waking up with perfect vision and nothing on her nose was weird, and would be for the rest of her life.

Which was likely to be much longer, now that she had crashed down in an era with something closer to modern medicine. More years stranded in the past—and not even the right past—without any hope of rescue or recovery. Was she even on the right *continent*? The navigation module that was supposed to drop researchers in the correct century also moved them, accounting for the movement of the planet itself during the intervening years, following some complicated quantum physics theory that she didn't understand beyond the assurances that she wouldn't be slingshot into the void of space when the machine engaged. She rolled onto her side, stomach clenching with a combination of fear and hunger.

"Good, you're awake," said a light female voice, from somewhere past her feet. Taylor shoved herself into a sitting position, shoving her hair out of her eyes, and found herself looking at a brown-haired woman in a dress almost appropriate to the time period she was supposed to be in, save for the clear evidence of machine stitching on the bodice, and the impossible perfection of the embroidery. "Do you remember where you are?"

"First aid tent?" ventured Taylor.

The woman nodded, apparently relieved. "Good. You passed out from dehydration—is this your first year at the Faire?"

"Yes?" It seemed like the safest answer.

"You need to remember to drink water and eat during your shifts," said the woman. She produced a clipboard and what looked like a ballpoint pen, making a note on the paper. "You could do worse than a glass of Gatorade every so often. Drink pickle juice if you want to stay a little truer to the period."

"I'm sorry, what?"

"The sun out here is brutal for the new fish. Are you even wearing sunscreen?" The woman crossed the tent in two long strides, grabbing Taylor's arm and twisting it so that the inside of her elbow faced the light. "Thought not. How are you not red as a boiled lobster?"

"I..." This wasn't going to get any easier the longer she waited. Taylor swallowed and asked, "What year is it?"

"What—oh *crap*, did you hit your head when you fell down before?" The woman released Taylor's arm and leaned closer, staring into her eyes.

The woman's eyes, Taylor noted dispassionately, were a lovely clear shade of hazel with flecks of green.

"Your pupils look normal," she said. "Does your head hurt?"

"I feel fine," said Taylor. "I just need to know the year." *How far off was the beacon?*

"Nineteen ninety-six," said the woman, pulling back. "You're at the Cleveland Renaissance Faire."

Taylor swallowed a gust of laughter that would surely have been enough to convince this stranger that she was far worse than concussed, although she *felt* concussed.

How was she supposed to explain that she was from the future, was supposed to be in the *actual* time period this little play-act was pretending to represent? Or that all her training and all her resources were literally four hundred years out of date? The purse at her hip was still there, light by modern standards but heavy enough for the peasant woman she'd been intended to become. None of her money was going to be any good here, not as anything other than an antique—and even that wouldn't work, since it had all been acquired through Deep Time artifact scoops. Meaning she had a purse full of 16th-century funds that had been struck from base materials less than a year before.

The reality of her situation was beginning to sink in, one tiny piece at a time, and Taylor was starting to feel like passing out again might be the only good option she had. She was completely unprepared to live in this time period. She wasn't trained for this, she wasn't optimized for this, she wasn't *vaccinated* for this. 1996 was before the first COVID outbreaks, before the swine flu and Ebola and the great rabies pandemic and—

And half of those were so far into the future as to be irrelevant. By the time they happened, she would be buried, probably in an unmarked pauper's grave somewhere in the middle of North America. Taylor blinked, the first tears escaping to roll down her cheeks, leaving snail's trails of moisture behind.

It was like a dam breaking. Her face crumpled, and she began to sob, great, racking sobs that shook her whole body until she pressed her hands over her eyes and blocked out the impossible, out-of-time tent and the woman with the hazel eyes, putting herself back into the comforting darkness of the transfer booth. All she needed was the smell of ozone, the flash of transmission coils engaging. All she needed was for this not to have happened, and for her to be going home to her apartment after the failed transfer, safe and secure in her own time zone for one more night.

"What—what's wrong?" asked the woman, her hand landing on Taylor's shoulder like an anchor, binding her to this impossible, unwanted future, this distant but not-distant-enough past. Taylor kept crying, and couldn't imagine a world where she was ever going to stop.

Not ever again.

THE FAIRE GROUNDS were gearing up for the Christmas Faire, which was a smaller, shorter affair than the Renaissance Faire, where the sun might be brutal, but didn't usually kill any of the tourists who were smart enough to at least apply sunscreen and keep drinking sugary, overpriced beverages throughout the day. The winter air was less forgiving, and the people who organized the Faires feared lawsuits if anyone got a sufficiently damaging case of frostbite. So they got two weeks instead of six, with as many indoor activities and period-inappropriate heaters as they could cram into the space.

Even so, attendance was lower, as fewer people could see the appeal of hanging around outside at a glorified craft fair. Not when there were other craft fairs in malls and senior centers that didn't involve the possibility of snow or sleeting rain or—on occasion—both at the same time.

Taylor helped Marianne drag the sign for the med tent out to the walkway, bracing it against the wind.

"You don't have to help me do this," said Marianne. "I'm sure this place must bring back some bad memories for you."

"Not a single one," Taylor reassured her, grabbing her gloved hands and giving them a solid squeeze. "This is where my life began."

"This is where you lost your time machine and got stranded in the wrong century."

"Mmm," said Taylor, noncommittally. Marianne had been willing to accept that she was a time traveler when confronted with enough evidence of the idea, including the scars on Taylor's legs and her uncanny ability to predict approaching world events; she was going to be really surprised in a few years, when Taylor's early stabs at the stock market made them both millionaires. But that could wait. What Marianne hadn't been able to make her accept was that she'd been intentionally marooned in the past. The idea of Deep Time's methodology was alien to her, as a woman who still lived in a world where people were treated like a precious resource.

She'd accepted the hopeful parts of the future Taylor described as the inevitable improvement of the universe, but she'd quietly and without much comment rejected the rest. The disastrous early decades of the 21st century, the politicization of pandemics and climate change, all the darker sides of what was to come, Marianne listened and sighed and set them aside as a problem for tomorrow. They had each other now. They had the next several decades to live through. They had a whole world in front of them, and while she was willing to work with Taylor to disrupt the world to come, they didn't have the resources to keep that world from coming in the first place. It was too big a hill to climb.

Instead, they climbed the hill of getting Taylor established as a denizen of the era in which she had found herself. Taylor was grateful she'd landed when she did, and not even ten years later, when her lack of records would have made this process a hundred times harder than it needed to be. No computer record of her birth? That was fine, she clearly existed, and she just as clearly had a Midwestern accent, making it unlikely that she'd smuggled herself in from Norway. No medical records? Well, she was healthy and had the marks of extensive dental work, she was probably fine.

The borders of her own time were iron walls compared to the barriers of 1996, which Marianne tore through with the precision and glee of a born bureaucrat, although some of the social barriers were surprising and horrific. The first time she had kissed Marianne in public, the other woman had pulled away as if she'd done something wrong, while the other people in the coffee shop had actively recoiled, expressions telegraphing shock and disgust, like they couldn't believe she'd done that outside of a bedroom. Explaining the state of human rights in her own time had made things a little easier to understand, but didn't remake society in an instant.

Still, she slept at night warm and comfortable, in the arms of someone who cared about her, and by now, Deep Time would have finished the excavation of the place where she'd been told to bury her notes; there was no reason for them to have waited even a little while, since she'd been intended to die, from their perspective, as soon as the booth closed behind her.

They weren't coming to get her. She didn't owe them anything. Her contract had never specified that she had to be successful for them to pay out; Emily would be taken care of.

And she would be able to found Taylor Swift's fan club.

"What are you humming?"

"Oh, nothing," said Taylor, with a bright smile. "A song I like. We'll hear it properly in about twenty years."

Reaching over, she took Marianne's hand, and the two of them walked together into the tent, into the future, and left the past to come to them.

I REMEMBER SATELLITES

Sarah Gailey

Hugo Award winner and bestselling author **Sarah Gailey** (www.sarahgailey.com) is an internationally published writer of fiction and nonfiction. Their nonfiction has been published by *Mashable* and the *Boston Globe*. Their short fiction credits include *Vice* and *The Atlantic*. Their debut novella, *River of Teeth*, was a 2018 Hugo and Nebula Award finalist. Their bestselling adult novel debut, *Magic For Liars*, was published in 2019. Their most recent novel is *The Echo Wife*.

EVERYBODY DRAWS THE short straw in the end.

It's part of the job. If a new recruit draws the short straw for their first trip back, someone usually steps in for them, an old-timer who will say that the shit luck can't keep running from them forever. Nobody's first trip back should be a short straw trip.

I wish I could say that was me. I wish my one-way

ticket was the result of some altruistic impulse to snatch a starry-eyed kid from the jaws of time. But the truth is, I always wished it on someone else. I loved my job—I loved my life—and I never wanted to have to trade it in for a different one, no matter how necessary that trade might be.

The air left the room when it happened. This job was a whopper, and everyone on the team knew it. Our crew was used to tough work, ugly work, but this one was going to be a misery even by our standards. There would be no quick death for me, no moral absolution, no promise of eventual escape.

I was going to have to do a dirty job, and then I was going to have to live with the results for a long, long time.

Nobody would look me in the eye. Nobody tried to save me, either. It was my turn and we all knew there was nothing to be done about that. The best thing I could do was go with dignity.

So that's what I did. I smiled a grim smile and made a joke about my mom's rotten old ghost being relieved that I was finally going to catch myself a husband. Someone slapped my back as I walked out of that silent circle. I knew that once I was gone, there would be a shuffle of feet as they moved to fill in the space where I'd once stood.

They were going to do everything they could to forget me. That's the job: to forget, and to be forgotten.

I walked away from them and cleaned out my locker. I didn't say any goodbyes, not even the ones that mattered.

I did slip an envelope into Dani's locker, an envelope with a letter in it that I'd had ready since the day we both joined the 30s—but a letter isn't a real goodbye. I knew that, even if I'd never admit it.

Then I headed for my briefing. I left my old name and my old relationships and my old life behind. I braced myself for a long few days: inoculations, a complete microbiome refresh, a new wardrobe, a new accent, a new identity. The person I had been before was, in effect, dead.

It was time for me to become Violet Anne Fitzwallace.

I WORE OPERA-LENGTH sixteen-button satin gloves and a strapless floor-length gown for my first run-in with my future husband.

Plenty of heads turned when I walked into the room. I had the right face for the job—excruciatingly pale skin, acres of forehead, not quite enough nose, teeth that weren't straight or white enough to look fake—so don't get the wrong idea. They weren't admiring me. They were gawking at me.

I was fresh blood.

My target, Prince Henry, stood at the very center of the action, nursing a martini. Opposite him was a slightly-younger man in a military uniform who looked bored to tears—his kid brother, Prince Martin, who nobody ever thought would really amount to much. The two of them flanked a gilt chair with a high back and a velvet cushion.

Seated on that velvet cushion, her spine as straight as

a ship's mast, was a chinless old woman in head-to-toe black crepe. My secondary target: the Queen Mother.

She was still in deep mourning for her recently deceased husband, but apparently she could still attend a few necessary functions, of which this party was one. She was probably there to supervise Prince Henry, who by all accounts had few social skills, no talent for diplomacy, and a weakness for drunken rants about phrenology. The Queen Mother would be taking every possible opportunity to improve him—a project that was undoubtedly becoming more and more urgent, what with his coronation just around the corner.

I intended to undermine that project.

I stared hard at Henry's profile for a few seconds, trying to inoculate myself to the sight of him. Then I forced myself to look away. It was time to get to it.

I worked the room in a loose spiral, dusting the place with my most sparkling laughter, gently pressing my gloved hand to the lapels of the wealthiest bachelors, lowering my voice to a conspiratorial whisper every time I mentioned my recent divorce. Nothing makes news spread faster than a good whisper. I pollinated the place with gossip, and all the while, I closed ever inward on the man in the center of the crowd.

I didn't look at him again, not past that first hard stare. I couldn't risk him catching my eye and realizing that he was the one I wanted. For this whole thing to work, he needed to think of it as his own idea.

"More champagne, ma'am?"

I turned to accept, my half-empty glass aloft, because yes, I did want more champagne. I didn't mind being a little drunk for my first meeting with the shitty man whose shitty choices were defining the shitty course of my life. There were perhaps fifty waiters at the party, an army of them, and this one shouldn't have been remarkable at all.

When our eyes met, the room shrank around us. Every voice that didn't belong to the waiter fell away.

"Oh," the waiter gasped, her false moustache trembling. "You're here already?" Her long brown curls had been cropped short and slicked back with pomade. I could make out the tracks of the comb she'd dragged through it. Her hair was shiny, unmoving, but I couldn't help thinking of how soft it would be once she'd washed the grease out of it.

She was paler than I'd ever seen her.

"You can't be here," I whispered back, a bead of sweat sliding down the inside of my arm toward the sixteenth button on my opera glove.

"I'm not," she hissed back at me. She filled my glass with a shaking hand, her full lips pressed into a flat, bloodless line. Her eyes darted away from mine. "You didn't see me. You don't know me. Go."

And she was right: I couldn't have seen her. I couldn't have known her.

I tried to forget her as I got back to work, maneuvering my way through the room until I was close enough to hear Prince Henry's voice—high, nasal, self-assured. I caught the attention of a nearby member of the peerage and let him crowd me, his brandy-breath suffocating me as he droned on and on about how the war would never come to *our* shores, and if it did, why, of course we would *flatten those bastards*. I coaxed him closer and closer, until he was standing on the hem of my gown.

Then I took a halting step backward and I let myself fall.

Ice-cold gin poured down the back of my neck. Hands that had never once had a callus caught me by the shoulders. I tilted my head back to show off the long, pale line of my throat, and I looked up into the eyes of the man with whom I'd spend the rest of my life.

"I—I say," he stammered.

"It's my fault, Highness," my unwitting assistant slurred. "I tripped the Lady—"

"Please, do forgive me," I drawled in an accent that screamed *I'm new money*. I didn't move to stand on my own two feet, not just yet. I needed to be in his arms just a few seconds longer. "I don't believe we've met, and here I am, wearing your cocktail."

"Quite, that's, all right, well." His fingers flexed on my shoulders and he gave an audible gulp, his eyes locked on the sliver of décolleté that peeked above my neckline. "I'm Henry."

I winked at him. "Hello, Henry. I'm Violet Anne. Thank you ever so much for letting me fall into you."

Just like that, he was mine. As Henry helped me upright, his hand lingering on my elbow, I glanced over his shoulder. A skin-warm drop of gin traced a slow finger down the back of my gown, along my spine, all the way to the small of my back.

There she was. The waiter, looking right at me, like I was a person she knew—a person who was supposed to be forgotten altogether.

I should have looked away.

I didn't.

THE FIRST RULE of going back in time is *No Contact*.

There are a thousand other rules. *No Contact* being rule one doesn't mean it's the most important, but it does mean it's one we can't ignore. Nobody can get away with saying 'I didn't know' or 'I forgot', because who forgets the first, simplest, most ironclad rule?

No Contact means: don't find each other. Don't coordinate. Don't overlap. When we go back in time, we have to blend in seamlessly. That means we act like our lives in the future don't exist at all. Total immersion is key. Total discretion is vital.

It's just too hard to keep that up if we're spending time with pals from our own time. The urge to connect with the things you know about—the things that don't exist yet—it's irresistible. One minute you're reminiscing with your fellow traveler about laptops, and the next thing you know, you're blithely dropping a Bill Gates reference at a garden party and everyone's looking at you like you're a maniac.

Worse still is the urge to talk shop. When you meet

someone who gets the stakes of the job, someone who understands the pressure and the isolation, it's too easy to give in to the urge to share why you got sent back. What you're there for. How important your work is. It's too easy to compromise your entire objective just for the sake of a moment of human connection.

The risk is too high. The rules are clear: if you spot someone you know, un-spot them. Our job is to forget who we've been, and to be forgotten by those we've known.

Absolutely no exceptions.

Not for anything.

THE PAPERS WOULD describe my romance with Henry as a whirlwind. The royal family would describe it as a scandal, an embarrassment beyond repair. I would describe it as a long battle with nausea.

Henry was everything the dossier had told me to expect: witty, dry, snobbish, smug, fashionable, petulant. Blazingly bigoted. He confessed the things he wanted in bed in a wet-lipped whisper that spoke to years of repression. I obliged him by blushing.

In all, using every tool at my disposal, it took three weeks to get him to fall deeply, profoundly, disgustingly in love with me.

"I will, you understand, be King soon," he murmured after a particularly dull evening, his thinning hair soaked through with sweat, his bed sheets tangled over both of our legs.

Of course I knew. Even aside from the fact that it was all anyone was talking about, the coronation was the entire reason I was stuck with him. It was the cause of my short straw.

"Oh, my love," I replied breathily, trailing my fingers across his sunken chest. "You know I don't care about all that. I just want *you*."

He caught my wrist in one soft hand. "Then you shall have me, my darling Vi. You shall have me. I don't care what anyone says."

"Anyone? Even *her*?" I put a little venom into the pronoun, because Henry hated his mother, hated her with all his might, and that hatred was the biggest lever I had. Leaning a little weight on it could go a long way.

"Especially *her*," he said, tugging on my arm gracelessly until I was on top of him, awkwardly straddling his hips. "All of them can hang. Who cares if you're a divorcée? In this day and age? Honestly," he tutted. "It's silly. An outdated rule. I'm sure nobody will care."

"Of course they won't care." Oh, they would *absolutely* care.

"Well, then." He kissed the tip of my nose. "It's decided. Call down to the kitchen for champagne, will you? We must celebrate."

I slid off him, numb with my terrible victory.

A job well done.

I wrapped a bed sheet around myself and leaned out the bedroom door, peeking into the hall, trying to catch the eye of anyone on staff. He'd wanted me to use the phone, of course, but I was naked, mussed, screamingly *premarital*. I wanted to be seen, to be the subject of torrid gossip. The conversation had to be out of his control.

I spotted a gray-suited butler about halfway down the hall, walking briskly away from me. A quick glance over my shoulder revealed an already-dozing Henry—honestly, he wore out as easily as a puppy at the beach—so I let the door shut softly behind me and darted out after him, the plush carpet enveloping my bare feet.

"Pardon me," I called softly. "Excuse me. You there."

The butler froze. He didn't turn around, but the back of his neck flushed. Maybe he'd been eavesdropping at the door, listening to the impressive performance I had put on for the Prince. I do have quite a decent vocal range.

"Would you fetch some champagne up from the kitchen, please?" I asked like it was a real question, not a command. If I played my cards right, they'd all be talking about how vulgar I was before Henry's refractory period was up. "We're celebrating, you see."

The butler nodded, but he still wasn't looking at me. This level of disrespect was better than I could have hoped for. If even the staff hated me, I could be sure of the ire of the family.

"Two glasses, please. And Henry's favorite dessert, too," I added boldly. "He'll want something special to mark our engagement."

At that, the butler's head whipped to one side. The sight of that profile took the wind out of me.

"Your what?" Her fake moustache was perfectly still.

All of her was perfectly still.

"Dani," I breathed. "What are you still doing here?"

Her eyes flicked down to my mouth at the sound of her name—a name that shouldn't exist anymore, that should have been devoured by whatever identity she'd assumed for this job—and then she blinked hard, like she was trying to clear her vision. "It's a mistake," she murmured. "I was supposed to be gone by the time you arrived. I was supposed to be out by now."

"You're on a job?"

"What are you celebrating? Say it again."

I swallowed hard. "Our engagement," I said, all the bright, stupid triumph gone from my voice. "Me and Prince Henry. We're going to be married."

"Champagne it is," Dani said, her voice as dull as tin. "My congratulations to you both."

She made to stride away, but I caught her. She turned to me whip-fast, stopping with her nose a threadbare centimeter away from mine. I breathed her in—the air around her tasted so familiar, tasted just like Dani. Like salt air, like thunderstorms, like warm flannel sheets on a cold winter night. "Do you remember satellites?" I asked, my fingers curled tight in the fabric of her sleeve.

It was wholly selfish of me: I wanted her to remember a future where satellites existed. I wanted her to remember staring up at them with me, tracing their paths across the sky.

After a long second she replied, her eyes shining and full. "Those don't exist yet. But I remember shooting stars."

With gentle fingers, she eased my grip off her sleeve. She gave my hand a fleeting squeeze—and then she was gone, down the hall and off to the kitchens to send up champagne so Henry and I could celebrate our engagement.

I crept back into the bedroom, the bed sheet clutched to my chest. I watched my new fiancé snore softly in his sleep, his slack chin vanishing into his neck, his future drifting ever so slowly in the right direction.

And my future drifting faster and faster toward him.

I WAS SO good at playing the concerned fiancée. "Darling, tell me what's the matter?" I asked as if I didn't know.

Henry shook his head, fastening his cufflink without looking at me. "Nothing, dearest. Nothing at all. Just the old bat up to her usual flapping."

"Oh?" I put my left hand on his sleeve, my ring sparkling aggressively. The diamond was as big as the lowest knuckle of my thumb. "Whatever is she squeaking about now?"

Henry heaved an enormous slump-shouldered sigh. "I— It's nothing. Truly." He gave me a thin-lipped smile that I'm sure was meant to be reassuring. "Just some to-do about the wedding. Nothing to fret about."

I returned his weak smile with a bright one and went back to hunting for my left glove. I couldn't remember where I'd put it the night before. I knelt beside the bed and lifted the bedskirt, peering into the shadows. There—a vague lump that might be a glove. I reached for it.

"The only thing," he continued. "The only thing is, well. I can't go on that drive we had planned for today. I've been summoned."

"Summoned?" I echoed him absently. "What for?" I fished under the bed, my fingers brushing kid leather. I almost had it.

"An audience. With Mother."

There. I grasped the glove at last and pulled it out. How it had wound up so far beneath the bed, I had no idea. "Is that usual?"

He sounded queasy when he replied. "Not as such, no."

"Well, too bad about the drive." I straightened, gave him a twinkly little smile. "Another time?"

"Another time," he agreed. I thought he'd talk to me about it more—about how his family didn't approve of the match, how they were going to forbid our marriage, how he was torn about what to do. I was all set to remind him to hold his ground. But he just kissed me and headed off, his head held high, his jaw clenched.

I sat on the unmade bed in the empty bedroom for a few minutes after he was gone. I hoped that he simply didn't need my encouragement as much as I'd predicted he might. I hoped that this wasn't a sign that he was less committed to our engagement than I needed him to be.

I needed him to be very, very, *very* committed.

There was no use sitting around. I needed to find out how thoroughly I'd managed to spread the news of our engagement. If the papers had it, the family would have to navigate things more carefully than they would if it was just a little gossip. I could apply a little pressure via the Fourth Estate, make sure the dreaded public had an interest in our romance. I shook my glove out and went to put it on, already thinking of the anonymous phone calls I'd need to make before morning dripped into afternoon.

It crinkled.

I frowned, peered inside the glove. There was something in one of the fingers—a piece of paper, all crumpled up. I couldn't imagine how it had gotten in there, but then again, the glove had been under the bed. Maybe a piece of trash, somehow.

Maybe some part of me knew. Maybe some part of me hoped. All I know is that I fished the paper out and, for no reason at all, instead of throwing it away, I smoothed it flat. There were three words written on it in familiar cursive, three words that made my heart twist.

I remember satellites.

HENRY'S CONVERSATION WITH the Queen Mother went deliciously awry. He related it to me that evening as we prepared to go out for dinner. Predictably, my divorce was a deal-breaker. I don't think she would have liked the match anyway, but the divorce meant there was legal precedent. She wasn't going to budge: our marriage was absolutely forbidden.

Henry was in a storm of temper, hurtling himself from one side of the room to another, livid and frothing. "As if I was a child! As if she has any right! I'm going to be King!

And then what power will she have? What authority to forbid anything at all?"

"Honestly," I purred, "this family doesn't deserve you."

He paused in front of the mirror, smoothing his hair down. "No," he snapped. "No, they don't. I should like to see how they'd fare without me. And with a war on the horizon. Oh, none of them believe it will happen, but that's precisely the problem, isn't it? They underestimated the power, the capability, the profound beautiful efficiency of the war machine in action—"

"They lack vision," I interrupted, draping myself over his shoulders, meeting his reflected gaze. "Your vision."

"Put Martin in charge for a while, why don't they, and see what happens," he muttered mulishly.

I walked away from him, heading toward my pocketbook as if there was something I needed from it. There wasn't—I just needed my face to be pointed away from his. I couldn't afford to let him see my incandescent triumph.

Almost there.

"That would be hilarious, wouldn't it?" I said, light as air, my voice holding almost steady. "Martin, on the throne. What a way to burn down the country. He could never hold his own in a war. We'd be overrun by fascism in no time at all."

The silence that answered me was electric. I let it sit for a good long minute, giving the idea time to sink into him. Giving it time to germinate.

"When is that reservation again?" I opened my pocketbook, casual as anything. The note from Dani was in there. I should have burned it or eaten it or thrown it into a river, but I hadn't been able to make myself do it.

"Seven." He was right behind me and I snapped the pocketbook shut at the feel of his hands resting on my hips, his lips on the nape of my neck. He pressed himself against me, throbbing and urgent. "But they'll hold the table for us, my brilliance."

We didn't leave until eight thirty. Under the pretense of fixing my mussed hair, I lingered in the bathroom, staring at myself in the mirror. I was flushed, bee-stung, and windswept. I smiled at myself and it all worked just fine together: I looked like I was in love with that man, that man who would be king, that man who had just gotten hard at the thought of his country falling to fascism during the looming war.

I looked like someone who could marry that man.

I was going to lose myself to this person I was becoming. That was inevitable. It was my job to abandon who I'd been, the life I'd had before, everything I'd ever known.

To forget, and to be forgotten.

But I wasn't ready yet. I wasn't ready to become that woman in the mirror, not all the way. I did what I had to do to stop myself from shaking apart, to stop myself from sinking into my own future faster than I could stand to.

Swallowing bile, I pulled the folded paper out of my pocketbook. *I remember satellites.* I turned it over and used my eyeliner pencil to reply in smudged black letters: *I remember watching them with you.*

I left the note tucked under the box of condoms on the

side of the bed that had rapidly become mine. By the time we returned, well past midnight, the bed was made and the note was gone.

THE NEXT MORNING, over tea, Henry told me that he would do anything for me. Go anywhere for me. He said that, in order to be with me, he would even be willing to give up the crown.

"But only if it came to that," he assured me with a soft smile. "And I don't think it will. They'll see reason. And besides, Martin is a simpering coward—he wouldn't want the throne, not really. Not to keep."

"They will," I agreed, and I meant it, even if I didn't mean it the way he wanted me to. "If you'll just excuse me for a moment? I need to powder my nose."

His lips twisted with distaste—even the suggestion of a bodily function was too much for him—and waved me off. I walked away and kept myself together until I was around the corner and out of his sight.

I was alone in one of the many endless hallways that would contain the rest of my life. I leaned against the wall, closed my eyes, and forced myself to breathe. Everything was going smoothly. I was functioning precisely as I was supposed to. We were ahead of schedule, even—he wouldn't need to abdicate the throne if he was never actually crowned. He'd never have any state secrets to funnel to anyone. I would be a footnote in his story, a little-known fact.

I would spend the rest of my life with him.

"Short straw getting heavy?"

I startled, my eyes snapping open, and there she was, Dani, just a few inches from me, in her staff uniform. She looked like a lifeline. She looked like home. I moved without thinking, the way a swimmer knows to gasp for air when her head breaks the surface of the water.

I grabbed her face and I kissed her like there was no future to worry about. She tasted just like I remembered, like shimmering heat and sea air, and I wanted to lose myself in her so I couldn't get lost in my own abominable fate.

She kissed me back with savage urgency, then pushed me away by my shoulders. "You can't," she whispered.

You can't, not *we can't*. Not *I don't want to*. "Why not?" I breathed back, my eyes locked on the swell of her mouth below her fake moustache. "It's not like they can write me up when I get back."

"I wish you'd said goodbye," she said. Not an answer. Her hands were still on my shoulders, holding me exactly where I was, not pushing me away any further. She leaned toward me just a little, still out of reach but not by much. "I know why you didn't, but..." She shook her head softly. "It's been four years for me, since you left."

Four years. I studied her. She looked older, now that I was looking for it, although not by much. Or maybe she just looked sadder. "I left you a letter," I said. "I can't believe they sent you here."

She didn't meet my eyes. "I didn't mention the potential

conflict of interest in my briefing. I thought I could handle it, if I ended up seeing you. I thought I'd be able to walk away. I should walk away."

"Dani," I said, because there wasn't anything else to say. She was right. We shouldn't do this. We *couldn't* do this.

But then again, my life was about to be permanently fixed to that of a spineless fascist sympathizer who was prepared to sell out his country to the first jackboot that asked for it, and Dani was here *now*, here right in front of me for who knows how long, and I was supposed to forget her, but I wanted to remember her.

I wanted her to remember me.

Her fingers flexed on my shoulders. She grimaced, glanced behind her, and I knew that face, oh, I knew that face, I had seen it so many times.

That face said *fuck it*.

"Powder room?" I whispered.

"Powder room," she confirmed, and then she pulled me down that endless hallway until we were both behind a door with a lock on it.

Henry would have to finish tea without me.

HENRY AND I met with the Prime Minister about our engagement.

Dani and I met in the garden and stared up at the moon together.

Henry and I snuck a statement to a hungry young reporter at the *Times*.

Dani and I snuck into an unused guest suite and pulled the white drop cloth off the bed.

Henry and I said it would only be a temporary move, a season or two out of town to show them they couldn't control his heart. We pretended not to know that we were going into a subtle kind of exile.

Dani and I said it would be the last time, every time. We didn't talk about the things that would have felt too hard to discuss, like the time she'd spent alone or the time I spent underneath Henry. We didn't talk at all about what her life had been like during those four years. It didn't seem worth it. It didn't feel like there was time for it. We pretended we were just saying goodbye to each other, the long way round.

Until, finally, it was time for me to go, and I had to stop pretending.

"I'm leaving tomorrow," I told her, winding a short lock of her sweat-damp hair around my middle finger. "They want us gone before the coronation, to which we are pointedly not invited. We're going to live in New York. He thinks it's just for six months, a year at the most, but..."

"But the war," she finished for me. She let her head fall pack onto the pillow and stared up at the ceiling. "They'll be dropping bombs on us by the time you've finished unpacking the silverware."

"That's the idea," I murmured. "No coming back while there's a war on. You should come with us. Stay on as household staff, avoid the bombing. I can offer you good pay." I traced a finger along the line of her throat. "And benefits."

Dani gave me a rueful smile. "You know we can't. Besides, I didn't come back just to visit you. I'm on a job."

"What's the job?"

She rolled her eyes. "I'm not telling you that."

"Come on." I kissed her shoulder. She shivered. "I'm going to be on a boat in the morning. I won't be able to get in your way. Who's so important that you have to stick around for them?"

Her fingers found the back of my neck, traced the path of my hairline as I trailed kisses across the plane of her belly. "I'm not telling," she said, her voice curling up like the corners of a smile.

I bit her hip just hard enough to make her gasp. "I could make you talk," I said, hoping she'd try to keep her secret just a little longer. "I could convince you to come with me. I have ways and methods."

But she tugged me back up toward the pillow, the playfulness draining out of her, her face falling into serious lines. "Violet Anne," she said.

"Ugh, please. That's not my name."

"It is now," she said. "And I need you to listen to me for a minute."

I sat up, gathering the bed sheets to my chest. Something was gathering in the air around us. Something I didn't like. "I'm listening."

"You didn't say goodbye to me," she said quietly. "I should have just walked away when I saw you in that ballroom. But I couldn't. Not without getting a chance to actually say goodbye to you, properly. And then I just kept not doing it, even though I know I have to. I have to say goodbye."

"Maybe it can just be 'until we meet a—'"

"No," she interrupted, her eyes bright. "No. Not 'until we meet again'. It has to be goodbye. You're on a short straw job. It's a miracle I haven't compromised you already. You have to be Violet Anne. You have to forget me, and us, and this. "

She was right. Total immersion. Total discretion. No contact.

I had to forget, and be forgotten.

"But I don't want to lose you," I said helplessly. "I don't want you to forget me."

Dani pressed her forehead to mine, holding me still, breathing me in. "This is our job. Love can't keep us from doing it. You said so in your letter, remember?"

"I didn't mean it." I gripped her hands, couldn't imagine letting them go.

She smiled and kissed me, her tears rolling down the length of my nose. "Yes, you did."

HENRY AND I were married on the boat that took us to New York. Martin was crowned and anointed, and became the king who would help the country survive the terrible war to come. History was solidifying in my wake: a job well done.

I smiled a lot. I kissed him in the morning and I made him cocktails in the evening. We moved into a townhouse. We bought a radio.

I looked up at the sky every night, and I looked at the unmoving stars, and I tried to forget.

HENRY OPENED THE mail over breakfast each morning. "Letter for you," he'd say, holding out an envelope to me without looking at me, so I'd have to put down my teacup or my fork and accept it.

It was a small annoyance. I was always on the verge of saying something about it. I wanted to pick at him, to erode his sense of contentment. My assignment was to stay married to him, to keep him in a state of righteous exile until his eventual death—but nothing said our marriage had to be a happy one.

I was still figuring out who, exactly, Violet Anne was. I was still figuring out just how miserable she could afford to make her husband. So, when we'd been married for six months, I decided on a little experiment. I decided to start a fight with him about the mail.

"Letter for you," he said, thrusting the envelope toward me.

"This instant?" I snapped, wiping my hands on my napkin in case of stray jam.

"Doesn't say who it's from," he added absently. "Hand-delivered, maybe."

I took the envelope and glared at him for a moment,

hoping he'd look up and ask what was the matter so I could snap 'Nothing' and look pointedly away. He didn't look up.

Too bad. I'd have to try again later.

There was no return address, just my name, typewritten across the front of the envelope. I turned it over, irritable. Most of my mail came from members of the social set that had cropped up around us in New York, all of whom were awful.

But the sheet of paper inside the envelope wasn't from one of our new friends.

It had a single line of handwriting on it. Five words. That's all it took to make the world fall out from beneath me.

I don't want to forget.

I told him I needed to put a reply letter in the box, and he didn't look up, didn't ask who I was writing back to, because of course he didn't. I was out the front door by the time he finished rattling the newspaper open and she wouldn't be there, she couldn't be there, she would surely be long gone already, but I still raced down the front steps as though I could catch her.

And there she was, like a miracle, like a shooting star in a dark sky. She was leaning against a lamppost with the collar of her trench coat turned up. A livid new scar cut a valley across her left eyebrow. My Dani.

She didn't make me find words. Not right away.

"I finished out my job," she said. There was an unfamiliar rasp in her voice, like she'd been shouting for the entire six months since I saw her last.

My bare toes curled against the pavement. "So you're headed home?"

She cocked her head, watchful. "Hope so."

"What's that mean?"

"The thing is... I spent that whole time trying to forget you. Trying to forget us. But I couldn't. So. Maybe I took a little too long to finish my assignment. Maybe I mistimed my extraction while the bombs were falling." She stepped toward me, close enough that I could smell the ghost of old smoke lingering on her. "My extraction point is rubble."

"Careless," I said softly. "That's not like you."

"A real blunder," she replied with a canny smile. Her eyes flashed, bright and burning. "And there's no way for anyone to know whether or not I was at the extraction point when it got hit. I suppose it would seem to them that my assignment turned out to be a short straw job after all."

I shook my head, not daring to hope. "I can't leave him."

"So don't leave him. You and I, we'll be one of history's great love affairs. They'll write songs about us."

I touched her cheek, her hair, the scar on her eyebrow. "The Agency will be furious if they find out."

She caught my hand and pressed a kiss to my palm. "Who is there for them to be furious at? I'm a dead woman, Violet Anne, and you're a short straw. They've forgotten all about us."

"That's the job," I said, a real smile creeping up out of me for the first time since I'd seen her last. "Forget—"

"—and be forgotten," she finished.

"I could stand to be forgotten. If I can be forgotten with you."

And then she pulled me around the corner, out of sight of the windows of the home I shared with the husband I hated, and she kissed me. She kissed me like there was a lifetime's worth of forgetting to do, and I kissed her back like I intended to remember.

And oh, how I intend to remember.

THE GOLDEN HOUR

Jeffrey Ford

Jeffrey Ford (www.well-builtcity.com) is the author of the novels *The Physiognomy, Memoranda, The Beyond, The Portrait of Mrs. Charbuque, The Girl in the Glass, The Cosmology of the Wider World, The Shadow Year, The Twilight Pariah, Ahab's Return*, and *Out of Body*. His short story collections are *The Fantasy Writer's Assistant, The Empire of Ice Cream, The Drowned Life, Crackpot Palace, A Natural History of Hell, The Best of Jeffrey Ford,* and *Big Dark Hole*. Ford's fiction has appeared in numerous magazines and anthologies from *Tor.com* to the *Magazine of Fantasy and Science Fiction* to *The Oxford Book of American Short Stories* and has been widely translated. It has garnered World Fantasy, Edgar Allan Poe, Shirley Jackson, Nebula Awards and a *New York Times* Notable Book of the Year.

I SAT WITH the time traveler in the apple orchard behind his lodgings at the Coach and Four. Barthus, the waiter from the hotel bar, for a healthy tip, didn't mind strolling out across the back parking lot and down a short path every now and then to serve us a round of lime and lavender gin. The conversation was unhurried, with long silences in which we heard the percussion of ripe apples falling at the end of summer. It never failed that he would mention in his musings that he was merely waiting for the time stream to reopen.

I never directly confronted him on the outlandish nature of his time travel escapades. I could see no gain in embarrassing him, and to tell the truth they were what I came for. All the while he spoke, in a faint and faltering tone, he was eating these little hard brown nuts he had a pocketful of in his jacket. I asked if I might try one, and he shook his head and gave a weak laugh. "Heavens, no," he said. "They're from the future, exceedingly bitter. One has to develop a taste for them."

He dressed like a scholar of a bygone era—tweed jacket, white shirt and tie, brown trousers, and a pair of black wingtip shoes that came to perilous points. He was always starched and creased, and his graying hair, what was left of it, he wore brushed back and held in place with what looked like a smear of bear wax. There was an autumn caterpillar of a mustache on his lip and his eyebrows were a tangle. An old man once told me that irony is the engine of the world, and so the tiny strawberry birthmark between his left eye and ear took the form of an hourglass. He often smoked a meerschaum pipe, the white bowl wrapped round by an eagle's talon affixed to the long stem. Sometimes, as the night settled in among the trees and a late summer wind carried the scent of the nearby bay, he'd puff his pipe and stare seemingly unconscious into the darkening corners of the orchard. Then I would quietly take my leave of him and walk back along a path through the Winesaps to my cheap motel in the cattails by the edge of the water.

I was really quite surprised that no one in the entire town of Wespire seemed to find his claims all that odd, but it was an easygoing backwater of a place. I was first introduced to him by Miss Host, the young woman who ran the newspaper kiosk where I bought my cigarettes and he, apparently, his pipe tobacco. She said to me, "Mr. Russell, have you met the time traveler?" I thought she was making a joke, but no, when I looked up, there he was with his gloved hand outthrust. I shook it, and said, "So, you're a time traveler," with a big grin on my face like I was in on the joke. I'm not exactly sure when the look of quiet desperation in Miss Host's big brown eyes made me realize they weren't kidding.

I wished them both a good day, and as I stepped away from the kiosk, the time traveler followed me. He told me that he was staying at the local hotel, "if you could call it that," waiting for the time stream to open back up so that he could resume his journey.

"Past or future?" I asked.

"Where the clues lead, young man. Where else?"

Of course, I wanted to ask him, "Clues to what?"

Before I could, he quickly inquired as to what my days were filled with.

"I'm holed up in the small motel over by the bay, under strict deadline, writing my third novel."

"About?"

"To tell the truth, I haven't written a blessed word. Maybe you'll be kind enough to regale me with tales of time travel I can use as inspiration."

To this he said, "Come by any late afternoon. If it's not raining, I'll be out in the orchard behind the Coach and Four Hotel. I've had them set up a table and two chairs back there. Summer is fading fast and its decline is beautiful amid the trees and tall grass."

"I will," I promised.

He nodded and headed across Main Street toward the library.

Two days later, the skies were clear and I left my room at the golden hour when the light turns the color of honey. The phenomenon doesn't last long. Still, I made it to the orchard and found the time traveler before the gold veneer dissipated into dusk. He sat in a foldout chair, next to a small round table. There was an empty chair across from his, and two crystal tumblers half-full of the violet lime and lavender gin that, I soon learned, was his favorite.

I approached him from behind, and when I drew close, without actually seeing me, he took the pipe out of his mouth and said, "Welcome, Mr. Russell. I've been expecting you."

I sat across from him and laid my notebook and pencil on the table. "Drink up," he said. "Barthus should be back with another round before long." The combination of flavors in the alcohol was stunning.

"What is it you want to know?" he asked.

"How do you time travel?"

"Very well," he said.

I lit a cigarette and took up my notebook and pencil.

"Time is not a mighty river, it's not a stream, nor a burbling brook. Time doesn't flow. It's one vast contiguous form like a giant wheel of cheese. This was proven by Professor Whelmer at the University of the West back at the end of the last century from this current date. She proved that the passage of time is an illusion. All time is any time and vice versa."

"I'm trying to picture you burrowing through a vast wheel of cheese."

"Precisely," he said. "That's why you have to understand that time travel is a function of memory."

"You mean you're simply daydreaming?"

"Oh, no. It's far more than that, and much more difficult to achieve. But because you can't actually go back to the physical moment in time, which never existed to begin with, you must settle for traveling at the impetus of your memory. It takes intense concentration, certain specific physical poses, a universal time travel mantra, and the power of the imagination. If you can get all of these windows to align, you do actually travel to the point initiated by your memory. Do you know of the experiments where Whelmer applied live electrodes to parts of a patient's brain? The patient acted and reacted as if she was reliving a moment from her life. For all intent and purpose, she was there. Once you achieve that, you can wander anywhere in the world of that memory."

"Sounds complicated," I said. "How did anyone discover this method?"

"It's been known by the sages and shamans of numerous cultures going back thousands of years. Some say that it was brought to our planet by visitors from the stars."

"Do you subscribe to that theory?"

"Do I look like a fool? No, I believe it's our reliance on and relationship with memory that drew inquisitive minds to discover the process."

"If not a metaphor for flowing water, what is the time stream that you refer to?"

"It's a term for the beams of focused recollection that you send streaming to your memory to achieve time travel. Depending on their strength, that is how adept you will be at the procedure. And one other rule, because time travel is a function of memory, you can only revisit those times that fall within the boundary of your life span or memory."

"You mean to tell me... Forgive me for asking, but what is your actual name?"

"Galen Thomas."

"You mean to tell me that right now, there is another Galen Thomas of some other age living in this world?"

He nodded.

I finished my drink and gave up on writing anything down. The moment was to be experienced with full concentration. Thomas's madness was intricate, confusing, and complete. There was a pause in our conversation in which I tried to analyze his methods but my thoughts ended in knots. When I finally rejoined the time traveler, he was off in one of his dazes. A mourning dove called across the orchard.

In the days that followed, I thought a great deal about the time traveler. I was fairly certain he was insane. I also wondered why, if he was so adept at the practice of time travel, he seemed as if he was stuck. Run out of time travel beams. I had every intention to go back for more a few days later, but when I left my motel room there was a luxurious black car out front. The window went down in back and there was the time traveler, wearing a hat and a pair of dark glasses. "Get in," he said. I did hesitate for a moment, but then noticed Barthus was driving, and he always seemed very pleasant. I got in.

We drove for a way in silence before Galen said, "I'm taking you to Oberidge for dinner. It's on me."

"Thank you," I said, and settled back.

The trip took only a quarter of an hour, and Barthus dropped us off at a sidewalk café across from the canal at the center of the small town. We had drinks and I asked Galen why he was stuck, why his beams were not streaming. He told me with a wistful expression, "I'm losing focus and energy as I grow old. Time travel is for the young. I'll get out of here someday, trust me.

And when I go, I probably won't have a chance to say goodbye."

The meal was served and it was quite good: roasted growl goose with potatoes and creamed peanuts. There were quite a few people at the café, some inside and some out on the street under an awning. The place was run by a husband and wife and two children. The four of them did everything from the cooking to the bussing of tables, to chatting up the customers. The young boy who brought us our drinks showed us a magic trick with a deck of cards he carried in his pocket. Galen gave him a tip for it and said, "You're a very bright young man. What's your name?" The boy smiled and said, "Galen."

"Is your last name Thomas?" I asked.

The boy pointed to the sign inside, over the bar. In large ornate letters it read Thomas Café. When he turned to point, I detected the strawberry hourglass between his eye and ear.

"Remarkable," I said to the time traveler. He nodded but said no more. We finished dinner and Barthus arrived to ferry us back toward Wespire. I was dropped off at the motel where I thanked the gentlemen for the evening out, and then I went to sleep for the first time with the new and stunning knowledge that time travel was possible. My sleeping mind couldn't wrap itself around the idea, and the conflict gave rise to nightmares of mathematics and feverish reasoning.

Autumn relieved summer in a graceful illusion of the progression of the year, and the temperature dipped to a condition not ungodly but at least brisk. I went one overcast afternoon to see the time traveler but found the chairs and round table knocked over by the wind and almost invisible in the long tawny grass. I went back again the following week, and, through a light snow squall, noticed the furniture had been removed. By then night had already fallen. I went back to my motel and my accursed third novel.

Not much writing got done but there was a lot of deep thought. By the bay, winter days were quiet save for the occasional screech of a seagull, or the pattering of mice in the motel walls. The rest of the place had cleared out and the owner let me keep my room through the empty season if I promised to do some light maintenance. You could fill all that quiet with memories, and I did. There was actually one specific recollection I kept returning to and worked on seeing and experiencing more of it, all of it. Of course, the time traveler's lesson was in the back of my mind.

It was just a ridiculously simple scene from when I was a child. It had snowed through the night and my mother, young and vibrant, and still alive, got out the sled and tied a rope to it and then around her waist. She ran through the snow with me on board. We were heading for the school where I was enrolled in first grade. I focused on it, the rhythm of her boots in the snow, the slush of the runners, the enormous flakes that fell slowly like in a dream. But it was no dream, I was certain of it. The more I concentrated on it, more became clear to me—my mother's coat with a fur-trimmed hood, my own bulky snowsuit, the kids we passed throwing snowballs at each other. One night, after sitting all day, staring out the window at the bay, and thinking of the incident, I felt the soul within me lurch.

I was certain I'd nearly traveled in time, positive that I'd nearly achieved an energy time stream to connect me to the past. It only lasted a second, but it was a revelation. I knew to go further I'd have to speak to Thomas. I was confident I could narrow down what I needed to know in no more than a dozen questions. Winter was formally upon Wespire and so I skipped the orchard and went straight to the Coach and Four. There, I encountered Barthus emptying the ashtrays in the solarium and inquired after the time traveler. He smiled and said, "Mr. Thomas is never in his room before nightfall. He has a visitor. A woman." I thanked him for the information and told him to have Thomas send for me when he had a free minute.

The following day, I walked downtown, dressed warmly with scarf and overcoat against the dark frigid day. Beneath my coat I wore a hooded shirt and kept the big hood pulled up to cover my head. All I cared to imagine were the beautiful breezy summer nights by the bay, and wished only to travel back to them. Upon reaching town, I visited Miss Host at the kiosk. She had a little barrel full of hot coals in her shop with her, and three of the four shutters of the little hut were closed against the wind. I pulled my hood off as I stood in line because I wanted to see Miss Host better and wanted her to see me. She was quite lovely. In addition, I had a question I wanted to ask.

Without me saying a word she brought me two packs of my usual non-filtered Galileos. I thanked her, paid her, and said, "Miss Host, have you seen the time traveler of late?" She smiled and noticed I was shivering. She said, "Please, come and stand inside with me." She opened the counter to her left and I had to duck in under the shutter. When I was in, she closed the counter and ushered me to a spot next to the barrel of coals.

"He still comes by for his pipe tobacco, but now he's here first thing in the morning rather than after lunch."

"I appreciate your having introduced me to him."

"Oh, I was so worried you'd question his sanity regarding time travel," she said.

"I could see it in your eyes."

"I had faith you were a kind person, Mr. Russell. I could just tell."

"What about Mr. Thomas?" I asked.

"He relayed to me that something on the order of a miracle had occurred in his life recently. His wife came through time to find him. And here she has. She arrived last Tuesday and they have been inseparable since. Stay in town today and you will assuredly see them pacing the sidewalks tittering and holding hands. It's adorable."

"She's here to take him home?"

"You see, years ago somewhere in the future, the time traveler insisted that he and his wife learn the time traveling techniques of the ancients. They did and traveled together for a while, but then their abilities diverged and Mrs. Thomas became the more powerful. They lost each other in time, and he has spent the last ten years searching for her in every year they'd lived, until, of course, he began losing his powers and was marooned here, in the year he was ten."

"So I suppose his wife must have been searching for him as well."

Miss Host nodded. "He told me once that he never realized he loved her so much as when she was some grand avalanche of years away with no clue where he was. He was sure he could find her if he could just find the focus and energy to travel."

"Think of the frustration."

"And this is all given you believe their time travel tales," she said.

"I believe them. I'm going to try to follow them and jot down the details of their remaining stay in Wespire. It has just struck me that my novel could be about these days where the time traveler's wife arrives in the time he's lost in and tries to train him to escape to their original time."

"Sounds like an enchanting story."

"You know a lot about them. Do you want to help me do my research? Come along with me, I guarantee you'll see that their claims of time travel are legitimate."

"I can come with you when I get off at dark. Meet me here."

My mind was adrift with the fact that Miss Host had acquiesced to assist me. To be honest, what really had my heart fluttering was how close I stood next to her in the kiosk. When she agreed to be my partner in spying on the Thomases, my throat closed up a bit. And when she took my hand to shake on our deal, and laughed as she pumped my arm, my heart was pounding. She gave me a free cup of coffee to go with my cigarettes and I wished her well and told her I'd be back at dark. I sat on a bench at the far side of the bridge in town, got a cigarette going and drank my coffee.

I was there for quite a while before I happened to look down at the bank of the frozen Alburk River. On the shore, in the fallen snow, they sat on a bench like the one I was on. It was the time traveler and his wife. She leaned into him as if to hide from the cold and he had his arm around her shoulders. I knew they were speaking from the puffs of smoke that came from their mouths. It was difficult to get a good look at her. Galen sat very stiff beside her and gently patted her shoulder. He'd added a brown hat with a broad brim and a crown with a crease down the middle to his brown suit and black overcoat.

I felt as if I was intruding on something very intimate, but I couldn't look away. It was all plot gold for the novel. I was concentrating on the time traveler with the same intensity as I did on the memory of my mother pulling the sled through the snow. I wanted to know more. The moment I thought that, his wife stood up and then helped him to his feet. He seemed weak and she held his arm. They stepped out onto the ice, and I caught a good glimpse of her—an aged but smiling face, eyes gleaming, a few pounds overweight, in a yellow satin jacket and earmuffs. Her hair was in gray braids that came to just below her shoulders.

They stepped out onto the ice, and she let him go. Staying a few steps in front of him, she slid on her shoes, swirling in circles and singing, as if luring him out across the frozen river. Galen staggered along behind her, left hand holding his hat in place. I watched for the half hour it took for them to cross the ice to the opposite bank. Once there, they disappeared into the early afternoon mist. I sat for a moment more and contemplated what I'd just seen, wondering if it was some exercise in time travel training.

When it got too cold on the bench, I retreated to the center of town and ducked into the Shut Eye for a late lunch. The place was fairly empty. I ordered a lime and lavender gin and a plate of steamed potatoes in a classic grim boy's gravy. No sooner had I dug into my lunch, when I heard the waitress seating someone in the booth behind mine. She made some small talk with the customers, and I was sure the voice I heard thanking her as she walked away was the time traveler's. Luckily, the back of my booth went way up past my head, so they couldn't see me. I turned my ear to it and eavesdropped on their conversation.

"You're going to have to do better, your time stream is limp," she said. They both laughed.

"A couple of trips across the ice, a few fast drives and I'll be back on the beam."

"You should've stayed in practice. Your memory's a mess."

"I meant to," he said.

"Well, let's just do what we have to do to get home. I miss being together on a quiet weekend. I can guide us back to only a few minutes before we left and we'll not have missed anything."

"I'll work extra hard," he said.

Their food came after that, and I heard no more conversation. Finally, I dropped enough money on the table to pay my bill with a nice tip and slipped out the back door. All afternoon I walked through the woods next to the river, waiting for nightfall. When it finally arrived, I climbed up the bank and crossed the bridge to stand outside the kiosk. A moment later, I heard Miss Host locking up for the night, and then she was standing in front of me with her big eyes like some denizen of the moon.

"I think we should head straight to the Coach and Four," she said, and took me by the hand. "The time traveler's room is the large one on the bottom floor. We can spy on them through the window if we're careful."

"How do you know this stuff?"

"Oh, the old man tells me everything," she said with a laugh. "When he stops by in the mornings now, it's as if he's confessing his life to me. He told me the other day that if he can't find the strength to focus and escape this time, he will shoot himself so that his wife might save herself from it."

"That's dire," I said and she stopped walking. The next thing I knew, she was kissing me and her tongue was in my mouth, not that I'm complaining. I could tell then there were a lot of secrets to discover about Miss Host. We left the main street that went directly over the bridge to the doors of the Coach and Four and found the bench from where I'd spied on the Thomases down on the frozen river. We had quite a session there in the dark, undisturbed, and time ran wild without our notice.

Who knew how late it was when we finally found ourselves in the back parking lot of the Coach and Four? As we approached the window of the room Miss Host said the time travelers were probably staying in, it appeared darkened to me, and I lost hope that we'd witness anything that night I could use in the novel. She put her finger to her lips and drew me closer. Then I saw them, on the other side of the room, sitting at a table with only the light from a single candle. They sat across from each other. Galen was leaning forward, his face in his hands, obviously crying.

Miss Host whispered in my ear that she was most likely telling him about the five years she spent living with another man in another time. She had been searching everywhere for him, and then, in that year he'd have been twenty, she met a man at a party one night and ended up staying with him for five years before traveling again to find Galen.

"How do you know that?" I asked her.

"Trust me," she said.

"Now she's crying. What do you suppose the reason is?"

"She's crying because even though she has found him, she realizes, without letting him know, that she's certain he will never have the focus and energy to escape now and return to their home and rightful time."

We watched them for a while more until their conversation turned to laughter, which we could actually hear vibrating in the window glass. They had another brief conversation and Miss Host said, "Look at his eyes, reflecting the flame and shining in the dark. She must be speaking to him about time travel."

"I wish I knew what she was saying," I said and then the candle went out and we moved carefully away from the window. We were freezing by then, having stood motionlessly for over an hour. I put my arm around her and we walked back over the bridge and along the cattail trail that led to my motel on the bay.

In the days that followed, while Miss Host worked at the kiosk, I snooped on the Thomases alone. Every day, I saw some very curious undertakings on their part. More than once she instructed him to stand in the snow-covered orchard and turn in tight circles. Every time I saw him do this, he ended up on the ground and she was forced to help him up. She wouldn't speak a negative word, but I saw when he couldn't, as she leaned over to get him, an enormous silent sigh. Of course, I was at a little bit of a distance, hiding behind a gnarled old apple tree.

A few days later, with my view from the bench on the

bridge, I saw her instruct him to remove his clothes, save for his boxer shorts—it had to have been the coldest day of the year—and to walk out on the river ice. Don't think I didn't wonder what walking on the ice had to do with time travel. Once he was standing in the middle of the frozen river, he sang a song, really belted it out as if on a stage in live theatre. He was too distant for me to hear all the words of the song, but I thought I did hear the phrase 'time is the mind'. On the other hand, he could have been singing, 'lime is so fine', in reference to his favorite cocktail.

Their antics grew more bizarre each day, and I couldn't say that Galen looked any better than he had before his wife showed up. She, on the other hand, looked great, exuding energy, even having lost weight, what with all their exercise. At night, after closing, Miss Host came to the motel. She'd undress and get in bed with me. I'd tell her what I witnessed the time travelers doing each day. We'd laugh and speculate until three in the morning when sleep would finally catch us.

It was late in the second straight week of his training that I encountered them on a sunny afternoon right at the apex of the town bridge. I was walking along, thinking to myself about the plot that involved Mr. and Mrs. Thomas without looking up and noticing that they were heading right for me. Just as I looked up, we passed. The time traveler was walking along, wearing a blindfold. His wife nodded to me and smiled as if to say, 'Isn't my husband a goofball?' Galen piped up and offered a hello to whomever was passing, even though he had no idea it was me.

After that, I didn't see them for a few days, and Miss Host didn't stop in after work for that same time. When I went to get my cigarettes, she told me that she had to take care of her ailing mother at night. She still seemed friendly and she still kissed me, but those days were lonely ones, as if I was cast away on a desert island in a run-down motel. The situation became so unbearable that I began writing my novel, the story of lovers lost in time, one too old to escape the years he'd landed in. I needed a prominent title. "Something simple," my editor instructed. "But something powerful and a tad profound. Not too profound. Just profound enough."

The knocking at my door one morning startled me and I jolted up out of bed. I wrapped a robe around myself and answered, expecting, hoping it might be Miss Host. It was most certainly not her. I needed to clear my eyes, before taking another look at my visitor. All I'd seen was a hulking form and a bald head. It came to me that it was Barthus. He said he had a message for me from Miss Host.

"What is it?"

"She said to tell you that the time traveler told her he was going to insist today that his wife leave him behind and return home or go where she might want to. He loved her too much to hold her here when it was clear he was never going to escape this time alive as a time traveler."

I thanked Barthus and gave him a tip. He asked me if I

needed a ride to town, and I accepted. It took me minutes to dress, and fewer minutes to get to the kiosk. I jumped out of the back seat and Barthus motored off toward the Coach and Four. As soon as Miss Host saw me, she pointed toward the bridge.

"Mr. Russell," she said. "I think the time traveler has shot himself. He had a gun and I heard it go off. Look, he's up on the bridge on the bench."

I didn't hesitate but turned and ran. There was Galen Thomas, slumped over, sitting forward on the bench overlooking the frozen river. I took a seat beside him. He looked over at me with pale surprise and said, "Russell, good to see you." I looked down at where he gripped his stomach and saw the blood burbling out from beneath his grip.

"Galen, you're wounded."

"So I am. And I shot myself."

"If you wanted to commit suicide, why not shoot yourself in the head? Faster and less painful than a gut shot. Can I get you an ambulance?"

"Most definitely not. The reason I went for the slow demise was because I wanted to see my wife, Muriel, heading out into time. Look, there she is." He pointed down onto the river.

I saw her moving along at a steady slow pace as if she had a tow rope tied to her, but there was no rope. She didn't move her legs or her arms, and she slid smoothly forward and away from us. Her hair was out of the braids and blowing back in the wind.

"Watch closely," said Galen.

I did, and like a light going out, she disappeared without a trace.

The time traveler waved as if she could still see him, but I don't believe there was any way she could have. He leaned over more and grunted. I could see in his expression, the life leaving him. Putting a bloody hand on my shoulder, he drew me close. "I had a memory the other day. It was late at night. Muriel was next to me in the hotel bed, sleeping peacefully. The lights were out, and I had a memory that was more like a vision it came in so strongly, so beautifully vibrant in its colors. I was a young child, in the first grade. It had snowed overnight, so that there were drifts in the street. My mother, looking young and full of energy, her black hair flowing, tied a rope around each handle of the sled, and then attached the rope around her waist. She ran and pulled me along the street. I heard the runners in the snow, and the percussion of her boots, like the orchard apples falling at the end of summer."

"Were the snowflakes enormous?" I asked.

He smiled and nodded. "They fell slowly, like in a dream," he said and then disintegrated, blowing away like sand and then salt and then smoke. And once he was gone, the town, our reality and time slowly began to vanish. The steepled church, the library, the woods on the opposite bank of the river. The boundaries of Galen's memory shrunk by the day. We realized we were all only part of this time in his focused beaming. His memory was all of us and everything. Miss Host predicted that invading nothing was herding us to the orchard behind the Coach and Four. We pitched a tent there and Barthus, one of the few left alive, brought us food and drink. She wept when we woke one day and found the kiosk gone. It had become the place where those who were left gathered every day to discuss the terror of living in a world that was the disappearing memory of a dead man.

Miss Host and I are writing my novel together. Something to do while the world shrinks. We're deep into the story, writing at night in the tent by flashlight with the winter wind whipping the apple trees all around us. We laugh and discuss and smoke cigarettes, and turn away for a moment when a memory of the mice in the motel walls seems too beautiful to resign to oblivion.

THE LICHENS
Nina Allan

Nina Allan (www.ninaallan.co.uk) is a novelist and critic. Her books have won several prizes including the British Science Fiction Award, the Grand Prix de L'Imaginaire, and the Kitschies Red Tentacle. Her short story 'The Art of Space Travel' was a Hugo finalist in 2017. Her most recent books are the novel, *The Good Neighbours*, inspired by the work of Victorian fairy painter Richard Dadd, and a new volume of her short fiction, *The Art of Space Travel*. Nina lives and works in Rothesay, on the Isle of Bute.

SHE BRUSHED THE earth aside, felt grit beneath her nails, felt the abrasive dryness of the sparse mountain soil. There was something here after all, the grey-silver gleam of metal pitted with age, with age or with pellet shot, small concavities choked with dirt, dirt so ingrained it looked immovable though Helen guessed it wouldn't be, not if you fetched a brush to it or a wad of wire, the same as you'd use to scour a fire grate or a boiled-dry saucepan.

She glanced down at her hands, the long lean track of them, the prominent wrist bones. You have lovely hands, Miss Stone, Pastor Acres had said to her, the hands of a ministering angel, pale and stern. The unexpectedness of the compliment had shaken her, though she sensed the man was being untruthful, not lying so much as pushing his advantage, which was somehow worse.

She was thirty-five years old. A teacher, Helen reminded herself, not a quarryman, though her hands were also the hands of a digger, a washerwoman, a woodcutter and a baker's wife, as likely to be dusted with flour or sawdust or soapsuds as with chalk. Or with the gritty grey-brown dirt of this mountain hollow.

Gleam of grey against the paler dust. Looked like stone but her hand said metal and the hand could often be trusted further than the eye. The eye was a mirror–it saw what you wanted it to see. The hand was not deceived so easily, or as often.

SHE HAD NOT told anyone, not her father, not Acres, not anyone, of the woman she met on the hillside the afternoon she stood on the crest and watched the redcoats swarming between the houses in the town below, Helen so overcome with anger, with despair as bitter as wormwood she'd scarce known where she was headed let alone the larger question of what she should do. The mist lifting off the firth like cobwebs, like a bridal veil, the dampness on her cheeks and in her gullet, the image of the town as a sacrifice, a biddy young thing skinny about the ankles still like Vida McBrady the year she'd been forced into wedlock at gunpoint with Jebediah Hearne.

Not the first time she'd thanked God for the luck of spinsterhood; astringent though that luck sometimes tasted, it did at least sharpen the mind, the mettle, the memory, indeed all her senses, and not merely, as men insisted, her devilish tongue. Better a maiden all her days than shackled to Jeb Hearne and it wasn't like he was the worst, just the closest to mind and with the wind and the recall and the red-coated soldier ants she, Helen, had gone tearing up the hill and in between the trees.

She had clasped the pine as a lover, hot tears wetting the bark and she could have sworn, yes she would have sworn, she could feel the tree breathing, cleaving to her like a paramour, its heartbeat soft and firm and even against her own and Helen sensed the pity of it, that she should seek consolation this way, that she should heed such febrile imaginings, that she had no one to hold.

What is it? came the voice then, the voice pure-toned and rounded and ethereal and so unlike her own. What's wrong?

The voice of the tree was a woman's voice, a fact that seemed less strange to her in that instant than that its accent was English. A Scots pine that addressed her in English? Were the redcoats so far advanced already they could turn the stones and trees of the hillside to the enemy cause? Helen sprung back, slivers of bark caught in mossy half-moons beneath her fingernails. Only then as she raised her head did she see she was not alone.

A woman, in a gabardine coat and with a canvas knapsack, the jersey leggings of a journeyman or of a soldier cast adrift from his platoon. The hood of her coat lay flattened against her shoulders, her hair, a tawny brown, cropped close about her ears. A nun, Helen thought, an English Joan of Arc. What woman would dare wear her hair that way unless a martyr or a saint, a madwoman confined to the cells of the Inverness Asylum?

The woman wore stout boots, not leather like her father's or the pastor's or Jeb Hearne's tackety boots made in Glasgow, but some other unknown material woven and shiny with a silvery sheen as if the woman had stepped in a puddle. Yet that was not it, Helen could tell, the boots were tight and dry and it was the boots more than anything more even than the soldier's crop gave Helen the sense that what she was seeing could not be real. More, *should* not be real, because why would a nun, a martyr in moon-boots, come from her place beyond the mountains to meet with the spinster schoolmistress Helen Stone?

I am a teacher, Helen said, stupidly, and it was only later at her desk in her bedroom, the fire burned down so low it was all but out she realized she chose the words not because her mind was gone but because they were the most the weightiest gift she had to offer.

For what was being a teacher if not her salvation? For what was being a teacher if not a curse?

Helen Stone, she added, the load of her name in her stomach like the thing it said it was.

My name is Joe, the woman said, well, Josephine, but everyone calls me Joe. My friends do, anyway.

Joan, Helen whispered. She felt weightless, bound by nothing, as if my blood were her blood, she would say to her god-daughter Janey some thirty years later, as if that were the moment my life became truly my own.

Were you scared, Nannie? Janey would ask. At the age of eight she was old enough to recognize the science of fear, still young enough not to question the art of belief.

No, Helen would reply, cautiously probing the question as if the response it inevitably yielded was still a mystery to her. I knew she meant me no harm.

I heard you crying, Joe said, in the present. I wondered if you were lost.

Which made Helen laugh because how could she be lost in these woods where she'd played as a child, where her sister Bessie who was now in America had taught her to forage for mushrooms where she had surprised Augie Dunseath her beloved kissing her best friend Martha-Mary behind a tree where she'd learned the name of every bird and plant before the age of ten?

I am not lost, she said, and the certainty of her statement lent her new courage. It is the soldiers. You must have seen them. They have taken the town.

You are a Jacobite, then? said the nun.

Helen stared at her in silence. I do not give myself that name, she said finally. I have no trust in politics. I have even less trust in the king's men, that is all. I have seen what they are capable of, their mistreatment of women. I know that while they are here in our town no one dares to speak their mind. Speaking my mind is something I value and if that makes me a Jacobite, those are your words, not mine. Are you also a soldier? she said, and her words once spoken seemed to crack open the air as a pick splits ice. A woman a soldier? The idea harsh and bright and piercing as a new pin. Your boots, she added, less certainly. They are like none I have seen before.

I'm not a soldier. The woman laughed a little. I am a scientist. I study plants. Well, lichens, she said. Lichens are—

Lichen is like moss. It grows upon trees and gravestones.

Among other places. The woman smiled. So you know about lichens?

I have not studied them in the way that you would understand the word. But I have observed and admired them in the forest when I go walking. I take pleasure in the wildness and variety of all living things. Helen could feel herself blushing. How foolish she must sound. And in my profession there is always the chance such knowledge may one day come in useful.

That's good to hear, Helen. I wish everyone felt that way about their environment. Joe reached out to touch the bark of the tree she had been leaning against. There are many thousands of species of lichens, all over the world. You might not know this yet, but they are amongst the oldest organisms on the planet.

Older than pine forests?

Many millions of years older, which makes lichens extremely useful for dating other organisms. Lichens are not ordinary plants. In fact they're not plants at all, they are more like fungi—like mushrooms and toadstools. Studying lichens helps us detect and measure changes in the environment, over long periods of time.

What kind of changes?

Like how wet an environment is, or how polluted. If you keep studying the lichen colonies in a single spot you'll notice alterations in color and density, sometimes in a single year, sometimes over decades. And as scientists pass on their research, over hundreds of years.

Helen imagined a parade of scientists, each handing on their discoveries to the one who came after her, a parade that marched ever onward and into the future. Even those who were dead, lying in the ground beneath the trees they had so lately studied would still be contributing their knowledge to the knowledge of all.

Like travelling through time, Helen thought. She remembered how as a child she liked to make paper dolls, folding a torn-off sheet of the butcher paper her father kept in the woodshed for lighting fires. Careful not to take too much or else her father would scold her for wanton wastage, though an edge he did not mind or at least pretended not to notice. Folding the paper as an accordion bellows, a concertina that could be squashed together to a single plane, that once extended would reach across the space between her outstretched arms.

Cutting carefully to create the outline of a human figure, then whoosh like the stirring of moths an unfolding line of them, each little neighbor identical to her paper sisters.

Paper sisters, paper teachers, paper stargazers, for although the Royal Society would not deign to admit a woman beneath its portals no one could stop a woman looking up at the sky. Helen liked to use her drawing pencils to give the figures clothing: smart dresses for the town meeting, sweeping gowns for the summer ball in the castle gardens, stout boots and gabardine capes for their hikes into the hills. Dolls that whispered and caroused, then folded themselves swiftly away when they wished to disappear.

Are you at a university? Helen said. They let you be admitted? She spoke quietly, as if to herself. This meeting with a stranger who spoke to her as if they might be friends, as if they might hold thoughts and actions in common, as if—she hardly dared think it—they might have met before. And yet who was she and where did she come from, silver boots and all?

None of this can be real, Helen thought. This is some temporary madness, an invasion of the senses. She thought once again of the red-coated soldiers, wondered if her mind might fall to enemy forces as easily as her town.

Men can be tiresome, of course, this quaint Saint Joan was saying. You know already what they are like. University men are no different, indeed some of them are worse, but we're all used to that. And there are some good ones, she added, grinning in a way that suggested her acquaintanceship with such goodness went a way beyond the formal. I don't have time to explain everything again—the durations are becoming shorter, just as I feared. Could you do something for me?

The woman's smile was gone suddenly, and with it her light-heartedness, the change in her demeanour so abrupt it was almost alarming. Helen remembered her paper dolls, the way they seemed identical but were not, how they could each be made to represent different aspects of the other.

I will if I can, she said. If I could I would turn the Earth for you, Helen thought her heart like the rattle of frozen stones upon an icy road. She remembered the days of her childhood, the dark winter evenings, being sent out to the log store to bring in wood for the stove. The thrill of panic in the gut that this time she would not be fast enough, that the fiends from the stories in her father's picture books—her father's *litho*graphs—would grab her this time for sure, the scolding herself *there were no fiends* yet still half-hoping there were because the nights were lithe as dreams and what were dreams without fiends, without bold imaginings? The terror that came with the darkness jostling at her elbow and her peace of mind, telling her there were worse things than being afraid, that the being afraid was what stopped you from freezing over from feeling nothing.

This is the greatest moment of my life, Helen thought. Greater by far than the love I felt for Augie. Greater than

I dreamed. The thought occurred to her once again that she and this Joan of Arc had met before.

In another life, she thought confusedly. Or a life to come.

There is a place at the edge of the forest, Joe said, not far from here—near where the quarry is? There is a small lake, and a strange little granite ridge, cutting out of the earth?

Libbet's Pond, Helen said. I know the place. It is always quiet there because there's no wind. The pond is not deep. Sometimes in the middle of summer it dries up completely.

There is a tree near the rock—a mountain ash. The mountain ash has a tenacious root system because it often finds itself growing in harsh environments. This tree is very old. It has well-established lichen colonies. I would like you to keep a record for me, if you can.

I would not be sure how to do that. I am not a scientist.

You don't need to be—and you needn't go there often, either. The kind of changes you would be looking for happen slowly. Make a note of the date, and time, and the weather, and then describe what you see. The size and location of the colonies, whether they have spread. And the colours—I especially need to know if the colours of the lichens have changed, and if so, how. Anything that occurs to you, that you feel might be important. If there is anything to be noticed, I'm sure you'll notice it.

I can try.

There is one other thing you might look out for. The next time the pond dries up, if you can, climb down into the hollow and scrape away some of the dirt from near the base of the ridge. If I am right—and I think I am— you will find something buried there. Something that shouldn't be there. Something old.

Something dangerous?

Not for you to touch. Not in the way you might think.

A weapon?

You might call it a weapon, though it was never designed to be one.

Why do you speak in riddles? Do you not have trust in me?

Joe smiled at her then, though it was a thin smile, almost like a frown. Trust is a rare emotion, Helen. Rarer than love, I think. Do you know how it feels not to be believed, to be made a fool of by those who deem themselves your superior through the single, unearned attribute of having been born inside a body that happens to be male?

Helen laughed. She clapped her hands, the sound ricocheting through the trees like a blast from a hunting gun. Only my whole life long, she said. Only by every man I have ever known, even those who have professed to care for me. I think especially of Pastor Michaelis who is now Bishop Michaelis, a kind man indeed and a learned one, yet still he found time to censure me for having the temerity to take solace in books that were not the Bible. To censure my father for allowing me to read such books even. I should count myself lucky that my father has no time for the church, that he somewhat enjoys the notoriety of having a witch for a daughter. Even so that has never prevented him taking advantage of my practical ability in darning overalls and chopping up trees.

How foolish of me. I'm sorry.

Sorrow is not in order. Not among comrades. Helen stepped forward and touched Joe's arm. There had been a part of her, even right up to and during the moment of contact, that doubted the other woman's physicality. That had believed—that in some sense still did believe—that her fingers would pass right through her, as through a ghost.

Instead there was her hand on Joe's arm, the heat of Joe's body faintly discernible through the layers of damp cloth.

You are truly here, Helen said. She laughed again, this time without bitterness, a soft peal of delight. I do not care where from or how you have come. I know only that whatever you may wish to tell me, it can scarcely be stranger or more impossible than your being here to tell it.

That is the nature of luck, Joe said quietly. You cannot predict it—it is what it is, blind chance. I might have wandered these hills a hundred times and never encountered you. And yet—here you are.

Luck has a name, Helen said. Her name is Fortune, and I owe her a great deal. I am sure that as a scientist you have no time for such superstitions, but I have felt her presence in my life too often to firmly deny it. Besides, she added, I have often wondered if Fortune might not be a master of the calculus in disguise.

I have never thought of it that way before—but I am sure she must be!

I have sometimes liked to imagine her in the guise of Hypatia of Alexandria, though I am inclined to believe her face will have taken on a more familiar aspect, next time I speak with her.

Helen felt the redness flare up in her cheeks again, though the woman in the silver boots did not seem to mind. Her expression was serious, as if she were engaged in a deep inner struggle with herself—should she say what was in her heart or let what had been said already be enough? Helen waited. She gazed at Joe intently, as if to fix her in stone. As if she feared that once the two of them were parted they would not meet again.

When Joe finally spoke the words burst forth unevenly, as if the doubter in her had been silenced but temporarily.

Helen—do you really not know me? Don't you remember last summer? Do you remember anything at all?

Helen's heart seemed to stop beating, to cease marking time, and she found herself thinking it must be time that was wrong here that had become confused. Not her and not Joe but the order of the world around them, which was not as it should be.

She recalled the woody scent of heather and a bank of wild roses. The bleached white light of a summer night to which dark never came.

She remembered a story she had thought to write once for the older children—the story of a sojourner-soul who learns how to fold time. To fold time over upon itself like the concertinaed paper she had once used to make her paper dolls. A warrior maid in sojourner's boots, linking hands with the schoolteacher in her Sunday best pinafore and the two of them laughing laughing laughing as they race up the side of the mountain the town so far below them so nearly out of sight they could be anywhere.

Yet the magical light of midsummer is the same in any year and still the story of the paper dolls remains unwritten. Helen remembered last autumn the encroachment of the darkness like a final farewell, the new minister, Pastor Dermot Acres, playing Bach all by himself in the candlelit church, the heavenly andante made pinched and peevish by the ancient wheezing pedal organ, an instrument that through generations of careless stewardship had entered the haunted twilight of its own dementia.

Miss Stone, Acres had greeted her. I have your father's permission to call on you. Shall we say four o'clock?

So here was her father's final attempt to secure for her what he would call *a life for herself*. One desperate last throw of the dice before the very idea of marriage became a dubious joke. And Dermot Acres was not unintelligent. He reads, at least, Helen thought. She wondered if it would be better she should surrender to what time had in store for her, like the organ. Those dreams of heather and roses? Simply dreams.

I think, she said to Joe, I think I am afraid to.

It isn't that you are afraid. I don't think you could ever be afraid. It's just the way this thing works. There are no memories for you to hold on to. Every time we meet it's like starting again.

It is like hearing an echo, Helen said quietly. You turn your head to catch the sound, and find it is gone. She fell silent, rubbing her eyes. I think it would be better if you simply tell me what you need me to do.

They stand facing one another, and Helen knows she will not say yes to Dermot Acres. As the town will never truly surrender to the swarming redcoats, she will cloak herself in stone and bide her time.

The artefact is buried, Joe said. You wouldn't be able to dig it up, not even with twenty men helping you, and you shouldn't try. I don't know how damaged it is, so I have no idea what the effects would be. Until I can find out more it's too dangerous to rely on guesswork. All I need to know for now is that it is there. Could you help me with that? Write down what you see—draw it if you can. Make a note of any details that seem important, the same as with the lichens.

And you have not seen this thing—this artefact—for yourself?

Joe shook her head. It's because of the lake—your Libbet's Pond. I know this is probably difficult for you to imagine, but in my time it's not a pond any more, it's part of the firth. The whole of that basin of land—where the quarry is now—has become completely submerged. In order to excavate it you'd need the cooperation of a professional underwater salvage crew—that's millions of dollars. The team I'm working with, we're just interested individuals, we don't have access to that kind of money. But you've already confirmed what I suspected, that at this point in time the floor of the quarry is still accessible, because the lake dries up during the summer months. We can at least confirm that the artefact is where I think it is.

What I would give to see Pastor Michaelis's face, were he to hear you, Helen said. He would swear we were daughters of Satan, and properly in league.

But what do you believe, Helen?

I believe I have reason to be glad of my father's insistence that I learn to till the land, to break clods and sow beans and parsnips as well as teaching the children of gentlefolk where and how they grow. I am used to feeling dirt beneath my fingernails. I believe that especially for a woman I am good at digging.

Take this then. Joe was smiling. It will protect what you write.

She handed Helen a journal, an impossibly fine ruled notebook, its many leaves threaded together with a spiral of wire. The journal was sealed inside a transparent envelope that appeared to be made of the same material as Joe's boots. Thrust down inside the metal spiral was a stylus, a writing instrument of some kind that, Helen discovered later, made a sharp indelible line, black as ink but without the concurrent hazards of smearing or blotting.

How can this even be? Helen asked herself. How can any of these things be? Yet she saw no purpose in asking questions that were their own best answers.

Will I see you again? she asked instead.

I don't know, Joe said. She shook her head. It's getting so I can't control my trajectory with any real accuracy. That's the curse of new technology—no one knows what they're doing. It's down to chance, I think.

Fortune, Helen said. She did not have the words to describe their situation, yet she found she understood it, nonetheless, she grasped its essence perfectly. Dermot Acres would speak of angels and visitations. Pastor Michaelis would speak of the devil, and the devil's works. Helen imagined herself without a map, trying to navigate her way through the dusk-laden streets of Edinburgh, a city she had visited only once, in the company of her father, and long ago.

Her recollections of the place were fragmentary and ever mutable, its landmarks possessing the aura of places in a dream: a narrow lane threading the boundary of a doctor's residence, a courthouse and a cathedral, a castle on a hill.

If travelling in time were possible, then it would surely be like this.

Use the mountain ash as your marker, Joe said. There's a small cavity in the trunk—a hollow—about three feet up. Each time you write a new report, tuck the notebook inside. That way I'll always know where to find it. The space is quite dry.

They embrace then, a brief, hard hug, the kind one soldier might give to their comrade on the eve of battle. Helen touches Joe's hair, the cropped brown silkiness, and feels her insides tremble like the needles of the pine, stirred to secret life by the summer wind.

THERE WILL BE a time, after the long dry summer when she first glimpses the artefact buried in the dusty soil of Libbet's Pond, after she learns that Dermot Acres has begun calling on Harriet Templar, ten years her junior, when Helen puts her hand inside the tree to retrieve the notebook and finds it gone. In its place is a small cloth-bound volume, which includes a series of colour plates that to Helen seem to be of exceptional quality. The book is called *The Lichens*, and is by James Morrison Crombie, a minister in the Church of Scotland and one of the first British naturalists to undertake a specialist study of these extraordinary organisms. Crombie died in 1906. The precise date of Helen Stone's death is unknown.

Inside the book on lichens there is a note: *Crombie was wrong to reject Schwendener, but his drawings are exquisite. I thought you might like them.*

Helen has no idea who Schwendener is—why should she, he hasn't been born yet—though she has no difficulty in guessing who has written the note. She agrees that Crombie's drawings are exquisite. She spends a long time examining them, turning the pages under the lamplight through the long winter evenings. Rain beats down upon the town and the surrounding countryside. Libbet's Pond fills up again, the dry grey dirt of its basin restored in the space of an hour to cloying black mud. Helen does not know this yet, but Libbet's Pond will never fully dry out again, at least not in this millennium. The changes have begun.

Helen continues in her post as teacher at the local school. After her father dies, she opens her own school, an institution for the education of girls whose parents cannot afford to send them to the bishop's academy. One of her pupils, Catherine Carraway, will become one of the first women botanists to sail down the Amazon.

Helen will later become godmother to Catherine's daughter Janey. It will be Janey who disposes of Helen's property after her death. Her furniture and personal effects are sold through Phillotson's Auctions, of Inverness. The little book on lichens ends up as part of a job lot, purchased by a university lecturer named McQuarie for just a few shillings. The lot includes a bound volume of letters, more than a dozen of them that were sent to Helen's father by his friend Captain Angus Stuart, written while he was a prisoner at Tilbury Fort. It is these letters in particular our lecturer is interested in. McQuarie is compiling a history of the Battle of Culloden and he has travelled all the way from Aberdeen to secure Stuart's letters.

The rest of the books are incidental, and the cloth-bound volume on lichens he barely glances at. Scottish history is his subject, not botany. McQuarie will live and die without ever noticing that Crombie's famous monograph has not yet been published.

* * *

"THEY'RE NOT GOING to give us the grant, so you might as well forget it," Kemal says. "They think we're cranks." Joe knows Kemal is exhausted—not just with the university and the grant committee, but with her. This is what happens in cases like theirs: exhaustion, infighting, recriminations, though they haven't sunk to playing the blame game and won't, they've known one another too long for that, they have too much at stake, not just as colleagues but as friends. Comrades, Joe thinks. As well as being a talented geologist, Kemal is her right hand. But still, it's easy to see why no true heretic ever gets to decide the course of history until after they've been burned at the stake: too little backup and too much lunacy. The end.

"But the lichens prove it, you said so yourself," Joe insists, though with less energy less fervor than last time or the time before that. She has been up all night filling in forms and she's almost out of craziness. "The lichens prove the anomalies in the soil are of alien origin."

"*Hitherto unidentified silicates*," says Kemal, quoting from the official lab report, which they both know by heart. "Which means whatever the lab guys want it to mean. We need to rethink our approach, conduct more analysis. And before you go off on one, I'm not talking about giving up, I'm talking about resting up. It has been ten years."

Ten years since Joe's first trip north in real time for the wedding of a school friend and although the little Scottish town had been a dull abstraction for her beforehand she had found herself falling in love with its remoteness. Five hours north from Glasgow, the stern grey buildings like stern grey ladies clustered together for warmth, for the easier communication of rumour and gossip. Then there was the book she happened upon in the town museum: *My Birthplace*, by Catherine Carraway, a local author the blurb on the back identified as one of the first female explorers to sail down the Amazon.

A first edition of the volume preserved carefully under glass in one of the galleries, a dozen copies of a recent paperback reprint readily available for purchase in the museum shop. Joe read the book on the train on her way back to London, and in amongst the predictable recollections of childhood memories—the two older brothers, the strict but adoring father and mildly depressed mother, the ironclad winters, the amethyst summers, the Christmases and funerals, the harvest festivals—there is the story told to them by their schoolteacher (her daughter's godmother) of the alien spacecraft buried in the muddy sediment of a flooded quarry.

Catherine Carraway does not write spacecraft, she writes artefact, antiquity, archaeological treasure. Just once and close to the end she adds: *Miss Stone would try and convince us that the artefact was a starship from beyond our galaxy.*

There is a playfulness to her words, a nostalgic longing for childhood secrets and family myths. *My friend Helen never married*, Carraway adds. *She was a woman of fierce intelligence, though I suspect she was lonely.*

*   *   *

THE BAN ON retrospective time travel is absolute, and final. There have been too many accidents, and Joe's original plan—that they could pay a company of quarrymen from Carraway's time to excavate the craft—has come to nothing, mainly because forming alliances with people in the past has turned out to be more difficult than anticipated. There has been plenty of the usual stuff— villagers believing they are gods or angels or devils or spies for the king. But the most troublesome aspect of retrospective communications comes down to the unreliability and impermanence of memory. Travellers to the past can be seen, touched, spoken to, killed, but it seems they cannot be remembered, or not systematically. For those living in the past, each contact with a future agent registers as a first contact, with all the shock and awe and suspicion such novelty entails. No one knows why this should be—no one has a clue, actually—but that's what's been happening. Without memories there can be no relationships and no forward progress. That idea everyone was so in love with, the Embassy of the Future? Forget it.

"We might as well be ghosts," Kemal says, disconsolately. "Who would have guessed time travel would turn out to be a technological cul-de-sac?"

"How can you even say that about a science that's still in its infancy?" Joe protests. "The big boys shut down the program because they want to control it, not because it's dead. You think they're not still conducting experiments behind closed doors?"

"What are you hoping to accomplish, anyway?" Eddie says. Eddie used to work in finance back in the day but as he is always saying computer skills are the most transferable on the planet. "Say we did find the artefact—there's not a lot we can do about it from here."

"How about providing proof of other civilizations and new technologies? Knowledge we can hardly imagine."

"And what if a little learning is a dangerous thing?" Eddie is old school so he believes in procedure and in protocol (put it down to that series of worldwide banking crashes in the 2090s) and in checking the balance of the roulette wheel before you place your bets. He is concerned about how any potential breakthrough might jeopardize what he calls the established order. Like stirring up a hornet's nest, he has said, repeatedly, and for what? Who knows what that thing is or where it came from? We don't know anything.

Ironically, it is Eddie who most believes. Ask him outright if he thinks the artefact is of extraterrestrial origin and he'll give you a flat no but Eddie buys it all right, or so their metallurgist Roxane says and she should know, she enjoys the dubious privilege of living with him. It's what he's been looking for all his life, she says. That's why he's so scared.

The only person who knows about Helen is Kemal. "She remembers me," Joe has told him. "Or at the very least she is becoming aware that there are gaps in her memory, stuff she should remember. Which suggests it's just a matter of patience. Patience and time."

"Time we don't have," Kemal says. "The artefact isn't crucial as a first proof anyway. We should be concentrating on the silicates."

"The silicates. You're as bad as Roxane."

"Roxane is a chemistry nerd. Concentrating on silicates is what she does."

"But where have they got us, Kem? Months and months of running tests when we already know the reason those compounds have never been identified is because the environmental changes that produced them are of alien origin. We need to get to the source."

"Meaning the artefact?"

"Meaning the spacecraft, yes." Joe sighs. They have been chasing each other in circles for months now. Ever since their access to the retro pass was denied, effective immediately, no rescind.

Joe has thought of putting in for one more transfer so she can say goodbye to Helen, try to anyway, but what would be the point? Those fuckers in central office will refuse her and probably try and get her removed from the project into the bargain.

Anyone forming a personal attachment blah blah blah.

One of the reasons she has never mentioned Helen in her write-ups is the underlying anxiety that she could put her in danger.

* * *

"EVERYONE TALKS ABOUT the wonder, the fount of knowledge, the untold riches of discovery," Eddie says. "What they don't talk about are the risks. This artefact of yours—have you ever thought about how it could wind up being worse than Hiroshima? You remember what Stephen Hawking said about being careful what you wish for. Ancient history I know but the guy knew what he was talking about."

"You're saying you're scared?"

"I'm saying my granddad fought in Afghanistan. I've seen what war can do."

"You're not thinking of going back?" Kemal asks her. "Going back illegally? If you jump without a passcode you'll be stuck there, Josephine. You do know that? I forbid you even to think about it."

"So you're my dad now?"

"I'm not your anything, you've made that clear. I care about you, that's all. Or is caring off limits now, too?"

JOE WONDERS WHAT it would be like to be stuck in the past forever, a woman in the north of Scotland at the time of Culloden. She could be a teacher, she thinks, like Helen. She and Helen could live together as women have done through the centuries hiding in the shadows two lonely old maids. How come men are so stupid sometimes? Why does it even matter?

She imagines how it will be when she arrives: sweet September dusk and with the year on the turn the forest yellow-gold the heather burned out the puddles on Quarry Lane rimmed blue with ice. She opens the gate with the squeaking hinge swears her fingers will freeze right off her hands one of these days and Helen is laughing you forgot your mittens then serves you right I warmed them on the stove for you and all.

Soon they will be planning for Christmas, mixing puddings, getting the logs in, making paper angels, the scents of ginger and woodsmoke and sweet dried apricots rising in the frosty air. They sit together by the fire and Joe tells Helen that story she loves, of how hundreds maybe thousands of years ago a starship fell from the sky and now they are the ones who must recover it discover its origins, find out what it wants.

We will help to stop a war, she will say to Helen. A war in the future.

Would you not say we have enough to do surviving the war in the here and now?

Will Helen still love her if she is not Joan of Arc but just another discontented woman biding her time? Her bright helmet of hair grown long and grey her books of learning just fairy tales her miraculous boots worn out in holes like any common pair?

Crazy old Josephine gone to the forest to dig for alien treasure?

How long will it be before Joe accepts that whatever they accomplish in the present she will never know the future, that even should their quest for the artefact succeed her own time is lost to her?

Does the fact that she is not in the history books mean she failed, or simply that time as a navigable river is more mutable and even less predictable than has thus far been proved?

Like hearing an echo, Helen said. You turn your head to catch the sound, and find it is gone.

KRONIA
Elizabeth Hand

Elizabeth Hand (www.elizabethhand.com) is the author of sixteen multiple-awarding-novels, among them the Cass Neary series of psychological thrillers, and six collections of short fiction and essays. She is a longtime critic and reviewer for many publications, including the *Washington Post* and *F&SF*, and is on faculty at the Stonecoast MFA Program in Creative Writing. Her supernatural thriller, *Hokuloa Road*, will be published by Mulholland Books this year. Under optimum conditions, she divides her time between the Maine coast and North London.

WE NEVER MEET. No, not never; just fleetingly: five times in the last eighteen years. The first time I don't recall; you say it was late spring, a hotel bar. But I see you entering a restaurant five years later, stooping beneath the lintel behind our friend Andrew. You don't remember that.

We grew up a mile apart. The road began in Connecticut

and ended in New York. A dirt road when we moved in, we both remember that; it wasn't paved till much later. We rode our bikes back and forth. We passed each other twenty-three times. We never noticed. I fell once, rounding that curve by the golf course, a long scar on my leg now from ankle to knee, a crescent colored like a peony. Grit and sand got beneath my skin, there was blood on the bicycle chain. A boy with glasses stopped his bike and asked was I okay. I said yes, even though I wasn't. You rode off. I walked home, most of the mile, my leg black, sticky with dirt, pollen, deerflies. I never saw the boy on the bike again.

We went to different schools. But in high school we were at the same party. Your end, Connecticut. How did I get there? I have no clue. I knew no one. A sad fat girl's house, a girl with red knee-socks, beanbag chairs. She had one album: The Shaggs. More sad girls, a song called 'Foot Foot'. You stood by a table and ate pretzels and drank so much Hi-C you threw up. I left with my friends. We got stoned in the car and drove off. A tall boy was puking in the azaleas out front.

Wonder what he had? I said.

Another day. The New Canaan Bookstore, your end again. I was looking at a paperback.

That's a good book, said a guy behind me. My age, sixteen or seventeen. Very tall, springy black hair, wire-rimmed glasses. You like his stuff?

I shook my head. No, I said. I haven't read it. I put the book back. He took it off the shelf again. As I walked off

I heard him say *Time Out of Joint*.

We went to different colleges in the same city. The Metro hadn't opened yet. I was in Northeast, you were in Northwest. Twice we were on the same bus going into Georgetown. Once we were at a party where a guy threw a drink in my face.

Hey! yelled my boyfriend. He dumped his beer on the guy's head.

You were by a table, watching. I looked over and saw you laugh. I started laughing, too, but you immediately looked down then turned then walked away.

Around that time I first had this dream. I lived in the future. My job was to travel through time, hunting down evildoers. The travel nauseated me. Sometimes I threw up. I kept running into the same man, my age, dark-haired, tall. Each time I saw him my heart lurched. We kissed furtively, beneath a table while bullets zipped overhead, beside a waterfall in Hungary. For two weeks we hid in a shack in the Northwest Territory, our radio dying, waiting to hear that the first wave of fallout had subsided. A thousand years, back and forth, the world reshuffled. Our child was born, died, grew old, walked for the first time. Sometimes your hair was gray, sometimes black. Once your glasses shattered when a rock struck them. You still have the scar on your cheek. Once I had an abortion. Once the baby died. Once you did. This was just a dream.

You graduated and went to the Sorbonne for a year to study economics. I have never been to France. I got a job at NASA collating photographs of spacecraft. You came back and started working for the newspaper. Those years, I went to the movies almost every night. Flee the sweltering heat, sit in the Biograph's crippling seats for six hours, Pasolini, Fellini, Truffaut, Herzog, Fassbinder, Weir. *La Jetée*, a lightning bolt: that illuminated moment when a woman's black-and-white face moves in the darkness. A tall man sat in front of me and I moved to another seat so I could see better; he turned and I glimpsed your face. Unrecognized: I never knew you. Later in the theater's long corridor you hurried past me, my head bent over an elfin spoonful of cocaine.

Other theaters. We didn't meet again when we sat through *Berlin Alexanderplatz*, though I did read your review. *Our Hitler* was nine hours long; you stayed awake, I fell asleep halfway through the last reel, curled on the floor, but after twenty minutes my boyfriend shook me so I wouldn't miss the end.

How could I have missed you then? The theater was practically empty.

I moved far away. You stayed. Before I left the city I met your colleague Andrew: we corresponded. I wrote occasionally for your paper. You answered the phone sometimes when I called there.

You say you never did.

But I remember your voice: you sounded younger than you were, ironic, world-weary. A few times you assigned me stories. We spoke on the phone. I knew your name.

At some point we met. I don't remember. Lunch, maybe,

with Andrew when I visited the city? A conference?

You married and moved three thousand miles away. Email was invented. We began to write. You sent me books.

We met at a conference: we both remember that. You stood in a hallway filled with light, midday sun fogging the windows. You shaded your eyes with your hand, your head slightly downturned, your eyes glancing upward, your glasses black against white skin. Dark eyes, dark hair, tall and thin and slightly round-shouldered. You were smiling; not at me, at someone talking about the mutability of time. Abruptly, the sky darkened, the long rows of windows turned to mirrors. I stood in the hallway and you were everywhere, everywhere.

You never married. I sent you books.

I had children. I never wrote you back.

You and your wife traveled everywhere: Paris, Beirut, London, Cairo, Tangier, Cornwall, Fiji. You sent me postcards. I never left this country.

I was vacationing in London with my husband when the towers fell. I emailed you. You wrote back:

oh sure, it takes a terrorist attack to hear from you!

That was when we really met.

I was here alone by the lake when I found out. A brilliant cloudless day, the loons calling outside my window. I have no TV or radio; I was online when a friend emailed me:

Terrorism. An airplane flew into the Trade Center.

Bombs. Disaster.

I TRIED TO call my partner but the phone lines went down. I drove past the farmstand where I buy tomatoes and basil and stopped to see if anyone knew what had happened. A van was there with DC plates: the woman inside was talking on a cell phone and weeping. Her brother worked in one of the towers: he had rung her to say he was safe. The second tower fell. He had just rung back to say he was still alive.

When the phone lines were restored that night I wrote you. You didn't write back. I never heard from you again.

I was in New York. I had gone to Battery Park. I had never been there before. The sun was shining. You never heard from me again.

I had no children. At the National Zoo, I saw a tall man walking hand in hand with a little girl. She turned to stare at me: gray eyes, glasses, wispy dark hair. She looked like me.

Two years ago you came to see me here on the lake. We drank two bottles of champagne. We stayed up all night talking. You slept on the couch. When I said goodnight, I touched your forehead. I had never touched you before. You flinched.

Once in 1985 we sat beside each other on the Number 80 bus from North Capitol Street. Neither of us remembers that.

I was fifteen years old, riding my bike on that long, slow

curve by the golf course. The Petro Oil truck went by, too fast, and I lost my balance and went careening into the stone wall. I fell and blacked out. When I opened my eyes a tall boy with glasses knelt beside me, so still he was like a black-and-white photograph. A sudden flicker: for the first time he moved. He blinked, dark eyes, dark hair. It took a moment for me to understand he was talking to me.

"Are you okay?" He pointed to my leg. "You're bleeding. I live just down there—"

He pointed to the Connecticut end of the road.

I tried to move but it hurt so much I threw up, then started to cry.

He hid my ruined bike in the ferns. "Come on."

You put your arm around me and we walked very slowly to your house. A plane flew by overhead. This is how we met.

"NOTHING SORTS OUT memories from ordinary moments. It is only later that they claim remembrance, when they show their scars."

Chris Marker, *La Jetée*

BERGAMOT AND VETIVER

Lavanya Lakshminarayan

Lavanya Lakshminarayan is the author of *Analog/ Virtual: And Other Simulations of Your Future*. She is a Locus Award finalist and is the first science fiction writer to win the Times of India AutHer Award and the Valley of Words Award, both prestigious literary awards in India, and her work has been longlisted for a BSFA Award. She's occasionally a game designer, and has built worlds for Zynga Inc.'s FarmVille franchise, Mafia Wars, and other games. She lives in India, and is currently working on her next novel.

THE FIRST RULE of temporal research is do not mess with causality. That doesn't apply to me. I have to destroy my future in order to save the past.

A vast and salt-stained desert lies where once there stood a city that dwarfed all that arose in its echo. I have a water skin from its ruins. I am covered in the dust from the night it was razed to the ground. There are carnelian beads from one of its greatest architects woven through my hair, and my heart is a bruise from when time stole it away.

I have to find my ship and go back to the beginning of the end, three days ago, four hundred years in the past, when the light of a new sun five millennia older than my own first shone upon my face.

Upon ancient waters that had passed into history, what appeared to be a curving longboat flickered into being, resting low in the water, its sails unfurled. My Temporal Research Pod, cloaked to blend into my impending present, slipped out of the narrow passageway of the wormhole and into the year 2501 BCE.

"Orumurai, reporting. We've made contact with the substrate of the past. Going dark for unbroken immersion." I cut off my feed to the Council of Time.

I deconstituted the vibro-glass of my cockpit's windshield to begin acclimatizing to my new point in space-time. The climate-control system in my suit kicked in. Its quantum intelligence had morphed it in the yoctosecond it took me to cross the threshold of the wormhole into the past. A knee-length cotton skirt was held in place by a slender leather girdle. My chest was covered by an elaborate array of beads, coruscant in the morning sun. An indigo cloak was intricately draped around my shoulders and midriff, indicating my social standing as someone with power. I had to find the quickest way to what I needed to save my home-world. I needed to understand the language of water from the first and only civilization to have ever mastered it.

T'ahnir rose to bridge the space between earth and sky, a shimmering mirage floating upon mirrors of silver. The city's sixteen reservoirs reflected the light of the sun into my eyes, blinding me momentarily. The river running to a standstill captured my breath, stealing it upon the wind into a past that was now my present. A slice of time that could save my future from its inevitable disintegration.

The harbor thronged with trade ships and fishing vessels, a moving tableau that teemed with overpowering scents and a cacophony of sounds. This wasn't my first visit to what we'd christened the Indus Valley Civilization—I'd spent a month upstream at Mel'or, posing as a researcher from Sumer across the sea. I'd studied its water systems and technology with some of its most brilliant minds. I knew T'ahnir, its southern neighbor, was the center of commerce for the entire Indus Valley, but all the reels I'd studied had never captured the sonority of its heartbeat. It thrummed through my bones as the past claimed me.

I slipped past the prow of a Sumerian ship made from woven reeds lashed together, a team of muscular men slicing its oars through the waters. I stilled my ship's nuclear core, steering it with mast and rigging, fitting in with the gentle pace of traffic on the river. Nudging the boat through the shallows, I looped a rope around a stake at the pier's edge.

Stillness. Silence. Serenity.

I meditated upon the temporal researcher's motto to steady my shaking hands. I fidgeted with the slender vein embedded into the skin of my left cheek, infused with bergamot essence. My personal relic was designed to be a permanent reminder of the slice of space-time I belonged to. Scent, the strongest summoner of memory, would always call me back to my world should I ever lose myself in the continuum.

I left my ship and stepped out onto perfectly symmetrical paving stones. A woman in an ornate headdress shoved past me, a squalling child in tow. A toy maker held a basket full of delights: woven dolls and wooden figurines of animals, colorful tops preserved in stillness, soon to be spun into motion only to be lost to time. The noise and bustle were archaic; the sheer number of human figures scurrying through the streets antiquated.

The eleventh prefecture of Nova-India, my home-world in the year 2451 CE, was a silent aggregate of icy glass spires piercing an azure sky; personal flight-craft leaving jet trails like whispers of an exodus across the clouds, hushed conversations in the ghostly hallways of deserted buildings, an absence of birdsong because there were no trees lining its streets. I was forged in a future on the edge of erasure, and I would vanish with its extinction unless I found answers here, in the vibrance of a forgotten time. I wove into the crowd and allowed the crush of bodies to carry me into the living past.

A wooden signboard, intricately inlaid with carved quartz, hung above the wide entrance to the city. *All is water. Water is all.*

The civ's vast vocabulary of symbols had been

indecipherable until a long love poem written in its script was unearthed in the 22nd century. Its language was lilting, a cadence of speech flowing like a stream. I was certain I'd never accomplish articulating it with grace.

"Oru Wellspring of Mel'or." I shortened my name to the brief syllables that characterized the time period and appended my alleged rank to my introduction. Qualifications were denoted by associations with the water, the least being 'Rivulet'. 'Wellspring' denoted someone with significant expertise, and that part held true for me, even if I'd earned my credibility five thousand years in the future. The only rank higher than the one I claimed was 'Earth-Heart'.

I produced my handheld from a simple cloth bag. My device cloaked itself as a wooden tablet, inscribed with details of my identity and the purpose of my visit. It bore the imprint of a seal from a city official in Mel'or—a humped zebu cow with an inscription. The harbor master glanced at it and looked back up at me.

Stillness. Silence. Serenity.

"Here to research the canal system, again? I thought it was all sorted out in Mel'or the last time one of you Sumerians visited."

"Dhōla—" I stopped myself from using the name given to this city by the future. "T'ahnir lies closest to the water's heart. We come here to reconnect."

The harbor master nodded, looking past me at the queue at my back.

"You'll want to meet Enre," he said. "Let me get you an

escort to the Citadel."

The course of time's river always runs forward.

I have to find a way to sail my ship upstream. I must unwrite the history we've etched into its banks. The city's docks no longer exist, and I cannot see my ship amidst the ruins. Has the Council of Time seized my time machine as punishment for my transgressions? Was it stolen by the T'ahniris during their frantic escape from the earthquake we caused?

I cannot stop searching, not now. To falter would be to condemn them to their doom, to live with the jagged edges of my heart in my hands and nothing but the memory of Enre wrapped up in the beads in my hair.

And so I wander these silent stones in solitude, climbing precarious and lopsided steps on my way to the Citadel, where only three days go, elegantly dressed city officials raced up and down the corridors carrying official missives, called greetings to each other in enthusiastic tones, and huddled in quiet circles whispering over state secrets.

I tapped my foot on the nearly smooth stone floor. Wooden doors, ornately carved with curling vines and lush tropical flowers, stood between me and my audience with Enre.

"Oru Wellspring." A clerk called my name. "Enre Earth-Heart will see you now."

I fought the urge to run my hands over the natural wood as I passed into the chamber. We didn't have many trees left in the future.

"Wellness and prosperity from the waters of Mel'or to

you," I said formally. "I am Oru."

"The blessings of T'ahnir's Earth-Heart Mother upon you," he responded, using the civ's favored metaphor for the river. "I am Enre."

Deep brown eyes twinkled in a suntanned face. His long dark tresses were pulled up in a topknot, held in place by a loop of colorful beads, streams of which were also woven intricately through his hair. He appeared to be barely older than me, and I was taken aback by the thought that I'd expected to see the likeness of a wizened Priest King, whose stone bust unearthed in the ruins of this civ had made his disposition a legend.

He indicated that I should take a seat at his table. I pushed a wooden bench back, touching the smoothened bole of a tree for the first time.

"May I pour you an infusion?" He reached for a set of painted ceramic pots and cups.

"Yes, thank you." I tried not to think about how alcohol from an ancient distillery might react with my system. To refuse would have been impolite.

Before I could sip from the brew he'd pushed my way, he flung a shimmering object at me. "Think fast."

Instinctively, my hand reached out and snatched a piece of metal from the air. I stared at it in confusion. It appeared to be a key from the late 19th century. It definitely was not from here or now.

"Where did you get this?" I asked.

"So you recognize that this is not from my time."

I froze.

"Listen, time traveler, let's drop the pretension." Enre sighed. "What is it you want?"

"What?" My palms began to sweat as my mind raced to comprehend what had just occurred. "What do you mean, *time traveler*?"

"Which sun-span are you from?" he said in a bored tone, dropping formal speech for the colloquial. A wary look crept into his eyes. "Five thousand sun-spans ahead? More? Don't insult my intelligence by feigning ignorance. That metal is not being forged yet. And the design of this device has never been seen before. Nothing like this exists here."

"How do *you* know what it is, then?" I blurted in panic. The fabric of my lies was beginning to fray, along with my composure.

He smirked. "I have encountered your kind before. One from five thousand five hundred sun-spans ahead, and another from five thousand eight hundred sun-spans. There might have been more. They tend to drop in, often carrying sentimental trinkets. I tend to divest them of their artifacts—shapes and objects that baffle my eyes, and my eyes have seen much of this world—before leaving them on a ship downstream with some food and water. Before you get dreamy-eyed, I'm not a noble savage from some golden age of the past. I just don't like spilling blood on the earth; it makes such a mess."

He clasped his long fingers together and leaned forward. Despite his short stature and wiry frame, he seemed to loom before me. "Now tell me. What is it you want?"

"I—I'm Oru, of Mel'or. Aqueduct Overseer. Rank: Wellspring," I said lamely, clinging to my story.

Enre started to shudder, and then a genuine laugh of delight spilled out of him. "Oh, you have... done this properly..." he said between choked breaths, clutching his ribs. "None of the others put in so much effort. Even your clothing fits right in. Most appropriate."

Head swimming with panic, I reached for the drink before me.

"Don't touch that!" Swift as the river's current, he knocked it out of my hands, spilling its contents all over the floor. "Poisoned. Can never be too careful."

He frowned at the remains of the infusion. "Hmm. Might have been a bit hasty in doing that. You could pull an outlandish weapon on me."

He whipped a cruel-looking metal knife out from somewhere behind the table. "I'll run you through if you even attempt it."

I raised my hands as a sign of surrender and realized that it was probably far too modern a symbol. I had no idea what it meant here. My fingers quaked. As a temporal researcher, I had no combat training. I wasn't equipped to deal with this.

"Whatever you're doing, stop it." He imitated the gesture. "I need to know what you want so I can figure out what to do with you."

"I—I want to understand the water." My voice shook. "I want to learn from you. *The language of the water, the story of the stream.*"

"What?" The dagger clattered to the table. His eyes widened in surprise.

A hush descended upon the room as he repeated my words, except he set them to a fragile melody. "Where did you learn that song?"

"It's a quote from an ancient love poem, unearthed in this city in the twenty-second century—four thousand seven hundred sun-spans in the future. It's our link to your language," I said. "I want to know what it means. *The river's endless loop, a circle in time, still and flowing.*"

The guarded shadows left his face, and a smile twitched at the corners of his lips.

My heart skipped a beat. A frisson of anticipation expanded to spark the air between us.

"Let me show you. Meet me here tomorrow."

The course of time's river does not consider the possibility of confluence when past and future collide in an infinite second.

A hot wind spirals through what I think must have been Enre's chamber on that distant day four hundred years ago, but only three days past in my living memory. The gust carries with it the dried leaves of stunted trees and the scent of parched and baking earth. I don't know what I hope to find here—his records on papyrus are crumbled to smears in the dirt, the furniture has been shattered, broken ceramic urns lie upended.

He is gone. I have to reunite our streams, torn apart by the cataclysm I helped cause. My earnest reports on the architecture of T'ahnir, detailed descriptions of its drainage systems, its reservoirs, of the central chamber of the citadel where rainwater was gathered from the sky, have led to an unspeakable crime.

I step onto the deserted streets of the city, shadows of a future I cannot reconcile leaning into each other and trapping me in their darkness. Two days ago, four hundred sun-spans nearer the source of the river of time, we strolled past the neatly structured residential neighborhoods in Middletown. Enre explained the construction of the aqueducts, the renewable cycle of water pumping through the canals, cisterns and reservoirs, all stemming from the river and returning to the river.

"These settling pools were built into the system—"

"—to collect sediment and allow the water to run back to the earth." I finished his sentence for him.

He let out an exasperated sigh. "You're familiar with the science, then."

"We've studied it extensively. It's considered... legendary." I hesitated.

He snorted. "Simple engineering. We aren't savages."

"You were—are—pioneers. That's what makes it so astounding."

"I don't need your approval." His tone was frosty.

"I didn't mean to condescend. I apologize," I said with genuine regret.

He quickened his pace, and I hurried to keep up with him. The deep burgundy cloak he wore swished through the hot, still air in a breeze of its own, or perhaps with the wind of his intensity.

"Tell me about your time," he demanded.

"Five-thousand sun-spans ahead, the place I am from is not too far away from where this city was—*is*. But cities are at least ten thousand times bigger, and mine is the largest for as far as the river runs," I said, using measures familiar to the T'ahniris. "Except we have few rivers. And fewer water reserves. Nearly no forests or farmlands."

The eleventh prefecture of Nova-India was the continent's largest megacity. By the turn of the 21st century, the world had moved past factories choking the skies with smoke to data centers devouring unsustainable energy sources for sustenance. At the dawn of the 22nd, a nuclear war had taken place, and most of the world stuttered through existence beneath ashy clouds of desolation. The 23rd had witnessed biological warfare lay waste to half the earth's population, while the other half had escaped to explore and colonize faraway planets. Those who stayed behind had desperately attempted to invest in a fragile peace. We'd inherited the hollowed-out husk that was the 25th century.

Enre frowned as he attempted to follow my description of the nuclear bomb, which I eventually explained as a raging fire that consumed everything within the blink of an eye. His scowl deepened at the mention of our trysts with the galaxies that lay beyond our own. "All this time spent on escaping a problem when you could be solving it instead," he said severely.

"There is hopelessness in the very soil of the earth; it spreads like a taint," I argued. "At least the stars hold mysteries, a future where we can start over."

"And yet you choose to stay?" he asked, sounding somewhat hopeful.

"I will persist while we still have water. Hope lies in its depths."

He lapsed into silence, thinking this over. We proceeded down the path to Lowertown, where the marketplaces and the craftsman's quarters beckoned. Verdant fields and farmlands, and the looping river, lay beyond.

"What survives us?" Enre asked, running the flat of his palm over the limestone walls of what he called Reservoir Seven, towering several meters above us into the sky.

"A city in the salt-desert lies, the triumph and ruin of an ancient people." I chose my words carefully.

"This is the sum of our ambition," he muttered. He stopped and spun around. I bumped into him and sprung back from the jolt that sparked its way across my skin. He stood his ground. "You should know, I've barely built any of this technology. I'm just a tinker, improving our systems every few years."

"That's exactly what I am in my time," I said, dismayed by his bitterness. "It's why I'm here, to learn from you. You were—are—masters of the river."

He took a step towards me. He caught my cloak and held it between his fingers. "Do you know why you wear this indigo cloak, Oru Wellspring?"

My heart juddered at his proximity, at the scent of vetiver and damp earth that clung to him. "It's my rank. A symbol of my expertise, of my status in this society," I said with certainty.

He laughed. "Five thousand sun-spans ahead and this is the advancement of thought that has emerged."

"What have I said wrong?" My shoulders tensed in defense, preparing for a confrontation I was unwilling to have.

"It's not you. It's what you've been trained to see." He tugged on the indigo fabric. "This is not a token of expertise, of social standing and privilege. Neither is the red cloak I wear as Enre Earth-Heart. It is a symbol of service; a lifelong commitment to the river and the rain, to the waters that run beneath us and to the endless seas beyond. What did you call us? Masters of the water? We are but its stewards."

I pressed myself into the wall at my back, pulling as far away from his physicality as I could. He stepped backwards, a flush deepening the bronzed skin of his cheeks. "You represent a future, a reality unimaginable to my own. You are living proof of my demise and of civilization's decline. It is hard to stare mortality in the face."

He turned and walked away.

I released a breath I'd been unaware I was holding.

The course of time's river swirls and eddies in unexpected truths.

I look upon the devastation caused by the Council of Time four hundred years ago to feed the desperation of a future thousands of years hence. They'd sent me to study techniques of conservation that our engineers, perhaps being so far removed from sources of water, might have overlooked. Or so they'd told me.

Instead, in a terrible violation of the laws of space-time, they'd pillaged an ancient river, stealing all its waters, siphoning them through reinforced portals spanning the space-time continuum. They chose to fuel our eroded future with the lifeblood of the fallow past. If I find my ship, if it still works, I will undo this wrong.

The walls of the reservoirs are bone-dry, cracking under an austere sun. I run my palm over the ruin of Reservoir Seven, haunted by the vanished light and sound of his presence, just as I was when he stormed away from me in disdain two days ago, four centuries upstream.

"Oru Wellspring, I apologize for my hostility," he said, returning to my side mere minutes after he'd left. "You're my guest here, even if you come from a time I cannot fathom. And you are not your people."

The wind whipped my loose hair about my face, and I struggled to push it off my forehead. He stretched his hand out, then stopped. "May I help?"

"Yes."

He reached out and tucked a strand behind my ear, pinning it in place with an ivory comb he produced out of a hidden pocket. "As I was saying, I apologize for my rudeness. Allow me to make it up to you. I would love to share an incredible discovery with you."

Lost for words at the brush of his fingertips against my cheek, I nodded.

We walked past crystalline creeks, flowing like threads of silver through the public orchards. Date and fig trees lined the avenues, interspersed by the sprawling canopies of mango and jujube. We were escaping the city's walls, Enre pointing out structures of interest, like the aqueducts that fed water into the cisterns, and the canals that irrigated the rice paddies in the distance.

Stewards of the water, Enre had said. *Not masters.*

"You manipulate the water," I said with a frown. "All these dams and reservoirs—you're controlling the flow of the river. That's not being a steward."

"We guide the water to meet our needs. We do not take more than it can give." Enre said seriously. "To thirst is to be alive, but to devour is to be monstrous."

We left the city through a concealed entrance and climbed a low rise covered in scrub and spiny grasses. The city curled into the crook of the river's passage, nestled against pools of water smoldering molten with the light of the setting sun. Enre sang a song to himself— I'd studied it as a love poem to the water while learning his language. His voice brought it to life, sending a shiver down my spine. Echoes from a future in which these words belonged to the past reached out across our continuum to hold us together in the present.

"Who wrote this poem?" I asked.

"I did." Enre's eyes shone golden.

I was growing to discover that the past had been written by the hearts of its people. I was beginning to see the world through Enre's gaze, through the eye of a mind that ran fathomless leagues deep, looking beyond the transience of the present and into the cyclical forever.

"You're not here to attempt to enslave our city?" Enre teased. "That was what the traveler from five thousand five hundred spans ahead wanted."

"No," I said, horrified.

"You aren't going to use our lands as a war zone? Unlike our visitor from six thousand spans ahead... who said something about a war in time." He grinned broadly, evidently enjoying my discomfort.

"No. Of course not!"

"This *is* a refreshing change." The cadence of his speech quickened in excitement. He was crossing the hillock already, scrambling down its other side. I hurried to keep pace and slid across the muddied ground.

"Watch your step!" He threw his hand out and grabbed me by the arm. A ripple of electricity galvanized my skin, spreading outward in waves and causing my breath to come up short. His long, rough fingers slid down my arm and he took my hand, pressing it into his callused palm. "I forget, you're unfamiliar with this terrain. We'll slow down. I will guide you by the hand if you'll let me."

"Yes." I squeezed his hand in response, my skin thrilling to his touch. We traversed the oozing mud and slippery rocks down the bluff until we encountered a rill, trickling its way through tussocks of knotted grass.

"Nearly there," he said, pulling me forward. We walked west towards the setting sun, rounding the hill and following the path of the stream. He stopped abruptly and spun to face me. I crashed into him.

"Easy." He laughed lightly. He let go of my hand, leaving my palm in the shadow of his warmth. He rolled a large rock away from the base of the low incline. A babbling, tinkling wave of sound spiraled outwards; the sound of a river's flood. I gasped and peered in through the narrow chasm.

"I give you the Earth-Heart."

A silence spanning several minutes wove past and future together.

"It's beautiful!" I said. Joy bubbled up through me like the river's song.

"It's an entire river system, running past the city and beneath it, out to the sea beyond. I've traced its path underground every day for the past sun-span."

"What an absolute wonder! Have you connected it to the reservoirs and aqueducts yet?"

"No."

I glanced upward and found him watching me intently, a look of sadness on his face.

"It's a secret," he said softly. "You're the only person I've shown."

"Why?"

"You betray the answer yourself. The minute the wider city knows... they'll want to use it. And we don't need this water. Not yet. The reservoirs are enough. The city's administrators, though..." His voice trailed off.

I turned, pressing my back to the wall of earth, ignoring the damp seeping through my modified suit. "But your civ—your city, it's not like mine, is it?"

"All people are the same, across cities and suns."

"Why me, then?"

"The secrets of this time are safe with you. You're here now, but soon you'll be gone, never to return."

My heart sank at the finality—and the truth—of his words. I tried to hide my inexplicable sorrow. "Don't you trust your own kind? I thought that's what set you apart. Your people's love for the water, its consecration."

His eyes swept across my face, then bored into mine with an intensity that caused my pulse to go jagged. "It's what sets you and I apart. Do you know what these beads in my hair are for, Oru Wellspring?"

He reached up and unbound a woven braid of his hair, carnelian glittering in the pink of the twilight sky. "Every jewel marks another moon-cycle I have spent bound to the service of the water."

He took a strand of my hair in his hand, curling it around his fingers. "Tomorrow marks the start of another moon-cycle. You should wear jewels of your own, and I shall give them to you."

I released the breath that had caught in my chest. "H-how?"

"Meet me here at moonrise." He let my hair drop back to my shoulder. I found myself unable to move, pinned in place by his searching gaze.

"Before you go, you should know. I lied to you," he whispered.

"What about?" My pulse quickened like a raging rapid.

"I knew you were a time traveler the minute you stepped into my room. It had nothing to do with that metal artifact I threw at you."

"How did you know?" My voice came out hoarse.

"Your scent is not of this time. What is it?"

"Bergamot," I said in my native tongue.

"Bergamot," he repeated, speaking my language for the first time.

I was surrounded by the scent of vetiver and wet earth, and it was him and it was everything around him, all I could sense, but for the heat in his eyes which were filled with the light of a thousand suns.

He leaned forward.

The course of time's river cascaded into me with the press of his lips against mine.

The course of time's river stood still, and I didn't believe it would unspool and come crashing down around me in a torrent of heartbreak and regret. And yet, here I am. A stranger alone in a strange time, responsible for the erasure of a culture, for the destruction of Enre's world, for the fragments of my heart, pierced and shattered by time's cruel arrow.

The course of time's river makes me yearn for a yesterday from countless suns away.

The thought of Enre's lips upon mine, the warmth of his chest pressing me back into the earth, the slope of his shoulders wrapped in my arms, consumes my every waking moment. The promise of all my future could have been had we left the past in place is a knife twisting its way through my chest. Hope for countless civilizations spanning five thousand years of human history, springing from an ancient way of looking at the world—lost to time because of the hand I played in its obliteration—forces me onward, one step at a time.

I fight a terrifying thought. I might never find my ship. My mind is blank, shrouded in the fog from last night, four hundred years past.

I couldn't believe what I'd heard.

The glimmering traversium alloy that made up the Council of Time's portals spun together in a dizzying blur, punching holes into the depths of continuum and preparing to bore wounds into the past.

A moment of silence spun out across the millennia.

"We expect you back in the next fifteen minutes, Orumurai. Leave before they discover their reservoirs emptying."

"You—you can't do this." I stuttered. "It could trigger an earthquake! Catastrophic effects—imagine the climate change. You'll erase an entire civilization."

The uniformed members of the Council of Time exchanged a significant glance between them. One of them sighed. "How do you think their civilization came to an end? It was always us, all along. Now get back here, and let history write itself."

I couldn't think. I threw up. My ship's systems deployed bots to take care of the spill. I was light-headed, the world spinning around me. I caught sight of the full moon glancing off the river behind me...

Moonrise.

Enre.

I had to warn him. I had to save him. I had to save them all.

I killed my video feed to the Council of Time.

I rushed from my ship and leapt out into the light of the full moon. I staggered, racing down the side streets. I pushed past revelers and courtesans in the marketplace, feet pounding against the stones as I raced up a low staircase and threw myself out the hidden entrance into the wilderness. Slipping and sliding on the mud and grass, I stumbled up the hill we'd climbed.

The air around me turned static. An electric charge singed the grass beneath my feet, and if it hadn't been for my temporal suit, I'd have been as charred as the blackened heads of the wildflowers I trampled.

I glanced behind me and saw the gaping maw of a portal, a machine-like claw tethered to something gigantic slipping through light and vibrance and onto the darkening soil of the past. My present. A world that seemed to call to me more than the future I belonged to. With alarming speed, it flung itself at me and caught me around my waist, dragging me back into the infinite space between times. The ground beneath my feet trembled and I fell, my hands scraping raw over the rocks as I clutched at sprigs of grass and vetiver in a desperate attempt to resist its pull.

The claw around my waist expanded, surrounding my limbs, boxing me into its traversium shell as a pod formed around me.

"Let me go! You can't do this!" I screamed.

"Sorry, don't know what your scene here is. I'm just leading this extraction on the Council of Time's orders. Gotta get you back in one piece."

My insides were squeezed as the pod was sucked into the wormhole.

"STOP!" I cried out. "STOP!"

I battered my hands against the vibro-glass and it held firm. I scanned the insides of the machine, desperately searching for a way out. A holo-dash monitored my vitals; it told me my heart rate was escalating and my breathing was ragged. It also told me where to find the emergency switch that would release the pod from its tether.

I slammed the only analog dial I'd ever experienced in my history as a time traveler, the only analog button that had ever mattered.

"What are you doing!" the voice yelled over the pod's intercom.

My capsule was flung forward and ricocheted off the fabric of the wormhole, bouncing as the world raced past me so fast it was as if all the universe stood still. I caught a glimpse of the portal ahead of me and willed the pod to fall through it.

It floated.

Agonizing seconds passed.

And then the force of space-time, of reality on the other side, reached out and began to suck me towards it, ripping me out of eternity and into the bright light of a foreign sun.

The pod struck the earth and shattered. Shards of vibro-glass rained down upon me, molecularly vaporizing before they pricked my skin. A sob wrenched its way through me, and I curled up on the ground for several moments before I could move.

Where am I?

I'd had no way to set my destination, not with the rudimentary controls in the pod. The wormhole had spat me out in an unknowable time, an unknowable place.

I forced several deep breaths into my lungs and opened my eyes. I lay by a familiar hill, but the grass was browned, the earth cracked. I got to my feet, unsteady and shaking, and looked around me.

No trees dotted the landscape of this world I'd known only yesterday. The rill Enre and I had followed no longer existed. The silver mirrors of T'ahnir were barren; the remains of its past glory lay crumbling in the dust.

In the stifling silence of a familiar world gone wrong, I heard a gurgle, like the heartbeat of a stream. I followed its sound. I hefted a boulder away from a crumbling crack in the rocks. Enre had made it look so easy.

At the entrance to the underground cavern, by the banks of the hidden river, lay a circlet of carnelian beads.

One for every lunar-cycle. There were a dozen.

Had Enre survived? I listened to the language of the water, the story of the stream. I heard Enre's voice singing its lilting words to me. I wove the beads into my hair and rolled the boulder back in place.

I sit by the Earth-Heart mother, weeping tears into her torrent.

I smell bergamot commanding my return. I ache for the scent of vetiver to root me in time.

I will destroy my future if it means saving the past. I will return the waters we stole. I will see Enre again.

I have to find my ship.

The course of time's river never did run smooth. It sweeps me up in its endless flow.

Author's Notes:

1.   The civilization being referred to in this story is the Indus Valley Civilization.

2.   The city of Mel'or is known to the modern world as Mohenjo-Daro, and T'ahnir is now known as Dholavira. However, since the script of the Indus Valley Civilization is yet to be deciphered, I have taken liberties with what the residents of the cities might have named their cities. Mohenjo-Daro literally translates to 'Mound of the Dead' and so it is unlikely that the living citizens of this city would have referred to themselves thus.

3.   The language of the Indus Valley is widely believed to be proto-Dravidian, and the linguistic foundation for all names in this story is Tamil, the oldest living Dravidian language.

4.   Owing to the absence of a Rosetta Stone, little is known about the Indus Valley Civilization's

customs and cultures. Those presented in this story are fictional. However, the descriptions of the geography, architecture, crafts and dress, including the prevalence of carnelian beads, are true to existing archaeological evidence. The denizens of Dholavira are widely believed to have been masters of the river.

5.   The civilization's demise is a mystery, and is often ascribed to an earthquake, or to climate change. I have chosen to reflect both these hypotheses in this story.

The Difference Between Love and Time
Catherynne M. Valente

Catherynne M. Valente (www.catherynnemvalente.com) is the New York Times bestselling author of forty works of speculative fiction and poetry, including *Space Opera*, *The Refrigerator Monologues*, *Palimpsest*, the *Orphan's Tales* series, *Deathless*, *Radiance*, and the crowdfunded phenomenon *The Girl Who Circumnavigated Fairyland in a Ship of Her Own Making* (and the four books that followed it). She is the winner of the Andre Norton, Tiptree, Sturgeon, Prix Imaginales, Eugie Foster Memorial, Mythopoeic, Rhysling, Lambda, Locus, Romantic Times' Critics Choice, and Hugo Awards. She has been a finalist for the Nebula and World Fantasy Awards. She lives on an island off the coast of Maine with a small but growing menagerie of beasts, some of which are human.

THE SPACE/TIME CONTINUUM is the sum total of all that ever was or will be or ever possibly could have been or might conceivably exist and/or occur, the constantly tangling braid of physical and theoretical reality, (steadily degrading) temporal processes, and the interactions between the aforementioned.

It is also left-handed.

It is, as you have probably always suspected, non-linear, non-anthropic, non-Euclidean, and wholly non-sensical.

In point of fact, it's a complete goddamned mess.

It has severe social anxiety.

And a weakness for leather jackets.

We first met when I was six. Our fathers arranged a play date. The space/time continuum looked like a boy my own age, with thick glasses in plastic army camouflage-printed frames, a cute little baby afro, and a faded T-shirt with the old mascot for the poison control hotline on it. Mr. Yuk, grimacing on the chest of time and space, sticking out his admonishing green Yuk-tongue. POISON HELP! 1-800-222-1222.

It smelled like lavender and bread baking in a stone oven.

I said I wanted to play Lego.

It looked helplessly at me with big brown eyes magnified into enormity by prescription lenses like hockey pucks.

It picked up a black block with an arch in it. Part of the drawbridge in my Medieval Castle Siege playset. The space/time continuum handed me the black arch and opened its mouth and the sound of a pulsar spinning, turning, thumping through silver-deafening radio static came out instead of "Where does this piece go?" or "It's nice to meet you" or "The idea of your shitty Lego drawbridge amusing me for even a nanosecond is hilarious on a geological scale."

The space/time continuum is a manifold topology whose coordinates can and frequently do map onto certain physical states, events, bodies. But that map looks like one of those old paper diner menus with a giant squiggle on it labelled *Enter Here* on one side and *You Win!* on the other.

And it changes all the time.

And you can't win.

And the crayon evaporates in your hand and rematerializes in your hospital bassinet under the *Welcome Baby!* card.

Or on the surface of the moon.

It doesn't care for television except for reruns of *Law & Order*. It cannot get enough of predictability. It says every episode is a bizarre upside-down bubble universe in which justice exists and things make sense.

The first real actual word the space/time continuum ever said to me was: "Nothing."

The first words I said to it were: "You can't just go around saying 'nothing' to people, it's weird. Do you want my extra Capri Sun?"

The space/time continuum wrapped its skinny baby arms around me and whispered it again in my ear: "Nothing."

I didn't like being hugged then. I yelled for my mom. She didn't come for a long time.

In high school, the space/time continuum looked like a scene kid with a million flannels and ironic shirts, a long black undercut, and a patch on his backpack from some band called Timeclaw. It got in a lot of trouble for drawing or carving or scratching its initial in desks all over the place, this funky *S* that kinda also looks like a pointy figure 8. But not lying on its side like the infinity symbol. Infinity standing up.

I've seen them everywhere. Still do. The space/time continuum gets around.

You've probably seen it, too.

It failed all its classes but shop. It was always punctual at the circular saw. It never failed to make a perfect version of the assignment from oak, birch, ash, even plastic. Every day, it brought me the objects it had been compelled to make by Mr. Wooton. A model PT Cruiser. A wooden orchid. A puzzle shaped like an iguana. My favorite was this bare green circuit board with a little lightbulb on it that flared to life if you put your finger in the right place. It used you to complete the circuit.

The space/time continuum and I sat behind the bike racks for hours after school smoking weed and putting our fingers in the right place.

Ocean Shores, WA is not the space/time continuum, though it is, of necessity, an inescapable part of it. Ocean Shores, WA is a city that used to be a pretty big deal and is now not even a little deal.

See, back in the sixties, the state of Washington thought maybe it would legalize gambling because fuck it, why not, and people started buying up all the land and building nightclubs and hotels and golf courses and bungalows and boardwalks so that when the legislature hit the buzzer, the good times would be ready to roll. All kinds of movie stars and rich people's girlfriends and purveyors of semi-legal entertainment poured in from California. But then the state of Washington thought maybe it would not legalize gambling so now there's just a lot of cold sand dunes and closed attractions and motels with names like Tides Inn or Mermaid's Rest Motor Court and Weigh Station.

Ocean Shores is hollowed out like a gourd someone meant to make into a drum for a beautiful party. But they wandered off and maybe even forgot what drums are to begin with so now it's just an empty, scraped-out dead vegetable lying on a cold beach nobody would ever hold a party on.

And then a seagull shits in it.

My mom and my dad and me used to always drive down for the last weekend of summer. Dad would always give me a riddle that I had to solve by the end of the trip. Like the one with the wolf and the chicken and the bag of grain or what has a ring but no finger? I'd play the twenty-year-old games on the last remaining boardwalk while my parents argued about what to do with me under the white noise of the waves.

Eventually, Dad left and it was just me and mom. We'd rent a bungalow that was once destined to be Jayne Mansfield's fuck grotto or whatever and sit in the moldy jacuzzi freezing our asses off, singing show tunes to the seals and shipping freighters out at sea.

The space/time continuum thinks Ocean Shores was at its best when only dinosaurs lived there.

I asked the space/time continuum who its mother was once. Did she have fluffy curly hair like mine, did she smell nice like mine, was her name Alice like mine, did she sniffle a lot like she was crying even though she usually wasn't like mine, did she always pack a fruit and a vegetable in its lunchbox (a Lisa Frank purple-blue cosmic orca one that I secretly coveted)?

The space/time continuum glanced nervously at the ashy green blackboard at the front of our classroom. This made me dislike the space/time continuum, as at the time many of the children liked to make fun of me for being dimwitted, even though I do all right. But it gave no other answer, and only a long time later did I consider that it was not looking at the blackboard at all, but the eraser.

When the space/time continuum stuck that black Lego arch over the scuffed blue moat pieces, it stopped being a Medieval Castle Siege playset and started being a Cartoon Sparkle Rainbow Geoduck playset.

Our dads didn't notice. They just kept drinking beers, one after the other, lifting the red and white Rainier cans to their lips and setting them down automatically after each rhythmic sip like they were beer-drinking machines stuck in an infinite recursion function.

The space/time continuum in the Mr. Yuk shirt smiled at me shyly. It was giving me a gift. It wanted desperately to please me. I was not pleased. I liked my Medieval Castle Siege playset a lot. It came with four different-colored horse minifigs. Geoducks are weird gross dumb giant clams that live in the mud for a thousand years and come with zero horse minifigs. Their shells aren't rainbow-striped and they don't have friendly eyes with big, long eyelashes and smiling mouths and they definitely don't sparkle.

I didn't even think Lego made a Cartoon Sparkle

Rainbow Geoduck playset.

But the space/time continuum's eyelashes were very long, too. So I said thank you.

It made the pulsar sound again.

You have to understand I was alone a lot of the time. It came and went as it pleased. But not because it was afraid to commit. The space/time continuum asked me to marry it when I was eight and we were pretending to fish with branches and string in the pond behind the primate research labs on the edge of town. I couldn't figure out why the fish weren't biting. I was going to bring my mom the biggest salmon you ever saw and she was gonna say how good I was and be so happy instead of staring at the dish soap for an hour while I watched the Muppets, but the stupid fish weren't on board with my plan.

That time, the space/time continuum looked like a girl my age with a red NO NUKES shirt on under her overalls. It said: *We didn't bring any bait. Or hooks. And there are no fish in this pond because it's not really a pond, it's a big puddle that dries up as soon as there's no rain for a week. Be my wife forever, limited puddle-being.*

I said: *Shut up, your face is a puddle.*

The space/time continuum lay its pigtailed head on my shoulder as the sunset sloshed liquid pink and gold and said: *We are a house and a hill.*

OK, weirdo.

But we were already holding hands so tight, without

even noticing it.

So it's not about commitment.

The space/time continuum just has a hard time with confined spaces. Like the public education system. And calendars. And apartments.

And bodies.

Its favorite album is the iconic 1979 *Breakfast in America* by often underrated British prog-pop group Supertramp. But its favorite song is 'Time After Time' by Cyndi Lauper.

I don't really have anything to say in defense of its weakness for easy listening.

I guess it just wants something to be easy.

The space/time continuum is holistically without gender.

Its pronouns are it/everything.

Or, to put it another way, it is a quivering, boiling mass of all physio-psychological states that will/are likely to/have developed across every extinct/extant/unborn species, making the whole issue pointless, irrelevant, and none of my business. The seventy-fourth time we met it looked like an Estonian woman who had just graduated from the Rhode Island School of Design, so you can see what I mean.

Butch on the streets, churning maelstrom of intersecting time and matter in the sheets.

Later, the space/time continuum told me that was only the second time we'd met in objectively perceived time. Which always meant its perception, never mine. It was freshly in love. I was forty and tired. It was July. Rain beat the streets down till they gave up. The puddle talk happened yesterday. Its hair was so long and fine I felt certain that if I touched it, it would all dissipate like smoke. But I really, really wanted to touch it anyway. It wore a pale blue leather jacket over a white T-shirt with a Frank Lloyd Wright quote on it in thin gray Arial letters. It looked so fucking cool. It was always so much cooler than me.

I took the continuum to that little Eritrean restaurant down on Oak. It ordered *tsebhi derho* with extra injera and ate like food had only just been invented, which, given the nature of this story, I feel I should stress it had not. I just had the yellow lentil soup. The space/time continuum cried in my arms. It thought it had lost track of me. I didn't answer its text messages.

If it was a commercial cereal brand it would be Cap'n Crunch Oops All Genders.

I would be Cinnamon Toast Chump.

Whatever it looks like, it always wears glasses. Safer that way. For all of us.

The Frank Lloyd Wright quote was: *No house should ever be on a hill or anything. It should be of the hill. Belonging to it. Hill and house should live together, each the happier for the other.*

We had our first kiss in middle school.

The space/time continuum took me to the winter dance. It wore white. I wore black. We looked like winter, the wide, deep snow and a bare tree. It picked me up at 6:45 and tied a corsage around my wrist. It said the flower was an odontoglossum orchid. Native to Argentina. Only grows in cold climates. Like me.

When the space/time continuum put its hands on my waist, lock-elbowed, stiff, uncertain, I smelled a lonely ultraviolet sea churning on a small world in the constellation of Taurus. It wasn't winter in the constellation of Taurus. It was spring, and the sea on that planet was in love with a particular whale-plant living inside it, and I understood a lot of things just then. When Bryan Adams hit his guitar solo, the space/time continuum kissed me, and I knew why it'd been wearing that poison control shirt when we first met, and also what it felt like to be a whale who is also a flower, floating inside a desperate sea.

The ninety-fourth time we met, the space/time continuum was on Tinder. It had a dog in its profile pic, even though it doesn't have a dog in real life. Its other pics showed it fishing, hiking, doing a color run.

This was its profile:

S, Young at Heart

>0.1 miles away

Hi, baby.

I'm sorry. I was wrong. I'm an idiot. I love you. I'll do better this time. I can be better. Come home.

But then I think it got nervous and confused because below that it said:

If you can't handle me at the peak of my recursive timeline algorithm, you don't deserve me when I'm an iguana.

The dog was a corgi. But not the orange kind, the black and white kind. Its name tag said *Snack McCoy*.

That's a pretty solid *Law & Order* joke. So it probably was the space/time continuum's dog. Somewhen. Elsewise.

I wonder if there was a version of me in the Snack McCoy universe. I wonder if there was a version of you.

I wonder if everything there was made out of crunchy biscuit treats.

I don't know why the space/time continuum stopped loving me. Maybe I worked too much, too hard, too late. Maybe it wanted more than cozy taco nights in a rooftop apartment above, in descending order, a comedy club, a Planned Parenthood, and a laundromat. Maybe it wanted less. Was I overly critical? (*Why the fuck do people just STOP at completely unpredictable points, what's wrong with you, why would you set it up that way? Sleep on the goddamned couch, you narcissist.*) Did I just *consistently* fail to put my dishes in the dishwasher right away? I could've done it any time I wanted. Cups go in rack not on counter. Easy. And yet. Did I not support its interests? Maybe I didn't understand its love language. Or how to set up a retirement account. Maybe I took too long to lose the baby weight. Maybe I didn't let it have enough me time.

Maybe I stopped really listening. Maybe the nexus of spatial and temporal possibilities was just sick of my shit.

Maybe I don't deserve to be loved.

That's probably it.

One time it showed our first grade teacher, Mrs. Aldritch, the drawing it made during quiet period and she cried spinal fluid out of her eyes so that was pretty intense.

It refused to show me. Even though it borrowed my black crayon to color with in the first place.

The space/time continuum's father looked very much like Mr. Clark, who used to run Dazzle Dan's Vintage Diner by the train tracks. Mr. Clark's name was not Dan.

It was Clarence Peter Clark. But the previous owner wasn't named Dan either. He was named Roderigo R. Rodriguez, which I am not making up. But it was pretty hard to be Mexican around here back then, especially if you wanted to sell all-American nostalgia burgers with lettuce, tomato, onion, and mayo, so he just went by Roddy.

Roddy was from Guadalajara. There's a cathedral there called the Catedral de la Asunción de María Santísima with two golden spires standing up into the sky and the birds together, completely identical. Clarence Peter Clark was from Yakima. There's nothing much in Yakima.

Nobody knows where Dazzle Dan came from.

By the time I was thirteen I was pretty sure the space/ time continuum didn't actually have a father, just a thing in its house like one of those old drinky bird toys that sat on the lip of a glass and rocked back and forth more or less forever, once you set it going. It needed a father to make sure no one suspected it wasn't actually a boy with glasses or a girl with pigtails or an Estonian exchange student. But it didn't need a *person*. Just a bobbing blob of weighted plastic wearing Mr. Clark's face, lifting can after red and white can of Rainier beer to its mouth in the background until the death of all matter in a fiery entropic abyss.

On our second play date we tried to play Cowboys and Indians. I heard the other kids doing it. Cowboys had horses, and I loved horses more than candy, so I was pretty excited.

But I never ever got to be the cowboy. The space/time continuum said: *Cowboy is just another word for the generational trauma inflicted by the colonizer's whole-ass inability to access empathy for anyone but himself and the debt to entropy incurred by his solipsistic commitment to almost unimaginable violence as an expression of personal potency.*

Then it poured the living memory of the surrender of the Nez Perce in the Bear Paw Mountains like molten platinum into my brain and blood shot out of my nose and my eyes at the same time and my pinky toe turned into a Suciasaurus rex tooth. The space/time continuum panicked, whispering *oh shit, oh shit, I'm sorry, I'll fix it*, whereupon it flooded my gray matter with golden retrievers and the smell of chocolate cookies baking and the exact emotional sensations experienced in the moment of era-defining scientific discoveries and a few old Bob Ross episodes just in case.

My appendix ruptured and I didn't speak again for ten months.

My parents sent me to specialists.

A lot of them.

The space/time continuum is a total slob and a nightmare roommate. It leaves its wadded-up proto-stars all over the floor. It won't do the dishes even when I cook, since it only pretends to eat. It washes clothes we haven't bought yet, then forgets to put them away for weeks. It has taken a moral stance against both mowing the lawn and dusting. It says doing so would only appropriate the culture of sequential cause and effect, which it has no right to wear like a costume.

It leaves a ring of quantum foam around the bathtub to just get crustier and crustier until I give in and scrub it off myself. Stare for fifteen minutes while my knees get sore on the badly grouted tile thinking about equal division of labor and if maybe we should get a chore chart, if that would even help, or if it just thinks this is my work because I'm the one who's going to die someday so it bothers me more. Finally, run the water and watch it all swirl down the silver drain into the waste infrastructure dimension.

"An alarm clock," I whisper to the slowly rotating water. "An alarm clock has a ring but no finger."

Every Valentine's Day, the space/time continuum wraps my gift in pink and red paper with hearts or baby angels or birds or radio signals all over it and practically climbs the walls with excitement waiting for me to open it.

Those are some of the best times I remember. The moments before I rip the baby angel bird hearts open.

There's never anything inside the box. It's just that after I open the box, I know a story about love I didn't know before I opened the box. And I mean I know it like it happened to me. Like it's my own story.

One year it was this: the Loch Ness monster was absolutely real. She lived to be about five hundred years old like that one ugly Greenland shark they found before a Swiss tourist hit her in the head with a boat propeller in 1951. There used to be two of them, even. A mating pair. Nessie had a single baby around the time of the Great Fire of London and I felt her love that baby monster fishosaur down in the dark and the cold that wasn't dark or cold to her at all. I felt the absolute safety and security of thousands of pounds of water pressure like one of those weighted vests for anxious dogs. I felt Nessie love her baby so much the temperature of the whole lake rose by one degree.

My gifts aren't as good. My gifts do not come from the time-pit out of which springs the Pleiades and ring-tailed lemurs and the Battle of Tours and Loch Ness, they come from my checking account.

Last year I gave it cufflinks. I don't fucking know, you try buying for a space/time continuum who definitionally has everything.

Here is an abridged list of things the space/time continuum and I fought about:

What movie to watch.

Whether or not I had a hostile tone this morning.

The exact dictionary definition of *narcissist*.

If it's technically gaslighting to make a fight never have happened.

Where it goes when we're not together.

Why it won't let anything last.

The whole thing about it allowing death to exist.

If it ever thought for one minute about consent before fucking about with my Lego and/or timestream.

Whether it has to pay rent.

Why it didn't tell me to go to the hospital that night because we both know it had to have known.

Why it is the way it is.

Why it refuses to change.

Why it decided capitalism had to be a thing.

Why everything sucks so much all the time.

Why I don't think a baby is a good idea.

This is what it looks like when the space/time continuum is mad at you: you wake up in the morning already late because your alarm clock now reads 1-800-222-1222. The auto-set coffee machine isn't left on for you and the taco leftovers from last night are all gone and its car isn't in the overnight guest spot and you can't find your phone and there's no dishes in the cupboards and there's no cute little Post-it note on the fridge telling you to have a nice day (PS we're out of milk) but there definitely *is* lipstick scrawled on the bathroom mirror. The expensive stuff, MAC Saint Germain, big swooping letters that read [*the speed of light in a vacuum is the same for all observers regardless of the directionality of the light source.*] *Asshole.*

You'll have to wait a few weeks for the space/time continuum to cool off and get a little cheeky over a couple of bottles of bodega rosé to find out that it one hundred percent ate all the leftovers just to spite you. But then it got sick and spewed total paralyzing awareness of causality all over the 98 bus and, like, *everyone* on that route is now loaded up with heavy sedation or Fields Medals but *ANYWAY* it's just *maybe* possible your phone is embedded in an extremely put-out pachycephalosaurus's eye socket.

But either way, you have to stop freaking out about the car.

The continuum doesn't have a car. It's never had a car. It doesn't drive. It doesn't even have a license so much as it *contains* everyone else's licenses. It's just that sometimes a pocket universe containing a reality in which Monet was never born looks *a lot* like a 2005 Inca Gold Pearlcoat PT Cruiser with a faded COEXIST bumper sticker half-peeled off the back and a leather frog keychain swinging from the rear-view.

Then the space/time continuum starts acting way too

nice. It lets you pick the movie and what kind of takeout to order and gives you a foot rub before admitting that your patterned cups and soup bowls and novelty pink octopus mug are currently making a long lonely pilgrimage around the frigid ring system of Saturn. Yes, it knows they were your mother's, and it's very sorry, it doesn't know what gets into it sometimes. It just loves you so much and, well, you know how you can be. So immature. So self-centered. So finite. You don't appreciate the emotional labor the space/time continuum puts into this relationship.

But that octopus mug is gonna make *big* news in about a hundred years, so let's focus on the positive, also don't be mad but your coffee ended up in the butt of Malmsey that drowned George Plantagenet. Because fuck you that's why. It was upset. You shouldn't have said that thing about the invention of death. There are just some things you do not say to someone you love.

But you make up. Always. Until you don't. And when your duck pad see ew with extra broccoli arrives in its pure white styrofoam container, twenty minutes before you put the order in, there's a pastel violet Post-it note inside that says: *please don't leave me.*

The space/time continuum enjoys baking, but you can't eat the pale green *prinsesstårta* it has worked so hard to perfect after seeing it on that reality cake show. You can only have eaten it. Or be going to eat it. Or sometimes one day will have been never eating it. That's pretty much how it goes for all its hobbies. It swears it knit me a gorgeous mauve cabled cardigan for my fiftieth birthday because I'm always cold.

I wouldn't know. I've never seen it.

Coming up on my sixtieth.

Still cold.

Dick.

The space/time continuum is not a dick.

Mostly.

My mom—you remember Alice, with the curly hair and the fruits and vegetables in every lunch? Well, Alice died a little while after the whole David and Susan thing. Paranasal tumors. I didn't even know you could get nose cancer. By the time they found it, Alice hadn't been able to smell or taste anything in years.

That's the worst part, she told me after the diagnosis, home, in bed with a couple of bottles of Ignoring Our Problems juice. *I can't smell anything. Not even you. I used to smell your head when you were a baby and it was the most amazing smell, better than Chanel No 5, I swear. Like lavender and bread baking in a stone oven. And sometimes, just once in a while, when you got older, you would be running out the door for a date with that kid in the flannel or putting groceries away or watching*

TV and I'd get a whiff of it again, like you were still so tiny and all mine and nothing bad could ever happen to us. And it's gone. I'll never smell you again ever.

She hated hospitals so by the time I managed to convince her to get her butt in a paper gown it was just all through her. It couldn't wait. Had somewhere important to be, I guess.

But she was wrong. The worst part was that I wasn't there. I wanted to be. But I had to work. I missed it. The last words my mother ever said to me were days and days before.

"Those things are rigged, honey."

But by then she was mostly morphine by volume, so.

One time the space/time continuum and I went to Mr. Clark's diner for burgers and floats. I was eleven. It looked eleven enough. I felt so grown up in that red vinyl booth all to ourselves, with my own money in my own wallet like some kind of real adult human who mattered. My dad had taken his curtain call three years before. But Mom and I were fine. Really. We carried the Christmas tree inside and set it up just the two of us. No men required.

I ordered a peppermint milkshake from Mr. Clark and there was a chocolate ribbon time loop inside it. I didn't find my way out until the school year was mostly over. I've been hard of hearing ever since.

I guess a lot of us spend middle school stuck in a time

loop. I'm not special.

Never have been.

The thirty-ninth time I met the space/time continuum it was a three-and-a-half-foot-long rhinoceros iguana named Waffles. Waffles was lounging on fresh shredded newspapers in the display window of Jungle Friends Exotic Pet Store and Bubble Tea Café. Waffles was marked down seventy percent for Presidents' Day weekend.

I ordered a black milk bubble tea from the counter wedged into the large parrots section.

The scarlet macaw said: *the problem with Einstein-Rosen wormholes is that the 'hallway' they create between two singularities is too small and open too briefly to ever permit transit by a living person.*

The African gray said: *You be good I love you see you tomorrow.*

The blue hyacinth said: *Fuckshit, Susan.*

Then it sang a few bars of 'The Entertainer' and cracked up laughing.

Not everything means something.

Waffles watched the parrots. Waffles slurped up a strand of wilted collard greens. Waffles licked his eyeball.

The owner-operator of *Jungle Friends Exotic Pet Store and Bubble Tea Café* brought me my drink and swapped the *70% Off!* sign for an *80% Off!* one. So I took Waffles home. I put him in a plastic sun-faded Rainbow Brite kiddie pool with the contents of a Sensible Plan brand EZ Ceezar Salad bag and some flat rocks from the last trip

I took with my mother to the Ocean Shores boardwalk, when I won every prize in the shitty Happy Claw prize machine one after the other. I warmed the rocks up in the microwave so Waffles could rest his belly on them. Then I sat back on my couch and drank the better part of a bottle of Bombay Sapphire because fuck George Plantagenet that's why.

That hadn't happened yet. But if you spend long enough around the space/time continuum you get this thing where your head turns into a Tetris game and all the falling pieces are memories spinning around, upside down, out of order, mostly missing the sweet spot so they can just pile up uselessly while the music goes faster and faster the closer you get to this person you love so much who is no less your life partner for being an iguana right now.

Also cancer.

Waffles stared at me for a long time. Then the space/time continuum chomped down on a ranch-seasoning crouton and said: *The traveler and their vessel would have to be smaller than an atom, far faster than light.*

P.S. We're out of milk.

That was probably our best date.

I married someone else. For a while. Right after college. Trying to get away, I suppose. Find out who I even was apart from the space/time continuum. High school relationships never last anyway, right? He was just a guy. Let's say his name was David. It doesn't matter.

The space/time continuum told me not to. It said we were not compatible because my cells were contaminated by long-term non-consecutive exposure to excited superliminal mass fields and David's cells were contaminated by long term exposure to being a douchebag.

By that time the space/time continuum wasn't an iguana anymore. It was a mid-market talk radio host of one of those raunchy-advice-for-the-unemployed-and-lovelorn shows they used to pump out like Xerox copies of Xerox copies. Tune in to KHRT 101.5 to hear the velvet voice of my ex, the unstably enfleshed and endlessly repeating moment of creation and destruction, give you hot tips for better oral sex. The trick is know to your core that nothing means anything and all life and feeling will end.

The space/time continuum was working through some stuff.

The seventh time we met, the space/time continuum was this gangly ginger kid who got hit bad with the freckle-gun and a broken arm. The cast had everyone's messy kid-handwriting all over it.

You should see the other guy.

You're cute!

That events do indeed occur sequentially is perhaps the greatest lie of all.

See you this summer.

"You wanna see something?" the space/time continuum

asked me just as the lunch bell rang. Seventh grade. We were gonna be discussing *The Westing Game* next period and I was so excited I could barely breathe. But I said okay anyway because it was wearing a shirt that said DON'T PANIC, so I figured the space/time continuum was on the up and up.

It took me to the teachers' lounge. It had a special key on a leather frog keychain. I didn't know what to think. The teachers' lounge was forbidden territory. As thrilling and terrifying as peeking in a crosshatched window at the surface of Mars.

"It's okay," the space/time continuum said. "I'm allowed."

Inside the teachers' lounge it wasn't the teachers' lounge. It was 1958 and we were outside and it was so hot. A man and a little boy were walking across a huge courtyard toward Catedral de la Asunción de María Santísima. Birds exploded into the air before them. The little boy was the most beautiful child I've ever seen, with the curliest hair and the biggest eyes. He practically glowed.

His father knelt down next to his baby and kissed his tiny cheek. He pointed toward the two golden spires.

"Look, Daniel!" Roderigo R. Rodriguez said. "Two of them! Just like you and me, mijo, forever and ever."

"It's Dazzle Dan," I whispered.

"Happy birthday," the space/time continuum answered. I said it wasn't my birthday. It shrugged. "It's always your birthday."

And then it wasn't 1958 anymore and it wasn't

Guadalajara, it was the teachers' lounge and it smelled like old pencils.

But the space/time continuum didn't do that kind of thing very often because it made my teeth bleed.

Anyway, David cheated on me eight or nine weeks after the wedding. Let's say her name was Susan. It doesn't matter. Let's say she looked just like me but younger and prettier and less contaminated by excited mass fields.

Fuckshit, Susan.

As far as I can tell, the space/time continuum owns every self-help book ever published. *The 7 Habits of Highly Effective People. The Power of Now. The 4-Hour Work Week. Hypatia's Commentary on Diophantus's Arithmatica. How to Win Friends and Influence People. Summa Theologicae. Truth in Comedy: The Manual of Improvisation. Awaken the Giant Within. Opticks, or, A Treatise on the Reflections, Refractions, Inflections, and Colours of Light. The Rules: Time-Tested Secrets for Capturing the Heart of Mr. Right. Gödel, Escher, Bach. A Brief History of Time.*

But I don't think it ever actually read any of them. It longed to improve itself, to access its trauma, discover its full potential, and rise above its faults. But it was terrified of actually *changing* anything.

I remember once, when we were moving from the

yellow apartment downtown to a bigger place over the river, the space/time continuum and me plunked down on cardboard boxes full of its comfort reading. I'd optimistically labelled them *Books to Donate,* but it was an arch lie and we both knew it. We ate cold pineapple pizza and drank warm merlot straight from the box. And the totality of existence said to me, with sauce on the tip of its nose and not a little chagrin:

For me, self-care is like the grandfather paradox. It might feel good in the moment, but at what cost? No butterfly could imagine the changes to the timeline that would go down if I truly discarded everything that does not spark joy.

Do you really want to live in a universe where the space/time continuum has become fully self-actualized?

The Suciasaurus rex is a two-legged carnivorous theropod, a cousin of the more famous Tyrannosaurus rex. It is the only dinosaur ever found in the state of Washington.

Once, we were lying naked at three in the afternoon in the uptown loft apartment we had for six months when I was twenty-five and the owner was on sabbatical in Paris.

I kissed the space/time continuum's chin and said, in that extra-soft voice that only comes out of you when you're just so happy: *Why me?*

What do you mean why you?

By definition, you could have chosen anyone, anywhere, in the whole cosmos. Why me? I'm just a person like everybody else.

The space/time continuum rubbed its nose tenderly against mine.

Because it's you. It's you because it's you because it's you because it's you. Haven't you ever been stuck in a stable time dome before?

Plus you smell really good. And you offered me your Capri Sun even though it was your favorite flavor.

And we laughed and snuggled and ordered sushi and champagne and watched the traffic go by in the snow thirty stories down. You got a point for every blue car.

Two for red.

But why are you here? Why are you in bodies and minutes and places at all?

The space/time continuum frowned. It finished the bottle.

Everyone gets stuck sometimes. Red car.

I went to a small liberal arts college upstate. Double major psych/physics. A very calculated choice. Inside/ Out, I used to say.

The space/time continuum wasn't allowed on campus. It would sit by the *University* sign on the bumper of its crumbling pickup truck chain-smoking angrily and reading through copies of *Omni* (for the articles) until

I was out of class. I'd run out every day like a movie montage, all long hair and long skirts and the long half-life of first love.

I was really pretty then. I don't know why I want you to know that. It's not important in any way. But I was.

The problem was that college isn't part of the normal timestream. Way too much angst and intersecting choice matrices. Warps the gravity fields and fucks with beta decay. It's an unsettling pocket universe of weird smells, meaningless gold stars, protective self-delusion, and leaking bodily liquid. Go ahead and try the double slit experiment on Friday night in a freshman dorm. You're safer with a Ouija board.

But the space/time continuum wanted to support my goals.

Ultimately, I ended up a bartender. Basically what I studied, in a roundabout way. And I only really do roundabouts anymore. Fluid dynamics. Classical conditioning. A festive arrangement of personality disorders and lost time. But I can make a mean Hammerhead Bowl, so who's to say I didn't come out on top?

We broke up junior year. It said we weren't putting the same effort into the relationship. I didn't make time for it. I laughed. It didn't.

Then David and Susan and my mom and student loans and better blow jobs through the power of drive-time radio and I didn't see the space/time continuum again for almost five years.

Sometimes things just don't work out. You want them to, but they don't want to, and their vote counts for more than yours, so they don't.

The space/time continuum says that no matter what, there is always a place where they *did* work out. So even if you're suffering, there's a version of yourself somewhere who isn't, maybe older, maybe younger, maybe she has one of those naked cats or something, and if you can't be happy, you can at least be happy for her.

I replied: *Fuck that bitch, I hope she drowns.*

The one hundred and seventeenth time I met the space/time continuum it was my mother's doctor. It had kind eyes and bifocals and a little felt bunny stuck onto the tip of its pen, just the perfect dusting of authoritative gray at the temples.

I cried and I cried and I told it to fucking *stop*, it wasn't cute anymore. It never was. Fix her or get out. What is the point of all this if it can't even fix one lousy directionally locked material entity?

It got out.

The hallway was so long and white and clean and quiet. The cool blue price display on the vending machine flashed on and off, on and off, like a lonely lighthouse in an antiseptic sea.

1.99.

Card only.

I thought I didn't see the space/time continuum for five years.

I got this idea in my head that having plants around would help my anxiety and ground me in the now. So I bought the first orchid I liked, one that promised spectacular colors that would last for weeks. I put it in the window and watered it and loved it and it died *immediately*.

So I got another one that looked just like it. The way you swap out a kid's dead goldfish for a ziplocked new one from the shop while they're at school and they never notice because who gives a fuck it's a goldfish.

That orchid also died. So fast it honestly felt kind of personal.

Lather, rinse, repeat.

All in all I had seventeen *Odontoglossa pulchella* and a lot of new, more interesting anxiety about maybe being the grim reaper of plants somehow. Or at least fundamentally incompatible with life.

The space/time continuum was all of them. It didn't mind waiting. Five years was nothing at all. Barely a ripple in a puddle that isn't a pond.

I wonder if the universe where everything worked out okay for me is also the Snack McCoy universe and the reason things can work out there but not here is because civilization is all or mostly corgis so there's fundamentally no real problems and also no climate change.

I wonder if I'm a corgi in the Snack McCoy universe.

The space/time continuum says I'm not.

I'm a cagey fucking greyhound and I still have anxiety.

The space/time continuum left me for good a couple years back. It was so ugly. Those scenes are always so ugly. It's your last chance to say the worst things you've ever thought about a person, so get it all out while you can, right?

But some things you can't come back from.

Maybe it was my fault. I said it first.

I'm not your fucking emotional support human. I just want the infinite embodiment of reality I fell in love with back. I just want everything to be like it was.

And the space/time continuum sneered at me. *I am exactly who you fell in love with! For me, the moment when I touched your Medieval Castle Siege drawbridge was half a second ago. I kissed you at the dance tomorrow. You're the one who's changed. But I don't have to sit here and take this. In a million other shards of reality beyond this completely stupid one, everything is precisely like it was. So fuck you very much. I don't want you like this. I can go find all the other versions of you in all the other timelines and love them and hold them close and give them everything while you stay here alone and drink yourself to death in this shitty town. And yes, I'm including the one where you're a greyhound. I'm going to pet her so good, and brush her and walk her and feed her organic raw food artisanal treats. We're going to enter agility competitions together and chase cars and have a trillion puppies. And wait till you see what we do in the one where you're a lamp. Yes there's one where you're a lamp, shut up! Stay here and have another drink, I'm going to go where everything is just as sweet and good and new as it was in the beginning and you're not fucking invited.*

It looked stricken. It put its hand over its mouth. But like I said, there's some things you can't come back from. Eventually, all loops degrade and fall apart and a way out of the squiggle opens up.

So that happened.

Or will happen. Or is happening. Or someday might inevitably be unhappened.

Maybe.

Nowadays I work the bar at the Neptune Room, home of the Hammerhead Bowl and extremely understated jewel of the Tides Inn Hotel. Too broke to retire, too stubborn to die.

It is *distinctly* shit here.

I am distinctly shit as well. And old. And angry a lot of

the time.

The decor is wall-to-wall plastic fish, seaweed garlands, and discount Christmas lights. The clientele come in drunk already when we open at four. The kitchen offers a limited menu of mystery bisque, French fries, and despair.

My knees hurt. I have a lot of time to think. Nobody bothers me except to grunt for another of whatever they've chosen to hurt themselves with tonight. I look out the picture windows at the town Ocean Shores was supposed to be and I think about the Suciasaurus rex and Mr. Yuk and corgis with lawyer names and David and Susan and the constellation of Taurus.

In the end, I get this place. We understand each other. I was supposed to be something better, too.

Today, I am mixing Hammerhead Bowls in the back. Don't get excited. It's just whatever's left in last night's well drunk bottles, Coke, and the syrup from the maraschino jar all dumped into a turquoise plastic tub shaped like a shark with two straws in it. I finish up and head out to flip over the CLOSED sign.

There's a box on the bar. Wrapped in pink paper with hearts and baby angels on it. But it's not Valentine's Day. My hands settle down on the ribbons. I look around for orchids or iguanas or whatever, but I'm alone.

The box is sitting on top of a hand-knitted mauve cabled cardigan.

Maybe I won't open it. Maybe I just let this be over for once. I'm tired. I don't believe in anything anymore.

Of course I open it.

I'm fourteen years old. Mom and I get in her little yellow Jeep and drive down the coast to Ocean Shores. It's the first year after Dad left. She's nervous about doing it all on her own from here forward into always, so she's smoking again, and interfering with the radio like there's some tuning on the dial that will bring back the life she thought she was going to have. But there isn't. She's alone. He's gone and she's alone.

But she's trying. Alice is trying.

So she gives me my riddle for the trip instead of Dad, instead of the man who couldn't handle us at the peak of our reclusive timeline algorithm, and my mother's riddle is this: *What is the difference between love and time?*

I'm stumped.

We get salt water taffy and hit the boardwalk, walking lazily down the rows of purple and pink and green neon flashing lights and tinny arcade machine action music. Tickets spit out of the bank of Skee Ball machines like cheeky blue tongues. A rusted-out mechanical pony plays 'The Entertainer' as we stroll by. I say low tide stinks something awful. Alice laughs. She doesn't smell anything.

Mom gives me $5 and says I can play whatever I want. We pass the Happy Time Entertainment Inc Treasure Claw Machine, whose decal stickers have peeled and blistered until it just says *Time Claw*.

I stop.

"Those things are always rigged, honey," Alice says

then, and later in a narrow white room with tubes coming out of her nose, and I hear it in both memories, in the same tone, at the same time.

But I promise her I can do it. I'm good at claw machines, always have been. I look over at her, at Alice, her face washed in all the colored electric lights, and she is so beautiful, she really is, so beautiful and so unfathomably young. You never think of your parents as young, but god, she's just a baby. And so am I.

I drop a couple of silver coins into the slot and press the glowing buttons with authority—left, right, over, just a little more. Release.

The claw descends.

It comes back up with a crappy stuffed starfish. Mom and I start screaming like I just won the MegaBucks, jumping up and down and hugging each other and she's kissing the top of my head and the WINNER lights are going soundlessly crazy because the machine's speakers are broken and then suddenly there's this kid standing next to me in a puffer vest and a Nirvana shirt and glasses and I know before I turn around who it is and was and will be.

"Wow," says the space/time continuum. "That was amazing! Can you win one for me?"

"Probably not," I say sadly. "Two in a row is pretty tough. And I'm out of money."

The space/time continuum hands me a dollar in quarters.

"I'll probably lose," I protest.

"It's okay if you lose," it says.

I look at my mom and she nods encouragingly. So in the money goes. I push the buttons again. I drop the Time Claw.

And what do you know? It comes up desperately clutching a giant toy it absolutely should not be able to lift with those pitiful skinny silver prongs. The claw looks like it's gonna break off the suspension for a minute. But it doesn't. It doesn't. It glides smoothly home.

I retrieve the mass of fluff from the prize bin.

It's a Cartoon Sparkle Rainbow Geoduck. With big friendly eyes and long lashes and a wide, smiling mouth. Geoducks are endemic to this coast. Some bright idea factory must have had a lot made up special for this specific arcade, in this specific, tiny, trash clam town.

I stare at it. Because this really happened and I forgot it ever did. I am both then and now, myself in the Neptune Room with shaky swollen hands and myself at fourteen, frantic with hope and hormones and I forgot this happened, because forgetting is so easy, little holes open up in the fabric of reality and you drop parts of yourself into them and you forget that your mother ever looked so pretty and so worried and so young, you forget that you won this ridiculous thing for a stranger in a tawdry arcade and Alice was so impressed. She looked at you like she was seeing you for the first time. Like you were a real live grown-up separate person and she only just noticed.

And then the Time Claw is gone and it's the end of the weekend and Alice and I are sitting in a hot tub with mold in every jet on a gray beach full of gray sand and hidden ancient clams. We finish singing 'Don't Cry for Me Argentina' and she smiles at me.

"Have you figured out my riddle yet, Miss Grand Prize Winner?"

She turns to me in the water and wraps up my cheeks in her wet hands and god, her eyes are so green, it is impossible than any human's eyes have ever been so green. Alice's face takes up the whole of the universe. She barely gets the first few words out before those green improbable eyes fill up with tears and she's crying and lying in that future bed listening to the radio and holding my hand while she whispers:

"Baby, the difference between love and time is nothing. *Nothing.* There is no difference. The love we give to each other is the time we give to each other, and the time we spend together is the whole of love. Things will get better, sweetheart, I promise. I love you so much. My darling baby. I love you. Don't forget. No matter what happens. The answer is nothing."

She hugs me and there is no difference. All the time spent in love is one time, happening simultaneously, a closed timeline curve of infinite gentleness. The continuum hiding in all the faces of people I have needed and wanted and cared for and grieved, the faces through which I loved the world, all one, all at once, memory and dreaming and regret and desire, injera bread and lentil soup and sushi and champagne and running toward a pickup truck in the yellow afternoon, red and white Rainier beer cans and rhinoceros iguanas and orchids and plastic army camouflage-print glasses and psychology and physics and circular saws and Dazzle Dan feeding the birds in front of the Catedral and the Loch Ness monster's ancient reptile heart beggared with love for her baby in the dark and plants that are whales and whales that are plants and Suciasaurus rex and middle school and the countless infinite loops we get stuck in like tar and an octopus mug in orbit around Saturn and the Washington State Legislature and KHRT 101.5 and golden retrievers and red cars and Bob Ross and the emerald dish soap on the sink that made Alice remember her bridesmaids' dresses and just stop like a watch in her pain and the puddle that comes and goes with the rain and a house that belongs to a hill and Cartoon Sparkle Rainbow Geoducks and the smell of a newborn's head and Snack McCoy running after a ball of light in a universe without pain and there is no difference, no difference between any of it at all, it is all one thing, the only thing small enough to fit through an Einstein-Rosen wormhole—all dumped together into a blue plastic shark bowl with two straws.

Love in the vessel of time.

That's where Alice left her loop. Not in that bed twenty years later not knowing who I was or where she was going, but there with her baby in Ocean Shores, WA, at twilight, somewhere between the water and the Time Claw, promising me ice cream for dinner while the space/time continuum looked on and kept the tourists at bay.

When she could still smell me a little.

When I was old and sorry, just so sorry.

There is no difference. There never was.

Nothing.

Nothing.

The lights twinkle in the Neptune Room. The space/time continuum looks like the Mr. Yuk kid all grown up, my own age still. It smiles from the doorway, silhouetted by sundown.

I'm holding something old and ratty and sodden with seawater in my hand. I don't even look at it, just sniff awkwardly and hand over the Cartoon Sparkle Rainbow Geoduck to the kid in the puffer vest.

"I won it for you, after all."

"Keep it," says the space/time continuum. "Happy birthday."

"It's not my birthday."

The space/time continuum looks just like it did in the beginning. And the end. And all points in between. It shines. And so do I and so does Alice and so does blasted, cursed Ocean Shores, WA and geoducks and all the ships at sea.

Cyndi Lauper starts playing on the long-defunct sound system because the space/time continuum is a cheesy fool and always will be. It takes off its glasses.

"It's always your birthday. Keep it. Keep it all. It's yours. I love you. I'm sorry. I'm an idiot. I love you. This you. Infinitely better than the lamp or the greyhound or the one I never made any mistakes with. I'll do better this time. I can be better. Come home."

UNBASHED, OR: JACKSON, WHOSE COWARDICE TORE A HOLE IN THE CHRONOVERSE

Sam J. Miller

Sam J. Miller's (https://samjmiller.com/) books have been called 'must reads' and 'bests of the year' by *USA Today*, *Entertainment Weekly*, *NPR*, and *O: The Oprah Magazine*, among others. He is the Nebula-Award-winning author of *Blackfish City*, which has been translated into six languages and won the hopefully-soon-to-be-renamed John W. Campbell Memorial Award. Sam's short stories have won a Shirley Jackson Award and been nominated for the World Fantasy, Theodore Sturgeon, and Locus Awards, and have been reprinted in dozens of anthologies. He's also the last in a long line of butchers. He lives in New York City.

HERE YOU ARE. Different, now. Not the brooding boy in the back row of my precalc class, nor the state-finals-champion martial artist so aloof across the college dining hall. Not the untouchable crush. Not the boy so tough he couldn't possibly be gay, so what's the point of staring at him so? Not the boy I stared at anyway, knowing, as I did so, that it was the first truly adult thing I'd ever done. You are something else, now. Streetlamps bronze your glossy black hair, gild your broad broken nose. Love sets you ablaze.

You are here. You are not dead. You pass a cigarette, not asking if I want one, knowing I don't, knowing I'll do whatever you want. Knowing how your black-brown eyes melt me. You press your nose against mine, swivel your cigarette to kindle my own, grind your scratchy cheek against my smooth one. You are my boyfriend; my first; the feeling so new I can barely say it for what it does to me inside. You are tough and strong where I am weak and smart. Or so I think, now. Here. *I am smart*, I think. The world is mine. Autumn night air fills my lungs like helium, sends me soaring. I had never guessed, all those nights in my bed at home, alone with Kleenex and my imagination, what sex really was. Easy to imagine the physical; impossible to guess at the emotional. How free I felt. How powerful, even in submission. One big hand pinning both of mine back. Instead of helpless I felt magnified. Your strength was mine, for the moment.

I smoke sadly, not wanting it to wipe away the taste of you. The taste of *all* of you, every piece a different marvelous flavor. Your armpit, your belly button, your ear, your hair. Your 'manhood', or whatever other euphemism you like.

Here we are. Out in the open—smoking on the back steps. Hands clasped. October midnight dries the sweat on both our brows. My dorm room radiator was overzealous, as were we. "Jackson," you say, for no reason, for the feel of my name in your mouth, for the shivers you know it sends through me. Jocks walk by in drunken gaggles, aim glares at us. And I am afraid. And I am ashamed. Boys have been bashed, lately, across campus. Panic makes me hate what I am, when moments before I thanked God and the Devil both for making me this way, for putting me on the path to the unutterable bliss of sex with you.

"Walk me home?" you ask.

And this time I smile. This time I nod. In this timeline I rise, and walk you home, and no one jumps you halfway there, no six men hold you down, break you, put you in the coma where you'll stay for the last six weeks of your life.

"Walk me home?" you ask. And this time I say, *Forget my roommate, you're staying here, you're sleeping with me*. We'll spoon on a twin mattress barely big enough for my own body. In the morning I'll blow you silently and you'll come without a whisper. Five feet away, my roommate will not stir in his sleep. In the morning we'll walk hand in hand to the dining hall for breakfast—and then lunch—and then a whole long life together.

"Walk me home?" you ask, and I don't panic. The love-lust obedience of moments ago doesn't crumble under the weight of my own cowardice. I don't fumble for excuses,

I've got to study, I've got to read this whole book by class tomorrow—when what I'll really do is wrap myself in sheets that still smell of you, and imagine all the times to come, not knowing our first time was our last.

"Walk me home?" you ask, and I do, and when the goons roll up on us I am a man possessed, rendered invincible by love, shattering all their skulls in seconds.

"Walk me home?" you ask, and I do, because I am no coward, no monster capable of letting the man he loves walk home alone to die. I am not ashamed of what I am. I am not afraid of what the world will do to me because of it. I am not full of apologies no one gives a shit about. I don't want to explain to Saint Peter or Shiva, *He was a martial artist, what good could scrawny, weak me have done?* I don't need to carefully not mention what I know in my heart: that if it was me they stopped I'd have run like hell and probably made it, whereas you, you big dummy, hopped up on hundreds of ring-fight victories, felt sure you could fight and win. I don't need to mention how for weeks I scanned the face of every baseball-capped boy, looking for the black eyes and cheek gashes I know you would have gifted them before they overpowered you.

You are here. We are here. I'm eighteen. I'm in college. The world feels wide and wonderful in a way it never will again. Because something broke in me, that night, or the next morning, when I learned what had happened. What I had done. The stars shattered; the sky shrunk. Something broke in me, and in breaking ripped the fabric of space-time wide open, tore a hole in the chronoverse just big enough for me to fall through.

And so. In supermarkets—at funerals—on dates—for decades—I'll time-skip back to here. Sometimes for a minute, sometimes for a week. I'll ignite a whole new timeline each time, a whole new life for you. For us. I'll feel your arm around me. Hold my fingers to my nose, grin till my face breaks at the lingering you-smell that is all I'll ever know of heaven.

But it doesn't matter how many timelines I take your hand in, and walk you home, that night. How many alternate universes you—and we—continue on in. Undamaged. Unbashed. How many different relationship life cycles we churn through: growing old and dying together; breaking up a week later when I catch you fucking your sparring partner; lasting a year or a decade and then letting life snuff out the spark of what we have, here, now. None of it erases the hurt of the knowing what I did, once; what that one Me out of untold trillions of Mes did to You.

Here you are. You smile. You squeeze my hand. I walk you home. I love you.

And still my stomach clenches with the acid-bile pain of what I did, and can't undo, no matter how many times I undo it.

An alternate-universe echo of 'Karina Who Kissed Spacetime', by Indrapramit Das.

ROMANCE: HISTORICAL
Rowan Coleman

Rowan Coleman (rowancoleman.co.uk) is the *New York* and *Sunday Times* bestselling author of several novels including *The Summer of Impossible Things* and *The Memory Book*. She also writes the *Brontë Mysteries* series, including *The Vanished Bride*, *The Diabolical Bones*, and *The Red Monarch* under the name Bella Ellis.

MADAM, WILL YOU *Talk?*

The novel by Mary Stuart sat in the middle of the countertop looking at Beth, and yet Beth could not remember it arriving there.

That wasn't so surprising. One of the reasons that Beth had taken the job as manager and sole staff member in the largely deserted and ancient King's Books, Bindings & Stationers on the Charing Cross Road (Est. 1822) was because, despite its central London location, it was rarely visited more than once or twice a day and even then, only ever in slightly apologetic awkwardness.

For Beth it was a near-silent haven of solitude to shelter in while the world streamed past outside in a thick, noisy herd. Being in the bookshop was the next best thing to being invisible and free from the constant requirement to decode and interact with other people. Here was the perfect place to spend the whole day not being here, wandering in and out of stories and daydreams on an endless meander that could lead her anywhere, as long as it was in the opposite direction to real life. She hardly felt fit for the modern world at all.

No one had been in the shop that morning. Yet there was the book, squarely placed on the oak counter as if determined to make itself known.

Things like this happened in the shop. Mr. King had told her that on her very first day. Books migrated and footsteps sounded overhead in empty rooms. Sometimes the bell over the front door would sound, although the door was still shut. It was only to be expected that in such an old building, that traces of the hundreds of gossamer lives that had passed through here would catch on something static, and leave a thread behind now and then.

So, as she had done several times before, she accepted the moment and picking up the book she turned it over in her hands, smoothing out one dog-eared page before returning it to Mystery: Cozy, where she slotted it into the gap on the shelf it had left vacant, and returned to the counter where it was waiting for her once again.

Beth stared at the book for one long, quietly alarmed moment, before she picked it up again. Yes, there was the same dog-eared page she had smoothed just minutes ago, still half-smoothed and still slightly bent at the same time.

When she was a small girl, her mum would kiss the top of her head, and mutter, "Always away with the fairies that one." She supposed she must have thought about putting the book back, without actually going through with it. A sort of reverse déjà vu. Very deliberately, Beth returned the book to the shelf, patting it once it was in situ, just to anchor the moment in reality.

Except when she got back to the counter some nine seconds later, there it was again.

"This is new," Beth said aloud, her voice sounding strange in the silence, as she looked around the room, considering what to do next, if anything.

On her first day Mr. King had told her to take care to make sure she knew where all the stock was, by which he meant the precise location of every single one of the many thousand books that lined the custom-built oak shelves that had been fitted over a century ago. They had been cleverly designed to double as floor-to-ceiling segment dividers, separating one large and lofty space into a labyrinth of category rooms, the books themselves acting as temporary bricks and mortar.

"Excellent, excellent," he'd said when Beth had promised she would do just that. "You never know when you might need to find your way back, you see."

"Back?" Beth had asked him, tilting her head.

"Yes, back," he said. "We don't want you getting lost, do we? Be an awful shame to lose another one."

He'd laughed, and supposing it was the thing to do, she'd laughed, too, none the wiser. He'd taken the creaking old staircase up to his attic apartment, where he now spent most of his hours, and Beth hadn't thought about the comment again. It seemed pertinent now, although Beth couldn't exactly put her finger on why.

It struck Beth that perhaps the bookshop was talking to her. The only polite thing to do was to try and talk back.

Grateful that she knew the stock inside out, Beth hurried to Mystery: Literary where she picked up a 1978 edition of Tony Hillerman's *Listening Woman* and left it out on the counter while she replaced the Mary Stuart once again. As soon as she had, she went to check the slot she had taken the Hillerman from. *Listening Woman* had returned. Beth ran back to the counter.

It was empty.

"What next?" Beth asked the empty air. There was no reply. All at once the air felt flat, one-dimensional as if something invisible had been subtracted. Whatever might have been happening, it seemed to be over.

For the rest of the afternoon she wandered listlessly around the bookshop, unable to settle back into her novel, finding excuses to take her eyes off the counter in the hope that another book might appear while she wasn't looking. None did.

As the evening drew in, Beth called up to the flat to say goodbye to Mr. King, and dawdled about closing up, lingering as long as she possibly could before she had to dash across the street to catch the bus back to her shared house, where she took a microwaveable meal to her room. Maybe it had been all in her head, a short string of coincidences that she had wound into a full-blown fantasy. They said she did that, the succession of people that had watched her grow up. They said she made things up.

Mum had always said she wasn't meant for this world. That was right before she had died, leaving thirteen-year-old Beth to navigate her way through a series of foster homes and cut-price college courses, until she turned eighteen and was told it was all up to her now. As soon as she had the choice Beth pursued a quiet life, insulated by books and as far outside the reach of time as she could be. A person as quiet and solitary as she was bound to come a little undone now and then, it was to be expected. And yet the feeling that she'd been stood up by someone lingered.

AT FIRST BETH didn't see anything on the desk as she opened the door, but when she switched on the lights she saw a small, flat picture book, its glossy cover gently gleaming.

Do You Want to Be My Friend? by Eric Carle. Beth picked it up and hugged it to her chest, all the common sense she had doggedly pursued during the night running out of her like watery ink in an instant. Running to Self-

Help she grabbed a copy of *Getting to 'I Do'* by Dr. Patricia Allen, put the book on the counter and waited.

Nothing happened. After a while Beth worried that perhaps she had been a little forward, putting a book about eliciting a marriage proposal on the counter. It was a bit early for that sort of thing after all. Taking two Post-it notes from the pad by the till, she covered up the 'Getting to' part of the title, and gave a thumbs up to the empty air.

Closing her eyes, she made herself count to thirty. Everything was perfectly still, there wasn't a sound or a rustle, and yet when she opened her eyes another book had presented itself. It was *The Invisible Man* by Ralph Emerson.

Beth took a breath, excited and elated, if a little unsettled. But then, she reasoned, if he, and he was a he according the last book title, was an evil entity then why would he be making small talk with her, even… almost… flirting? Still, it was sensible to check he wasn't a ghostly serial killer or something, so she ran to fetch a copy of *Dangerous Liaisons*, adding a Post-it note question mark next to the title.

This time Beth did not close her eyes. She waited, determined not to blink, and sure enough saw with her very own eyes the book she had set down disappear to be replaced with *In Search of Lost Time* by Proust.

It was not exactly a reassurance, but even so it was somehow comforting. Just the title of that book spoke of memory, a kind of ennui and deep sadness. Whoever was talking to her was intelligent, lost, and perhaps even as lonely as she was. Who knew how many decades he had been quietly waiting? Waiting for someone just to know he existed. It was a feeling that Beth was familiar with.

Beth set down a copy of *Brave New World* and he replaced it with *One Hundred Years of Solitude*.

"You must be lonely," Beth said aloud, "but how can I help you? Do you have some unfinished business, or were you the victim of a terrible crime?"

Just as she was trying to think of titles that might best express her question another book appeared in answer. He could hear her! Of course he could. This would make things much quicker.

A Tale of Two Cities. What was he trying to tell her?

"Are you French?" she asked.

The Fatal Englishman. The next book to appear.

"Are you a ghost then?"

Dead and Alive, a novel by Hammond Innes, appeared. Dead, but also alive. What did that mean?

As the question formed in her mind, the extraordinariness of what was happening caught up with Beth in a rush. High-definition reality buckled her knees and punched the air out of her lungs. Beth steadied herself; after all she had spent her whole life in training for this moment, preparing unreservedly to believe in the impossible. It was the only thing she had any talent for.

Going to the door, she opened it a crack to gulp in the warm exhaust-filled fumes of the busy street outdoors and let her heart slow a little. Perhaps she had fallen asleep at the desk, she rationalized, and woken in a start to find it was all just an *Alice in Wonderland* ending?

But when she turned around there was a new book on the counter.

To the Lighthouse, by Virginia Woolf.

Beth frowned at the title, puzzled. There didn't seem to be a message here, so what could he mean. Did he want her to go to Maritime History? The sound of something falling off a shelf in the back of the shop grabbed her attention. That's where he wanted her to go, he did want her to go to the lighthouse. The little ancient and dusty ceramic model that occupied a space on the shelf between Travel and Historical Romance. Besides dusting it now and then, Beth had stopped noticing it long ago, almost forgetting it was there. That was until now.

Beth went and stood in front of the model.

Hesitatingly, her hand hovering for a moment in the air, she picked up the lighthouse, which left a gap of around a square foot, and as she expected on the other side of the shelf was the Historical Romance room. And him. A young man's face, slight and pale with blue eyes and sandy hair, smiled shyly at her.

"Hello," he said. "I'm George King, I work here too, though not exactly at the same time as you."

Beth screamed. Grabbing the lighthouse by its top, she wielded it like a club as she charged around to the adjoining room with the intention of, well, she wasn't really entirely sure what her intention was. As it happened it didn't matter, because when she arrived the room was quite empty. No sign of George. She went to the space she had made on the shelf and looked into Travel. Empty. Slowly, uncertain of what she was hoping for, Beth walked back into Travel, back to the gap in the shelf and made herself look. There was George.

"Sorry to alarm you," George said. "I've been trying to work out a way to talk to you without upsetting you for weeks, and in the end, I thought, George, there's no easy way of explaining that you discovered a hole in time. You just have to crash on. So, I did."

"A hole in time?" Beth said.

"That does seem to be the only logical explanation," George said. "This gap, just here, bridges your Tuesday afternoon in your time to my Tuesday afternoon in 1914."

"What?" Beth blinked.

"It is rather unusual," George smiled again. "Takes a bit of getting used to."

"But…" Beth could only stare at the young man, who watched her patiently, waiting for her to catch up. After a moment the face retreated a little and a hand with long slender fingers extended through the gap and waggled at her.

"How do you do?" George said.

"Hang on. Don't move."

Beth went to end of the shelf so that she had a view of both Travel and Romance at the same time. Sure enough, the Romance room was empty, but George's hand was still waving about in Travel.

Returning, Beth took George's hand in hers. It was

warm, it was real, as was the man it was attached to.

"How is this happening?" Beth asked.

"I've wondered that myself," George said, letting go of her hand reluctantly. A rosy flush spread over his cheeks and nose. "I noticed it, the hole, a few months ago. I was dusting in here, moved the lighthouse and there you were, sitting on the stool reading. I came round to see if I could offer you any help, and you weren't there. You weren't there, and were there at exactly the same moment." George dropped his gaze for a moment. "It did make me worry I was a bit of a lunatic, at first. And it felt wrong to watch you when you didn't know I was. But... well, I started to look out for you, every day, I'd hope to see you through the gap. But you hardly ever came."

"There's been a lot less travelling done recently," Beth said. "And people don't really buy travel guides anymore. But wait, it's 1914 on your side of the shelf?"

"Yes," George nodded.

"Then how did you put out books published decades after your time for me to see?"

"There is this hole," George said, "and about a week ago I discovered what I call the veil. It's not a hole, but a sort of *thinning*. If I time it right, I can get into the veil through The Classics, and if I try really hard, move things around on your side. It frightens me a bit, I don't mind saying. Like it might be somewhere I could get lost if I'm not careful." He smiled. "But it was worth the risk."

"So, you can move things in my time, from behind this veil?" Beth asked. "What is it like?"

"Like looking at something through a waterfall or seeing the two separate images in a stereograph, one laid over the other, except they are not quite the same. I see the shelves as they are now, here, and how they are in your time, in the future. And if I let myself almost come apart, then I can push and pull at the meniscus and move things. That's when I realized I could try and contact you, after a fashion. When I thought I might even be able to talk to you and bring you here." He smiled suddenly and his face was transformed by pleasure. "It worked."

For a moment neither of them said anything, they just watched each other through the gap, each one standing back a little so they could see the other's face. George's face wasn't the sort of face that would be given to the hero in her novel, and yet it was a singularly nice face. Gentle and open, sweet and tender. It was a face that invited possibility. What George was thinking about as he returned her gaze, Beth couldn't tell, but crucially his gaze didn't make her want to run away and hide. She even felt a little emboldened. Maybe it was because he was on the other side of the bookshelf, more than a hundred years in the past. Maybe that was what had been missing from all the awkward dates she had endured.

"So, what now?" Beth asked him.

"How about a cup of tea?" George said.

GEORGE BROUGHT TEA in a rose-patterned pot, which he poured into matching cups and saucers. Beth brought a packet of digestives, which he picked up through the gap, examining the wrapper with a great deal of curiosity.

"That's nothing," Beth said, as she sipped her tea, still hot after its passage over twelve inches and a century or so. "Wait until you get a load of this." She unlocked her phone and showing it to him slid her fingers over the screen.

"That's the Internet," she told him. "In your pocket. It tells you everything that has ever happened, and anything you might want to know, quite a lot you don't and some things you can't unsee, and all in a fraction of a second."

"Is this why the shop is so empty there?" George asked.

It wasn't exactly the sort of amazed reaction that Beth had been expecting, but she supposed George had just accidentally discovered inter-dimensional time travel, so he would be hard to impress.

They drank tea in silence for a while, observing one another with brief glances answered in half-smiles. George was her type, Beth decided, having not previously ever known that she had one.

"So, is there another place, another portal where you can come all the way through, like this one? Perhaps, if we took all the books off the shelves, you might be able to wriggle through entirely?"

"I tried that, it doesn't work," George said with a sigh. "For some reason it's just this space here, maybe it was bigger once. Or smaller. But this is all we have as far as I can tell. It is rather astounding, it feels wrong to be disappointed about the limitations." He looked down, coloring. "And yet I am."

Beth felt a little glow in her chest flare with sudden intense heat. Was George flirting with her? She wasn't sure, but she thought the best way to find out was to treat him just like any other boy she had ever liked and hoped liked her.

"So," she said after a pause. "What's your favorite book?"

AND SO IT began, their romance. Weeks went by marked by cups of tea and talk of books. Whenever they could Beth and George would meet at the intersection between Travel and Historical Romance to talk, laugh and wonder at one another. And every morning Beth would find a new volume waiting for her on the counter in greeting.

Great Expectations had been the first book after their initial meeting, making her heart skip a beat. Later that day, at their appointed tea break, they had talked over Dickens at great enthusiastic length, George rather taken aback that Beth wasn't so fond of the great man as he was. As they talked Beth had found herself resting her chin on the shelf, as did George. They were so absorbed in one another, they hardly noticed they were close enough to kiss, while at exactly the same moment it was all their bodies could think of, as if each atom of one of them strained toward the other in desperate longing.

A few days later *Portrait of a Lady* waited for Beth as she skipped into the shop. At first, she had been puzzled, but that afternoon George passed a pencil sketch he had made of her in the hours they had been apart. His hand had been trembling when he passed it through the gap, fearful of what she would think.

"This is…" Beth's eyes filled with tears as she looked at the drawing that had been executed with such tender care it felt like a caress. "You really see me like this? But she's so beautiful."

"You are so beautiful," George had blurted out, adding: "Forgive me. I didn't mean to be forward. It's just that when I am not with you, I can't stop thinking of you."

"I don't mind you being forward," Beth had said. "Anyway, I think you are beautiful, too."

ONE DAY THEY had the idea that they could creep back in after hours for a night-time tryst. George's family lived off the premises, and Mr. King went to bed at 6pm. So Beth locked up as usual, went around the corner to Costa, changed into her long button-down floral dress in the loo, and brushed out her usually tied-back hair until it rippled in coppery waves collapsing down her back.

When she returned George was waiting for her dressed in his Sunday best. They each lit a candle on their side of the shelf. Beth presented George with Chinese food and a bottle of wine. Neither of them was used to drinking, and after one or two glasses of wine they were both a little tipsy.

"Beth, I…" George faltered.

"What, George?" Beth pressed him. "You can say

anything to me, you know."

George nodded, squaring his shoulders for courage.

"I'm glad this miracle has happened, Beth, because," he took a deep breath, "I've fallen in love with you and if I could simply hold your hand for ten minutes a day for the rest of my life it would be more joy than I have ever known, or could ever hope to know."

"George," Beth said. "I love you, too."

One hand reached for another, fingertips touching before their hands entwined. George drew Beth's towards him, kissing first her palm, and then the place on her wrist where her pulse raced. Drawing back, Beth leaned her face into the space.

"Kiss me?" she asked.

"I never have before," George said. "Kissed anyone, that is."

"Just put your lips on mine," Beth said. In the moment that he did Beth vaguely considered the possibility that their kiss might explode the universe somehow, and it did, at least for them. But not in a Large Hadron Collider kind of way, so that was good.

They kissed for hours, lips the only point of contact, all of their longing and desire for each other flowing through that one portal. It was delicious, it was tortuous delight. After a long while they parted.

"I've never wanted someone as much as I want you," George told Beth. "If I could only hold you, touch you, I think I might die of happiness."

"Me too," Beth said. She thought for a moment, and

took another long draft of wine for courage. "We can't see all of one another through the gap, but we can see *bits* of each other." She turned as red as the wine in her mug. "What I'm saying is that we can touch and kiss each other all over, just not all at once. If you would like to, that is?"

"I would really like to," George had said with a swallow.

Taking a step or two back, Beth began to unbutton her dress.

THE SPRING TURNED into summer. In the heart of that huge restless city, Beth's whole life existed in a space twelve inches square. Every moment she was away from George she thought of being with him again, of his hungry touch and her own searching fingers and lips.

Tender is the Night, George left for her after that first kiss. *A Room With a View* a few days later. One day she laughed out loud when she picked up a copy of *Wuthering Heights.* Yes, they certainly had reached some wonderous heights in their explorations of one another. And then a copy of the *Metaphysical Poets* opened flat on a verse by John Donne.

"Oh, my America, new found land."

It was more than just physical pleasure though, so much more. They would sit and talk late into the night, their fingers entwined, passing through the events of the day, their hopes and dreams, just like any other couple might.

"What will happen, I wonder?" Beth asked one night

as the candle burnt down. "Do you think we will still be here when we are old and grey, making kinky bookshop love in our nineties?"

George's fingers stiffened.

"There's talk of war here," he said. "Beth, I think it will happen within the month."

"Of course," Beth whispered. "You never spoke of it, so I hoped it wasn't going to happen."

"I didn't want to spoil our time together, but I can't hide from it anymore. I have to join up, Beth," George said. "But don't worry, they say it will all be over by Christmas. It will only be a few months. Can you wait a few months for me?"

"Of course I can, of course I will." Beth bit her lip. George had never asked her what she knew about his time, and she never mentioned it. The horror of the long bloody combat. The millions of lives that were lost trampled in the mud. What she knew of that war had been a vague sadness before, an abstract loss of so much hope. Now, raw fear ran through her veins, and desperate grief for what she had not yet lost threatened to overwhelm her.

"Or we could find a way for you to be here, to really be here," Beth said, urgently. "To bring all of you through to my time at once, and then we can be together where you will be safe."

"I'll be safe. Beth, I swear it. The British Army is the best in the world. We'll have that lot beaten before you know it, and then you'll be able to say your young man is a war hero."

"People die in wars," Beth said. "I can't lose you, George. All I'm saying is let's just see if there is a way for you to come to me. Even if just because, if you have to go away it would mean we could *really* say goodbye."

George drew back a little, sensing her fear.

"What do you know?" he asked her.

Beth hesitated. She had to be honest with him, he deserved that.

"It's a dreadful war, George," she whispered. "It will last for four years and millions die. Thousands of young men just like you never come home."

George leaned away from her for a moment, letting her words sink in.

"And that thing on your phone, the instant library thing. If you put my name into that, would it tell you what happens to me?"

Beth bowed her head.

"I... I don't know," she said. "I don't want to look."

"Do it, Beth," George said.

"George, I don't know if..."

"Do it, please. I have to know."

Reluctantly, Beth did as she was asked, and after a moment of silently searching she passed the phone to George.

George King, son of Mary and Edward King, Hammersmith
Rifleman

Service Number S/10232
The Rifle Brigade 7th Battalion
Killed Friday August 18th 1916

George dropped the phone on his side of the shelf, shocked and shivering.

"George." Beth reached her arm through the gap, all the way to her shoulder, her hand searching out his trembling shoulders. "George, it's okay. I'm with you."

"I don't want to die," George said. "I don't want to leave you."

"We have to find a way through," she said. "A way to make you safe."

"But even if we could, how can I leave my brothers, my mates? How can I leave them all behind and save myself?"

"I don't know, if we find a way, we could bring them through too," Beth suggested frantically.

"And all the others?" George asked her, wiping tears from his face. "All the others that are lost? Every single one of them? I don't want to die, Beth, but I couldn't live with myself if I found a way to run away and left all of them behind."

"Could you try?" Beth pleaded. "Please, George, if you love me, try for me. Please?"

George straightened up, turning his pale, tear-streaked face towards hers. Beth wept to see the struggle and fear on his dear, sweet face.

"For you, I'll do anything," he said.

*   *   *

THE DAYS AND nights that followed were spent searching, almost together and yet so far apart. There were places in the building where Beth could feel George near. Not physically, there wasn't even a disturbance in the air. It was more a kind of electricity that hummed in the atmosphere when he was around her, a sense that his soul was tantalizingly close to its mate. In the veil, as George called it, she could almost see him, almost touch him but not quite. She'd feel a cold shiver sometimes, catch a glimpse of his blue eyes, but it was in jagged judders that made her head ache and her stomach lurch. Objects could be moved in the veil, but hands could not be joined. Methodically, they covered every section of the old building from the top to the bottom, looking for a door that might let George through into her present. And found nothing.

"At least we have this," George said later, taking Beth's hand through the gap. "It's better to have loved and lost and all that."

"I don't know how I will stand it," Beth said. "To live without you."

"You must do more than stand it, Beth," George said. "You must do your best to enjoy it, to live it, to embrace it. To make every breath you take, every food you taste, everything you do count double for me."

"Are you afraid?" Beth asked him.

"Not anymore," he said. 'At first I was, and then I was

angry and so, so sad. But then I realized, how can I be any of those things for long when I can see for myself what a miracle the tried universe is? I won't be gone, not really, I'll just be transformed into something else wonderful that makes up the fabric of everything. I will still be with you, somehow. Now come here and let me kiss you."

Just as she was about to comply, Beth had a thought.

"We haven't tried Mr. King's flat," she said, drawing back.

"We've got tenants in it here," George said. "I can't just wander in. They've got daughters."

"But we have to try, George," Beth said. "I need to know we tried everything. They will all be asleep now, won't they? If we are quiet, they won't know."

George sighed.

"For you," he said. "I'll meet you up there."

MR. KING KEPT the spare key to the flat on a nail outside the front door. Holding her breath Beth removed the key, slotted it into the lock, and opened the front door. A slice of light from the doorway fanned across the floor. The flat was small, a living room, an adjacent kitchenette and the bedroom, with adjoining bathroom. Closing the door quietly behind her, Beth tiptoed into the middle of the small but comfortable sitting room, searching the still air for any trace of George. All was still, the air was empty. Carefully, she searched every inch of that room, opened every cupboard and drawer in the kitchen, half-expecting to see one beloved blue eye peering out at her. There was nothing, which only left the occupied bedroom and bathroom to check.

Mr. King slept in a sitting position, a book open on his chest, emitting gentle, steady snores. Beth's heart was in her mouth as she opened the wardrobe doors, and then, after a moment of hesitation, peered under the bed. Whatever was there it wasn't George. And then she heard a movement in the bathroom, the creak of a floorboard.

Beth didn't dare switch the light on as she tiptoed into the bathroom, where she thought she saw a shadow shift behind the drawn shower curtain. Catching her breath, she drew it aside.

"Hello, Beth," George whispered.

George took Beth's hand as he stepped out of the bath and into her arms. They held one another there in the dark for a long time, cheek pressed to cheek, thundering heart to thundering heart, arms entwined around one another in a hungry embrace.

And then Beth and George quietly tiptoed downstairs.

"I KNOW ONE thing," George said as they lay under a blanket on the large beanbags in the Children's room. "I love you, Beth, I love you so much."

"I love you, too, George," Beth smiled. "And now you are here, you are safe. You and I can grow old and have kinky bookshop sex together for years and years, and have children and grandchildren and people will talk about how much we loved one another, they will write about us, I expect. It will be called…" She thought of the place they had met, Romance: Historical.

Even as she smiled at the thought Beth knew what was coming next.

"I have to go back," George said, taking her hand. "You know that I have to go back, don't you?"

"Yes," Beth said, without looking at him. "I know you do. I know that no matter how much you love me you couldn't run away from your family, your friends. You're just not that sort of man. It's one of the reasons I love you."

George kissed the top of her head.

"What we have is more than some people get in a lifetime," he said. "And besides, we have a few weeks left before I have to join up. And a couple of years when I might get back now and then."

"Yes," Beth said, rolling over to face him. "That's why I've made a decision too, George."

"What's that?" George asked her.

"That I'm coming back with you, to live in your time," she said. "If you don't mind."

"Would you really do that for me?" George asked her. "Leave Chinese food and instant libraries for me instead of just visiting now and then?"

"Yes, I want to be closer to you, even when you are not here. I never was really made for this world anyway. I'm much better suited to yours," Beth said. "And besides, George, I'd do anything to be with you."

*　*　*

ROMANCE: HISTORICAL

"Now, what's really important," Mr. King told Steve as he showed him round the shop on his first day, "is that you get to know the stock inside out. We don't want you getting lost, do we? Be an awful shame to lose another one."

"Of course." Steve laughed because it seemed like the right thing to do. "What an amazing shop this is, Mr. King. Wow, look at this photo, are they your relatives?"

It was a wedding photo, a young man in uniform arm in arm with his bride.

"Oh yes, that's my Grandpa George, just after joining up. He died a couple of years after this was taken sadly, in France. And that's my grandmother, Elizabeth King. Now I come to think of it, she reminds me of someone I know. I can't think who, though."

"Well, she is your grandmother, Mr. King," Steve said.

"Oh yes," Mr. King said, chuckling. "I expect that will be it."

THE PLACE OF ALL THE SOULS
Margo Lanagan

Margo Lanagan has published two dark fantasy novels (*Tender Morsels* and *The Brides of Rollrock Island*) and seven short story collections, most recently a collection of micro-fiction, *Stray Bats*. She collaborated with Scott Westerfeld and Deborah Biancotti on the New York Times bestselling trilogy, *Zeroes*.

Her work has won four World Fantasy, nine Aurealis and five Ditmar Awards, and has been shortlisted in the Nebula, Hugo, Bram Stoker, Theodore Sturgeon, Shirley Jackson, International Horror Guild, British Science Fiction Association, British Fantasy, and Seiun Awards, and twice made the James Tiptree Jr Honor List. Her books and stories have been widely translated. Margo lives in Sydney, Australia.

From anecdotal evidence, notably collected
by Ngoe and Pederson (2018), the experience

263

of time travelers in the transitional interval known variously as 'the interchange', 'Bardo™', 'the between-times' or 'the place of all souls' bears notable similarities to the pupal phase of the insect life cycle. No radical remodeling of the body takes place during the transition, however. It is an adult that is thus broken down, then reconstituted on the destination plane from the imaginal cells and discs.

—Jean Swimmerdam, *The General Treatise on Intertemporal Travel*

A DREADFUL HOWLING climbed through Ciarán's dream. He sat up, and the dream fell away directly, but the noise remained: a terrified woman, in unbearable pain. He sat up staring. Cool air rushed into his fever-damp nightshirt. The room had a just-exploded feeling, though the bare bluestone walls were intact, the white vault steady above.

He was on a camp bed, in the orphanage cellar. He had a vague memory of being carried down here for Mrs. Mac to keep an eye on through the night. He could hear her now, trying to calm the howling woman.

A howl broke off into frantic apologies, hisses, spits. "Just got to let it out my *mouth*!" the woman cried, and another bellow burst from her.

Ciarán threw back the blanket. Across the bricked floor he ran, even lighter than usual after two days with only water and soup-sips. To the archway, to the pouring light.

He poked his head around the corner.

It was like a holy painting in there. Jacob wrestled the angel, or a soul was pitched into Hell. On the table a magic lantern apparatus rattled and blared light, casting huge shadows on the whitewashed wall. There was a strong smell of fresh-mown grass and hot metal.

The woman—tall, naked, white, with a cataract of dark hair—reared and lunged, waving her left fist in the air. She shrank from her own hand, begged it for mercy, fell to her knees beneath it, sprang up again to fight it.

How small that fist was, how wrong! Smooth as the knob of Da's Tipperary blackthorn stick, the skin gleamed white against the cramped and crowded bones inside, flamed red and purple otherwise. It was folded as a hand was never meant to fold.

"Bring an axe!" called the woman. "For God's sake, cut it off me!"

"Ciarán!" Relief lit Mrs. Mac's face. "Run for Mr. Polk!" she cried, wrestling with the woman's free arm. "Tell him to bring his spirit-bottle to the kitchen, and as many lamps as he can find. And Doctor Popplewell!" She called louder as he fled for the stairs. "Tell him there's a woman needing surgery. And Captain Douglas. No one but them, boy, whoever else you see! Tell them I sent you. They'll know where to come, at this hour. And shut every door behind you as you go, hear me?"

"I hear!" He sprang up the stairs, fever-light, fever-bright. He pushed open the weighty cellar door. The woman's cries resounded dangerously in the kitchen; he shut them away behind him. Now the loudest noise was his own heart agallop. Then he was running, fast and smooth as a panicked rat, across the cold flags, towards the outer door.

IT WAS PERFECT weather for the school fête, sunny but with a cooling breeze. The crowd was large, cheerful and constantly changing, and every stall and activity was doing healthy business.

Della was there with her eldest daughter Cara. Cara had just paid for two mixed trays at the plant stall when the music over the PA system cut out. A calm voice said, "If there's a doctor or a nurse here today, could they please go immediately to the café marquee to attend to a medical emergency? To the café marquee, please, urgently."

Cara thrust her tray into Della's arms and was gone.

"Paramedic," said Della to the plant-stall lady.

"Oh, how lucky!"

Della put the tray on the end of the trestle table and shook her hand in its prosthetic Glove. It was baulking a bit at spontaneous demands lately—she must check when the next service was due.

"I hope she can help," said the plant-stall lady.

"Can I leave these trays with you while I nip over there?"

"Of course, of course!"

Della hurried through the wandering fête-goers to the crowd gathering below the COFFEE banner. "Excuse me.

Coming through. Pregnant lady coming through." People jumped aside at that, and frankly stared at Della's belly as she passed. Seven months along, she was entering the galleon-under-full-sail stage: smocked, regal, her silver-streaked hair part caught back with clips, part flying free.

You hardly ever saw a visibly pregnant woman in public these days—they were put away and watched and tested and kept very still and peaceful. But pregnancy had always treated Della well; she was sixty now, and this was her twenty-sixth—three babies of her own, twenty-three sponsored. The sponsors paid to keep her strong, flexible, and well monitored. The extra lease of youth and fertility from her old IITT work took care of the rest.

She broke through the innermost circle, arriving at the sandalled feet of a man, maybe mid-fifties, lying unconscious on the well-trodden grass. Cara was at work on his sternum, compressing twice a second just like she'd used to wedge clay at that pottery workshop when she was a teen. The man's wife was kneeling over him, holding his head, dripping tears onto his face. "Christopher! Chris, come back to me!" She was slim, with well-dyed, well-tethered hair. People had backed away from her passionate emotion, leaving a wide arc of grass around her.

Della edged around and squatted beside her. She put a hand to the woman's shoulder. "Maybe give him a bit of room to breathe?" she said, gently but firmly. "Cara's onto this, don't worry." Hmm, she didn't like the purplish tint of the husband's lips.

The woman didn't look at her, but sank back to sit. She took a pressed handkerchief from the pocket of her neat beige three-quarter pants and dried her tears.

"He's only a hundred and twenty!" she said. She caught Della's startled gaze. "I know. He was a sojourner. Nice work when you could get it."

Della tipped her head, agreement that could be taken for ignorance. "He looks in good nick," she said. His lips were pinker now. "If anyone will pull through, he will. Cara's my daughter. She's very experienced."

Christopher. Della had never met these people, but she'd seen them around the neighborhood for years. Their children had attended a different school from this one, where Della's and Dan's had gone. The other public school, probably—no private-school parent would deign to come to a state school fête.

She stayed squatting there as the woman pulled herself together. The husband lay mercifully unaware of the gawkers all around him.

He was strong-bodied, leaner than Dan. His face was somewhere between pleasant and handsome, his silvering hair thick and a bit too long, his beard redder among the frosty streaks.

"My name's Della, by the way," she thought to say to the wife. "I don't think we've met, but I've seen—"

"*Is* it now?" the woman said. She turned slowly towards Della. "Just Della *by the way*, is it? So casual."

"I'm sorry?"

The woman looked Della up and down. "Of course

you're here," she sneered. "Of course you're a local person. Oh, how delightful. How convenient. How very nice to meet you."

Della rocked back, rose to standing. A school-age boy and his dad pushed through the spectators, the dad bearing the school's defibrillator.

"Great!" said Cara, continuing to pump. "Open that case up, would you mind?"

The wife was not distracted. She gazed up at Della with extreme dislike. "I always wondered when you would *pop up* and blow my life apart—"

"I think you're mixing me up with—"

"And could you, ma'am," Cara said loudly to the wife, "unbutton Chris's shirt for me so I can stick the pads on?"

"Oh, I'd like to believe that." The woman threw the bitter words over her shoulder at Della, kneeling forward again. Swiftly, she undid the first few buttons. "I'd like to believe I'd made a mistake, I really would."

She flicked aside the shirt panels almost with disdain. Sitting back on her haunches, she watched Della, working her mouth as if about to spit on her.

Della kept her eyes on Cara so as not to look at the wife's angry face. Cara stuck the second pad to the man's left side. A tattoo covered much of his flat, tan belly. It looked like handwriting, several paragraphs. Even back to front as it was, even upside down, it made Della go cold all over—cold, deaf, and very still.

Below his navel, the mirror-written closure, *All my love*. The mirror signature, *Della*.

The wife leaned at Della and yammered silently up at her. Cara spread her hands above the man like a magician, checking that no one was touching him, interrupting the wife to move her back. In the sunlight the man lay exposed, oblivious. In the silence he jolted on the ground as if someone had kicked him.

Della turned from the sight. The baby swirled inside her and a Braxton Hicks contraction gently clenched around him. She searched the crowd for an older, kind-looking woman. She waved her forward, into place beside the wife.

She walked away through the craning, jostling crowd. An ambulance siren flowed into the silence like a faint pennant undulating in the wind. Flashing lights slid to a halt at the far edge of the fête.

Then she was at the plant stall. The plant-lady was serving someone, thank heaven. Della stood over the trays Cara had chosen, examining the hopeful seedlings, the confident sprays of herbs, the variegated leaves of the ornamental plants.

"Christopher," she whispered. He wasn't Christopher. There were Christophers in his family tree, on his mother's side. But he was Alfred, Alfred John Aspall. *Her* Alfred. The name was tattooed on her memory, if not on her skin. No one else could conceivably have her signature on him. Could have *All her love.*

Time raced and ambled past her. Through the crowd she saw the ambulance officers wheeling 'Christopher' down the playground on a trolley. He said something, making one of them laugh. The plant-lady was free now, and chatty with relief. Della heard herself swapping platitudes with her, soothing them both.

Christopher's wife was ushered into the passenger seat of the ambulance. And then Cara was making her way back up the slope as the van pulled away.

"Well done, darling!" said the plant-lady. "I'd be so proud of you if you were my daughter."

Cara gave her a quick smile and picked up a tray. "Let's get these home." Della couldn't read her, couldn't tell how much she'd heard, what she'd seen, what she thought.

She flexed her Glove-fingers and picked up the other box. "Thanks again," she said to the woman, and sailed off after Cara. The fête-goers bustled from bric-a-brac stall to pony ride to jumping castle. Death had flown in close, touched them with its wing tip, then decided after all to fly on.

Now that the shock of being shouted at was wearing off, Della felt something like laughter well up. So many years she'd searched for him, wondered about him! Now all the possibilities had suddenly narrowed down to one actual body, one life, a life very much like hers, and near enough to reach out and touch. Whatever came of the discovery, there was at least a moment's peace to be enjoyed, now that she knew.

DEEP IN THE night in the cellar, Doctor Popplewell went to work on the woman's hand. Ciarán stood ready to hold down the unhurt arm, should she rouse and struggle, while Captain Douglas guarded her blanket-covered legs. Mrs. Mac, at the woman's head, only smoothed and gathered her hair, waved the chloroform cloth under her nose when she stirred, and watched everything the doctor did.

The lantern that had stood on the table was doused and removed, and its hot-metal-and-grass smell was almost completely gone. Now lamps encircled them, brought by the gardener Polk to the cellar door and carried down and lit by Ciarán.

He could only bear to glance at Doctor Popplewell's work now and then. The unfolding hand looked worse than the blackthorn knob had. But the doctor professed himself quite pleased. "She will still have a hand of sorts," he said, dabbing the poor writhen thumb with his cloth. "And a hand of sorts is better than no hand at all."

"How did she come to be so hurt?" Ciarán heard his own small voice ask Mrs. Mac.

"Oh, my dear," she said, "you hardly need to know."

"No," agreed the captain. "Best you forget everything you have seen and done tonight, lad." He passed fanned fingers in front of Ciarán's face like a mesmerist entrancing someone.

"Here, now." The doctor straightened over his work and dabbed more blood away. "It seems there is an object concealed in the lady's grip." He scratched at something more solid than flesh with the tip of his scalpel blade. "I will need to free a finger to release it."

"What, has she tried to pick up some keepsake along the way?" said Mrs. Mac.

"From what I am told," said the captain, "nothing in the place of interchange can be grasped and retained."

"And they are forbidden, are they not, to bring items from their own times?"

"They undertake not to attempt it, yes. All that is to be exchanged between the zones is information, and that only verbally. That is why the Institute chooses whom it chooses, for their faultless recollection of detail. Mrs. Holcombe here is marvelous for her memory."

"Oh, I know. She can recite like a book come to life."

"But she is an educated woman and takes her responsibilities seriously. I cannot conceive that she would disobey the terms of the license."

Doctor Popplewell wiped the object of blood, but when he placed it on the table next to the woman's shoulder, it was still red. It was imprinted with the tight grip of the woman's fingers, like a knapped flint or an odd kind of seashell.

"Is it sealing wax?" Mrs. Mac said.

The captain bent to examine it, taking care not to obstruct the doctor's light.

"It must contain something," said Popplewell. "Why would you deform yourself so, or inflict such deformity on another, for only a ball of wax?"

"We must have you open it for us, Popplewell."

The doctor gave a distracted glance and a laugh. "I shouldn't imagine it requires surgical skills, captain." He clapped down a second scalpel, almost identical to his own.

The captain blanched.

"What harm do you fear from it?" Mrs. Mac said.

"Believe me," said the captain, "The future holds unpleasant surprises. Destructive weapons such as we can hardly conceive of. Diseases more virulent than the Great Plague—"

"But *is* this from the future?" said Mrs. Mac. "Or is it from that timeless place *between* now and what's to come?"

"About which we know even less," the captain said. "And where there is no possibility of implementing any form of scientific method."

Ciarán found breath to whisper, "Has this lady come *from the future*?" He peered at the apparatus behind Mrs. Mac. It was too dimly lit to properly see, but perhaps it was not so similar to a magic lantern as he had first thought. It was certainly larger. "And has she put herself, a whole live person, through that... between-place, to get here?"

Mrs. Mac pursed her lips, glancing at the captain, who still stood paralyzed. The doctor worked on calmly, his breath whistling slightly in his moustache.

Ciarán reached across and picked up the scalpel.

"Take care," the doctor said absently. "It will be sharper than any knife you have handled."

Ciarán took up the capsule. "Oh, it's quite heavy. Heavier than only wax, I think."

He made a first light cut. The warm wax split easily. He pulled the split gently apart. A pattern of fine, close diagonal lines shifted and shone in the bottom of the split.

"It is paper!" he said. "Very fine paper, rolled up, edged with gold."

He laid the opened capsule on the blanket over the woman's front. The doctor peered at it. "India paper," he said. "Someone has cut the blank pages from the end of their Bible. Or several Bibles, by the look."

The paper lay in a tight roll. The outermost page was blank, stained pink by the wax. Ciarán peeled it away.

The inner pages were covered front and back to the very edges with script that an ant would have been lucky to read, written in black ink with what looked like a needle tip. One page included a fairy map, and others bore careful fairy drawings of what looked like piles of horse dung. The doctor having a magnifying glass among his accoutrements, the captain applied himself to deciphering the writing, but the minuscule letters defeated him.

"Oh, I would have no hope," said Mrs. Mac when he offered her the glass. "But Ciarán is a good little scholar."

"Do you think?" The captain hesitated.

"I think the cat is well and truly out of the bag with this boy, captain," Mrs. Mac said. "But maybe his sharp young eyes can serve us."

"It's a letter," Ciarán was able to assert, after studying a few of the leaves. "'Dearest you' it begins on this page, and the name at the end is 'Alfred John Aspall'. And the date at the head is Friday the second of October, nineteen thirty-one. Is that when she is from?" He gazed wide-eyed at the unconscious woman.

"Goodness, no," said Mrs. Mac. "She is from much later. He is only, what, seventy years hence? 'Dearest you,'" she murmured. "It is a personal letter, then."

"What is all *this*?" The captain nudged forward the paper curls with the map and drawings.

Ciarán took the map page, held down its corners and examined it.

"It is of a place called Evan's Crown," he said.

The captain shook his head. "Have you heard of such a place, Mrs. MacAinch?"

"Roads lead off to Ta-ra-na," said Ciarán, "and to Bat... to Bathurst. That's west of Sydney Town, isn't it?"

"He could not be suggesting a *meeting*, surely?" said the captain.

Ciarán peered at the script crowding around the map, at the labels of the drawings. "He is telling this lady where she might bury a letter herself. An answer, I suppose. Under a certain rock at this Evan's Crown—these are formations of rounded rocks. He says he will visit there on one of his assignments, either to the past or the future—can they go both ways, then?" He had not thought he could be more astonished.

Mrs. Mac and the captain shifted uncomfortably.

Ciarán shuffled his dozens of questions, trying to decide on the most sensible one. "And so, can he not tell, in that between-place, where she's from, or when?"

"He cannot," said Mrs. Mac. "There are no names in

the between-place, no dates, no way to tell where they started out from, or where they're bound. These two are lucky to have found themselves on the same side of the globe!"

The captain shook his head. "Lover's notes! This goes directly against the provisions in the licensing agreement. The Institute will have to be informed. I should imagine there will be most severe consequences."

"For whom?" said Mrs. Mac. "Not for Mrs. Holcombe, surely? This Aspall fellow looks to have forced this letter on her. She is an innocent victim here."

"Certainly *he* will be penalized. I should imagine his sojourner's permit will be rescinded. And his area of operations closely examined, to discover how he was able to transmit this material." He began gathering up the curled papers.

Mrs. Mac put out her hand as if to stop him, but he shooed it away.

"I think Mrs. Holcombe has a right to read her own correspondence," she said crossly.

"This should go straight to the Institute regulators." Tetchily, the captain continued snatching up the papers.

"Come now," said Mrs. Mac. "The damage won't be done for seventy years!"

He gathered; they glared at each other.

"Let the boy make a fair copy for her," Mrs. Mac said finally, in her most reasonable voice. "You could do that, could you not, Ciarán? You seem good enough at your letters."

"I—I'm sure I could, given a good light and a glass as strong as the doctor's." He tried to sound doubtful and grown-up, like them, to hold down the heady excitement bubbling in him. He was still unsure that this was not all a fever dream. "It would take time, though—so many pages and such tiny writing."

"There will be time," said Popplewell. "She must heal somewhat before she returns. These stitches would be foreign objects. They would not travel with her. All my work would come undone."

Mrs. Holcombe made a noise in her throat then, as if adding her voice to the argument. The captain watched Mrs. Mac make another pass with the chloroform cloth, the officiousness draining from his face and posture.

"And it's not as if he is urging her to breach the license terms further," said Mrs. Mac gently. "It's not forbidden, is it, to bury a letter in one's own time, for someone else to find?"

DAN KNOCKED AND poked his head in the History Hut door. "You okay?"

Della emitted a high of-course sound, bringing up her email to cover the browser window.

"Cara said there was an 'incident', up the fête."

She made an ambiguous face. "We-ell, it's never nice to be shouted at."

Dan stepped in. He came around the desk, glanced at the screen. Almost idly, he reached down and switched windows, and there were her search results for 'christopher john brace', the name the wife had given the ambulance officers, which Della had got from Cara. Here were the tabs for the articles in the local paper (Chris Brace protesting overdevelopment, coaching squash and technology prize-winners), for his record in the Medical Corps, for his professional profiles in prosthetic medicine, for some seniors sports listings…

"Ah." Dan straightened and gave a big, weary sigh. "It was only a matter of time, I guess." He went heavily to the door.

A small bomb went off in Della's head. "What do you mean, 'ah'?"

But he was gone out the door.

"What do you mean, 'only a matter of time'?" She stormed after him.

He was halfway across the yard, his gait that of a man approaching the gallows.

"Are you saying you *knew*?" All flying hair and Braxton Hickses, holding her belly, she scuttled around him to block the concrete path.

He stood there as if he didn't have the will to simply walk around her on the grass. The look he gave her was moving water, one moment half-seen depths, the next glossy surface, blameless sky.

"You knew and you didn't *say*? For how long?"

"Oh…" He consulted the air above her head and shrugged.

"All along? Since it happened? Twenty-whatever years?"

"Oh... I pecked away at it, over time."

"So did I, pecked and *pecked*!"

He looked at his feet.

"Then how did *you* find out?" Why was it given *him* to find out, she meant, about *her* soul mate?

He looked up, shamefaced. "I started from the basis of any fellow in our orbit. Any *well-preserved* fellow. Weeded out the wealthier ones who'd bought themselves Elixir or Silverfount. Checked out the rest for any that might have been sojourners. That took a while. They're all over the bloody joint. What an enterprise. What a gigantic... maze of bad ideas."

Stubbornly, Della held his gaze.

"So, ah, friend of Sam Perini's, at work, did the name-change search for me—"

"Highly illegal."

Another shrug. "That would've been, ah, ten-twelve years ago?"

"And you sat on it."

"Well..." He gave a low, pained laugh, his eyes on the kitchen window. Cara was playing music in there, and scrubbing out that casserole dish Della had told her to leave; it clanked in the sink. She'd be watching every move. They were ludicrous out here in the sunshine, with their pegged underwear flapping around their heads, the blushing bear of a man and the stout woman with her dress and hair blowing out sideways.

"Why would I tell you?" said Dan. "What would be in it for me?"

"Look me in the eye." She felt sick.

He did so, but sidelong, his face reddening further.

"What did you do?" she whispered.

"Nothing. Like you said," he said determinedly, "I sat on it."

"You couldn't lie to save yourself."

His gaze dropped again.

"You spoke to him."

A glance, half shame, half satisfaction.

"You confronted him. You and he—" the words nearly choked her "—came to some kind of, bloody... *gentlemen's agreement*."

All shame now. He twisted as if his boots were clamped to the concrete.

"About me!" She leaned over the lumpish, lucrative nuisance of the baby. "About me!" In her head she was shrieking it, but it was coming out half-strangled. "Without consulting me! Leaving me in the dark! Out of the equation!" She swept a hand across the air, erasing herself from their thoughts. "For *years*! The pair of you!"

"To be fair, *he* wanted you to have your say."

"But you managed to persuade him otherwise?" She cocked her head, radiating irony from her every angle.

"I threatened him," Dan said to his boot-toes. "I threatened his family. I said I'd tell his wife. Destroy their peace."

"You—"

She squinted up at him, hangdog lummock that he was. The anger fell away, and the sarcasm.

"Jesus bloody Christ, Dan."

"I know." His voice was leaden.

"I don't know whether to hit you or hug you."

His eyes were a hundred percent sincere, a little glint in them. "I'll just sit quiet over here, then, while you decide."

INSTITUTE STAFF AND sojourners had called that place the between-times, but it was out of the flow of time completely. *And* it contained all times at once: past, future, and ongoing present.

People were least and most themselves there—if there were such things as selves. The place threw that into serious doubt, even as it affirmed that there most certainly were. It was a place of paradox, which paradoxically set all anxieties and puzzles to rest. This is the ultimate truth, it said—and here, its opposite, this is also true. It was a joke played endlessly on the tininess of human minds.

The darkness there was washed like a sleeper's sight with dim light, many-colored. She could 'see' nothing else, but she could apprehend everything. Her usual five senses were just the tip of the iceberg. The sensation beyond distinctions of temperature was the least of it; there were also the pulses behind the silence behind sound; the mouth-filling, being-filling taste of eternity; the smell like amniotic fluid gone feral, where planets and suns had floated unborn, galaxies, universes. Everything was essential here, fruitful, purposeful, free of moral weight.

Her self was in pieces. Some of it had lost form entirely, and cell by cell joined the vast general matter. Other parts were now compressed into templates or seeds, dormant pattern-pieces of great beauty and complexity. Though these were scattered far and wide in the matter, light years apart as far as distances existed, she felt no fear of losing them. They knew how to cohere again, whenever time summoned them.

From arriving and being suspended here, she saw quite clearly how simple was the mechanism for stepping outside time, how it was no great mental leap for a certain kind of mind to arrive at it. She saw, too, how readily, how fluidly, the future could change, and the past be adjusted so as to seem singular. It was accomplished here, that change. Everything was done here, anything. The scale of the potential for beings and things to exist, their endless generation, continuance, metamorphosis and inevitable ceasing, filled what could collectively be called her self— sexless, nameless, eternal—with wonder, with a kind of joy, a kind of relief. How insignificant were the concerns and experiences of her time-bound days and nights! Yet how crucial they were to this seething busyness, as crucial a part of it as any other.

Once returned into time, she could never recapture the place's at-once-ness. She would aim her thought at it in a hopelessly linear stream. She would expend endless words failing to describe it, puzzling over the memory— if indeed it was a memory, when it remained all around her, with the 'real' slid into place just in front of it. She learned when to stop trying, before a normal mortal's eyes glazed over. It was something only her colleagues could understand, and they had no need to explain it to each other, to talk about it at all.

Cara, can I ask a favor?

ooh spelled out my name, must be serious. fire away 🔫 ♥

It's about that bloke you resuscitated the other day.

yeeeees?

I've been trying to visit him at the Hearthouse, but his wife is adamant that I can't see him. I'm thinking you could talk to her? She might be a bit more receptive to the woman who saved her husband's life?

C, you there?

do you just want to find out how he's tracking?

Yes PLUS, I need to see him face to face, at some point when his eyes are

open and he's functioning normally
behind them. If he is, that is.

if she lets me in, what do you want
me to ask him?

No, it needs to be me. Do you think
you could talk her around?

C?

yebbut just, how much of what that
woman said is her being upset and
unhinged, and how much is true?
like, will I regret this?

Didn't hear all of it, but I suspect ratio
is about 9:1. I honestly can't say if
you'll be sorry. The main point of the
meeting is actually to find that out.

oh

fuck, mum

I know. I'm sorry to put this on you. I
can't think of any other way.

* * *

DELLA HAD GONE to Evan's Crown too early, before her hand was fully repaired. With only one arm to dig with, in the confined space under the belly of Alfred's rock, it took her a crazy amount of time to break up the well-settled earth there, to dig deep enough for her letter to be out of reach of rabbits or wombats.

She had booked one night in the Bathurst motel and a flight home the next day, thinking to bury and be gone in an afternoon, to minimize the disruption to Dan and the children. So when her labors turned up a small, flat, rectangular package, wrapped in oilcloth and tied with string, she was aghast with exhaustion and indecision.

She stared up from among the granite tors, at the restless clouds, the restless treetops waving like a warning. Dimly, she thought through the logistics of extending her stay, of extending her letter, of returning to bury it, thought through the costs and the conversations and the time that all those things would entail.

Finally, she took her letter as it was, in its sealed plastic time capsule, and placed it at the bottom of the excavation. She pushed the dirt back into the hole, packed it flat, spent some time making it look as weathered, as insignificant, as the ground either side.

She roamed, then, among the boulders, in the fitful wind, the spitting rain, the letter inside her jacket, against her grubby shirt. She almost didn't want to read it, to have read it and not have it to look forward to. She felt a little mad; she wanted to inhabit this moment forever, alone among these giant hard haunches and flanks of rock, trimmed with tenacious eucalypti.

She must go home to her family, or at least for now to the motel room. She must open the letter and absorb its contents. It would be difficult, whatever they were. And she must decide whether to show Dan. How badly should she frighten him in the name of honesty and openness?

Yet still she stood, hungry and tired, at the lookout. The clouds' skirts hid and revealed the green fields spread below, seamed and scattered with dark trees. A farmhouse sent up a thread of chimney smoke. A single car beetled along the Tarana road. Birds cried and caroled, speaking of her and for her. And then the rain began to come down harder, and she put up her hood and followed the signs down to the car park.

Later in the motel room, showered and fortified by trail mix and tea, the bar-fridge miniature of Johnnie Walker Red in a battered motel tumbler at her elbow, she ceremoniously untied the stiff string from the package, unfolded the cloth. She felt only a negligible tremor of doubt about this packaging, only a moment's surprise at the even hand in which the several pages were covered. So different from the needle scratches on the India paper! But then, of course it would be, with all that space at Alfred's disposal.

But then, opening the folded pages, she saw the date at the top of the first one. For a slippery moment she thought she had someone else's mail in hand, some other sojourner reaching out to their colleague. What, she would have to bury this again?

My dear Mrs. Holcombe, it said, though. *You may well not recall me—*

She snatched away the last page from the others, and turned it over. "Oh!" The scowl cleared from her face and the dread from her heart. For it was not to be difficult at all, this reading; it would not test her loyalty to Dan. It wouldn't need to be hidden, or only revealed with care for his feelings.

"Oh!" She gazed sightlessly at the wall of the cheap plain room that could never dispirit her now. She pressed her eyes into the sleeve of her windcheater and took some steadying breaths. Then shakily she laid the pages on the pale woodgrain Laminex tabletop, and began to read the letter, every word, from the very beginning.

DAN WAS VERY quiet as they entered the hospital. He was not great in hospitals at the best of times.

God, no, he'd said when she suggested he come.

To sit with the wife, I mean. It might calm her down, someone else in the same... position.

Let me think about it, he'd said reluctantly.

She herself, as she led him through the corridors and across the garden walkway to the Hearthouse, was full of scrambling emotions. The baby seemed to have picked this up, somersaulting and pushing at her ribs and bladder with its feet. Braxton Hickses crawled over her belly like lightning roaming a thundercloud.

They came along a corridor to the glass wall of the lounge.

IN THE PLACE of all the souls, recognition had hit them at first gently, like fingertips interlacing. A soft startlement had taken her. Then she was seeing, against the galaxies of other people's pattern-pieces, uniformly dim and mysterious, one other's clearly, cell by bright cell, wheel by bright wheel. The closer she observed a piece or a cell, of his or of her own, the more depth, patterning, color or subtlety of structure it revealed. This constellation was as scattered and as intricate as her own, as everyone's. And all his pieces were drawn to all of hers, two murmurations approaching, combining, together taking wing.

It was not that they aligned like identical stained-glass windows pairing up to make the light more vivid. Neither were they perfectly complementary, yin-and-yang-ly. Each called energy out, struck sparks, goaded the other to a kind of cellular laughter, urged the other to complicate and transform. They set each other racing, like two vines clambering together towards the light, twining and bracing to be twined upon. They improvised entanglements wherever they sensed each other near.

All this happened timelessly, placelessly. It was explicable only within the conditions of that between-planes existence. The first time concurred with the several other times; they were separate, coupled and collective all at once. One instance might resolve into Della unravelling from this play of joys and surprises to arrive intact and mission ready in the orphanage cellar. Another might land her uninjured in the Institute reception chamber, there to dress and file her report, log out and go home to

Dan and the children. And then in that one case, as her limbs had extended from the pattern-pieces, her hand had distorted and crushed itself as it emerged. The pain had bloomed brighter and sharper, and the noise had begun as her throat began, and grown as it grew, pouring forth the horror and surprise. The 'darkness' had faded and the beauties and the galaxies receded. A glare replaced it, of light from the apparatus on the whitewashed wall, and the smell morphed from newborn baby through hot machine oil to damp bluestone and gum leaves. And the knowledge moved with Della between dimensions, transforming as it came, from exhilaration at shifting their discovery into the stream of time, to the stark knowledge that the movement entailed a wrongness being committed on her that endangered them both and yet remained as right as, and righter than, that fabulous play, that glorious mingled flight.

THE WIFE—ALICE—had not wanted him to look his best this morning. His silvering hair was uncombed, and stubble was breaking out beyond his beard's usual clipped lines. The hospital gown had slipped from one shoulder to show the patches and wires leading to the monitors beside him. From his face, she knew that he would have adjusted the gown, had he known how vulnerable that bare shoulder, those sensors, made him look.

He'd been focused on the doorway, waiting. His chin had come up when she appeared there and his lips clamped closed. The monitor's quiet beeping accelerated for a few beats, and settled back to slightly faster than before, but every angle of him denied the sound. He watched her warily for a few seconds, and then, "Mrs. Holcombe," he said. A rumble of a voice, used to being obeyed.

"Alfred."

He neither smiled nor winced. "Please," he said, with a sketch of a look at her belly, "come in and sit down."

She went to the end of the bed, and grasped the white rail at its foot, keeping their eyes at the same level.

"I'm told we have an hour." He looked at the wall behind her, where she assumed there was a clock. "In which to..." He raised his eyebrows. There was so much leashed energy in his expression, in his tensed body. He was so clearly *him*, so clearly the one she had known, and who'd known her, so completely.

"In which to establish... a way forward." She must try to stay *here*, to stay *now*.

He shrugged, looked away, looked back. "I don't see why we shouldn't all go on as before, do you?"

"Are you serious? Of course we can't. Everything is completely different now."

"Everything is almost completely the same. We each have families, responsibilities. You are happy in your marriage, I in mine. The time is surely past when either of us would be tempted to destroy everything we've achieved in the name of a moment's dalliance? In a place we're not sure even exists outside our own imaginations?"

She gave him the gently incredulous look she had

perfected with her children. "Would I be here," she mused, almost to herself, "if it were so trivial?"

"Believe me," he said, marginally less blustery, "I have thought this through many times—"

"*Strangely enough,* so have I."

"Of course you have. It seems to me, that though you and I came together so neatly in *that* realm—"

A snort burst from her. "'Neatly' is hardly the word."

"Though we fitted together so perfectly there..." He gave an ironic, checking-with-her look. She looked blandly back. "...it is nonetheless *here* that we must live out our lives, partnered with people who have never had the advantage of perfect acquaintance on another plane."

Heat rose in her face. "I wish you would stop trying to *kill this off* with words."

"A way forward, you wanted," he almost snapped. The beeps sped up as if in irritation.

She dropped her gaze to the peaks of his feet under the waffle-weave hospital blanket. She breathed deeply. "You are a hundred and twenty and have just had a heart attack," she said. "That would tend to make you cling to what you've got, I should think. Perhaps we should have our hour when you're further recovered."

"You *want* to break our two families apart?"

"What I want is for you to at least acknowledge..."

"Acknowledge what?"

She shifted on her feet, the child pressing its hard head against her pubic bone. "Acknowledge the scale of what happened."

The beeping eased. He almost visibly reached for a prepared script.

"I thought I had. In my letter. But I was so young, so full of illusions when I wrote it. About love, about everything. I can't remember half the guff I wrote—"

"I can. Every word. I could recite it to you if you wanted."

"Oh, please don't!" He laughed, perhaps the cruelest sound he had made so far. "I'm a different man now. I believe differently."

She watched him, letting that lie. When the bluster left him and he next fidgeted, "I think that isn't true," she said in a low voice.

"We have to be practical, Della—"

He stopped abruptly, flushing red. Her name had fallen out between them for the first time, laden with familiarity, having been turned over in the silence of his own mind, decade after decade. It carried, too, all the feelings he was not admitting to, the attachment he was affecting to toss aside so cavalierly. All this in two rapid syllables—and yet they both heard how it broke through and betrayed the words, the tone that had gone before.

But he ploughed on. "All the work we've put into our marriages. We can't pretend that here in the real world, our own marriage wouldn't also need such labor. There's still all the outer surface to be adjusted, the whole dismal domestic business, learning what 'pushes each other's buttons', all that. It hardly makes a difference whether two souls have melded in perfect knowledge of each other in an instant, or stumbled towards each other over years, working it all out as they go."

Della swayed slightly, gripping the bed-bar for balance. Perhaps she would surrender and sit down soon. For now she only watched Alfred perform, as calmly as she could.

"One might even argue that the latter was more rewarding," he said, "having been striven for rather than simply bestowed."

"One might," said Della coolly. No, she must not sit. "But if you believe all this, I have to ask, Alfred, why did you change your name? Why did you come here from Sydney? Why did you transplant your family, transfer your work, set yourself up so close to me and mine?"

He closed his lips on some swift, inauthentic answer, looked out the window beside him. A wing of the Hearthouse extended below, its roof an architect's fantasy of angled metal and glass. The beeping ratcheted up and stayed there.

She didn't care how irritated he was. She was about to hammer home her point when his chin twitched in an unmistakable way, and his eyes glistened.

"Because—" His voice cracked. "Because if I couldn't have you, I wanted at least to see you now and then."

She made to go around the bed to take up his hand, but "Don't," he snapped. His hands came up like a dowager's frightened by a mouse. He glared at her, ignoring the tear that dashed down his left cheek. "Don't understand. Don't be sympathetic. You know it's best for both of us."

She halted, one hand on the bed's side rail. "I *don't*

know, actually," she said. "And neither do you, however much you pretend. But I agree with what I think you're saying, behind all this nonsense. There are many other people to consider. I don't know if I've got it in me to cause the amount of pain that would lie ahead for them if we decided to be together, here in this... realm."

"I know," he said, both earnest and angry. "I knew you would say that. I knew that would be your thinking. And I'm not going to try to talk you out of it. I told myself I wouldn't. Even though—" He was tearless now, and stern. "Even though I *could* find it in myself. Even though I *could* cause such pain. Even though that's exactly what I want to do. All I want to do. Now, up to now, beyond now." Then he looked away again, and she did too, to the roof's clever origami under the blue, cloud-puffed sky.

They endured through long moments together. Della was glad her own body was not betraying her through a beeping machine.

"My wife," he said wearily, "she's half-mad with this. She can't weep and rage at me about it because—" He indicated the monitor, the wires, the prison of the bed. "I've heard her exploding at you, at your daughter, and I'm sorry. Though you both seem more than strong enough to handle her. I'm sorry it had to come to this. I'm sorry I was stupid enough to collapse and betray us."

"You're getting tired," she said softly.

He held up the hand with the clip on the finger. "Let me finish. If she says—if my wife—says we have to move away, move somewhere where you and I can't run into one another? Where she doesn't have to see you or your husband ever again? I will probably do it."

Della regarded him calmly. She wasn't as wretched with this as he was—but then, her heart was half the age of his, and not recovering from a recent assault. And Dan wasn't Alice, all raw nerves and terror. Protection was the last thing he wanted from his spouse.

"I probably *can* do it now." He raised dull eyes to her face. "Now that we've met, now that the barriers are down, now that it's awkward between all of us, instead of just my secret—mine and Dan's, I mean."

Their gazes held, and she nodded, the smallest nod. She stepped up and took the hand without the clip, which he had in his weariness let fall to the blanket. She was close to him; his whole body was there, lean, *well preserved*, as Dan had said, inaccessible under bedclothes and medical paraphernalia and... everything else. All this. Her letter, its final paragraphs inscribed to be read in any mirror, whenever he needed, was hidden by the hospital gown, her name, her *All my love*.

She had meant it to be a chaste and chastened kiss, a sweet goodbye. But his other hand came up, his fingers into her hair. He held her there, not forcefully but fearfully, tenderly, held them joined at the mouth in the kiss that must do for a long lifetime's lovemaking, from fresh discovery to deeply sown habit. She sank away into it, the fullness and the familiarity, the rightness, the intense pleasure, the sharp grief.

It finished. Their faces were close, their eyes open. "No

regrets," she commanded in a whisper.

"Oh," he said, gently pushing her away, "*huge* regrets. Are you mad? Wild, gigantic regrets. We don't get away as easily as that. Regrets that you were reduced to *this*, for a start." Helplessly, he gestured to her belly.

"Reduced?" she said, stepping back. "Do you know how rich I am from this? How well cared for? How envied? I'm the luckiest—"

"And still it's a series of humiliations you'd rather not undergo."

She had never said it to anyone, not even herself. She stood back winded from the bed, from Alfred, from the need to lean in for a second kiss, which would change their minds, which would bring ruin on both their houses. She was not even tempted to say—which it had been in her mind to say—*There'll come a time. I'll be a widow, and you a widower...*

He watched her with a solemn, fond gaze as she computed what he had done. He watched her outrage melt away to solemnity, to fondness.

She backed across the room. "Take care of yourself, Alfred—Christopher—whoever you are."

"I'll always love you, Della." He said it steadily, but the beeping sounded urgently beside him.

She nodded. She blew a kiss. She was in the doorway again. She was gone from his sight, and he from hers. She stood in the white corridor, hand against the wall holding her upright, hand on the baby massaging its life, her livelihood.

Then she was walking away, his heart-beeps fading behind her, the light from the glass-walled lounge brightening the corridor ahead.

...AND HERE I come to the nub of this letter, dear Mrs. Holcombe, which is a matter perhaps for the scientists of your day—for those of my own who know of the Institute's efforts profess a blithe lack of interest in my observations. I was but a child, they say, recently orphaned and seeing what I wished to see, rather than any objectively observable phenomenon.

It was not a matter of seeing, as you well know. Even if no twenty-first century person of science cares to listen, I suspect that you yourself will be keenly interested, this being a matter close to your heart—not to mention Mr. Aspall's and perhaps many other souls'—but also because you flattered me by professing interest in almost any observation I cared in my youthful frankness to make. I know that your interest was to some extent a professional one in gathering information to illuminate the genealogies of your employer's clients, but the warmth and kindness with which you always addressed me and the enthusiasm with which you received the almost-nothings I contributed to your project make me certain that I will find a ready audience simply in yourself.

So I say—after this voluminous preamble! which I am sure you in your kindness will tolerate:—

On that night, once Mrs. MacAinch and the captain

had lit the apparatus and allowed its energies to build to the requisite level, the noise of it separated us from each other. You will recall that the light the machine produced was very bright on the wall, and very flat. We looked at almost anything else for preference—the machine itself, the cloth screen rippling between us and it, the captain noting down his figures and Mrs. Mac waiting with her hands at her waist. I watched your face, because it would be gone from my sight soon and I wished to recall every detail. I had little hope that I would be admitted here again. And if I were, from what I had learned, it was unlikely that you would be permitted to return.

And I do recall you, in your shift, with your hair down, your arms covered in gooseflesh and your good hand cradling your injured one, healed but still terribly malformed. Look at it, Ciarán, you had laughed to me once, Is it not like a kangaroo's paw, the feeble fingers, the mangled thumb?

The time came. The captain's shouted figures climbed. There would be only a matter of moments where the field generated was strong enough to accomplish the task. You slipped behind the screen, then. You blew kisses to me and to Mrs. Mac. The captain had his head down over his meter and his figures and he kept it there—the better, I am sure now, not to engage with the next few moments' reality. No kiss did he receive, and no revelation.

The apparatus screamed, on the verge of overheating. The captain shouted the numbers with sudden urgency. Mrs. Mac and I called out our farewells. You turned from us towards the white wall.

And as the light swelled, as it swallowed you, an instant occurred in which the between-times leapt free of its boundaries and inhabited us. In which we, and our century, and our world, were unmade and remade. And perhaps because I was an orphan who had been shown some kindness and now was losing it; perhaps because, as the Institute professors say, I wished so strongly to perceive it, I saw in the lightning-fast interval between the unmaking and the remaking that vast terrain, material and yet of no kind of everyday matter I have encountered before or since, which you had so despairingly, so cheerfully, so stumblingly and yet so accurately described to me during our days of shared recuperation, during our evenings toiling over our books and papers by lamplight and our mornings taking the air on our gradually extended strolls, recovering our respective strengths.

I did not sense in that flash—and I am as glad as I am disappointed, Mrs. Holcombe!—any intimation of the kind of connection you found and formed with Mr. Aspall. I suspect there was not time for such to occur, from your description. Though it be a timeless place as you say, an all-times and a no-times place, traveling through it must surely immerse one more deeply, more wholly in the experience than merely glimpsing it from the entrance with the distractions of one's own time present around one. Or it may be that, being only of tender years, my consciousness was not sufficiently matured to alert that of my perfect mate, to draw that person to me or to detect their component pieces among my own, among all the world's, afloat in that wondrous place.

Mrs. Mac saw the lightning flash, I know from the glance she gave me. She may have even seen her love there, her eyes were so bright, her face so suddenly youthful, open, amazed. She noted, too, that I had seen it—she was eager that I do so, and gratified when I did. The apparatus wound down from its crisis, its fans clattering into action. The captain, his eyes fixed on the cooling engine, continued to call out his numbers and scratch them on his paper, as if those annotations were the things of greatest import in that cellar, not the flash-and-unflash of our immortal selves, not the glimpse of what you had once called, laughingly, *the stuff behind all things*.

Then there was only the dissipating scent of immortality, and the cacophony of the fans, and your shift upon the floor, collapsed where you had departed from it. And we three people, fixed rather than sojourning here, each in her or his small life, so riddled with ordinariness—and that ordinariness itself revealed as a wondrous quality by what we had been permitted to see. What a gift was that seeing! I thank my illness for having brought me to that cellar and made its glimpsing possible. And I thank you for bringing the gift to me, though I must lose your friendship forever to take delivery of it.

My dear Mrs. Holcombe, I find myself at the end of my tale, yet casting about for more to tell you, reluctant to take my leave of you as I was desolated in my boyhood to see you depart us and our time. But the only business left me is to conclude by wishing you, your family and all your dear ones long and happy lives, good health and prosperity all the way. And by hoping that, when my end comes, when my labors for this land, its peoples and the planetary body it rides on are done, there will be sufficient of my soul remaining, my self-such-as-it-is, that we may greet each other, you and I, in the marvelous beyond, and that you will recognize me then, as I am now, as your friend,

Ciarán Damon Cahill

TIMED OBSOLESCENCE

Sameem Siddiqui

Sameem Siddiqui (sameemwrites.com) is a speculative fiction writer currently living in the United States. He enjoys writing to explore the near-future realities people of South Asian ancestry and Muslim heritage will face in the coming centuries. His stories explore issues of migration, gender, family structure, economics, and space habitation. He's attended the Tin House and FutureScapes workshops and his stories have appeared in *Clarkesworld* and *ApparitionLit*. Some of Sameem's favorite authors include Kurt Vonnegut, Octavia Butler, and Haruki Murakami. When he's not writing, Sameem enjoys reveling in fatherhood, watching '90s *Star Trek* or *Avatar: The Last Airbender* and tinkering with data and music.

IT'LL BE HARD when they tell you that you can no longer be a Memographer. "Synaz," the doctor will say between slurps of peppermint tea, "just one more temporal dip could lead to permanent psychosis." You'll knock the tea out of his hands and shout about how you're still good enough to work, but the truth is, Temporally's new DipDrones will have made you obsolete years earlier.

There'll be a small niche market for you, though. People who'll love the daring charm of a handmade Memie, no matter the cost. So, you'll keep doing it, despite the known health risks, because you'll hope it'll give you another chance to find *her*, to see her deep brown eyes somewhere on a job, as if she'll coincidentally show up in the right place and time again.

Just as she'll show up the first time.

You'll be watching the nawab dip his naan into a floral blue bowl filled with nihari when you'll notice her walking in the gardens outside the palace. You won't think much of her at the time, but you'll certainly remember her because she'll look at you as if you don't belong there.

As soon as you can, you'll slip away and walk out to the gardens, to find her. She'll be stalking a peacock that'll be nonchalantly clucking along, pretending it doesn't know it's being followed. You'll be reluctant to interrupt her, but she'll pause and turn to look at you before you can say a word. She'll wave you over, her fingers moving back and forth slowly, indicating that you should move as gently as possible.

When you're beside her, you won't know what to say so you'll just ask who she's there to Memify. You'll apologize, knowing she won't violate Temporally's customer privacy agreements.

"Did you know," she'll whisper without turning her attention away from the anxious bird, "that this very bird was used as a model for the peacocks on Shah Jahan's vaunted throne?"

"You know," you'll whisper back, "I haven't spent much time with animals, but I'm fairly certain a four-century life span is somewhat uncommon for this creature."

"So, you know a thing or two about history then?"

"Research rabbit holes are a bit of an occupational hazard, aren't they?"

She'll turn and study the pattern on your grey jama carefully. She'll be deeply familiar with the detail of your PublicTour Memies, but she'll never have stopped to think about what you must have done behind the scenes to blend in.

"You really take the outfits quite seriously, don't you?" she'll say with a smile.

You'll shrug, uncertain of what to say, but even if you knew there'll be too many people around to talk much longer and you can't risk getting flushed for timeline infractions and missing another deadline. Besides, your Temporally credits will expire momentarily.

As if she'll know this, she'll turn, lean over and whisper to you a place and a time.

While you'll struggle to move her words from your ear to your memory, you'll stare at the peacock as it turns and flares its tail. You'll watch the feathers swirl and expand as the folds of space-time contract and pull you back to 2347. Back to your home in Topor, Mars. Back on to the plush copper-toned armchair in your dimly lit study.

You won't want to waste any time, so you begin setting up your Temporally ad targets to find anyone who may have had ancestors near Bridalveil Fall in California on May 7, 1982, and hope that you can convince them they want a Memie.

You'll get some false positives at first, mostly people asking about the wrong Bridalveil Falls. Then you'll get a few people who lead you on for weeks without providing a DNA sample. But finally, three months in, you'll find the perfect request. The descendants of Supriya Rao, who'll have a poorly preserved photograph of her in front of Bridalveil with a date stamp of May 8, 1982.

It'll be close enough.

"You're dipping for just one job?" Ilkay will say, only half-concerned because you'll have been married long enough for him to know how your occasional bouts of artistic eccentricity lead you to these decisions.

"So few requests come up for then and there," you'll say, steadily observing yourself to make sure your excitement won't give away your true plans. "I thought it'd be a good time and place to make a PublicTour while I'm there."

Ilkay won't respond because he'll be chasing Olma through your home, trying to get him ready for school.

"Abba! Don't go!" Olma will wail as he escapes Ilkay and leaps toward you with his backpack jangling. "I'm gonna miss you too much."

"Oh, beta," you'll whisper as you wrap him up in a hug. "You won't even notice I'm gone."

You'll hug him extra tight, to hide the fact that you're just desperate to leave. Desperate to see someone whose name you won't even know yet. Desperate to see if she'll really want to meet you. And to ask her why.

So, you'll be disappointed when you arrive and find her sitting under an oak tree, thumbing at a paper book with absolutely no clue who you are. You saw her only fleetingly three months ago so you won't be sure it's really her.

But, she'll begin to laugh as if the passing gust of wind makes off with her confusion and blows it up through the leathery leaves above. "I have a habit of playing jokes on myself," she says standing up, "and I fear you may have simply been my punchline."

You'll get the sense that something is amiss, but as her laugh softens you'll get distracted by her subtle smile. She'll introduce herself as Myna Pervez and you'll stumble over words and twigs as you introduce yourself.

"Synaz Ranpir," she'll repeat with thick confidence as if she's more sure of who you are than you are yourself.

Before you can interpret the calm on her face, she'll point toward the trail and ask, "Would you like to join me for a climb?"

I suspect you would rather sit and talk, but this won't be the only time you won't know how to say no to her.

You'll ask how long it's been for her and she'll say,

"You know in those moments in between, I wish time would just stand still. I could do without those times, to be honest."

"I'm not sure thawing out of cryo every couple of days will really be worth the trouble," you'll say.

She'll smile at you before grabbing you by the waist and turning off the path into the trees and up to the rocky wall. Without looking up, she'll firm her grip on you and will boost both of you off the ground and up to a ledge a hundred feet up.

You'll panic, your face inches away from the damp rock face, knowing with just a glance that the ledge is barely deep enough to fit your shoes. But she'll sit, audibly inhale and look calmly over the valley's treeline.

"It's okay, I won't let you fall," she'll say, before knocking on the metal frame lacing your ankles under your sterile beige pant leg. "And if you do, you're wearing an exo, you'll be fine."

"A g-assist exo, not armor," you'll squeak between shivers.

"Just trust me," she'll say with a smile.

It won't be very reassuring, but you'll realize you can't stand there forever, so you'll gradually crumple your body until you're sitting beside her, staring at a passing cloud and counting down from thirty while your breath evens out.

"You know, it's funny," you'll say, once the awkward silence becomes more nerve-racking than your vertigo, "they call the war against the indigenous communities that lived here the Mariposa War."

"What's funny about that?"

"The area was named after a creek not too far from here and the creek was named so by early Spanish explorers who had never seen so many butterflies in their lives. But, as much as they were enamored by the sight, they were irritated at the butterflies' persistent attempts to swoop toward them." You'll sigh and finally feel brave enough to look down. "It's almost as if, from that very moment the butterflies were fighting to expel the new entrants to the valley. So, it just feels fitting that the war should be named for them, too."

"Wow. Was discovering random historical factoids what drew you into this line of work?" she'll ask.

"It was definitely part of it," you'll say, ignoring the possibility that she may be mocking you. "But my great-grandfather was Kursheed Ranpir, so I suppose it's a bit of a family tradition."

"Oh…" she'll say, with a look of surprise, but also clarity. As if she's now certain of a hunch. "Have you thought of commissioning yourself? To go back and find out what happened?"

"Every few years, I splurge on it. But each time Temporally pulls me back warning of timeline infractions, no matter how careful I am not to pierce the temporal perimeter of the accident. It's as if his entire life has vanished."

"That's kind of what they used to do, isn't it?"

"I guess."

"Have you ever considered that maybe he regretted his

role in enabling all of this?" She'll wave her hand around the scenery, but what she'll really mean is your presence in that time. "What if he didn't believe one's life should be accessible after death, even if just to their descendants."

"But what would he have to hide?"

"I don't know," she'll say, frowning slightly. "Is it so unfair to want to take some secrets to your grave?"

You'll close your eyes and think about this for a moment, but it's a foreign concept that's difficult to process. You'll never have considered that there are secrets worth keeping once you're dead. You won't know this, but it's a concept your Temporally training will have carefully steered you away from considering. But you decide to let the idea stew in the back of your brain for the time being.

She'll ask if he's the only reason you keep doing these dips.

"At some point I learned to enjoy it," you'll respond, "mostly for the moments I'm so completely immersed in recording that I really do disappear. Those moments when I'm just flowing through the scene like rapids in an invisible river of time."

She'll touch your cheek and when you turn your head you'll see she's staring at your lips. You won't notice until that moment how much taller she is than you, but before you can process that, she'll lean in and plant a soft kiss on your cheek.

While you're confused about why she studied your lips so closely, only to kiss your cheek, she'll wrap her arm around your waist again and kick her heel on the rock face. You'll clutch her shoulders as she bounces off a few ledges and makes it to the top of the mountain.

She'll lead you over to the trees beside the waterfall and before you can pick a tree to lean on, she'll spin you around and kiss you, firmly on the lips this time.

It'll be a stiff kiss, as if you're frozen in time, both holding your breath. It's the way first kisses are sometimes, to either savor the moment or keep from ruining it with some imprecise movement.

But you'll melt the kiss when you let out a soft moan letting her know you're relieved she's kissed you and that you're waiting for more. And she'll oblige you for the next hour, beneath the tree cover, under the weight of the sound of water crashing hundreds of feet to the earth.

When it's over she'll ask you if you've been to Europa.

"Once..." you'll say. "...kind of. When I was twelve we did a flyby during a Jovian cruise. It was lame in retrospect."

"Well," she'll say standing up. "I'm taking you ice skating."

"Would you believe that I can't ice skate?" you'll say, pulling on your dip suit.

"Prepare to learn. There's an old sealed-up café stall, semi-submerged on the surface outside Delsiki transit station." She'll lean in for one more kiss. "February 25, 2191. I'll see you there."

She'll take a step back and you'll watch as her outline folds into a blur and she dissipates.

As you set up to record Supriya Rao's day, you'll be

scheming about your next ad targeting, anxious to get back and set up some targeting experiments.

But when you return and see Ilkay's green eyes glinting under the purple swirling living room lights he'll have designed himself, you'll feel compelled to take him out and do something nice.

At times like these you'll call me up and say, "Oh Aqsa, Olma thinks the world of you." I'll usually remind you that no matter how long it's been since I nannied him full time, the feeling will always be mutual, so I don't need to be charmed. But, you and Ilkay will insist on telling me how you couldn't imagine raising Olma without me. That I'll truly always be part of your family.

Ilkay will wrap your arm around himself as you strap into the ToporTransitPod. He'll watch you as you prepare to state a destination, but before you can come up with something he'll say, "Alexay's Cavern on Firdos Ridge, please." His one grey beard hair will tick up as he smiles at you and says, "It's okay, my love. I was touched that you wanted to take me out."

The embarrassment you'll feel for never being good at planning these things will be washed away by the intense love you'll feel for being known so intimately. You'll pull his hand from your lap and kiss it softly and tease his fingertips with your tongue. He'll let out a soft sigh and will unfold his fingers.

"How long were you gone this time?" he'll say as he leans his head back. "You seem to have worked up an appetite."

You'll laugh and give his thumb a nibble before putting

his hand down.

"About thirty-six hours," you'll tell him honestly and not just because it's easily verifiable.

"Plenty of time to work up an appetite, I guess, but you can wait a few more hours."

"Of course," you'll say, hoping the smile on your face is the one you hold for him and no one else. It won't be unusual for either of you to see other people, but you'll hold back as if you already know this time is different.

When you arrive at Alexay's, you'll both be relieved to find your favorite booth is empty, the one overlooking the valley of greenhouses below. Ilkay will recall how there was just one struggling greenhouse down there when you came here on your first date. By the end of that date you'll be confessing that you'd been admiring him since you saw his talk on neo-communal living spaces.

"I can't remember if it was your multi-family, multigenerational spiral dome design that impressed me first or if it was these," you'll say as you slide your hand up his arm and give it a squeeze. You'll melt a bit every time you do that, no matter how long you've been married.

Ilkay will wrap you up in his arms and ask, "What's on your mind, my love?"

You'll take a deep breath and pause because you're not even sure where to start. But Ilkay will be used to your scattered brain and will occupy himself with his own thoughts while he waits for you to gather yours.

"Can you imagine," you'll say as the fog in your mind

clears, "when we're gone and the fifty-year waiting period expires, Olma's grandchildren might order a Memie of this very moment?"

"I try not to think about that. It'd just make me perpetually self-conscious."

You'll smile at him and stare off at the landscape again. "Are there any moments you'd lock away and keep just to yourself if you could?"

"I don't think so. I trust you memographers and Temporally's filters to remove anything too sensitive from any final Memies." He'll pause for a moment. "Is there a reason I shouldn't?"

"Well, you won't be there to complain if they don't, will you?"

"Are you having second thoughts about your Khursheed par-dada trip this year?" Ilkay will say as he brushes the hair from your forehead. "It's okay to take a break."

"I just wonder, if maybe it wasn't an accident? If it was intentional. I can't imagine him hiding some wrongdoing, but what if, on principle, he just wanted to be forever put to rest?"

"I didn't know anything like that was possible," Ilkay will say as he massages your neck.

"It's not supposed to be. But if it were, then maybe I need to respect his wishes?"

He'll kiss your forehead and say, "Whatever you need, you know I'll support you."

When you return home, I'll swing my feet off your lime-green couch and slip my book back into my purse.

As I head out I'll smile and tell you how seeing the love between you two always brings me such joy. You're lucky to have found one another at the right place and time.

"There's love out here for you yet, Aqsa," you'll say, "worry not."

I'll laugh and say, "Oh, it's possible. But, for now, it's just enough to see joy in others. Good night, you two. Don't stay up too late," with a wink.

When I return home that night, Zaneel will message me. His panicked, sun-deprived face will sneer at me as he once again spouts rumors that Temporally is days away from announcing time-life encryption. He reminds me that if QuantKey doesn't get there first, he won't be able to pay down the debt I'm accruing daily. I'll tell him it's a delicate matter that will need to unfold slowly. He'll know I'm right and that there's nothing he could do to rush me, but he'll always be impatient and imperious as if he owns my every move. But whatever his role in bringing me to this world, I know my debts won't define me.

The next morning you'll begin entering parameters for your next campaign and soon you'll get a request from Harshal Wong. He'll tell you of his great-grandfather who spent some time at Delsiki. He won't have any solid information to go on, but will hand you a silicate orb.

"This is all I have," he'll say as you run your fingers over it. "I don't know what it's for, but it seemed important enough for my grandmother to hide in the safety deposit box I inherited."

You'll hold it up to the light and study the metal key encased inside. *DELSIKI ABODES 914* will be engraved along the handle.

"My father said she never spoke of her time on Delsiki. Too traumatic."

You'll scour records and find 914 was occupied by Malvay Tolson in 2193. You'll suppose there's a chance that there's a family scandal afoot, but the DNA records confirm that she's of no relation to Harshal, so you won't be able to help him.

But you'll use this new name to target any Tolsons who might have had family at Delsiki and that does the trick. You'll get a request from Zuzana Tolson who'll want to know what her great-great-grandmother was doing on her birthday on March 12, 2192.

You'll make up an excuse about an anomaly that year that'll make it difficult to get a good quality Memie, but ask her if 2191 would be all right. She'll confirm that Malvay moved there in 2188 so any year before the 2203 incident will be fine.

A dip of sixteen days will cost you about three days, so you'll give Ilkay the PublicTour excuse again and arrange for me to come help while you're gone.

While you slip into your beige dip pressure suit, you'll watch yourself in the mirror carefully. You'll try to decide if you look an artist driven by reckless inspiration, or if you look like the desperate fool that you feel like. But through the glare of your helmet, you'll see yourself as Temporally encourages all their memographers to see themselves: as a sterile, invisible instrument inserted into yesterday and removed with a sample for examination.

You'll sit back in your armchair and brace yourself for a slippery entrance. Your suit will handle any stability issues, but still the idea of being on ice feels disempowering.

You'll emerge right by the café and Myna will be leaning against its walls, dressed in a dark purple pressure suit dotted with white, as if she's wearing the Europa sky itself.

"That's not standard issue, is it?" you'll say, once you find the right frequency.

"I find you can hardly standardize any issue in this profession."

You'll laugh as you take a step toward her. She'll bend a bit to reach for your hand and will slide you over to her as she grabs it. You'll feel the muted clink of glass in your ears as she rests her helmet on yours in an embrace.

"I missed you, in the in-between," she'll say.

"How long has it been for you?" you'll ask.

After a shrug, she'll maneuver you around and set you both off streaking down the rough icy surface. Even by this year, the once-primed smoothened surface areas will be left in a state of disrepair as the Moon wrestles with the gravity of its insatiable abuser.

When you get to a large shank of ice you'll stop and rest, but she'll begin climbing atop it, so you'll feel obligated to follow.

"It's hard to believe," she'll say, surveying the small settlement, "that this all ends up embedded in ice in just a few years."

"I don't think it's hard to believe," you'll scoff. "They built a settlement on tectonically active ice."

"Maybe not logically, but look at it all," Myna will say, pointing at the grey wedged-shaped buildings bolted to the ice. "Can you imagine? One day all evidence of this community might get churned through the ice sheets and wind up sinking into the ocean."

"Like a shipwreck, just waiting for capable looters."

She won't respond and when you turn and look at her she'll be staring at you with a serious face and you'll suddenly remember that she's a person outside yourself whom you know less about than you might feel you do, and that you can harm and offend her with callous missteps.

"I'm sorry, I didn't mean that we're looters. I just—"

She'll stop you with a smile and you'll relax back into yourself.

"Come, I've got a surprise for you," she'll say as she takes your hand and leaps off the ice mound. She'll guide you behind a small icy mountain where you'll find a ship waiting. She'll see you hesitate to even approach the ship.

"It's fine," she'll say. "You know as well as I do that Temporally will pull us before we can cause any timeline interference."

"And getting caught committing an infraction is comforting, why?"

She'll sigh through your helmet comms. "Don't you ever wonder if you're important enough to really make a dent in the timeline?"

You'll just stare at the ship for a moment. You'll have spent so much time training for infraction prevention, that you'll never second-guess the threat you pose.

"I just meant, we aren't going to break the universe. Relax."

You won't relax, but you'll ease a bit, because you just don't know if you can handle seeing any disappointment in her face again.

It'll be a short trip to the orbital bubble hovering below Jupiter's southern pole. You will have flown by and gawked at Jupiter's colossal swirling storms, but this will be the first time you'll see the gem-like blue spirals at the south pole.

As soon as you enter the orb you float up and stare at the sunlit half of the clouds. You'll feel a strange sense of calm as you watch the clouds fold into one another seemingly endlessly.

"Amazing," you'll say without looking away, "that something that's constantly changing could constantly look the same."

"An illusion," she'll say, floating up next to you. "Nothing is ever staying the same. We take for granted that, from a distance, we can remain ignorant about the pain and suffering experienced by others as the universe grinds at the thin membranes encasing them."

You'll turn and look at her, wanting to kiss her, but realize you're still in your pressure suit. You'll watch her hair radiating out from her scalp as she reaches over to unlatch your helmet.

As soon as it's out of the way, you'll pull her close and kiss her as hard as you can. This is the first time you're together in zero-g and it makes you forget she's taller than you, which, for some reason, makes you feel the need to be dominant. But it only lasts a moment before you'll be melting in her arms and letting her take the lead.

And so she'll make love to you in that orbital bubble as it swings around those sapphire clouds. It won't be the only time you have sex on this trip, but for her it'll be the most memorable because it's the only time you come simultaneously and for just that moment she'll feel like she's not done anything wrong. That suddenly a part of the universe that she has no control over has synced with her existence and she no longer feels out of step.

It'll be fleeting though, because a few days later, as you make your way back to Europa to begin working on that Memie of Malvay Tolson, Temporally will pull you back. You'll reach for Myna as you feel yourself dissociate. You won't be able to touch her, but you'll hear her voice on your comm whisper, "ChandOrb, 2143, under Ghazi's Lal Shamiana," as the view of your study begins to seep back in.

You're not sure why she thinks you'll ever be allowed to dip again, because you'll assume the next time you see her will be during an infraction hearing.

But then you'll notice the emergency callback notifications pulsing in your periphery. You'll pull it forward and see the urgent messages from Topor Hospital.

You'll tear off your pressure suit and run through the

house looking for Ilkay and Olma, but it'll be empty. You'll rush out front and board a TransitPod to the hospital.

The desk attendant will try to keep you calm as he waits for someone to escort you to the emergency ward. When they finally lead you to a room in the back, you won't recognize the face of the person they've brought you to see, but you'll know who it is.

You won't remember this later, but you'll scream and shout and beg and plead for someone to tell you what is going on. A doctor will finally come in and you'll squeeze your eyes shut to see if you can, by sheer force of will, dip back eighteen hours to when the doctor says the seal on Ilkay's construction lift shattered and left him momentarily exposed to the Martian atmosphere. You'll open your eyes and take a deep breath as the doctor tells you how lucky Ilkay is to have survived, unlike some of his colleagues on the lift.

You'll relax and look at Ilkay's bruised face as the doctor tells you that this will all heal. But you'll tense again as they list the damage to organs you're not entirely sure you could point to.

"My love," you'll say, resting your head next to Ilkay after the doctor leaves, "I'm sorry I wasn't here. I won't ever leave your side again."

And for seven years you won't. Months later, Ilkay will have mostly recovered and will gradually return to work, but you'll still refuse any new Temporally requests. I'm not certain if this will be your way of coping with the fear of something going wrong while you're away. Or if you'll just feel the need to punish yourself for leaving on a lie.

Ilkay will encourage you to return to work at first, but eventually you'll convince him that you've lost your passion for it. That the passion was drying up even before this all happened. That you'd been wanting to take a break and just focus on raising Olma and that this was just the sign you needed to be more decisive.

I'll continue to come and care for Olma when you and Ilkay want to get away. And often, I'll come around unannounced, with biscuits for tea and we'll sit and talk for hours about the harmless trouble Olma will cause and the lives we've all come to build on Mars.

Zaneel will pester me each time I visit you, to see if I've learned anything new about your great-grandfather. For someone so obsessed about encrypting their own time-life, they will have little qualms about being so invasive. But I'll assure him I'll venture off to search for what he wants as soon as I've lived what I want.

Sometimes I'll ask you about Temporally, and I think you can tell that I'm less convinced than Ilkay that you truly were ready to quit. But, I never press you on it. Instead I'll just listen to you tell stories about clients that should definitely remain quiet. And this is why I'm still not sure you'll ever understand what your great-grandfather's work was really about.

When Olma is seventeen he'll present you with his acceptance letter to ChandOrb University. You'll have helped him with his applications, but you'll still yelp in certain disbelief that he's grown up so quickly. Over the years you'll have gradually steered him away from a life in memography and into a more fruitful pursuit, like atmospheric reconstruction.

But, you'll become anxious thinking about taking him to the Moon. The next afternoon you'll collapse into your suitcase as you have a full-blown panic attack. Ilkay will insist he can take him, but you can't imagine being apart from both of them for two weeks. So, you'll ask me to take him instead.

I will be reluctant to leave you and Mars and the carefully tuned enclave I've carved for myself there. But I'll be thrilled to get this time to connect with Olma one on one for a few weeks.

While we're gone, you'll stare at your Temporally equipment, trying to resist the memory of Myna whispering "…ChandOrb, 2143…" as it swirls repeatedly in your head. With Olma grown, you'll worry you'll forget what it means to be useful and that once you're no longer of use to anyone else, you won't be of use to yourself either. So, you reactivate your Temporally account and set up some new targets.

It'll take you a week to figure out all the new Temporally processes, but when you do, you'll refine your targeting toward people who have a tendency toward connoisseurship. As much as you've avoided paying attention, you'll know that Temporally's DipDrones are all the rage, so you'll only be sought after by those with expensive and detail-oriented tastes.

Eventually, you'll hear from Rupaz Sampa, who'd love a view of their great-great-great-great-grandparent's wedding outfits. All five days' worth.

It won't be until you're mid dip that you'll suddenly worry that you've aged beyond recognition, or attraction. You'll wonder if you should have been more patient and enhanced yourself cosmetically before leaving.

When you emerge, you'll be on a promenade balcony, overlooking the top of the Ghazi's Red Shamiana. You'll throw your beige sherwani on top of your dip suit and run down the green glass stairs.

Inside the shamiana, a crowd will be bustling around a buffet. Laughs of elaborately dressed guests talking over one another will brew into a cacophony of sound spilling over the whole scene.

You'll wander around, doing your best to look like you belong. Kids will play on the low-g dance floor, while a photographer tries to get just one shot of the bride, groom and their friends all smiling and looking at the camera at the same time. Even at this point, this kind of photography is an obsolete practice, but you'll appreciate the desire to maintain a tradition of craft long after necessity disappears.

It's not until the bride and groom stand up that the two peacocks adorning the roof of stage decor will catch your gaze. You'll laugh, because you're certain that this is a detail Myna brought you here to see.

After wandering around the entire shamiana several times you'll admit to yourself something might be wrong. You'll calmly exit and stroll along the brightly lit ChandOrb promenade. But she won't be there either. There's a bench under a terra vista and you'll lie there and stare up at the white clouds swirling over Earth.

The Moon's orbit will be above the South Asian subcontinent and you'll close your eyes and remember the blues and greens of the peacock that shimmered in the sunlight as Myna stalked it. Beads of sweat will emerge from your forehead and slide into your graying hair as you wonder if this is what you were to her. A beautiful creature to stalk and toy with for a while, before moving on with life. If this is the reason why you always met in dips and never at home, in your own timeline.

As you feel the tears seep out of your eyelids you take a deep breath and walk back down to get to work on your Memie.

A few years after this trip, they'll recall your Temporally equipment, but you'll still sit in your armchair sometimes, squeezing your eyes shut tight, hoping you'll somehow end up in a dip again.

Once, as you clench your fists around the wilting armrest, you'll think you hear a voice whisper, "I'm sorry," and you'll gasp and open your eyes. Your shock won't be entirely unwarranted, because I won't normally come in there.

"Aqsa!" you'll say as you get up to hug me, but I'll insist you sit down. I'll pull up a chair beside you and look you in your milky, aging eyes before saying, "I'm sorry you weren't ever able to find her."

"Why," you'll say, clearing your dry throat, "did you wait until now to say something?"

"Probably the same reason you never said anything."

"It was difficult," you'll say, patting my head gently, "stifling my curiosity and remaining willfully ignorant. But the risk of losing you to an infraction made it well worth it."

You'll lift my chin and look into my watering eyes before saying, "Just tell me, beti, before you go," you'll take a deep breath, "who *exactly* are you, to me?"

"Your daughter, of course."

You'll smile, a calm and steady smile. I'll be able to see you brimming with questions, but holding back for fear of triggering Temporally too soon. "You certainly got your mother's cavalier attitude. How have you avoided an infraction for so long?"

"Things are different in 2942." I'll stand up and look at the family portrait on your desk. "Timeline infractions that are deemed inconsequential won't get you pulled…" I'll take a deep breath "…if you can pay for them."

As you let yourself piece it together, you'll pause and ask, "What happens to her?"

"I'm afraid sometimes even inconsequential changes lead to… insurmountable debts."

You'll shake your head gently as I continue.

"I think she knew I'd come and watch it happen. I think that's why she stared stoically at the ceiling above the hospital bed as the nurse pulled my newborn body from her arms and handed me to my adoptive parents, who promised Amma they'd keep me safe from Zaneel."

You'll nod gently, hoping that a more subtle realization will slow any infractions. "What will it be that he wants hidden so badly?"

"I couldn't tell you, even if I knew. But he's so convinced Khursheed par-dada is the key that he went through great lengths to scheme me into existence. When Amma refused to hand me over, he let her drown in her debts."

You'll be sobbing as you take my hands and hold them to your cheeks.

"Before they took her, the Temporally retrievers asked her once more if she was certain that it was her life and not mine that she wanted to return to the void. She looked somewhere past them and said, 'She is the universe, pierced through my membrane. With or without her I am already lost. So please, let her life shine so brightly and beautifully that those around her will be too blinded to see the pain.'

"I wanted to unveil myself and enter the scene and stop her, but I knew any infractions would just add to our family debt. So, I just watched as her body blurred and she silently faded from my future."

When I look up, you'll be clutching your ears, as if you're not certain you wanted to know what the future holds.

"If Temp credits were no object," I'll ask you, fiddling with the bracelet on my left arm, "would you want to bring her back?"

You'll study my face until you understand.

"No. I couldn't." You'll wrap me in a hug. "Like she said, you're the universe. You're too important to me, to our family."

I'll smile, but I won't be satisfied with your answer, because I'll know that you'll have had time to get over the trauma of loss.

But you haven't experienced any of it, yet. So, my question to you is: will you let me live or will you send me into the abyss of inexistence?

A LETTER TO MERLIN

Theodora Goss

Theodora Goss (www.theodoragoss.com) is the World Fantasy, Locus, and Mythopoeic Award-winning author of the short story and poetry collections *In the Forest of Forgetting*, *Songs for Ophelia*, and *Snow White Learns Witchcraft*, as well as novella *The Thorn and the Blossom*, debut novel *The Strange Case of the Alchemist's Daughter*, and sequels *European Travel for the Monstrous Gentlewoman*, and *The Sinister Mystery of the Mesmerizing Girl*. She has been a finalist for the Nebula, Crawford, and Shirley Jackson Awards, as well as on the Tiptree Award Honor List. Her work has been translated into fifteen languages. She teaches literature and writing at Boston University and in the Stonecoast MFA Program.

MY ENEMY, MY friend:

How many times have I written you this letter? More than ten, perhaps more than twenty. The first time I was sent here, I did not write to you, nor the second time. It was not until the third time that I realized what you must be, where you must have come from. The third time, I wrote to you, from this same desk under this same window. Perhaps I have written to you more than thirty times, I don't know. I have lost count of how many times I have lived this life.

Below me in the courtyard, gray doves are walking back and forth in the herb garden, among beds of thyme and tarragon, marjoram and rosemary. The bushes are softer now, no longer neat and trim as they were earlier in the year. In autumn, everything gets a bit straggly except the lavender, which has just been harvested. The nuns walk back and forth, going about their tasks like gray doves themselves. I like them, these women of God, in their neat habits, with their kind, worn faces. They have been kind to me. They do not judge the disgraced queen.

No matter what else happens in this life, it always ends here, in what will someday become Glastonbury, between these stone walls. To be honest, I have come to welcome these quiet years, in which I can grow old and remember.

IT WAS THE third time that I began to suspect you were like me, an interloper, a—what shall I call us? An implant, an insertion? I would use the term secret agent, but I do not know where you are from, exactly. In your timeline, were there governments and corporations to spy on each other? Surely there were. Surely those are endemic to late humanity.

Every time I wake in this body, I breathe deeply. The air here is pure, almost effervescent. It is air a thousand years before factories, and it affects me like wine. Feeling a little drunk, I get up and look in the mirror to find this now-familiar face looking back at me, achingly young and beautiful, with light blue eyes and masses of red hair falling over a linen shift. The beauty is important— it is what will make him fall in love with me, and later facilitate my betrayal.

Do you know that already, on the first day—that I will betray him? When I walk down the steps to the great hall in my blue peplos, with my hair in a long braid down my back, a gold circlet on my brow, and they announce the arrival of Princess Guinevere, do you already know? Do you ever feel sick in your stomach, knowing that the man standing beside you, himself achingly young and beautiful, Arthur, king of a small kingdom that he would like to extend by marriage, will die in agony and we will be the instruments of his death? For I hold you culpable, Merlin—as culpable as I am. Did we not come to this place, this time, to enact a tragedy?

DO YOU REMEMBER the flat gray place where they trained us and fed us and kept us, until we could sleep again? Once, I asked the Chronographer where it was. She said the buildings had been military barracks in an ancient war, when the moon had rebelled against the Earth. Sometimes at night I could see the full disk of the barren

Earth, gleaming in the sky.

Nothing relieved the gray of that place—the buildings made of some concrete composite, the bland food (it reminded me most of liver). Those of us who were temporarily awake were different from one another, yet somehow the same—different colors and heights and ages, yet dressed in identical gray garments that reminded me of medical scrubs, our heads filled with dreams. At least the nuns here have white wimples to relieve the monotony of God's uniform.

Sometimes, in the waking intervals, I made friends. There was a woman named Melina 9—she and I became close for a while. She had also come from North America, although the western coast, before San Francisco sank beneath the waves. Her specialty was assassinations. She said she had poisoned kings, shot presidents. She once told me, "I wish they would stop giving me Lucretia Borgia." But we have little choice of where we go, what life we are given. Once we develop a specialty, we are sent back again and again. How many times have you been Merlin?

If I had a choice, would I come here time after time? Would I continue to play Guinevere? Yes. I would, for him, for those early years.

THE FIRST TIME I saw him, I thought it must be a trick of the light that he seemed to shine more brightly than anyone else in the great hall of Cameliard. Even you,

Merlin, with your long gray beard and imposing robes embroidered with stars, were a pale figure beside the young king. He seemed to burn like a flame.

How much of that early love was me, how much Guinevere? The underlying Guinevere, the seventeen-year-old into whose mind I had been inserted, like a cuckoo's egg into a nest, to hatch and take over? Another word for us, I suppose, is usurper. Or parasite. I could feel her there, the pampered daughter of King Leodegrance who had never been denied anything. Privileged, pious, a little vain, a little scared of life, fundamentally conservative. Ten years later, would she betray her husband? I was here to make certain she did.

And there he was before me, standing in the sunlight. Then my father was presenting me, with the air of one showing a prized heifer he was about to offer for sale—the price being an alliance between Cornwall and England, or whatever we are to call Arthur's kingdom, that loose conglomeration of Angles and Britons and Celts that was eventually to stretch from Rheged to the Atlantic. We may as well call it England, although that name will not be spoken for centuries.

Did she love him, that Guinevere? She must have been infatuated and gratified—he was a king, he was handsome, his brown hair short in the Roman fashion, although like most men after the withdrawal of the legions he wore a short beard. He must have increased her sense of her own worth. If she was a prize heifer, she was an expensive one. And I-in-Guinevere, did I love him then? Not the first time. It was only after a lifetime of walks in the palace garden, of riding through the forests around Camelot and conversations at night in our bedroom, a lifetime of him calling me Ginny, that I loved him. The second time, when I saw him again, I almost burst into tears. But we do not break character, do we, Merlin?

WHERE WERE YOU born? When were you born? How did your world end?

I was born in New Cleveland, on the north side, near the Towers—a cluster of government projects that jutted into the brown sky. They had been built for the working class when Old Cleveland was leveled and the new city was built, farther inland, away from the encroaching waters of what was then called Lake Erie. The middle class had moved to the gentrified neighborhoods of the south side, protected by the flood wall, or into the Columbus suburbs. The wealthy who had once lived in those suburbs had long ago decamped to the orbiting stations, to enjoy filtered air and a simulated world. I was told there were artificial windows looking out onto a blue sky with white clouds. I had never seen such a sky myself. The tops of the Towers were wreathed in perpetual smog. From our windows, halfway up, all I could see was a landscape of rust and iron. When I was a child and the pollution was not so bad, we could sometimes see the lights of Copernicus City, until the Great Recession hit and the lunar settlements were abandoned.

Both of my parents died in the second wave of Black Spot, leaving me and my sister Angelina. A woman from Child Welfare, Delilah Watson, said there was no more room in the orphanages. She helped me apply for guardianship of Angie and got me a FlexCare account with a dependent child allowance so we could buy groceries in the supermarket on the fifth floor or the bodegas at ground level. Delilah had been born in Detroit and told me what it had been like before the waters of the Huron Sea closed over it. She made sure the Housing Cred for the apartment was transferred to my name, and I arranged with a man named Johnny Duvall that no one would try to take it away from us. You had to pay for protection in the Towers, one way or another. Johnny had an old-fashioned notion of chivalry. He was rapacious with honor, not much different than most of Arthur's knights.

Angie went to the Towers school, next to what had once been a community center but now housed the homeless who were too sick or drug-addled to apply for FlexCare, or Housing Credit, or any of the other benefits that, thanks to Delilah, were coded into my FlexBand, which mostly worked except when we had rolling internet blackouts. On the north side, I could never be sure when my FlexBand or Angie's tablet would connect. I had just turned seventeen, so I dropped out of school and started working as a waitress at a restaurant on the south side, which paid in cash at the end of each week, although by then the federal government in Chicago was in such disarray that I don't think the IRS would have noticed. Ohio was part of the Secessionist movement, convinced it would be better for the northern states to ally themselves with Canada and form a North American Union.

Does any of this sound familiar? Are you from my disaster or another? There were so many, the Chronographer told me. Humanity, she said in her dry, clipped, precise voice, has an infinite appetite for self-destruction. The details are boringly repetitive: war, famine, pestilence.

It was pestilence that got me in the end, despite the yearly vaccinations. I made sure Angie and I got whatever the government was offering that year, wherever it came from—we all knew Indian vaccines were the best, but after the famines, we could rarely get them. Anyway, that year's Black Spot was a new and more virulent variety. It came in a shipment of bananas from the USSA—there had been a bad outbreak in Ecuador. It hit on the East Coast first—Virginia, Kentucky, Tennessee, all around the Gulf of Carolina—then made its way inland. Once I started coughing, once I had difficulty catching my breath, there was no need to see a doctor, even if we could afford one. We knew what an X-ray would show: the telltale black spots on my lungs. I went into the bedroom where our parents had died, shut the door, and told Angie to keep out. It was all I could do for her.

One night, as I was coughing myself to death, I heard the door open. I was about to shout at Angie, telling her to get out, stay away from me, but it was Delilah Watson. She came and sat on the edge of the mattress.

"Janelle," she said, "I've transferred your FlexCare and the apartment to your sister. You're going to be dead in twenty-four hours. Would you like to save the world?"

HOW DO YOU tell a love story without sounding like one of those old Hollywood movies from before the San Andreas earthquake, especially when you have lived it twenty or thirty times already? My memories are a palimpsest—the first time Arthur and I walked alone together in the apple orchard at Cameliard as a betrothed couple, the second time, the third time. Each time was a little different, as each timeline is a little different. It was like acting in a play that required continual improvisation, although the play was my life—Guinevere's life, stolen by me.

"Lady," he said, "would you really like to be wedded to me? I know the king your father commands it, but I would not wish to wed unless you so desire."

Forgive me, I am trying to translate from early medieval Anglish, for I cannot call it English, into a language that only you and I can understand. By the time it is spoken anywhere in the world, this rough paper, made of beaten linen by the nuns for keeping their household accounts, will long ago have disintegrated. Only the vellum codices of the monks will have survived. I am aware that I sound like a bad edition of Shakespeare. (Once or twice, I was Anne Hathaway. It was a relief being the faithful wife.)

"Yes, your highness," I said, or something like that. "I also desire..." To kiss you again after all the years apart.

338

Of course, I did not think that the first time. I knew only my lines, my duty in this lovely teenage body.

How did I fall in love with him, my husband? It did not happen in those early days in Cornwall. I was still playing a part assigned to me by the great computer, if that's what it is, in the Temporal Observatory—those golden strings stretching upward, each representing a timeline. Strings, threads, cables—I don't know what to call them. Streams of information going up and up, all the information for each timeline stretching upward as far as humanity survives, and then going dark where the information ends. Where humanity has destroyed itself again. Every single string, except one—the only one that stretches into the darkness. The final timeline of humanity.

That first time, I had not been a cuckoo long. It was, I believe, only my fifth assignment. Only my fifth attempt to make the timeline stretch just a little longer. All my roles had been young women, I suppose because the Chronographer thought it would be easier for me. Since then, I have played many roles, of many ages—who knows how old I am now, after so many lifetimes? But my best role remains Guinevere. I play it perfectly so they will send me back again.

My wedding coat was embroidered by three Cornish women, like the three fates, and took two months to complete. It was covered with stylized flowers—lilies for purity, roses for love. Nothing like it had been seen before in Cornwall, and some of the ladies-in-waiting whispered that it was a Frankish fashion. As we stood over my marriage contract, while my father signed it, I could see my beauty reflected in Arthur's eyes. He was not in love with me yet either—perhaps with the princess of Cornwall, but not with me.

On our wedding night, I realized he was not much more experienced than I was. After all, he had spent his life trying to stay alive as the bastard son of King Uther and then consolidating his kingdom. He was only twenty-three, but looked older. He had fought battles, led men. There had been no time for gentler things. We had to find those together, create them between us.

Nights sitting by the fire at the castle in Camelot, he would say, "Ginny, tell me a story, something Cornish. A fairy tale, or something with giants." I would reach into her memory, or remember something in the databases I had studied at the Library, when I was learning as much as I could about early 6th-century Britain—sometimes I could not tell the difference. Which was my mind, which hers? And I would tell him a story. Halfway through, he would close his eyes, tired out from the endless negotiations of being king over a fractious kingdom. I would stroke his hair, his eyebrows, run my finger down his nose. The tenth time, the fifteenth time, I would think, *Remember this, when you believe I have been unfaithful. Remember me like this, when our world has fallen apart.*

I remember a conversation we had in Camelot. The barons were being particularly obstreperous, fighting each other rather than banding together against the Saxon settlements in the south, as Arthur wanted. He knew the threat they posed—they had been mercenaries settled there by the Romans, and made regular incursions into Arthur's kingdom. I could not tell him that one day, Angles and Saxons would fight together against the French.

"Go to the people," I said.

He looked at me, confused.

"Go directly to the people. As the Roman senators did."

Thank you, Merlin, for giving him a classical education. I saw a light in his eyes at the idea that he could bypass the quarreling barons and speak directly to the populace. It became the cornerstone of his diplomacy. This was the early middle ages, after all, before feudalism had really taken hold. Britannia was still an island of opinionated freemen. If he could get the people behind him, the barons would have no choice but to follow.

Sometimes he would stroke my hair back from my forehead and look at me with such love in his eyes that I felt as though I might drown in it. "When I married you, Ginny, I received so much more than I expected. My wife, my love, my queen." And then he would kiss me, so tenderly, so completely, as though his soul was in that kiss.

Yes, I could not help thinking. *You got two in one, what a bargain.* Guinevere and Janelle. The beautiful Cornish princess and the implant from a world in which representative democracy had already failed, where the rich lived in space while the people coughed and stumbled at ground level through brown fog, unheeded and unheard. Forgive me if I sound bitter. I know that he loved me in her, and yet he also loved her in me—her beauty, her grace, her gentility. He would not have loved me as a waitress from the north side of New Cleveland.

Once, I asked one of the librarians what the hosts we entered experienced—whether the underlying Guinevere was aware of me. "Only as part of herself," came the answer. "You nudge her toward different actions, different decisions. You are like an impulse in her mind, a sort of conscience telling her what to choose. But she has no access to your thoughts, if that's what you're asking."

Did he love her or me? I suppose it does not, in the end, make much of a difference.

This is what I remember, this is why I am glad and relieved to be sent back, time after time: sitting together in the garden at Camelot, my ladies-in-waiting sent away for an hour, him reading to me from an ancient, precious scroll from his foster-father's library, where Ector saved all the Roman literature he could, while I embroider some random piece of knightly regalia. That, I learned from Guinevere—you cannot learn embroidery from a database. Or at night, lying together in bed by candlelight with my head on his shoulder, his fingers tangled in my hair, talking about his childhood wandering through the forests with Kay, learning to be a knight. Him turning to me, saying, "Make love with me, Ginny." Both of us forgetting politics for a while. Those private moments away from the court and its constant bickering—among knights for precedence, among their ladies for flirtatious attention.

We had seven years. It is those seven years I am glad to come back for.

The first time, I did not understand why you avoided and seemed to dislike me. I understood the rest of Arthur's family, his inner circle. His foster brother Kay resented that as queen, I was a new locus of power at court. I came between him and the absolute control he held over the royal household as Arthur's steward. His half-sister Morgan, in her rare appearances at Camelot, resented me for the same reason she resented Arthur. After all, Uther had seduced her mother. She had no love for her young half-brother, and I was simply an extension of him, no more important in her eyes than the spoon with which he ate his soup. Her dislike for me was almost a reflex. She was always a direct, practical sort of person, interested only in power and how she could obtain it. Arthur's nephews, Gawain and Gaheris, both liked and looked up to me, the way teenage boys will idealize an older woman who is comfortably out of their reach. I might as well have been a film star. As for Mordred—I don't wish to write about Mordred, Arthur's son and murderer.

But you—why did you seem to be my enemy? It puzzled me, that first time. Of course I know now. We are alike in so many ways, Merlin. You loved him too, as a teacher loves his brightest and most promising pupil. Neither of us wanted to be the agent of his destruction.

Seven years. That's what we had, Arthur and I, before he arrived—the Breton knight who would later become Lancelot. I might as well call him by that name. I might as well call us all by the names we will be given in the stories. After all, what matters in the end is the legend we created, isn't it, Merlin, Myrddin, whoever you are? The truth was burned to the ground with Camelot, and out of it grew a tree called the Matter of Britain, and what does it matter how our names were spelled in the beginning?

Have I mentioned yet that once, in another Camelot, I was Jacqueline Kennedy? It was not my best role. I am not good at playing the grieving widow.

We had seven years of love and happiness. Seven years before I had to betray my king, my love, my husband.

IT WAS THE third time, as I have said, that I began to suspect you. Arthur was in Mercia, subduing another rebellion. At midnight, I was supposed to meet Lancelot in the chapel, where we would declare our love and make plans to flee Camelot together. He would enter through the chapel door as though to pray. I would sneak in through a back door that opened directly into the sacristy. I had done this twice already, in two different timelines. But this time, the door was locked. The key was missing.

What was I to do? This script had been written long ago—I had only to play my part. But suddenly, I had lost my cue.

That was when you appeared in the stone hall, by the light of my flickering candle, with the key in your hand. "The priest left this in his vestments," you said, handing it to me. I was so astonished that I could not say anything.

Without another word, you disappeared into the darkness.

That was when I wrote you my first letter—I mean, after my plans with Lancelot were discovered, after I was tried for adultery and almost burned at the stake, after I retired to this abbey. I remembered something I had almost forgotten, a small detail from the databases in the Library— that Merlin was supposed to live backwards through time. And I started to wonder.

I no longer wonder. I am certain. In the seventh lifetime, you brought me a letter from Lancelot that his squire had accidentally dropped in the courtyard. In the twelfth or thirteenth, I don't remember which, you tripped the servant who would have lit my pyre too soon and burned me to a crisp before Lancelot arrived. Time after time, you have corrected glitches in the system, places where the script did not work for one reason or another. You have untangled knots in the timeline.

In other words, my friend, my enemy, you are like me. You are of the tribe of cuckoos.

Tell me if this is true. I have sent you this letter so many times. Each time, I am patient—I wait to write it until we have both fulfilled our tasks. Yesterday, I received news that my beloved is dead and Camelot has fallen again. So write to me, Merlin. Just once, acknowledge my letter. Reply.

"WHY?" I ASKED the Chronographer the first time I met her in the Observatory.

I had already seen the training videos, already been

shown the chamber of sleepers—hundreds of them floating in oval tanks that nourished their bodies while their consciousnesses were lost in time, inhabiting the bodies of Genghis Khan, Marlene Dietrich, or countless men and women whose names were no longer remembered but whose actions had changed their timelines in some small but important way.

"Janelle 13," our receptionist had said, "you might be interested to see your recruiter, Delilah Watson, or as she is known here, Ifeoma 7. You will find that you perform best in certain roles. You will develop an affinity for certain eras, genders, nationalities, professions. But Ifeoma 7 can become anyone, at any time. She is equally good as Nefertiti and Sir Francis Drake. Only the best are asked to become recruiters."

I looked down into the tank before me, shaped like an egg and filled with some sort of gel in which floated the woman named Ifeoma 7, her eyes closed in sleep. I did not recognize her. Her skin was darker than Delilah's, and she was younger, more muscular, with long braids of hair floating around her bare shoulders. I looked at all the oval tanks in that room, as large as a sports stadium. Each one was filled with a sleeper living a different life. I could not imagine being one of them.

Someone in our small group of recruits asked a question, but it was in a language I did not understand—at that time I did not speak Mandarin, and even now my understanding is only elementary. The receptionist answered in that language, then explained to the group in two other languages before she said, "Hoda 2 and Janelle 13, Xiang 27 wanted to know about the recruiting process. I told him that each recruiter identifies suitable candidates for this type of work. Intelligent, practical, adaptable, able to put the needs of others before their own—and about to die. At the moment of their death, with their prior permission of course, the recruiter transfers their consciousness here. Only consciousness, what some might call the soul, can cross the barrier between timelines, and only at the moment of physical dissolution. It's difficult to find the right sort of person, particularly from late enough in the timeline to understand the technology we use here. From each timeline, we are able to recruit only two or three candidates. So you see, each of you is precious to us. We have tried to replicate your previous bodies as closely as possible based on your genetic code, although they are not entirely biological. I hope they are satisfactory. They will age very slowly, and there are no pathogens here, but it is possible to injure them. Please tell one of us if you require medical care. In the meantime, we still have a lot to do. Later today you will each meet with the Chronographer—I suppose you could call her the CEO of this place. Tomorrow you will begin your training."

"Training in what, exactly?" asked Hoda 2. I could not place her accent—she told me later that she came from the Republic of Ghana, during the Great Migration that followed the water wars.

"In repairing the timelines," said the receptionist.

"Saving humanity."

"Why do the timelines need to be repaired?" I asked the Chronographer, later that afternoon. The training videos had been technical. They had not answered that question.

"Come, I'll show you," she said, waving me forward. We reached a central console and walked around the circular room, whose perimeter was filled with golden threads rising up, up into the darkness. Hundreds of them, perhaps thousands. She stopped.

"This is your timeline," she said. It looked no different to me than any of the others—like a fiber-optic cable, flickering along its entire length as it rose toward the distant ceiling, stopping several meters above my head. "We have already extended it twice. Originally, it was destroyed in 1956, during the Cold War. You and your sister could be born because a sleeper named Xandi 11 decided not to push a button when he was ordered. We will never send you back into that timeline—no one ever re-enters their own timeline. But there are other timelines, with other Janelles and Angelinas. The work you do here may allow those other Janelles and Angelinas to live. It may give them clear skies and clean water so their parents do not die of Black Spot. It may prevent the Northern Secession. Angelina may not have to fight or die at the Battle of Ottawa. Each time we make an insertion into the timeline, we try to keep humanity alive a little longer." She looked around at all the golden timelines with a weary look on her face. I wondered how old she was—she looked both ancient and ageless.

"Who is we?" I asked. "I mean, who are you? Those of you who are not us—not recruits." I felt as though I had walked into a science fiction movie. "Are you aliens?"

She looked surprised, then broke into a laugh. It made her sound much younger. "There are no aliens. In all the millennia that human beings have survived on Earth and the moon, and briefly on Mars, no alien intelligences have introduced themselves. Perhaps they're avoiding us—I would not blame them. As far as we know, in the darkness of space and time, there is only us." She frowned and gestured at all the golden threads. "Us, destroying ourselves again and again. We—that is, myself and the receptionists who showed you around, the librarians you will meet later, the technicians who keep this place running, all of us working here in the Temporal Observatory, inhabit the last timeline of humanity. Look." She pointed upward, and I could see one golden thread rising above the others, disappearing into the darkness. "We are flickers of light, bits of information dancing at the top of that column. And soon we too will be gone. We have learned to extend our physical lives, but we no longer reproduce. No children have been born in a thousand years. When we die, humanity will be over. The universe will go on without us." Her voice was sad.

"How many of you are there?" I asked.

"Less than three hundred."

I was silent. Here we were, in an ancient military barracks on the moon, high above the uninhabitable Earth. Less than three hundred human beings remained in the universe. This was all that was left of humanity.

* * *

I wish I could ask a favor of you, Merlin. I know you were there at the last moment of Arthur's life, when he lay in the mud after the Battle of Camlann, killed by Mordred's sword. I know you will be there again, in the next lifetime. At that moment, I wish you could lean down and say to him, "Guinevere loved you every moment of this life, and she will love you again in the next, and the next, and the next," as many times as they send me back here. But you would not do that, and I will not ask you to. We both have our duty to do, you and I. All I dare, in this lifetime, is to send you this letter, now that our tasks are done and we are waiting for death to free our souls again. Please, if you can, write back to me. This time, next time, the time after, send me a reply so I know that you understand. I need someone, in all the golden streams of time, to understand that I loved him and will love him, as long as humanity lasts.

Or perhaps we will find each other in the Observatory. There is only a small chance that we will be awake at the same time and recognize each other. And after all, perhaps you are not one Merlin but two or three. Perhaps there are a number of sleepers who have been you. But I persist in believing that, lifetime to lifetime, you recognize me. When you awake, come find me—ask for Janelle 13.

I must go to compline. The nuns are waiting for their Abbess, the final role I play in this place and time. I shall walk through the herb garden, scattering gray doves, and crush a bit of thyme or sage between my fingers to inhale the sharp fragrance. Perhaps there will be a final sprig of lavender fallen on the path. Only such small pleasures are left to me—but they are enough.

The next time I see you again, I will be seventeen years old. You will stand beside Arthur in the great hall of Cameliard and stare at me disapprovingly as I curtsey to my future husband, thinking of the days to come, when for a little while I will once again be with my love.

Until then, affectionately,

Guinevere

DEAD POETS

Carrie Vaughn

Carrie Vaughn's (www.carrievaughn.com) work includes the Philip K. Dick Award-winning novel *Bannerless*, the *New York Times* bestselling Kitty Norville urban fantasy series, over twenty novels and upwards of one hundred short stories, two of which have been finalists for the Hugo Award. Her most recent work includes a pair of novellas about Robin Hood's children, *The Ghosts of Sherwood* and *The Heirs of Locksley*. She's a contributor to the Wild Cards series of shared world superhero books edited by George R. R. Martin and a graduate of the Odyssey Fantasy Writing Workshop. An Air Force brat, she survived her nomadic childhood and managed to put down roots in Boulder, Colorado.

I say someone in another time will remember us.

– Sappho, trans. Diane J. Rayor

THE STUDY OF literature is the process of continually falling in love with dead people.

A sentence can do it. A well-turned phrase. Nearly all we have of Sappho are well-turned phrases, and she has survived more than twenty-five hundred years on that. I tell my students, you will fall in love with these dead people, copying their poems in your notebooks, memorizing them because you can't help it. You will tell yourself you love the poems, not the poets. But you will love the poets, too.

Even though so many of them were difficult people. Opinionated, prone to locking themselves in rooms, drinking too much, and betraying their long-suffering lovers. We forgive them because of the words. But no matter how much we peel back those words, looking for the people who created them, they're all we have. And it's so easy to fall in love with someone who can't respond, whose difficulties you never have to confront. They can't reject you. They can't cheat on you or hurt you.

You can love an idea of someone to the core of your heart, seal that idea in amber, sink it in a well of longing, and never suffer any consequences. You will get tenure for the dispassionate papers you write and congratulate yourself that at least you were able to turn that love into a career. You understand that your love is for an image, a construct, and that is fine. You tell yourself you're satisfied with that.

* * *

I SNEAK INTO the archeology department lab after hours, and using my credentials I'm able to steal a small package. No, not steal. Borrow. I'm only borrowing it.

Safe at home, door locked, curtains drawn, I open the box, pull away the packing material, and reveal the artifact. It is an ancient kylix: a wide, shallow drinking cup with a sturdy foot and two slender handles. It's in extraordinarily good condition, an example of black-figure pottery, red terracotta with gleaming black images of elegant figures: a woman sitting in a curving chair, her tunic draped in folds. She is holding a lyre. Her expression is intent.

I had examined the cup earlier, at the request of an archeologist who made some speculation and wanted an unofficial opinion. Just to give my thoughts on the matter. There is no way of knowing for certain. Ancient poets didn't write their names on the bottom of their mugs so they wouldn't get lost in the dishwasher in the department break room. But yes, Sappho would have owned a cup very like this.

I need both hands to hold it. Drinking from it would mimic the motion of drinking from my cupped hands. It is approximately twenty-six hundred years old, and was excavated on the island of Lesbos. I want to believe with all my heart that this cup belonged to Sappho.

This is the point where that irrational love makes one just a little bit crazy. Where one's imagination goes a bit sideways. Where frivolous self-indulgence has made me break a pile of university rules, to bring this cup home.

At a specialty wine dealer I find a Vin Santo, a sweet white wine, from Santorini, the closest I can get to a wine that comes from Lesbos. They're both islands, at least. The grapes that made this wine could not possibly have grown on vines that were alive when Sappho was. It's as close as I can get. I can pretend she would have drunk a wine much like this. I have a clay oil lamp—a modern reproduction, but cast from an ancient example. She might have written at night by the flame of a lamp just like this. Too bad I'm in Boston and not Greece.

The sweet tang of the wine rises up and tickles my nose. The weight of the cup is steadying. The glow from the lantern is warm, flickering, casting shadows on the clutter of books and the cheap drapes closed over the window. I can almost imagine a more atmospheric setting: the courtyard of a villa at night, the texture of a tiled wall.

I put my lips on this two-thousand-six-hundred-year-old piece of pottery and imagine that her lips once touched the rim of this same cup, like a kiss. A sting on the tongue, as the sweet wine hits it.

It's a silly idea, reaching across the centuries to try to touch someone beyond her words. Thrilling, nevertheless. A striking image to share. I'll have to write it down, get a poem or two of my own out of my frivolity.

The light changes. My eyes are closed, but even so I can sense the surge from buttery yellow to bright red. My heart yearns into my throat, the room grows hot, like a sun has come to life in it. The floor opens up and seems to turn into a door and—

* * *

I OPEN MY eyes. I'm standing in a stone room that smells musty. Through a narrow window I can see an overcast sky, fading at dusk. Embers burn in a small fireplace. I shiver, maybe from the cold.

Why am I disappointed that this is not a Greek island? I should be on a sunny Greek island, looking down from a vantage on the edge of a cliff with a view of a distant trireme plying blue Aegean waters. On the warm air drift the gentle notes from a lyre, which I follow to a marble courtyard, where poets have gathered and where she—

I have no reason to expect such a thing. To expect anything but feeling silly, and maybe aghast that I have poured wine into a priceless artifact. But somehow I'm standing in a chilled stone room that might be part of a castle, and there is a man, age thirty or so, lying on a cot in the corner. He seems dramatic, flung back, arm draped over his face. He's wearing a loose linen shirt, an unlaced doublet, rumpled breeches, and is stocking-footed.

My academic brain tells me his clothes are from 16th-century England. Given the scant furnishings in the irregularly shaped room, I think he might be a prisoner. A high-ranking prisoner, entitled to a cot and a fireplace, a table and a jug of something with a cup to drink from, but not much else. The window looks over the castle yard, a river beyond...

Oh. I know where I am.

I have loved many poets in my time. You don't subject

yourself to a Ph.D. in literature without being in love with words, and who made them.

This is ridiculous. I'm furious that I'm here in the Tower of London and not on a beautiful Greek island. I drank Vin Santo from an ancient kylix, not sack from a pewter cup a mere five centuries old.

The cup is still in my hands, the taste of wine still on my tongue. I set it down on the nearby rickety table before I drop it, because my hands are shaking. I rub them together.

Sir Thomas Wyatt still has not moved his arm or apparently noticed the strange woman standing in his cell.

I have to say something. I have to, but my stomach is churning. I know his words, the lines I fell in love with, but I don't know him. I have a lot of questions, but the questions I have when I read his poems sound silly now.

"Um. Hello?"

He starts, flinching back on the cot, pressing his back to the wall.

I'm not sure what he sees when he looks at me. A flushed woman in her thirties in what must seem like very strange clothes to him, striped yoga pants and an oversized sweater, my brown hair pulled back with a ragged headband. His eyes are wide, gleaming.

"A ghost has come to torment me," he says. His voice is... pleasant. A little rough, but clearly from exhaustion and stress. He has a light tenor that probably sounds lovely when he sings. Many of his poems would have been sung, lyrics written to entertain the ladies of court, accompanied by the lute. My knees go a little weak, thinking of him singing.

Sappho's poems were meant to be sung as well, and I suddenly wonder about my attraction to poets who also sang.

It's madness. It's all madness.

"No, I'm not—" But I don't know how to explain, and maybe it's best if he thinks I'm a ghost. "Um. Hi."

This man wrote the first sonnets in English. Within the formal structures of English Renaissance poetry he poured a mountain of emotion. He inserted his own biography into his work, barely dressed in metaphor. If I could ask him anything, say anything—

"What are you?" He shifts to the edge of the cot. His hands clench as if reaching for a sword or knife.

"I don't know what I am," I say. "I think I'm having a dream."

He studies me. "If this is your dream then what am I?"

He is tragic. He is a painting. He is unpeeled from the formality of the era's portraiture, the polished, glowing images with their details of embroidered doublets and gold lace trim. Those serious faces, filled with inscrutable mystery. Or simply the images of people who are bored with sitting for an artist. If they had known how those portraits would live after them, they might have been more interested.

His beard is ragged, but he seems to have one of those faces that gains an alluring edge when it loses its polish.

His dark hair is swept back, a little greasy. A man who has been lying in bed, despairing, for days.

I shake my head a little, wincing, as the history comes back to me, the date and context, along with a sinking feeling. "What day is it? The date?"

"The darkest," he says and moves to the window, leaning against the stone to look out.

He was imprisoned in the Tower because he was one of the men suspected of being Anne Boleyn's lovers. The lore is that he watched her execution from his cell. He wrote a poem about it. *These bloody days have broken my heart...*

"Is it true?" I asked. One of the questions anyone would ask him. He makes a disgusted sigh, and I realize I should have specified. Not *that* question, if he really was one of Anne's lovers. The other one. "Did you see it happen? Some people say you did, and some say you couldn't have, but it's such a good story—"

"It has only just happened, not these few hours past, and there are stories?"

It's been almost five hundred years, I don't say.

"Why should they even speak of me? I am nothing here." He slumps, his gaze still out that window. Riveted by the view, it seems.

"You write about it," I say. "Everyone wants to hear stories of unrequited love, of tragedy. Of irony." Because if Anne had chosen Wyatt, she wouldn't have died here, like this. "It appeals to the sense of the dramatic, to think you watched from your cell."

He chuckles. "To write about it I will have to survive it. That seems unlikely now."

"But you will," I say. "Maybe that's why I'm here. To tell you that you'll survive." A vision. An omen. His dream, not my own. He was imprisoned in the Tower twice and escaped with his life both times. He is charmed.

I'd sit but there isn't an extra chair. His interrogators, Thomas Cromwell and the rest, must have brought their own when they came to speak to him.

He says, "I cannot remember what it was like to be in love with her. All I see now is the blood."

Ink stains his fingers, though there's no paper or anything to write with in the room. I know from his words, all the words of his I've read, that nothing I say will comfort him. I think of all the well-turned sentences this man wrote, that I loved. *I am not he such eloquence to boast to make the crow singing as the swan...*

He glances over. "Everyone loves her, at first. That is her talent. She sweeps her gaze up your body and looks away before she can possibly have the measure of you. It makes you wish to cry after her, wait, look again, see me. Please see me. You want her to look because you want to see her eyes again. Those gem-like eyes. As deep as a mine that is sure to collapse and bury you. But why do I tell you this, you cannot understand what it is to look upon a woman and feel pain."

No one knows what Sappho looked like. If I had a time machine... it's a silly question, a party game. If you had a time machine, where would you go? If I drink from that cup again, maybe I can get to the Greek island this time and learn what Sappho looked like.

"Every man loves her," he says again. "She captures them. And then she leaves them, but still they love her. Even as they hate and curse her, still, they love. But when she captured the king, we were all lost. Fitting, that it took a king to devour her."

This is a man who has spent his life using words, arranging them, making pictures with them, lining them up until they did just what he wished. He did this in a culture that valued the masterful use of words. He takes the skill for granted.

"You don't believe women can love at all, do you?" I ask.

"Of course not," he said. "Women are cold and feel no passion. They torture men because they must, it is their nature. They are driven by devils to ruin us."

Nothing he has said surprises me. It's all right there in his work, the words he wrote. He saw himself as a man brought low by women who mocked his pain.

He turns his back on them and so never sees the longing in their eyes.

"*I say nothing, my tongue broken, a delicate fire runs under my skin, my eyes see nothing, my ears roar...*"

"Yes, just so. Who wrote that? Whose words are those?"

"Sappho. A woman."

"Ahh." He breathes this out, a sigh. "I suppose, then, you want me to reconsider."

"You've had your heart broken, I get it. So have I. We all have."

"And do you write poetry about it?"

"I might," I confess. "Some. It's not any good. And don't tell me it's because women can't write poetry."

"You could perhaps recite for me—"

"No! Just... no." I don't want an impromptu critique from Thomas Wyatt. I might never recover. Not to mention having to explain postmodernism. "It would probably be better if I tried to write about something other than love."

"All poetry is about love," he says. "It can be about court or a journey or a war or God and it is still about love, when passion drives the words. It isn't only women who've broken my heart." He leans against the wall of the Tower, where he has been imprisoned by the councilors of Henry VIII, whom he has served loyally. So many loyal servants died here.

"You keep looking at the window," he says. "Come, and I will tell you what I saw." He shifts aside, to make room. I can't resist, not when I've come so far, and move beside him to see.

There is just enough light to reveal the scene. The wall of the keep encloses the green; on the outer wall beyond the green a guard stands watch.

On the green, the scaffold is still in place, the raised platform allowing all to see the deed. There was no block—Anne Boleyn had been executed by sword. The swordsman would have stood to the side. Where would her head have fallen? Would it have tumbled back? Did anyone worry that it might fly out into the crowd? I don't know anything about these things. There were dozens of eyewitness accounts of the moment. It's said that the coffin they used was too small and so they had to nestle her head by her feet when they carried her away.

I suppose I could ask.

"There is still blood on the dirt," he says. "Do you see it?"

The stretch of gravel before the platform is pale, and if I squint I can see one or two dark spots on the edge. They might just be shadows. It's too dark to see color.

He is at my back. He puts his hands on my shoulders to shift my angle, to see just what he sees. To picture the exact scene. The yard would have been filled with people. I try to imagine the sounds of it.

"Was the crowd silent or did they murmur? Did they cry out?"

"They were quiet. No one has ever executed a queen before. They were thinking of history, but, you see, I loved her. She was never mine, but I did." His breath touches my hair. His hands are still on my shoulders, just resting. How long has it been since he had any human contact?

"They hated her, because of how she made the world turn around her. She would not have fallen so hard, otherwise. She was brave. She did not weep nor beg. But I hoped... I hoped she might look this way, just once."

What else is there to say? "I'm sorry for your loss."

"It is a crime, to mourn the death of a traitor. No one will wear black for her." Wyatt's doublet is black.

I laugh a little. "They'd have to catch me before they could punish me."

He chuckles. His smile is bright, bringing a glint to his eyes. The old portraits never show anyone smiling, so that it's easy to think they never did. His smile changes him. *A delicate fire under my skin...*

He says, "When you go back to whatever spirit realm sent you, might I go with you?"

When I turn, just a shift of my shoulders, he is right there. His face near mine, hands still touching me. His lips part as if to say more, to tell yet again how much and how tragically he loved her. Yes, yes, I want to say, we all know, he can't shut up about it.

He kisses me.

And I let him. My hands grip his arms, his fingers stroke my neck and then tangle in my hair. Does he even see me or is he still looking out the window?

I kiss him back, arms closing around him as he presses me to the wall.

"I don't even know how I got here," I say.

His gaze lights on the kylix, sitting on the table across the room.

It is 1536. I'm trying to remember the dates, the timelines. Renaissance England is my hobby, not the focus of my research. I teach a survey class every other year. I'm trying to remember: what year is it that Wyatt first translates Petrarch from Italian, and introduces the sonnet into English? Is it after 1536?

He can't go, he has too much left to do, and I don't

know if he understands that. He still thinks he's about to die.

There's a knock at the door. Supper, maybe. I don't know how meals work in the Tower. Wyatt flinches back; my eyes go wide. The door is about to open, and so I scramble away from him—

"Wait," he says, reaching. "What is your name—"

But I have already lifted the cup with both hands and drunk down the rest of the wine.

They flee from me that sometime did me seek
With naked foot stalking in my chamber...
It was no dream: I lay broad waking.
But all is turned thorough my gentleness
Into a strange fashion of forsaking...

WYATT NEVER WROTE about ghosts. Not literally, not overtly. Still, all his writing looks different to me now.

Or maybe it's my imagination and it never happened at all. A bad batch of wine.

In my apartment, no time has passed. I'm standing right where I was, with an empty ancient cup in my hands. I'm appalled that I might have done damage to this artifact by pouring actual wine into it, but I'll have to worry about that later. Immediately, I set it down and grab a spiral notebook and pen. I want to remember every moment, every detail, the feel of his beard on my cheek, the sooty smell of the fireplace. The faint light on the green, the longing in his voice when he said he could see the blood there. He was looking for a point of connection, no matter how faint.

I write it all. The great tangled mess of it. There is a struggle, trying to manage the words. Some embarrassment, this falling in love with dead poets. There is confusion: I've fallen in love with a dozen other poets, why not send me to another? To Emily Dickinson, to demystify nearly everything about her. To Frank O'Hara, who never would have loved me back but wouldn't it be nice to just have coffee with him? Why did I meet Wyatt when I wanted to meet Sappho?

Maybe Wyatt needed to hear someone tell him he would live. Maybe this was about him and not me.

I write it all down because it's no hardship to do it. Paper and pen are right there, and the lamp is still burning. In the morning I will pack away Sappho's kylix and return it to the archeology lab before anyone knows it's gone.

"Um. Hi."

My pen smears across the page as I'm startled by the voice. Gasping, I turn in my chair to look behind me.

"Oh! It's you! It's really you!" An intruder stands there, a woman. I hadn't heard her come in, I could have sworn the door never opened. Was I so wrapped up in the work that I wouldn't have noticed? Possible.

I stammer out, "What are you—"

Then I notice. She is holding a clay cup. A Greek kylix. There is a shining drop of wine still on the edge.

TIME GYPSY
Ellen Klages

Ellen Klages (www.ellenklages.com) is the author of three acclaimed MG historical novels: *The Green Glass Sea*, which won the Scott O'Dell Award and the New Mexico Book Award; *White Sands, Red Menace*, which won the California and New Mexico Book Awards; and *Out of Left Field*, which won the Children's History Book Prize and the Ohioana Book Award. Her adult novel, a historical fantasy, *Passing Strange*, won the World Fantasy and British Fantasy Awards in 2018. Her short fiction has been translated into a dozen languages and been nominated for or won multiple Hugo, Nebula, Locus, Mythopoeic, and World Fantasy Awards. "Time Gypsy" was her first published story. Ellen lives in San Francisco, in a small house full of strange and wondrous things.

Friday, February 10, 2006. 5:00 p.m.

As soon as I walk in the door, my office mate Ted starts in on me. Again. "What do you know about radiation equilibrium?" he asks.

"Nothing. Why?"

"That figures." He holds up a faded green volume. "I just found this insanely great article by Chandrasekhar in the '45 *Astrophysical Journal*. And get this—when I go to check it out, the librarian tells me I'm the first person to take it off the shelf since 1955. Can you believe that? Nobody reads anymore." He opens the book again. "Oh, by the way, Chambers was here looking for you."

I drop my armload of books on my desk with a thud. Dr. Raymond Chambers is the chairman of the Physics department, and a Nobel Prize winner, which even at Berkeley is a very, very big deal. Rumor has it he's working on some top-secret government project that's a shoo-in for a second trip to Sweden.

"Yeah, he wants to see you in his office, pronto. He said something about Sara Baxter Clarke. She's that crackpot from the '50s, right? The one who died mysteriously?"

I wince. "That's her. I did my dissertation on her and her work." I wish I'd brought another sweater. This one has holes in both elbows. I'd planned a day in the library, not a visit with the head of the department.

Ted looks at me with his mouth open. "Not many chick scientists to choose from, huh? And you got a postdoc here doing that? Crazy world." He puts his book down and stretches. "Gotta run. I'm a week behind in my lab work. Real science, you know?"

I don't even react. It's only a month into the term, and he's been on my case about one thing or another—being a woman, being a dyke, being close to thirty—from day one. He's a jerk, but I've got other things to worry about. Like Dr. Chambers, and whether I'm about to lose my job because he found out I'm an expert on a crackpot.

Sara Baxter Clarke has been my hero since I was a kid. My pop was an army technician. He worked on radar systems, and we traveled a lot—six months in Reykjavík, then the next six in Fort Lee, New Jersey. Mom always told us we were gypsies, and tried to make it seem like an adventure. But when I was eight, Mom and my brother Jeff were killed in a bus accident on Guam. After that it didn't seem like an adventure anymore.

Pop was a lot better with radar than he was with little girls. He couldn't quite figure me out. I think I had too many variables for him. When I was ten, he bought me dresses and dolls, and couldn't understand why I wanted a stack of old physics magazines the base library was throwing out. I liked science. It was about the only thing that stayed the same wherever we moved. I told Pop I wanted to be a scientist when I grew up, but he said scientists were men, and I'd just get married.

I believed him, until I discovered Sara Baxter Clarke in one of those old magazines. She was British, went to MIT, had her doctorate in theoretical physics at twenty-two. At Berkeley, she published three brilliant articles in very, very obscure journals. In 1956, she was scheduled to deliver a controversial fourth paper at an international physics conference at Stanford. She was the only woman on the program, and she was just twenty-eight.

No one knows what was in her last paper. The night before she was supposed to speak, her car went out of control and plunged over a cliff at Devil's Slide—a remote stretch of coast south of San Francisco. Her body was washed out to sea. The accident rated two inches on the inside of the paper the next day—right under a headline about some vice raid—but made a small uproar in the physics world. None of her papers or notes were ever found; her lab had been ransacked. The mystery was never solved.

I was fascinated by the mystery of her the way other kids were intrigued by Amelia Earhart. Except nobody'd ever heard of my hero. In my imagination, Sara Baxter Clarke and I were very much alike. I spent a lot of days pretending I was a scientist just like her, and even more lonely nights talking to her until I fell asleep.

So after a master's in Physics, I got a Ph.D. in the History of Science—studying her. Maybe if my obsession had been a little more practical, I wouldn't be sitting on a couch outside Dr. Chambers's office, picking imaginary lint off my sweater, trying to pretend I'm not panicking. I taught science in a junior high for a year. If I lose this fellowship, I suppose I could do that again. It's a depressing thought.

The great man's secretary finally buzzes me into his office. Dr. Chambers is a balding, pouchy man in an immaculate, perfect suit. His office smells like lemon furniture polish and pipe tobacco. It's wood-paneled, plushly carpeted, with about an acre of mahogany desk. A copy of my dissertation sits on one corner.

"Dr. McCullough." He closes his laptop and waves me to a chair. "You seem to be quite an expert on Sara Baxter Clarke."

"She was a brilliant woman," I say nervously, and hope that's the right direction for the conversation.

"Indeed. What do you make of her last paper, the one she never presented?" He picks up my work and turns to a page marked with a pale green Post-It. "'An Argument for a Practical Tempokinetics'?" He lights his pipe and looks at me through the smoke.

"I'd certainly love to read it," I say, taking a gamble. I'd give anything for a copy of that paper. I wait for the inevitable lecture about wasting my academic career studying a long-dead crackpot.

"You would? Do you actually believe Clarke had discovered a method for time travel?" he asks. "Time travel, Dr. McCullough?"

I take a bigger gamble. "Yes, I do."

Then Dr. Chambers surprises me. "So do I. I'm certain of it. I was working with her assistant, Jim Kennedy. He retired a few months after the accident. It's taken me forty years to rediscover what was tragically lost back then."

I stare at him in disbelief. "You've perfected time travel?"

He shakes his head. "Not perfected. But I assure you, tempokinetics is a reality."

Suddenly, my knees won't quite hold me. I sit down in the padded leather chair next to his desk and stare at him. "You've actually done it?"

He nods. "There's been a great deal of research on tempokinetics in the last fifty years. Very hush-hush, of course. A lot of government money. But recently, several key discoveries in high-intensity gravitational field theory have made it possible for us to finally construct a working tempokinetic chamber."

I'm having a hard time taking this all in. "Why did you want to see *me*?" I ask.

He leans against the corner of his desk. "We need someone to talk to Dr. Clarke."

"You mean she's alive?" My heart skips several beats.

He shakes his head. "No."

"Then—?"

"Dr. McCullough, I approved your application to this university because you know more about Sara Clarke and her work than anyone else we've found. I'm offering you a once-in-a-lifetime opportunity." He clears his throat. "I'm offering to send you back in time to attend the 1956 International Conference for Experimental Physics. I need a copy of Clarke's last paper."

I just stare at him. This feels likes some sort of test, but I have no idea what the right response is. "Why?" I ask finally.

"Because our apparatus works, but it's not practical," Dr. Chambers says, tamping his pipe. "The energy requirements for the gravitational field are enormous. The only material that's even remotely feasible is an isotope they've developed up at the Lawrence lab, and there's only enough of it for one round trip. I believe Clarke's missing paper contains the solution to our energy problem."

After all these years, it's confusing to hear someone taking Dr. Clarke's work seriously. I'm so used to being on the defensive about her, I don't know how to react. I slip automatically into scientist mode—detached and rational. "Assuming your tempokinetic chamber is operational, how do you propose that I locate Dr. Clarke?"

He picks up a piece of stiff ivory paper and hands it to me. "This is my invitation to the opening reception of the conference Friday night, at the St. Francis Hotel. Unfortunately, I couldn't attend. I was back east that week. Family matters."

I look at the engraved paper in my hand. Somewhere in my files is a Xerox copy of one of these invitations. It's odd to hold a real one. "This will get me into the party. Then you'd like me to introduce myself to Sara Baxter Clarke, and ask her for a copy of her unpublished paper?"

"In a nutshell. I can give you some cash to help, er, convince her if necessary. Frankly, I don't care how you do it. I *want* that paper, Dr. McCullough."

He looks a little agitated now, and there's a shrill undertone to his voice. I suspect Dr. Chambers is planning to take credit for what's in the paper, maybe even hoping for that second Nobel. I think for a minute. Dr. Clarke's will left everything to Jim Kennedy, her assistant and fiancé. Even if Chambers gets the credit, maybe there's a way to reward the people who actually did the work. I make up a large, random number.

"I think thirty-thousand dollars should do it." I clutch the arm of the chair and rub my thumb nervously over the smooth polished wood.

Dr. Chambers starts to protest, then just waves his hand. "Fine. Fine. Whatever it takes. Funding for this project is not an issue. As I said, we only have enough of the isotope to power one trip into the past and back—yours. If you recover the paper successfully, we'll be able to develop the technology for many, many more excursions. If not..." He lets his sentence trail off.

"Other people *have* tried this?" I ask, warily. It occurs to me I may be the guinea pig, usually an expendable item.

He pauses for a long moment. "No. You'll be the first. Your records indicate you have no family, is that correct?"

I nod. My father died two years ago, and the longest relationship I've ever had only lasted six months. But Chambers doesn't strike me as a liberal. Even if I was still living with Nancy, I doubt if he would count her as family. "It's a big risk. What if I decline?"

"Your postdoc application will be reviewed," he shrugs. "I'm sure you'll be happy at some other university."

So it's all or nothing. I try to weigh all the variables, make a reasoned decision. But I can't. I don't feel like a scientist right now. I feel like a ten-year-old kid, being offered the only thing I've ever wanted—the chance to meet Sara Baxter Clarke.

"I'll do it," I say.

"Excellent." Chambers switches gears, assuming a brisk, businesslike manner. "You'll leave a week from today at precisely 6:32 a.m. You cannot take anything—underwear, clothes, shoes, watch—that was manufactured after 1956. My secretary has a list of antique clothing stores in the area, and some fashion magazines of the times." He looks at my jeans with distaste. "Please choose something appropriate for the reception. Can you do anything with your hair?"

My hair is short. Nothing radical, not in Berkeley. It's more like early Beatles—what they called a pixie cut when I was a little girl—except I was always too tall and gawky to be a pixie. I run my fingers self-consciously through it and shake my head.

Chambers sighs and continues. "Very well. Now, since we have to allow for the return of Clarke's manuscript, you must take something of equivalent mass—and also of that era. I'll give you the draft copy of my own dissertation. You will be also be supplied with a driver's license and university faculty card from the period, along with packets of vintage currency. You'll return with the manuscript at exactly 11:37 Monday morning. There will be no second chance. Do you understand?"

I nod, a little annoyed at his patronizing tone of voice. "If I miss the deadline, I'll be stuck in the past forever. Dr. Clarke is the only other person who could possibly send me home, and she won't be around on Monday morning. Unless—?" I let the question hang in the air.

"Absolutely not. There is one immutable law of

tempokinetics, Dr. McCullough. You cannot change the past. I trust you'll remember that?" he says, standing.

Our meeting is over. I leave his office with the biggest news of my life. I wish I had someone to call and share it with. I'd settle for someone to help me shop for clothes.

Friday, February 17, 2006. 6:20 a.m.

THE SUPPLY CLOSET on the ground floor of LeConte Hall is narrow and dimly lit, filled with boxes of rubber gloves, lab coats, shop towels. Unlike many places on campus, the Physics building hasn't been remodeled in the last fifty years. This has always been a closet, and it isn't likely to be occupied at 6:30 on any Friday morning.

I sit on the concrete floor, my back against a wall, dressed in an appropriate period costume. I think I should feel nervous, but I feel oddly detached. I sip from a cup of lukewarm 7-11 coffee and observe. I don't have any role in this part of the experiment—I'm just the guinea pig. Dr. Chambers's assistants step carefully over my outstretched legs and make the final adjustments to the battery of apparatus that surrounds me.

At exactly 6:28 by my antique Timex, Dr. Chambers himself appears in the doorway. He shows me a thick packet of worn bills and the bulky, rubber-banded typescript of his dissertation, then slips both of them into a battered leather briefcase. He places the case on my lap and extends his hand. But when I reach up to shake it, he frowns and takes the 7-11 cup.

"Good luck, Dr. McCullough," he says formally. Nothing more. What more would he say to a guinea pig? He looks at his watch, then hands the cup to a young man in a black T-shirt, who types in one last line of code, turns off the light, and closes the door.

I sit in the dark and begin to get the willies. No one has ever done this. I don't know if the cool linoleum under my legs is the last thing I will ever feel. Sweat drips down between my breasts as the apparatus begins to hum. There is a moment of intense…sensation. It's not sound, or vibration, or anything I can quantify. It's as if all the fingernails in the world are suddenly raked down all the blackboards, and in the same moment oxygen is transmuted to lead. I am pressed to the floor by a monstrous force, but every hair on my body is erect. Just when I feel I can't stand it anymore, the humming stops.

My pulse is racing, and I feel dizzy, a little nauseous. I sit for a minute, half-expecting Dr. Chambers to come in and tell me the experiment has failed, but no one comes. I try to stand—my right leg has fallen asleep—and grope for the light switch near the door.

In the light from the single bulb, I see that the apparatus is gone, but the gray metal shelves are stacked with the same boxes of gloves and shop towels. My leg all pins and needles, I lean against a brown cardboard box stenciled Bayside Laundry Service, San Francisco 3, California.

It takes me a minute before I realize what's odd. Either those are very old towels, or I'm somewhere pre-ZIP code.

I let myself out of the closet, and walk awkwardly down the empty hallway, my spectator pumps echoing on the linoleum. I search for further confirmation. The first room I peer into is a lab—high stools in front of black slab tables with Bunsen burners, gray boxes full of dials and switches. A slide rule at every station.

I've made it.

Friday, February 17, 1956. 7:00 a.m.

THE CAMPUS IS deserted on this drizzly February dawn, as is Telegraph Avenue. The streetlights are still on—white lights, not yellow sodium—and through the mist I can see faint lines of red and green neon on stores down the avenue. I feel like Marco Polo as I navigate through a world that is both alien and familiar. The buildings are the same, but the storefronts and signs look like stage sets or photos from old *Life* magazines.

It takes me more than an hour to walk downtown. I am disoriented by each shop window, each passing car. I feel as if I'm a little drunk, walking too attentively through the landscape, and not connected to it. Maybe it's the colors. Everything looks too real. I grew up with grainy black-and-white TV reruns and '50s Technicolor films that have faded over time, and it's disconcerting that this world is not overlaid with that pink-orange tinge.

The warm aromas of coffee and bacon lure me into a hole-in-the-wall café. I order the special—eggs, bacon, hash browns, and toast. The toast comes dripping with butter, and the jelly is in a glass jar, not a little plastic tub. When the bill comes it is 55¢. I leave a generous dime tip, then catch the yellow F bus and ride down Shattuck Avenue, staring at the round-fendered black Chevys and occasional pink Studebakers that fill the streets.

The bus is full of morning commuters—men in dark jackets and hats, women in dresses and hats. In my tailored suit I fit right in. I'm surprised that no one looks '50s—retro '50s—the '50s that filtered down to the next century. No poodle skirts, no DA haircuts. All the men remind me of my pop. A man in a gray felt hat has the *Chronicle*, and I read over his shoulder. Eisenhower is considering a second term. The San Francisco police chief promises a crackdown on vice. *Peanuts* tops the comics page and there's a Rock Hudson movie playing at the Castro Theatre. Nothing new there.

As we cross the Bay Bridge I'm amazed at how small San Francisco looks—the skyline is carved stone, not glass-and-steel towers. A green Muni streetcar takes me down the middle of Market Street to Powell. I check into the St. Francis, the city's finest hotel. My room costs less than I've paid for a night in a Motel 6.

All my worldly goods fit on the desktop—Chambers's manuscript; a brown leather wallet with a driver's license, a Berkeley faculty card, and twenty-three dollars in small bills; the invitation to the reception tonight; and $30,000 in banded stacks of fifty-dollar bills. I pull three bills off the top of one stack and put the rest in the drawer, under the cream-colored hotel stationery. I have to get out of this suit and these shoes.

Woolworth's has a toothbrush and other plastic toiletries, and a tin 'Tom Corbett, Space Cadet' alarm clock. I find a pair of pleated pants, an Oxford cloth shirt, and wool sweater at the City of Paris. Macy's Men's Shop yields a pair of 'dungarees' and two T-shirts I can sleep in—69 cents each. A snippy clerk gives me the eye in the Boys department, so I invent a nephew, little Billy, and buy him black basketball sneakers that are just my size.

After a shower and a change of clothes, I try to collect my thoughts, but I'm too keyed up to sit still. In a few hours I'll actually be in the same room as Sara Baxter Clarke. I can't distinguish between fear and excitement, and spend the afternoon wandering aimlessly around the city, gawking like a tourist.

Friday, February 17, 1956. 7:00 p.m.

BACK IN MY spectator pumps and my tailored navy suit, I present myself at the doorway of the reception ballroom and surrender my invitation. The tuxedoed young man looks over my shoulder, as if he's expecting someone behind me. After a moment he clears his throat.

"And you're Mrs....?" he asks, looking down at his typewritten list.

"Dr. McCullough," I say coolly, and give him an even stare. "Mr. Chambers is out of town. He asked me to take his place."

After a moment's hesitation he nods, and writes my name on a white card, pinning it to my lapel like a corsage.

Ballroom A is a sea of gray suits, crew cuts, bow ties, and heavy black-rimmed glasses. Almost everyone is male, as I expected, and almost everyone is smoking, which surprises me. Over in one corner is a knot of women in bright cocktail dresses, each with a lacquered football helmet of hair. Barbie's cultural foremothers.

I accept a canapé from a passing waiter and ease my way to the corner. Which one is Dr. Clarke? I stand a few feet back, scanning name tags. Mrs. Niels Bohr. Mrs. Richard Feynman. Mrs. Ernest Lawrence. I am impressed by the company I'm in, and dismayed that none of the women has a name of her own. I smile an empty cocktail-party smile as I move away from the wives and scan the room. Gray suits with a sprinkling of blue, but all male. Did I arrive too early?

I am looking for a safe corner, one with a large, sheltering potted palm, when I hear a blustery male voice say, "So, Dr. Clarke. Trying the H. G. Wells route, are you? Waste of the taxpayer's money, all that science fiction stuff, don't you think?"

A woman's voice answers. "Not at all. Perhaps I can change your mind at Monday's session." I can't see her yet, but her voice is smooth and rich, with a bit of a lilt or a brogue—one of those vocal clues that says 'I'm not an American.' I stand rooted to the carpet, so awestruck

I'm unable to move.

"Jimmy, will you see if there's more champagne about?" I hear her ask. I see a motion in the sea of gray and astonish myself by flagging a waiter and taking two slender flutes from his tray. I step forward in the direction of her voice. "Here you go," I say, trying to keep my hand from shaking. "I've got an extra."

"How very resourceful of you," she laughs. I am surprised that she is a few inches shorter than me. I'd forgotten she'd be about my age. She takes the glass and offers me her other hand. "Sara Clarke," she says.

"Carol McCullough." I touch her palm. The room seems suddenly bright and the voices around me fade into a murmur. I think for a moment that I'm dematerializing back to 2006, but nothing so dramatic happens. I'm just so stunned that I forget to breathe while I look at her.

Since I was ten years old, no matter where we lived, I have had a picture of Sara Baxter Clarke over my desk. I cut it out of that old physics magazine. It is grainy, black-and-white, the only photo of her I've ever found. In it, she's who I always wanted to be—competent, serious, every inch a scientist. She wears a white lab coat and a pair of rimless glasses, her hair pulled back from her face. A bald man in an identical lab coat is showing her a piece of equipment. Neither of them is smiling.

I know every inch of that picture by heart. But I didn't know that her hair was a coppery red, or that her eyes were such a deep, clear green. And until this moment, it had never occurred to me that she could laugh.

The slender blond man standing next to her interrupts my reverie. "I'm Jim Kennedy, Sara's assistant."

Jim Kennedy. Her fiancé. I feel like the characters in my favorite novel are all coming to life, one by one.

"You're not a wife, are you?" he asks.

I shake my head. "Postdoc. I've only been at Cal a month."

He smiles. "We're neighbors, then. What's your field?"

I take a deep breath. "Tempokinetics. I'm a great admirer of Dr. Clarke's work." The blustery man scowls at me and leaves in search of other prey.

"Really?" Dr. Clarke turns, raising one eyebrow in surprise. "Well, then we should have a chat. Are you—?" She stops in mid-sentence and swears almost inaudibly. "Damn. It's Dr. Wilkins and I must be pleasant. He's quite a muckety-muck at the NSF, and I need the funding." She takes a long swallow of champagne, draining the crystal flute. "Jimmy, why don't you get Dr. McCullough another drink and see if you can persuade her to join us for supper."

I start to make a polite protest, but Jimmy takes my elbow and steers me through the crowd to an unoccupied sofa. Half an hour later we are deep in a discussion of quantum field theory when Dr. Clarke appears and says, "Let's make a discreet exit, shall we? I'm famished."

Like conspirators, we slip out a side door and down a flight of service stairs. The Powell Street cable car takes us over Nob Hill into North Beach, the Italian section of town. We walk up Columbus to one of my favorite restaurants—the New Pisa—where I discover that nothing much has changed in fifty years except the prices.

The waiter brings a carafe of red wine and a trio of squat drinking glasses and we eat family style—bowls of pasta with red sauce and steaming loaves of crusty garlic bread. I am speechless as Sara Baxter Clarke talks about her work, blithely answering questions I have wanted to ask my whole life. She is brilliant, fascinating. And beautiful. My food disappears without me noticing a single mouthful.

Over coffee and spumoni she insists, for the third time, that I call her Sara, and asks me about my own studies. I have to catch myself a few times, biting back citations from Stephen Hawking and other works that won't be published for decades. It is such an engrossing, exhilarating conversation, I can't bring myself to shift it to Chambers's agenda. We leave when we notice the restaurant has no other customers.

"How about a nightcap?" she suggests when we reach the sidewalk.

"Not for me," Jimmy begs off. "I've got an 8:30 symposium tomorrow morning. But why don't you two go on ahead? The Paper Doll is just around the corner."

Sara gives him an odd, cold look and shakes her head. "Not funny, James," she says, and glances over at me. I shrug noncommittally. It seems they have a private joke I'm not in on.

"Just a thought," he says, then kisses her on the cheek and leaves. Sara and I walk down to Vesuvio's, one of the bars where Kerouac, Ferlinghetti, and Ginsberg spawned the Beat Generation. Make that *will* spawn. I think we're a few months too early.

Sara orders another carafe of raw red wine. I feel shy around her, intimidated, I guess. I've dreamed of meeting her for so long, and I want her to like me. As we begin to talk, we discover how similar, and lonely, our childhoods were. We were raised as only children. We both begged for chemistry sets we never got. We were expected to know how to iron, not know about ions. Midway through her second glass of wine, Sara sighs.

"Oh, bugger it all. Nothing's really changed, you know. It's still just snickers and snubs. I'm tired of fighting for a seat in the old boys' club. Monday's paper represents five years of hard work, and there aren't a handful of people at this entire conference who've had the decency to treat me as anything but a joke." She squeezes her napkin into a tighter and tighter wad, and a tear trickles down her cheek. "How do you stand it, Carol?"

How can I tell her? *I've stood it because of you. You're my hero.* I've always asked myself what Sara Baxter Clarke would do, and steeled myself to push through. But now she's not a hero. She's real, this woman across the table from me. This Sara's not the invincible, ever-practical scientist I always thought she was. She's as young and as vulnerable as I am.

I want to ease her pain the way that she, as my imaginary mentor, has always eased mine. I reach over and put my hand over hers; she stiffens, but she doesn't pull away. Her hand is soft under mine, and I think of touching her hair, gently brushing the red tendrils off the back of her neck, kissing the salty tears on her cheek.

Maybe I've always had a crush on Sara Baxter Clarke. But I can't be falling in love with her. She's straight. She's fifty years older than I am. And in the back of my mind, the chilling voice of reality reminds me that she'll also be dead in two days. I can't reconcile that with the vibrant woman sitting in this smoky North Beach bar. I don't want to. I drink two more glasses of wine and hope that will silence the voice long enough for me to enjoy these few moments.

We are still talking, our fingertips brushing on the scarred wooden tabletop, when the bartender announces last call. "Oh, bloody hell," she says. "I've been having such a lovely time I've gone and missed the last ferry. I hope I have enough for the cab fare. My Chevy's over in the car park at Berkeley."

"That's ridiculous," I hear myself say. "I've got a room at the hotel. Come back with me and catch the ferry in the morning." It's the wine talking. I don't know what I'll do if she says yes. I want her to say yes so much.

"No, I couldn't impose. I'll simply—" she protests, and then stops. "Oh, yes, then. Thank you. It's very generous."

So here we are. At 2:00 a.m. the hotel lobby is plush and utterly empty. We ride up in the elevator in a sleepy silence that becomes awkward as soon as we are alone in the room. I nervously gather my new clothes off the only bed and gesture to her to sit down. I pull a T-shirt out of its crinkly cellophane wrapper. "Here," I hand it to her. "It's not elegant, but it'll have to do as a nightgown."

She looks at the T-shirt in her lap, and at the dungarees and black sneakers in my arms, an odd expression on her face. Then she sighs, a deep, achy-sounding sigh. It's the oddest reaction to a T-shirt I've ever heard.

"The Paper Doll would have been all right, wouldn't it?" she asks softly.

Puzzled, I stop crinkling the other cellophane wrapper and lean against the dresser. "I guess so. I've never been there." She looks worried, so I keep talking. "But there are a lot of places I haven't been. I'm new in town. Just got here. Don't know anybody yet, haven't really gotten around. What kind of place is it?"

She freezes for a moment, then says, almost in a whisper, "It's a bar for women."

"Oh." I nod. "Well, that's okay." Why would Jimmy suggest a gay bar? It's an odd thing to tell your fiancée. Did he guess about me somehow? Or maybe he just thought we'd be safer there late at night, since—

My musings—and any other rational thoughts—come to a dead stop when Sara Baxter Clarke stands up, cups my face in both her hands and kisses me gently on the lips. She pulls away, just a few inches, and looks at me.

I can't believe this is happening. "Aren't you—isn't Jimmy—?"

"He's my dearest chum, and my partner in the lab. But romantically? No. Protective camouflage. For both of us," she answers, stroking my face.

I don't know what to do. Every dream I've ever had is coming true tonight. But how can I kiss her? How can I begin something I know is doomed? She must see the indecision in my face, because she looks scared, and starts to take a step backward. And I can't let her go. Not yet. I put my hand on the back of her neck and pull her into a second, longer kiss.

We move to the bed after a few minutes. I feel shy, not wanting to make a wrong move. But she kisses my face, my neck, and pulls me down onto her. We begin slowly, cautiously undressing each other. I fumble at the unfamiliar garter belts and stockings, and she smiles, undoing the rubber clasps for me. Her slender body is pale and freckled, her breasts small with dusty pink nipples.

Her fingers gently stroke my arms, my thighs. When I hesitantly put my mouth on her breast, she moans, deep in her throat, and laces her fingers through my hair. After a minute her hands ease my head down her body. The hair between her legs is ginger, the ends dark and wet. I taste the salty musk of her when I part her lips with my tongue. She moans again, almost a growl. When she comes it is a single, fierce explosion.

We finally fall into an exhausted sleep, spooned around each other, both T-shirts still crumpled on the floor.

Saturday, February 18, 1956. 7:00 a.m.

LIGHT COMES THROUGH a crack in the curtains. I'm alone in a strange bed. I'm sure last night was a dream, but then I hear the shower come on in the bathroom. Sara emerges a few minutes later, toweling her hair. She smiles and leans over me—warm and wet and smelling of soap.

"I have to go," she whispers, and kisses me.

I want to ask if I'll see her again, want to pull her down next to me and hold her for hours. But I just stroke her hair and say nothing.

She sits on the edge of the bed. "I've got an eleven o'clock lab, and there's another dreadful cocktail thing at Stanford this evening. I'd give it a miss, but Shockley's going to be there, and he's front runner for the next Nobel, so I have to make an appearance. Meet me after?"

"Yes," I say, breathing again. "Where?"

"Why don't you take the train down? I'll pick you up at the Palo Alto station at half past seven and we can drive to the coast for dinner. Wear those nice black trousers. If it's not too dreary, we'll walk on the beach."

She picks up her wrinkled suit from the floor where it landed last night, and gets dressed. "Half past seven, then?" she says, and kisses my cheek. The door clicks shut and she's gone.

I lie tangled in the sheets, and curl up into the pillow like a contented cat. I am almost asleep again when an image intrudes—a crumpled Chevy on the rocks below Devil's Slide. It's like a fragment of a nightmare, not quite real in the morning light. But which dream is real now?

Until last night, part of what had made Sara Baxter

Clarke so compelling was her enigmatic death. Like Amelia Earhart or James Dean, she had been a brilliant star that ended so abruptly she became legendary. Larger than life. But I can still feel where her lips brushed my cheek. Now she's very much life-size, and despite Chambers's warnings, I will do anything to keep her that way.

Saturday, February 18, 1956. 7:20 p.m.

THE PLATFORM AT the Palo Alto train station is cold and windy. I'm glad I'm wearing a sweater, but it makes my suit jacket uncomfortably tight across my shoulders. I've finished the newspaper and am reading the train schedule when Sara comes up behind me.

"Hullo there," she says. She's wearing a nubby beige dress under a dark wool coat and looks quite elegant.

"Hi." I reach to give her a hug, but she steps back.

"Have you gone mad?" she says, scowling. She crosses her arms over her chest. "What on earth were you thinking?"

"Sorry." I'm not sure what I've done. "It's nice to see you," I say hesitantly.

"Yes, well, me too. But you can't just—oh, you know," she says, waving her hand.

I don't, so I shrug. She gives me an annoyed look, then turns and opens the car door. I stand on the pavement for a minute, bewildered, then get in.

Her Chevy feels huge compared to the Toyota I drive at

home, and there are no seatbelts. We drive in uncomfortable silence all through Palo Alto and onto the winding, two-lane road that leads to the coast. Our second date isn't going well.

After about ten minutes, I can't stand it anymore. "I'm sorry about the hug. I guess it's still a big deal here, huh?"

She turns her head slightly, still keeping her eyes on the road. "Here?" she asks. "What utopia are you from, then?"

I spent the day wandering the city in a kind of haze, alternately giddy in love and worrying about this moment. How can I tell her where—when—I'm from? And how much should I tell her about why? I count to three, and then count again before I answer. "From the future."

"Very funny," she says. I can hear in her voice that she's hurt. She stares straight ahead again.

"Sara, I'm serious. Your work on time travel isn't just theory. I'm a postdoc at Cal. In 2006. The head of the Physics department, Dr. Chambers, sent me back here to talk to you. He says he worked with you and Jimmy, back before he won the Nobel Prize."

She doesn't say anything for a minute, then pulls over onto a wide place at the side of the road. She switches off the engine and turns toward me.

"Ray Chambers? The Nobel Prize? Jimmy says he can barely do his own lab work." She shakes her head, then lights a cigarette, flicking the match out the window into the darkness. "Ray set you up for this, didn't he? To get back at Jimmy for last term's grade? Well, it's a terrible joke," she says, turning away, "and you are one of the cruelest people I have ever met."

"Sara, it's not a joke. Please believe me." I reach across the seat to take her hand, but she jerks it away.

I take a deep breath, trying desperately to think of something that will convince her. "Look, I know it sounds crazy, but hear me out. In September, *Modern Physics* is going to publish an article about you and your work. When I was ten years old—in 1985—I read it sitting on the back porch of my father's quarters at Fort Ord. That article inspired me to go into science. I read about you, and I knew when I grew up I wanted to travel through time."

She stubs out her cigarette. "Go on."

So I tell her all about my academic career, and my 'assignment' from Chambers. She listens without interrupting me. I can't see her expression in the darkened car.

After I finish, she says nothing, then sighs. "This is rather a lot to digest, you know. But I can't very well believe in my work without giving your story some credence, can I?" She lights another cigarette, then asks the question I've been dreading. "So if you've come all this way to offer me an enormous sum for my paper, does that mean something happened to it—or to me?" I still can't see her face, but her voice is shaking.

I can't do it. I can't tell her. I grope for a convincing lie. "There was a fire. A lot of papers were lost. Yours is the one they want."

"I'm not a faculty member at y*our* Cal, am I?"

"No."

She takes a long drag on her cigarette, then asks, so softly I can barely hear her, "Am I...?" She lets her question trail off and is silent for a minute, then sighs again. "No, I won't ask. I think I prefer to bumble about like other mortals. You're a dangerous woman, Carol McCullough. I'm afraid you can tell me too many things I have no right to know." She reaches for the ignition key, then stops. "There is one thing I must know, though. Was last night as carefully planned as everything else?"

"Jesus, no." I reach over and touch her hand. She lets me hold it this time. "No, I had no idea. Other than finding you at the reception, last night had nothing to do with science."

To my great relief, she chuckles. "Well, perhaps chemistry, don't you think?" She glances in the rearview mirror then pulls me across the wide front seat and into her arms. We hold each other in the darkness for a long time, and kiss for even longer. Her lips taste faintly of gin.

We have a leisurely dinner at a restaurant overlooking the beach in Half Moon Bay. Fresh fish and a dry white wine. I have the urge to tell her about the picture, about how important she's been to me. But as I start to speak, I realize she's more important to me now, so I just tell her that. We finish the meal gazing at each other as if we were ordinary lovers.

Outside the restaurant, the sky is cloudy and cold, the breeze tangy with salt and kelp. Sara pulls off her high heels and we walk down a sandy path, holding hands in the darkness. Within minutes we are both freezing. I pull her to me and lean down to kiss her on the deserted beach. "You know what I'd like?" I say, over the roar of the surf.

"What?" she murmurs into my neck.

"I'd like to take you dancing."

She shakes her head. "We can't. Not here. Not now. It's against the law, you know. Or perhaps you don't. But it is, I'm afraid. And the police have been on a rampage in the city lately. One bar lost its license just because two men were holding hands. They arrested both as sexual vagrants and for being—oh, what was the phrase—lewd and dissolute persons."

"Sexual vagrants? That's outrageous!"

"Exactly what the newspapers said. An outrage to public decency. Jimmy knew one of the poor chaps. He was in Engineering at Stanford, but after his name and address were published in the paper, he lost his job. Does that still go on where you're from?"

"I don't think so. Maybe in some places. I don't really know. I'm afraid I don't pay any attention to politics. I've never needed to."

Sara sighs. "What a wonderful luxury that must be, not having to be so careful all the time."

"I guess so." I feel a little guilty that it's not something I worry about. But Stonewall happened six years before I was born. By the time I came out, in college, being gay was more of a lifestyle than a perversion. At least in San

Francisco.

"It's sure a lot more public," I say after a minute. "Last year there were a half a million people at the Gay Pride parade. Dancing down Market Street and carrying signs about how great it is to be queer."

"You're pulling my leg now. Aren't you?" When I shake my head she smiles. "Well, I'm glad. I'm glad that this witch hunt ends. And in a few months, when I get my equipment up and running, perhaps I shall travel to dance at your parade. But for tonight, why don't we just go to my house? At least I've got a new hi-fi."

So we head back up the coast. One advantage to these old cars, the front seat is as big as a couch; we drive up Highway 1 sitting next to each other, my arm resting on her thigh. The ocean is a flat, black void on our left, until the road begins to climb and the water disappears behind jagged cliffs. On the driver's side the road drops off steeply as we approach Devil's Slide.

I feel like I'm coming to the scary part of a movie I've seen before. I'm afraid I know what happens next. My right hand grips the upholstery and I brace myself for the oncoming car or the loose patch of gravel or whatever it is that will send us skidding off the road and onto the rocks.

But nothing happens. Sara hums as she drives, and I realize that although this is the spot I dread, it means nothing to her. At least not tonight.

As the road levels out again, it is desolate, with few signs of civilization. Just beyond a sign that says *Sharp*

Park is a trailer camp with a string of bare lightbulbs outlining its perimeter. Across the road is a seedy-looking roadhouse with a neon sign that blinks *Hazel's*. The parking lot is jammed with cars. Saturday night in the middle of nowhere.

We drive another hundred yards when Sara suddenly snaps her fingers and does a U-turn.

Please don't go back to the cliffs, I beg silently. "What's up?" I ask out loud.

"Hazel's. Jimmy was telling me about it last week. It's become a rather gay club, and since it's over the county line, out here in the boondocks, he says anything goes. Including dancing. Besides, I thought I spotted his car."

"Are you sure?"

"No, but there aren't that many '39 Packards still on the road. If it isn't, we'll just continue on." She pulls into the parking lot and finds a space at the back, between the trash cans and the ocean.

Hazel's is a noisy, smoky place—a small, single room with a bar along one side—jammed wall-to-wall with people. Hundreds of them, mostly men, but more than a few women. When I look closer, I realize that some of the 'men' are actually women with slicked-back hair, ties, and sports coats.

We manage to get two beers, and find Jimmy on the edge of the dance floor—a minuscule square of linoleum, not more than 10 x 10, where dozens of people are dancing to Bill Haley & His Comets blasting from the jukebox. Jimmy's in a tweed jacket and chinos, his arm around the waist of a young Latino man in a tight white T-shirt and even tighter blue jeans. We elbow our way through to them and Sara gives Jimmy a kiss on the cheek. "Hullo, love," she says.

He's obviously surprised—shocked—to see Sara, but when he sees me behind her, he grins. "I told you so."

"James, you don't know the half of it," Sara says, smiling, and puts her arm around me.

We dance for a few songs in the hot, crowded bar. I take off my jacket, then my sweater, draping them over the railing next to the bottles of beer. After the next song I roll up the sleeves of my button-down shirt. When Jimmy offers to buy another round of beers, I look at my watch and shake my head. It's midnight, and as much as I wanted to dance with Sara, I want to sleep with her even more.

"One last dance, then let's go, okay?" I ask, shouting to be heard over the noise of the crowd and the jukebox. "I'm bushed."

She nods. Johnny Mathis starts to sing, and we slow-dance, our arms around each other. My eyes are closed and Sara's head is resting on my shoulder when the first of the cops bursts through the front door.

Sunday, February 19, 1956. 12:05 a.m.

A SMALL ARMY of uniformed men storms into the bar. Everywhere around us people are screaming in panic, and I'm buffeted by the bodies running in all directions. People near the back race for the rear door. A red-faced, heavy-set man in khaki, a gold star on his chest, climbs onto the bar. "This is a raid," he shouts. He has brought reporters with him, and flashbulbs suddenly illuminate the stunned, terrified faces of people who had been sipping their drinks moments before.

Khaki-shirted deputies, nightsticks in hand, block the front door. There are so many uniforms. At least forty men—highway patrol, sheriff's department, and even some army MPs—begin to form a gauntlet leading to the back door, now the only exit.

Jimmy grabs my shoulders. "Dance with Antonio," he says urgently. "I've just met him, but it's our best chance of getting out of here. I'll take Sara."

I nod and the Latino man's muscular arms are around my waist. He smiles shyly just as someone pulls the plug on the jukebox and Johnny Mathis stops in mid-croon. The room is quiet for a moment, then the cops begin barking orders. We stand against the railing, Jimmy's arm curled protectively around Sara's shoulders, Antonio's around mine. Other people have done the same thing, but there are not enough women, and men who had been dancing now stand apart from each other, looking scared.

The uniforms are lining people up, herding them like sheep toward the back. We join the line and inch forward. The glare of headlights through the half-open back door cuts through the smoky room like the beam from a movie projector. There is an icy draft and I reach back for my sweater, but the railing is too far away, and the crush of people too solid to move any direction but forward. Jimmy sees me shivering and drapes his sports coat over my shoulders.

We are in line for more than an hour, as the cops at the back door check everyone's ID. Sara leans against Jimmy's chest, squeezing my hand tightly once or twice when no one's looking. I am scared, shaking, but the uniforms seem to be letting most people go. Every few seconds, a car starts up in the parking lot, and I can hear the crunch of tires on gravel as someone leaves Hazel's for the freedom of the highway.

As we get closer to the door, I can see a line of black vans parked just outside, ringing the exit. They are paneled with wooden benches, filled with the men who are not going home, most of them sitting with their shoulders sagging. One van holds a few women with crew cuts or slicked-back hair, who glare defiantly into the night.

We are ten people back from the door when Jimmy slips a key into my hand and whispers into my ear. "We'll have to take separate cars. Drive Sara's back to the city and we'll meet at the lobby bar in your hotel."

"The bar will be closed," I whisper back. "Take my key and meet me in the room. I'll get another at the desk." He nods as I hand it to him.

The cop at the door looks at Sara's elegant dress and coat, barely glances at her outstretched ID, and waves her and Jimmy outside without a word. She pauses at the door and looks back at me, but an MP shakes his head and points to the parking lot. "Now or never, lady," he says, and Sara and Jimmy disappear into the night.

I'm alone. Antonio is a total stranger, but his strong arm is my only support until a man in a suit pulls him away. "Nice try, sweetie," the man says to him. "But I've seen you in here before, dancing with your pansy friends." He turns to the khaki-shirted deputy and says, "He's one of the perverts. Book him." The cop pulls Antonio's arm up between his shoulder blades, then cuffs his hands behind his back. "Time for a little ride, pretty boy," he grins, and drags Antonio out into one of the black vans.

Without thinking, I take a step toward his retreating back. "Not so fast," says another cop, with acne scars across both cheeks. He looks at Jimmy's jacket, and down at my pants and my black basketball shoes with a sneer. Then he puts his hands on my breasts, groping me. "Loose ones. Not all tied down like those other he-shes. I like that." He leers and pinches one of my nipples.

I yell for help and try to pull away, but he laughs and shoves me up against the stack of beer cases that line the back hallway. He pokes his nightstick between my legs. "So you want to be a man, huh, butchie? Well, just what do you think you've got in there?" He jerks his nightstick up into my crotch so hard tears come to my eyes.

I stare at him, in pain, in disbelief. I am too stunned to move or to say anything. He cuffs my hands and pushes me out the back door and into the van with the other glaring women.

Sunday, February 19, 1956. 10:00 a.m.

I PLEAD GUILTY to being a sex offender, and pay the $50 fine. Being arrested can't ruin *my* life. I don't even exist here.

Sara and Jimmy are waiting on a wooden bench outside the holding cell of the San Mateo County jail. "Are you all right, love?" she asks.

I shrug. "I'm exhausted. I didn't sleep. There were ten of us in one cell. The woman next to me—a stone butch?—really tough, Frankie—she had a pompadour—two cops took her down the hall—when she came back the whole side of her face was swollen, and after that she didn't say anything to anyone, but I'm okay, I just…" I start to shake. Sara takes one arm and Jimmy takes the other, and they walk me gently out to the parking lot.

The three of us sit in the front seat of Jimmy's car, and as soon as we are out of sight of the jail, Sara puts her arms around me and holds me, brushing the hair off my forehead. When Jimmy takes the turnoff to the San Mateo bridge, she says, "We checked you out of the hotel this morning. Precious little to check, actually, except for the briefcase. Anyway, I thought you'd be more comfortable at my house. We need to get you some breakfast and a bed." She kisses me on the cheek. "I've told Jimmy everything, by the way."

I nod sleepily, and the next thing I know we're standing on the front steps of a brown shingled cottage and Jimmy's pulling away. I don't think I'm hungry, but Sara makes scrambled eggs and bacon and toast, and I eat every scrap of it. She runs a hot bath, grimacing at the purpling, thumb-shaped bruises on my upper arms, and gently washes my hair and my back. When she tucks me into bed, pulling a blue quilt around me, and curls up beside me, I start to cry. I feel so battered and so fragile, and I can't remember the last time someone took care of me this way.

Sunday, February 19, 1956. 5:00 p.m.

I WAKE UP to the sound of rain and the enticing smell of pot roast baking in the oven. Sara has laid out my jeans and a brown sweater at the end of the bed. I put them on, then pad barefoot into the kitchen. There are cardboard boxes piled in one corner, and Jimmy and Sara are sitting at the yellow Formica table with cups of tea, talking intently.

"Oh good, you're awake." She stands and gives me a hug. "There's tea in the pot. If you think you're up to it, Jimmy and I need to tell you a few things."

"I'm a little sore, but I'll be okay. I'm not crazy about the '50s, though." I pour from the heavy ceramic pot. The tea is some sort of Chinese blend, fragrant and smoky. "What's up?"

"First a question. If my paper isn't entirely—complete—could there possibly be any repercussions for you?"

I think for a minute. "I don't think so. If anyone knew exactly what was in it, they wouldn't have sent me."

"Splendid. In that case, I've come to a decision." She pats the battered brown briefcase. "In exchange for the extraordinary wad of cash in here, we shall send back a perfectly reasonable-sounding paper. What only the three of us will know is that I have left a few things out. This, for example." She picks up a pen, scribbles a complex series of numbers and symbols on a piece of paper, and hands it to me.

I study it for a minute. It's very high-level stuff, but I know enough physics to get the gist of it. "If this really works, it's the answer to the energy problem. It's exactly the piece Chambers needs."

"Very, very good," she says smiling. "It's also the part I will never give him."

I raise one eyebrow.

"I read the first few chapters of his dissertation this afternoon while you were sleeping," she says, tapping the manuscript with her pen. "It's a bit uneven, although parts of it are quite good. Unfortunately, the good parts were written by a graduate student named Gilbert Young."

I raise the other eyebrow. "But that paper's what Chambers wins the Nobel for."

"Son of a bitch." Jimmy slaps his hand down onto the table. "Gil was working for me while he finished the last of his dissertation. He was a bright guy, original research, solid future—but he started having these headaches. The tumor was inoperable, and he died six months ago. Ray said he'd clean out Gil's office for me. I just figured he was trying to get back on my good side."

"We can't change what Ray does with Gil's work. But I won't give him *my* work to steal in the future." Sara shoves Chambers's manuscript to the other side of the table. "Or now. I've decided not to present my paper in the morning."

I feel very lightheaded. I *know* she doesn't give her paper, but— "Why not?" I ask.

"While I was reading the manuscript this afternoon, I heard that fat sheriff interviewed on the radio. They arrested ninety people at Hazel's last night, Carol, people like us. People who only wanted to dance with each other. But he kept bragging about how they cleaned out a nest of perverts. And I realized—in a blinding moment of clarity—that the university is a branch of the state, and the sheriff is enforcing the state's laws. I'm working for people who believe it's morally right to abuse you—or me—or Jimmy. And I can't do that anymore."

"Hear, hear!" Jimmy says, smiling. "The only problem is, as I explained to her this morning, the administration is likely to take a very dim view of being embarrassed in front of every major physicist in the country. Not to mention they feel Sara's research is university property." He looks at me and takes a sip of tea. "So we decided it might be best if Sara disappeared for a while."

I stare at both of them, my mouth open. I have that same odd feeling of déjà vu that I did in the car last night.

"I've cleaned everything that's hers out of our office and the lab," Jimmy says. "It's all in the trunk of my car."

"And those," Sara says, gesturing to the boxes in the

corner, "are what I value from my desk and my library here. Other than my Nana's teapot and some clothes, it's all I'll really need for a while. Jimmy's family has a vacation home out in West Marin, so I won't have to worry about rent—or privacy."

I'm still staring. "What about your career?"

Sara puts down her teacup with a bang and begins pacing the floor. "Oh, bugger my career. I'm not giving up my *work*, just the university—and its hypocrisy. If one of my colleagues had a little fling, nothing much would come of it. But as a woman, I'm supposed to be some sort of paragon of unsullied Victorian virtue. Just by being *in* that bar last night, I put my 'career' in jeopardy. They'd crucify me if they knew who—or what—I am. I don't want to live that way anymore."

She brings the teapot to the table and sits down, pouring us each another cup. "End of tirade. But that's why I had to ask about your money. It's enough to live on for a good long while, and to buy all the equipment I need. In a few months, with a decent lab, I should be this close," she says, holding her thumb and forefinger together, "to time travel in practice as well as in theory. And that discovery will be mine—ours. Not the university's. Not the government's."

Jimmy nods. "I'll stay down here and finish this term. That way I can keep tabs on things and order equipment without arousing suspicion."

"Won't they come looking for you?" I ask Sara. I feel very surreal. Part of me has always wanted to know *why* this all happened, and part of me feels like I'm just prompting the part I know comes next.

"Not if they think there's no reason to look," Jimmy says. "We'll take my car back to Hazel's and pick up hers. Devil's Slide is only a few miles up the road. It's—"

"It's a rainy night," I finish. "Treacherous stretch of highway. Accidents happen there all the time. They'll find Sara's car in the morning, but no body. Washed out to sea. Everyone will think it's tragic that she died so young," I say softly. My throat is tight and I'm fighting back tears. "At least I always have."

They both stare at me. Sara gets up and stands behind me, wrapping her arms around my shoulders. "So that *is* how it happens?" she asks, hugging me tight. "All along you've assumed I'd be dead in the morning?"

I nod. I don't trust my voice enough to say anything.

To my great surprise, she laughs. "Well, I'm not going to be. One of the first lessons you should have learned as a scientist is never assume," she says, kissing the top of my head. "But what a terrible secret for you to have been carting about. Thank you for not telling me. It would have ruined a perfectly lovely weekend. Now let's all have some supper. We've a lot to do tonight."

Monday, February 20, 1956. 12:05 a.m.

"What on earth are you doing?" Sara asks, coming into the kitchen and talking around the toothbrush in her mouth. "It's our last night—at least for a while. I was rather hoping you'd be waiting in bed when I came out of the bathroom."

"I will. Two more minutes." I'm sitting at the kitchen table, rolling a blank sheet of paper into her typewriter. I haven't let myself think about going back in the morning, about leaving Sara, and I'm delaying our inevitable conversation about it for as long as I can. "While we were driving back from wrecking your car, I had an idea about how to nail Chambers."

She takes the toothbrush out of her mouth. "It's a lovely thought, but you know you can't change anything that happens."

"I can't change the past," I agree. "But I *can* set a bomb with a very long fuse. Like fifty years."

"What? You look like the cat that's eaten the canary." She sits down next to me.

"I've retyped the title page to Chambers's dissertation—with your name on it. First thing in the morning, I'm going to rent a large safe deposit box at the Wells Fargo Bank downtown, and pay the rent in advance. Sometime in 2006, there'll be a miraculous discovery of a complete Sara Baxter Clarke manuscript. The bomb is that, after her tragic death, the esteemed Dr. Chambers appears to have published it under his own name—and won the Nobel Prize for it."

"No, you can't. It's not my work either, it's Gil's and—" She stops in mid-sentence, staring at me. "And he really *is* dead. I don't suppose I dare give a fig about academic credit anymore, should I?"

"I hope not. Besides, Chambers can't prove it's *not* yours. What's he going to say—Carol McCullough went back to the past and set me up? He'll look like a total idiot. Without your formula, all he's got is a time machine that won't work. Remember, you never present your paper. Where I come from it may be okay to be queer, but time travel is still just science fiction."

She laughs. "Well, given a choice, I suppose that's preferable, isn't it?"

I nod and pull the sheet of paper out of the typewriter.

"You're quite a resourceful girl, aren't you?" Sara says, smiling. "I could use an assistant like you." Then her smile fades and she puts her hand over mine. "I don't suppose you'd consider staying on for a few months and helping me set up the lab? I know we've only known each other for two days. But this—I—us—Oh, dammit, what I'm trying to say is I'm going to miss you."

I squeeze her hand in return, and we sit silent for a few minutes. I don't know what to say. Or to do. I don't want to go back to my own time. There's nothing for me in that life. A dissertation that I now know isn't true. An office with a black-and-white photo of the only person I've ever really loved—who's sitting next to me, holding my hand. I could sit like this forever. But could I stand to live the rest of my life in the closet, hiding who I am and who I love? I'm used to the 21st century—I've never done research without the Internet, or cooked much without a microwave. I'm afraid if I don't go back tomorrow, I'll be trapped in this reactionary past forever.

"Sara," I ask finally. "Are you sure your experiments will work?"

She looks at me, her eyes warm and gentle. "If you're asking if I can promise you an escape back to your own time someday, the answer is no. I can't promise you anything, love. But if you're asking if I believe in my work, then yes. I do. Are you thinking of staying, then?"

I nod. "I want to. I just don't know if I can."

"Because of last night?" she asks softly.

"That's part of it. I was raised in a world that's so different. I don't feel right here. I don't belong."

She kisses my cheek. "I know. But gypsies never belong to the places they travel. They only belong to other gypsies."

My eyes are misty as she takes my hand and leads me to the bedroom.

Monday, February 20, 1956. 11:30 a.m.

I PUT THE battered leather briefcase on the floor of the supply closet in LeConte Hall and close the door behind me. At 11:37 exactly, I hear the humming start, and when it stops, my shoulders sag with relief. What's done is done, and all the dies are cast. In Palo Alto an audience of restless physicists is waiting to hear a paper that will never be read. And in Berkeley, far in the future, an equally restless physicist is waiting for a messenger to finally deliver that paper.

But the messenger isn't coming back. And that may be the least of Chambers's worries.

This morning I taped the key to the safe deposit box—and a little note about the dissertation inside—into the 1945 bound volume of *The Astrophysical Journal*. My office mate Ted was outraged that no one had checked it out of the Physics library since 1955. I'm hoping he'll be even more outraged when he discovers the secret that's hidden inside it.

I walk out of LeConte and across campus to the coffee shop where Sara is waiting for me. I don't like the political climate here, but at least I know that it will change, slowly but surely. Besides, we don't have to stay in the '50s all the time—in a few months, Sara and I plan to do a lot of traveling. Maybe one day some graduate student will want to study the mysterious disappearance of Dr. Carol McCullough. Stranger things have happened.

My only regret is not being able to see Chambers's face when he opens that briefcase and there's no manuscript. Sara and I decided that even sending back an incomplete version of her paper was dangerous. It would give Chambers enough proof that his tempokinetic experiment worked for him to get more funding and try again. So the only thing in the case is an anonymous, undated postcard of the St. Francis Hotel that says:

Having a wonderful time. Thanks for the ride.

FIND US ONLINE!

www.rebellionpublishing.com

/rebellionpub /rebellionpublishing /rebellionpublishing

SIGN UP TO OUR NEWSLETTER!

rebellionpublishing.com/newsletter

YOUR REVIEWS MATTER!

Enjoy this book? Got something to say?

Leave a review on Amazon, Goodreads or with your
favourite bookseller and let the world know!